Judith Tarr

THE
EAGLE'S
DAUGHTER

TOR®

A Tom Doherty Associates Book
New York

This is a work of fiction. All the characters and events portrayed in this novel are either products of the author's imagination or are used fictitiously.

THE EAGLE'S DAUGHTER

Cover art by Donato

A Tor Book
Published by Tom Doherty Associates, Inc.
175 Fifth Avenue
New York, NY 10010

Tor Books on the World-Wide Web:
http://www.tor.com

Tor® is a registered trademark of Tom Doherty Associates, Inc.

ISBN: 0-812-55083-8
Library of Congress Card Catalog Number: 94-47225

First edition: April 1995
First mass market edition: January 1996

Printed in the United States of America

0 9 8 7 6 5 4 3 2 1

To
Jane Butler
Who believed that this *Eagle* could fly

Previous books by Judith Tarr:

Praise for
JUDITH TARR

"Tarr is an excellent writer. Her prose is graceful and her plots are carefully constructed. She is as confident in describing the battlefields of war as she is in exploring the conflicts of love. . . . Tarr takes the time to ensure that the settings for her novels are solidly constructed. Her efforts result in thoughtful, well-written entertainment."

—*The Washington Post Book World*

"In this carefully researched, well-crafted novel about Antony and Cleopatra, Tarr weaves Rome and Alexandria, wars of conquest, pageantry and personality, earthly as well as supernatural powers together in a marvelously entertaining tapestry."

—*Booklist* on *Throne of Isis*

"Judith Tarr's *Lord of the Two Lands* moves away from her previous medieval efforts to the story of Alexander the Great. This is Alexander seen from a viewpoint similar to that in Mary Renault's *The Persian Boy*—someone who joins his campaigns in mid-course. . . . Alexander is as compelling as ever as a central figure for a novel, and Tarr has done her research and writing as well as ever."

—Chicago *Sun-Times*

"Judith Tarr's *Lord of the Two Lands* is an exciting story of Alexander the Great and his move into Egypt, told through the eyes of Pharaoh Nectanebo's daughter, Meriamon. Tarr has portrayed, in a remarkably believable story, a rich sense of time and place. Since the plot does not turn on those elements, her use of oracles and the occult is entirely appropriate for the period in this well-researched and entertaining work of historical fiction. I simply could not put it down until I had turned the last page."

—Jean M. Auel, author of *Clan of the Cave Bear*

Acknowledgments

This novel could not have been written without the help of the following:

Gillian Bradshaw, who gave support and early encouragement.

Professor Jaroslav R. Pelikan of Yale, who introduced me to Gerbert of Aurillac.

Harry Turtledove, especially in matters Byzantine; any errors herein are entirely my own.

Katharine Kerr, but for whom Ismail would be a very different character.

The members of my class in writing the historical novel at Wesleyan University in Middletown, Connecticut, and Dr. Margaret Lindsey of the Graduate Liberal Studies Program, by whose good offices I discovered that teaching writing can be a remarkably efficacious cure for writer's block.

The Holy Roman Empire A.D. 972

PROLOGUE

Aachen

Christmas, 983

It was a splendid day to crown a king. Cold but diamond-clear, snow like a glittering mantle over the roofs and walls of Aachen, the sun offering what warmth it might in the shadow of the solstice. The people who filled the city to bursting, hardy Germans all, stood bareheaded and even bare-armed under the blue vault of heaven, and sent up their roar of approbation, acclaiming their new lord: Otto, son of Otto, son of Otto of the Saxons.

Under the vault of Aachen's chapel, under the eye of Christ the King, Otto who was about to be king moved slowly through the rite of his consecration. He was extraordinarily patient, Aspasia thought, craning to see past the lordly figures of the bishops and their scarcely less lordly acolytes. Small as she was among all these great hulking barbarians, she was never as small as the King of the Germans, the heir of the Holy Roman Emperor, the august and illustrious prince, the seal of the peace between the Germans and their too often distant overlord. Otto the king, son of

Otto the emperor, was well grown for his age and, while Aspasia had anything to do with it, most well trained. But he was only three years old.

He had objected once to forsaking the bright free air for the musty darkness of the chapel. There was very nearly an incident; a tantrum, Aspasia would call it. But she had seen it coming, and she had caught his eye even as he opened his mouth to howl. He was a wise child. He scowled, but he let himself be led away from her into that glittering place which Charlemagne had built.

He did not sulk long. He loved the music, and the sheen of a thousand candles on floor of marble and walls of porphyry and roof of mosaic as magnificent as any in Byzantium, and the shift and shimmer of gems and silks and furs on the backs and arms and heads of all the great lords of Germany. His own lords, though he was too young still to understand what that meant. His father was emperor of both Germany and Italy, and had perforce to give half his mind and most of his presence to his realm south of the Alps. The younger Otto was his hope and promise in the north; his proof that Germany was not forgotten. The empire had an heir, and that heir was Germany's king. It was wise, and politic.

Germany's king was a child with his father's red-fair Saxon hair and his mother's great dark eyes, stiff almost to immobility in robes of imperial silk: a child invested with a sword a handspan taller than himself, and armlets vast enough to swallow both his arms in one, and a cloak which enveloped all of him but his small pale face, and scepter and staff cut to the measure of a man and a king. A man would bear them all at once. This child was given them one by one; then each was taken away.

Otto was much too small a prince for the regalia of a king, but one mark of his rank at least was made to his measure: the golden circlet of the diadem. The bishops anointed his brows with oil from Jerusalem and bound them with the diadem. He did not fret with it as Aspasia had half feared he would. He bore it easily, as a king should.

Aspasia's eye moved past him. The empress stood where these lords and prelates had made her stand, in the upper sanctuary behind the throne, almost out of sight of the people below. Almost, but not quite. She looked, with her daughters about her, like an image of Hagia Sophia in Byzantium where she was born: the moon and her attendant planets, lofty and imperially beautiful. No one would ever have guessed that she was angry. The Germans thought themselves subtle in setting her so high and yet so far apart: remote and powerless. Theophano would teach them what subtlety was.

Aspasia, having surrendered her charge to the lords and the bishops, managed to come no closer to the throne than the chapel directly below it. They had used the throne in the portico that was proper to the German kings; it was that to which Otto had been raised for his election and acclamation. Now they led him up the spiral of the stair to the upper chapel, and in it the high seat, the throne of Charlemagne with its six steep steps.

He mounted them one step at a time, as a child will. A bishop walked on either side to steady him: John of Ravenna, Willigis of Mainz, Italy and Germany brought together to crown the new king.

It was a terrible height for a child, and a long fall if he stumbled: down from the summit of the high chapel into the lower with its press of people. He looked for a moment as if he would cry. Then, as he reached the top and turned and saw them all below him, faces turned upward like flowers to the sun, he laughed. The choir had paused in its antiphon. His laughter rang out alone, light and clear and giddily exultant.

The echoes died. The bishops readied themselves to seat the king on his throne. The cantor drew breath to begin the first phrase of the *Te Deum*. The people waited, caught in time, in the instant between crown and throne, between prince and consecrated king.

A roar shattered the silence. "Rome! Word from Rome!"

Tumult burst through the chapel. Cries of outrage; shouts of protest; a woman's shriek. The great bull-bellow that had begun it sounded louder now, full beneath the throne, clear above the rising uproar. "Rome! Word from Rome, and true, I swear to God! The emperor—the emperor is dead!"

Aspasia was born a Byzantine; she intended to die one. She could be calm even in pandemonium. Even at the end of a world. She rocked in the flood of grief and shock, disbelief and stunned belief. She knew the bitter taste of truth. It had a tang of irony. Otto, twenty-eight years old, was dead in Rome. Otto, three years old, lived in Aachen, poised to take the throne of Charlemagne.

The bishops had forgotten him. No one else was close enough to remind them. The empress had disappeared. Of her daughters, only Sophia was visible, eldest and most un-willing to understand why her infant brother should be crowned here, and not she. Her face had drained of all its high color, its scowl of temper slackened into shock. No tears. Sophia only ever wept for rage.

Otto eyed the long descent and the near-riot below. The crown slipped; he steadied it with a hand. His glance found the tall chair behind him and reckoned its use as a haven. Calmly, while his people reeled to find themselves bereft of an emperor in the moment of gaining a king, he turned his back on them and clambered onto the broad stone seat. He settled there, wriggling a little for the stone was cold even through the cushion, and set his hands on the arms as he had seen his father do. His head was high under the crown, his face composed. He did not know yet what death was, or what it meant. But he knew that he was king.

I

PORPHYROGENITA

⊕

Constantinople and Rome

968-972

One

It was raining hard with an edge of sleet, scudding across the Sea of Marmora, rattling against the shutters of the Sacred Palace. Even with every brazier stoked red-hot and the hypocaust roaring below, the halls were as cold as they were beautiful. It was a fortunate functionary who could take refuge in his own house, with a warm wrap about him and a hot cup in his hands.

Aspasia did not need to think about hot wine. She could have had it where she was coming from, for a price. It was, aptly enough, the festival of winter's beginning, the Brumalia, and little in it of Christian charity even after six hundred irreproachably Christian years. The great ladies of court and city would be struggling toward the palace through the wind and the wet, each to receive her length of imperial silk from the empress' own hand, and all together to dine at the imperial table. Aspasia should have been there in the flock of attendants about the Basilissa. She would slip in later; with luck, her gracious majesty would never have noticed the gap in the ranks.

Swift feet sounded behind her. There were always people in the teeming city-within-a-city that was the palace, but they seldom ran; and never in the empress' domain. Aspasia made herself smaller in the plain dark mantle over her court dress, and hoped that she was invisible.

She was the only living thing in that passage, and it was not a public one; no pillars or statuary to hide behind, not even a scrap of hanging. The runner was mantled as closely and darkly as herself, like a shadow in the gloom, but the voice was human enough, breathless as much with laughter as with exertion. "Aspasia! Aspasia, will you wait?"

Aspasia waited. She was almost as displeased as she tried to look. "Did I ask you to come with me?"

"Did you think I wouldn't follow?" The pursuer came to a halt, gangling-graceful as a yearling foal. She was going to be a beauty, Aspasia reflected dispassionately. At the moment she looked like a hoyden, with the color high in her cheeks and her eyes sparkling and her hair doing its best to fly out of its plaits. She had managed to get out of the swathings of court silks and into something sensible. Aspasia hated her for it.

"Here," she said, pressing something into Aspasia's arms. "You can change here. I know just the place to hide your robe until we come back."

So did Aspasia, maybe better than she. Aspasia was as native to this place as the other was, and had begun rather higher in it. She did not say so. She rid herself of her state robes and put on the plain wool gown with its skirt that let her stretch her stride, all without a word to the one who brought it.

Nothing short of the empress' wrath could cow Theophano. "I told Mother I had a headache and needed to lie down. She was busy: she believed me. We could probably escape the banquet if we wanted to. Shall I have a very bad headache?"

"You will if your mother finds out that you lied," said Aspasia. Not, alas, as severely as she should. She was beginning to be amused.

"My lady mother, long life to her sacred majesty, is going to be counting out ells of our second-best silk until nightfall. I don't envy her at all," said Theophano. "Or want to watch her, when I can play truant with you."

That was breathtakingly daring and quite worthy of a reprimand, except that time was flying. Aspasia settled for a repressive scowl and a long stride past Theophano.

Theophano's longer stride matched itself easily to Aspasia's haste. Aspasia was utterly Byzantine: small, dark, and bird-boned. Theophano had the Macedonian height and fairness, although she had her mother's eyes. Ox-eyes, great and brown and deceptively soft. Her mother the Basilissa was the most beautiful woman in Byzantium. The Basilissa usually was. It was a requirement of the office, like fecundity; but unlike noble lineage. Her sacred majesty was born a tavernkeeper's daughter. She had no shame of it, nor felt she needed any.

Her daughter had her wits as well as the promise of her beauty, and a goodly share of her stubbornness. "I don't know why you thought you could creep out without me. You never have yet."

"I'll never stop trying." Aspasia slowed a fraction. "What if I'm going to an assignation with my husband?"

Theophano was too well-bred at least to laugh. "At midmorning? On the Brumalia? With Demetrios? Now, if it were Cousin John—"

Aspasia blushed, and was furious at herself. "You know perfectly well that I can't abide that puffed-up peacock. What the rest of you silly geese see in him, I'll never understand."

"*I* don't like him," said Theophano. "He's short. And

too thick. And going bald in front. But you have to admit, he's handsomer than—"

"My husband is quite as handsome as he needs to be. And only a little bald. And he has a beautiful beard. And he's taller than anybody, even some of the Varangians."

Aspasia paused for breath. Theophano grinned at her and skipped, looking a good deal less than fourteen years old. Then all at once she sobered. "When I marry I want to have a husband like Demetrios. Warm and kind, and not always scheming for his own advantage. He doesn't need to be handsome. My father was, and what good did it do him? He still died, and Mother married an old man because he would be good for the empire."

"Not so old," said Aspasia. "And not so loud."

Theophano shook her head, mutinous, but she did not argue. Even a princess royal did not speak too freely of the emperor. Particularly if she was the daughter of his predecessor and had a better claim to the throne than he ever would. It was one certain way to death, or to the life-in-death of a convent.

Aspasia must have said it aloud, without thinking. Theophano said, "You weren't sent away when my father died. Grandmother and the other aunts were, but not you."

"Because of you, catling. You raised such a shriek as these old walls had never heard. And I had Demetrios, and he is the Autokrator's cousin: a miracle in itself, considering who I was and what I was supposed to be. My father was indulgent; I was the youngest, and headstrong, and I was not about to bow meekly to the necessity of keeping a royal female unmarried while there are heirs enough without her. So I was given to a nobody with no ambitions beyond the scholarly, except that he persisted in wanting me. For myself, God knows why. Not for the purple I was born in."

"I know. It's scandalous." Theophano was a little ahead; she put her weight to the door that ended the passage, gasping as sleet smote her face. They darted together into the lee of the next pavilion, with no eyes for beauty that, in summer and in sunlight, amply earned the name of paradise. It was all grey now, and slicked with ice.

There was warmth within, blessed waves of it, and a scent of wine and spices. Aspasia loosed a surreptitious breath. It was all as she had ordered it. In these days, under this emperor, one never knew.

The object of it was there and, from the look of him, had been there for a goodly while. He looked as comfortable as he ever could.

Liutprand was not a comfortable man. He was a Lombard, and Lombards were big men, ruddy and fair, but Liutprand had older blood; he looked remarkably like Aspasia, small and dark and quick, with a great Roman nose and a fierce Italian temper. That temper was barely held in check now. Maybe it was only that he had another of his endless coughs, and his nose would not stop running. He glared through reddened eyes, but he did obeisance without the edge of parody which he had been known to give it, and said politely enough, "Welcome to your own palace, my ladies. It was gracious of you to come. I trust my request gave you no difficulty?"

Aspasia let the lone servant take her cloak, offer her a chair, ply her with heated wine. She folded her hands round the cup, welcoming the pain of thawing fingers. "No difficulty," she said, "your excellency." He scowled at that; she kept her face somber, but let her eyes dance. "Why so formal, Liudo? Have we done something unforgivable?"

"You," he said, biting off the word, "no." He went back to his chair and his cup, and sniffed loudly. "God be my witness, you have never been anything but hospitable. Which is more than I can say for others in this pestilential city. Full half a year I've been here, do you know that? Scorching in the heat. Freezing in the cold. Was Constantine a madman, to build the capital of his empire here of all the places in the world?"

"Maybe he surveyed the site in the spring," said Theophano. "We do have a beautiful spring."

The Lombard snorted. "Well, thank God and His holy Mother, I won't be here to see it."

They both stared at him. Aspasia said it first. "You're not staying? You're leaving?"

"Yes, I'm leaving." He sneezed explosively. "Damn." They were not excessively shocked, although he was a bishop. "I'm leaving. I know when I'm getting nowhere. I should have known it the day I came here, when they bivouacked me—lodged is far too elegant a word—in that ramshackle barn and afflicted me with that tribe of insolent servants, every one of them bent on robbing me blind. His most gracious majesty has no intention, now or ever, of honoring my embassy. He keeps me here like a tame ape, to dance for his amusement."

"It's not as bad as that," said Theophano. "He's been preoccupied. There have been battles, and armies to raise and pay and feed, and precious little time to think about more peaceful things."

"No, and there never will be. Nikephoros Phokas has no intention whatever of giving me a bride for my prince."

"Well," said Theophano. "You have to understand his side of it. Your prince's father is claiming the western half of the Roman Empire. If our emperor gives your emperor a princess for his son, people might think that he's sanctioning the rest of it, too. Letting a German barbarian call himself the equal of the one and only Autokrator of the Romans."

"My emperor *is*—" Liutprand stopped, drew a deep breath, closed his eyes. "Never mind. We've fought it all before. I'm tired; I'm going home. I wanted you to know. As soon as the weather allows, we sail."

"That might not be till spring," Aspasia said.

"God forbid." He glowered into his cup, found it empty, held it out for the servant to fill. "And God forbid that you be punished for trying to make my life bearable. I shouldn't have allowed it."

Aspasia met him glare for glare. "Who said you did? I summoned you the first time, as I remember, because I'd heard that you were interesting, and I wanted to see for myself."

He smiled as if he could not help it. "And I came because I was spitting nails over my latest audience with his majesty, and I thought I might get at him through you. You were honest with me about the hopelessness of that. I was so shocked that I was honest right back."

"You threatened to put me in a book," said Aspasia. "I was delighted. Are you going to be as deliciously nasty to me as you were to Queen Willa?"

He had the grace to blush. "Devil take the day I told you that. I must have been off my head."

"Only honest, Liudo. That girdle of hers . . ."

Theophano looked from one to the other, bright-eyed. "Girdle? Aspasia, you never told me that one."

Liutprand's blush deepened to imperial purple. "She has not, and she will not."

"No," mused Aspasia. "Maybe later. When you're grown."

"I am grown," said Theophano, stung. "I've been a woman since Easter. I know about men and women, and babies, and—"

Aspasia shook her head in a way that Theophano would not, if she was wise, mistake. "Later, Phania." She turned to Liutprand. "I'm afraid I've never been that scandalous. Truth to tell, I'm rather dull."

"Because you know the meaning of prudence." He was unwontedly quiet and unwontedly somber. "You shine here like a pearl in a herd of swine. You wallow in the mud of their intrigues, but you never let it stain you. Pray heaven they never open their eyes and see what you've done; or remember who you are."

"I'm my father's daughter," said Aspasia.

"Exactly," Liutprand said. "He knew how to efface himself; how to keep himself both clean and unmurdered. He outlasted them all, and in the end he held the throne as he was born to hold it, with no regents or usurpers to stand against him. He died in his bed, and not of poison. So, God willing, shall you."

"I don't intend to die an empress," said Aspasia. "I never want a throne. The Basilissa does. She has one. She'll hold it till she dies, and share it as she pleases, with whoever best suits her purpose. All I ask of the world is that I live in it, and not immured in the walls of a convent."

"You'll never make a saint," said the Bishop of Cremona.

Aspasia grinned at him. "Neither will you, my friend, and well you know it. I'm sorry to see you go. I'm glad you're going home. We've treated you badly, I confess it; I'd redress it if I could."

"You've done more than you know." He rubbed his eyes angrily, muttering about winter rheums. He stood and bowed with astonishing grace. One could see then what a statesman he could be when he was not beset with imperial insults. "God and His Mother keep you."

He left quickly, at a pace just short of discourteous. Neither princess minded.

"He'll be back," Aspasia said. She did not know how she knew.

Theophano nodded slowly, eyes dark and liquid-soft as a fawn's. She looked exactly like her mother. Aspasia shivered lightly. When the Basilissa wore that melting expression, it meant inevitably that she was up to something; usually something lengthy, intricate, and subtly dangerous.

The Basilissa's daughter blinked and was herself again. She stood and shook out her skirt, eyeing her sodden cloak without pleasure. "We had better go back," she said. "Before we're missed. Unless you'd rather I had that headache?"

Aspasia did not smile. "No. I think you can reckon yourself quite recovered."

Theophano looked unhappy, but she let the servant settle the mantle over her shoulders, and led the way into rain that had turned, all unnoticed, to snow.

Two

Aspasia was pregnant again. That was nothing new, in nine years of marriage to Demetrios; but this time, by all that was holy, she would bear a living child.

"I will," she said to Theophano, fiercely. "I *must*."

Theophano held her hand tightly and tried to smile. "I'm sure you will. We've all been praying, and you've got the best doctors in the world."

"And they've got me tied to my bed." Aspasia struggled up in the mound of cushions, glaring at the maid who leaped to catch her. She endured a flurry of clucking and settling, wanting to scream but knowing better than to try. Then the baby kicked, and she could not care about anything but that. "Phania! Phania, did you feel it?"

Theophano laughed with her, and cried with her, too, pushing aside a tottering heap of books to coil beside her on the bed.

The baby left off kicking. They left off carrying on, regarding one another a little ruefully. "This is a fine pass for a woman to come to," Aspasia said. "No wonder men call us weak."

"You aren't," said Theophano. "Are you frightfully bored?"

"Catling, you can't imagine." Aspasia picked up a wayward book, dropped it again. "I thought I'd study Arabic. But how many hours a day can a Christian read the Koran? I sleep too much. I don't eat enough, they tell me, though I stuff myself till I'm like to burst. People come and talk, but all the women want to do is tell ghastly tales about their own pregnancies. When I try to change the subject, they either leave in a huff or tell me I shouldn't be thinking about such alarming things as whether the German emperor will send another embassy like the one that left last winter. Even Demetrios can't seem to remember that I'm Aspasia and not an image of the Great Mother. He keeps touching me and going pale, and threatening to faint."

"Poor thing," said Theophano. "He's terrified."

Aspasia's hands tightened over the swell of her belly. "I'm not going to lose this baby. I *won't*." She shook her head once, hard. "Enough of that. Talk to me. Tell me what's happening in the palace."

Theophano obeyed her. But there was something in her manner: a constraint; a distinct air of clinging to trifles. Aspasia watched her narrowly. She kept her eyes down, her face serene, her voice low and calm.

"Phania," Aspasia said. "You haven't mentioned your mother. Is she well?"

Theophano stiffened just perceptibly. "Yes. She's well. There's nothing to tell."

"Is there?"

"Yes. No. Nothing."

Aspasia let the silence stretch.

Theophano flung up her head. Her eyes were angry. "I'm not supposed to upset you!"

"You aren't," said Aspasia. "But you will if you hide it from me much longer. What's wrong, Phania?"

What was wrong was her mother. And Cousin John. "She and he," said Theophano. "He does have a handsome face and that yellow hair, though he's losing some of it. And he's spirited, like one of his own stallions. I suppose, after the emperor, he must be like sun in a dark place. But it's treason, Aspasia. Do you know what he does? He goes up to her every day in the afternoon, and they lie in her bed, and he calls her by her titles. *Glory of the purple, joy of the world, most pious and most happy Augusta, Christ-loving Basilissa.*" Theophano swallowed hard, as if she wanted to retch. "And then—and then, Aspasia, he goes away, and at night she goes up to the emperor, and he never suspects a thing. They're going to kill him, Aspasia. They'll murder him, and John will be emperor."

Aspasia put her arms around Theophano, who had begun to cry. "Hush," she said. "Hush." But her heart was cold. Nikephoros was her safety: a hard man, but fair, and fond of his cousin Demetrios. He had sent a gift of embroidered silk for their child's christening robe. John was less hard, but all the less fair for that, and ambitious. Ambitious enough not to care whom he trampled, if only he won the throne. And Demetrios would be a threat. Demetrios, whose wife was *porphyrogenita:* a child born in the Purple Chamber, princess royal, daughter of a ruling emperor. Born, if she had willed it, to be empress; to give the right of empire to the man who married her.

"Have you tried to tell the emperor?" Aspasia asked. Her voice was perfectly calm. She was surprised.

Theophano tensed against Aspasia's arms. Aspasia let her go. She sat up straight and composed her face. It was royal, that art, and frightening to see. "I can't tell him. Whatever my mother is, whatever she does, she is still my mother."

"Others must know."

"Everyone knows," said Theophano. "The emperor won't listen. He laughs, or he preaches sermons on jealousy and false witness. He's blind and deaf."

"Men are, when they grow old and their wives are young and beautiful."

"He'll die for it."

Aspasia crossed herself. "God guard him." She meant it with all her heart.

Theophano went away soon after that. Aspasia lay in the bed which she had come to hate, for once hardly aware of it, thinking hard.

She was still thinking when Demetrios came. He brought a breath of free air with him, cold and clean, and a gift of honey sweets. He could not stay long. "I'm dining with the emperor tonight," he said. He was the only man in the world who could say it without either fawning or boasting. "I'd rather stay with you. I'll come back early. God knows, I have an excuse."

She laughed because he wanted her to, and hugged him. He was all bones and angles, but lately he had begun to thicken a bit in the middle. "You're keeping me company," she said.

Only a little while ago he would have leaped on her and kissed her into submission. Now he settled for a glare. "Is that any way to address the father of your child?"

"The mother of your child is delighted with any diversion she can find." Before he could answer that, she laid a finger on his lips. "No. Don't stay. You have to go. There's something you have to do."

She told him what Theophano had said. At first he tried to interrupt, but then he was silent, tight-lipped. When she finished he ran his fingers through his beard, tugging at it. His brows were knotted over his mild brown eyes: though they were not so mild now. "Devil take that child," he said.

"You know!"

His scowl deepened. "Yes, I know. I'd hoped you didn't.

That's what this dinner is. An attempt to persuade him to see sense."

"Go, then," Aspasia said. "Do it." She all but pushed him toward the door.

He stood at arm's length, gripping her small hands in his great bony ones. "And you," he said, "stop fretting. The emperor is the emperor, but you are the only wife I have, and I want to keep you, and the baby with you."

"I'm well enough," she said.

He wanted to believe her. He kissed her warmly—almost too warmly for her comfort, even six months gone in pregnancy—and went to dine with his emperor.

Aspasia dozed. She kept starting awake. The house was quiet but for the song of wind about it. Too quiet for her taut-strung nerves. She restrained herself by main force from getting up and stalking through the rooms.

When the door opened, she started up with a cry. Demetrios was still in his court dress, glittering in the night-lamp's light, as impossibly elongated as a saint in a basilica. But he was smiling as no saint ever did, simply to be here with her, and knowing what she carried.

"Tell me!" she demanded.

His smile faded. He came in and sat by her and raked his hands through what was left of his hair, making it stand up in comic disarray. She could have hit him for taking so long to get to it. "Nothing happened," he said, "though something tried to. Someone—one of the priests—sent his majesty a letter telling him that there was a plot to kill him this very night, and the empress was in it, harboring the murderers in her own chambers. He had to pay attention to that. He sent Michael the chamberlain to search, and Michael found nothing. The emperor decided to laugh. 'Someone has ghastly taste in jokes,' he said. We stayed a little longer, but nothing happened; then he dismissed us. He did promise to double the guard on his rooms. What more can anyone do?"

"Nothing," said Aspasia, though the taste of it was bitter. She caught Demetrios' hand and held tight. "Stay with me tonight," she said.

He hesitated. "The doctors—" he began. "The servants—" He shook his head suddenly. "They don't need to know."

He dropped his clothes and came in beside her. She fitted her swollen body to his familiar planes and angles, drinking in his warmth. He smelled of wine and myrrh. She wound herself about him and clung, willing the night to pass, and her terrors with it.

There had never been a night like it, nor ever would again. The story, like the dalliance that had begun it, was no secret, once it was irrevocable.

The empress went up to the emperor as she did every night, taking with her no weapon but her beauty. Tonight she barely lingered. She had guests to see to, she said, but when she had done that, she would come back. Would he leave his door unlatched for her?

All that he had was hers, and well she knew it. He forgot, or chose to forget, that he had ordered a doubled guard. She would never harm him. Maybe she did not love him; love was not a luxury for emperors. But she was his lady and his consort, and she still found him handsome, although he was no longer young.

He paused to assure himself of that. He was by no means a tall man, but he was broad and strong, honed to a keen edge in years of campaigns. His hair was thick and black; his beard was greying round the jaw but soft and silken, a pleasure to the touch. She loved to stroke it, to call him her lord and captain, to bid him conquer her as he conquered the enemies of Byzantium. He was strong in that still, as strong as he had ever been.

He approached the icons that had pride of place in his bedchamber, and knelt before them, and began to pray. In a little while, hearing no sign of his lady's return, he stretched out on the leopardskin that had cushioned his knees, and slept.

The Basilissa left him as unwitting of danger as a newborn child. What she thought or felt, no one ever dared to ask. Maybe her heart beat hard; maybe, for an instant, she wavered. Maybe she steeled herself for what she had determined to do. He had never been more to her than a means to the stability of the empire. Dark, squat, shaggy little man, as indifferently clean as any soldier or saint, happier in stinking rags on the floor than in silks in his great bed. But he was a gifted general, and the empire needed him. For that she had swallowed her disgust and pretended that she wanted him. One learned that art early, in the tavern where she was born.

Now there was John, who had all that Nikephoros had, and beauty, too. She would make him emperor. He would remember to whom he owed his throne; he would bend to her will.

She found her allies in the room in which they had hidden, where Michael the chamberlain had never troubled to look. "Now," she said to them. Their eyes gleamed: fear, excitement, a flare of bloodlust. She smiled and let them loose.

The night advanced toward midnight. The wind rose, shrilling out of the north. Snow rode on the back of it.

Down below the walls of the palace, where a stone image stood by the sea, stone lion springing upon stone bull, John beached the boat that he had bought for a handful of silver. The empress' men stood watch above. They leaped at his signal and lowered a basket, drawing up his men one by one, then John himself. They braced themselves against the parapet, hauling hand over hand. The basket swayed and spun.

The wind was loud in their ears; the waves crashed on the shingle. Snow blinded them.

The basket struck the parapet. John heaved himself out of it, cursing, and kicked it into the sea. But then he laughed, though softly, lest anyone hear: a deep rumble of mirth. "Now, lads. To the hunt!"

The emperor's chamber was just beyond the place where John had come up, with windows on the sea. One was unlatched. They paused, firming their grips on their swords, and burst through it.

The bed was empty, the nightlamp flickering low. Those in the lead stared at one another, eyes rolling white. One yelped and bolted for the window. His companions hauled him back. In the shadows someone hissed: a signal, and safe, though they started like deer. The one who had given it minced into the light, one of the empress' beardless pets, smirking at their disarray. "He never sleeps in his bed," said the eunuch. "Come, bold lions. Follow me."

He led them through the shadowed opulence of the great chamber to the niche with its shimmer of icons: Christ the King and the Mother of God and John the Baptist, great-eyed dark faces haloed in gold. In front of them lay a heavy scarlet cloth, and on it a leopardskin, and on the leopardskin, snoring, the emperor.

John paused, standing over him, sword loose in his hand. His face was empty of expression. He drew back. The others surged past him, spreading to circle the sleeping man, grinning at one another. There was a long pause. John sat on the bed, sword across his knees. "Now," he said.

They moved in. One meticulously judged toe dug into the emperor's side. His snoring stopped. Another prodded him. He started; his head came up. "What—"

He never saw the sword that swept down. "Mother of God!" he shrieked. "Help me!" Blood streamed from the great wound in his brow. He thrashed, blinded. They caught him, pinned him.

"Bring him to me," said John.

They dragged him across the floor, trailing blood. He could not kneel; they held him half-sprawling. John regarded him in disgust. "And you call yourself an emperor."

"Mother of God," Nikephoros said over and over. "Sweet Mother Mary, have mercy."

"Mercy?" asked John. "You ask for mercy? When did you ever give it? When did you give even gratitude? Who raised you to this eminence? Who set you here, and supported you with all that was in him, and asked nothing of you but the smallest fraction of what he was due? And how did you repay me? You sent me away. You cast me out. Then when my shame was complete you brought me back— and made me bow my head and serve you, and never a word of thanks for it. You gave me nothing but dishonor."

Nikephoros tossed his wounded head, gasping, scrabbling feebly at the floor. "No," he said. "No."

"Yes," said John. He caught the emperor by the beard, twisting his fingers in it. "You took my honor and my power. I repay you in kind." He pulled, merciless. His wolves laughed and smote with fists and hilts. Teeth shattered. Nikephoros dropped. John kicked him. He convulsed. John clove his skull.

They hewed him, and when they had hewn him they struck his head from his shoulders. They dragged his body to the window and flung him out. He wheeled in the snow-shot darkness like a great ungainly bird, and fell to the shingle above the sea. There he lay, broken and headless in the snow, through the night and the day; nor did anyone dare to touch him.

The Emperor Nikephoros was dead. The Emperor John, having taken the crimson buskins and set himself on the throne, set about securing his power in this empire which he had seized.

* * *

Thunder startled Aspasia out of a troubled, tossing sleep. She felt Demetrios pull out of her clasp, and clutched him, but he escaped her. She struggled against the fog in her brain, straining to hear. Someone shouted outside. Someone else burst into the room. It was one of the cousins, wild-eyed and covered in snow. "For God's sake, Demetrios, run while you can! Those are John's men, they're coming for you, they—"

Demetrios tried to push the man out of the room, but Aspasia's cry stilled them both. "What is it? What has happened?"

Cousin Diogenes was never the most tactful of men, even when he was not distraught. He answered her bluntly, though Demetrios looked ready to throttle him for it. "Nikephoros is dead. John murdered him. The Basilissa abetted it. John has seized the throne. The Varangians have acclaimed him. Now he's securing his victory." He turned to Demetrios. "He wants you. You could be a rival, he says; you're best disposed of."

Demetrios did not look at all afraid. He went to the window, opened the shutter a fraction, peered out. "They're breaking through," he said, perfectly calm. He turned. "Diogenes. Wake the steward; tell him to ready the litter for my lady. Or if there's no time, fetch someone who can carry her without jostling."

Diogenes nodded and ran. Aspasia struggled out of the bedclothes. "Where are we going?"

"I'm sending you to the palace," Demetrios said. "I may be mad; I should probably send you to one of the convents; but I think you'll be safest in plain sight."

"And you?" she asked sharply. "Are you coming?"

He shook his head.

She staggered up, reeling more with rage than with dizziness. "You can't stay here."

"I won't," he said. "I'm going to try to run."

He was lying. She could see it in his eyes. He was going to

stay and try to delay the hunters, until she and the baby could escape.

She seized him and shook him. "You can't stay. They won't touch me. The worst they'll do is pack me off to a convent. But you they'll kill." His face was set hard against her. She pulled his head down, eye to blazing eye. "Go, Demetrios. Take what you can and run. I'll stay here; I'll be monumentally indisposed. I'll keep them as long as I can."

"No," he said.

He was beyond reason. All he could see was that she was his woman and she was threatened, and he must defend her. Never mind that he was the one who needed defending.

The uproar at the gate rose to a crescendo. Demetrios moved feverishly, bundling together whatever belongings came to hand. He would not let Aspasia help him. She nearly wept with frustration. "Please, Demetrios. If you love me. *Go.*"

He set the bundle in her lap as she sat on the bed, and reached the door in two long strides. Neither Diogenes nor the servants had come. He wavered as if torn.

"I'm safe here," she said again, one last desperate time. "Go, Demetrios. Save yourself. We'll find a way to get you back."

She watched her persuasion take hold, bitterly though he fought it. His face twisted; he looked ready to weep. But she had won. He sprang for the garments which he had discarded when he went to bed, and began to pull them on. They were hardly suitable for a fugitive, but the cloak would cover them, and there was wealth in them: gold and silver thread, jewels at collar and hem, and the silk itself, woven on imperial looms.

Feet thudded in the corridor. Metal rang. "Varangians," said Demetrios. "He's taking no chances."

"The back door," Aspasia said. "The garden. Quickly."

He strode toward it. She dropped the bundle and kicked it under the bed, and drew up the coverlets. For once she was glad to look so ghastly: sallow, owl-eyed, and visibly pregnant. She did not need help to look terrified.

Demetrios opened the inner door. She would always remember him as he was then. His narrow glittering figure with the dark cloak flung over it; his long pale face; his eyes fixed on her, committing her to memory.

It was that pause which betrayed him. The emperor's men broke down the door. They were a blur of scarlet and gold, great, braided, bearded men, armed with axes. They took no notice of the woman in the bed. They surged toward Demetrios.

He stood unmoving. He carried no weapon; he would not have known how to use one if he had. His head was up. He was almost smiling.

"Run!" she screamed at him.

He backed through the door. He was not afraid; not of dying. She understood him perfectly. He did not want her to see him fall.

Aspasia fought against the blankets' grip and her own body's weakness. The Varangians stalked her husband. Her eyes darted. A weapon—if she could find a weapon—

Demetrios backed out of sight. Maybe he would run. Please God, maybe he would escape.

The Varangians checked, poised, charged. She heard a sound that she would never forget. The song of an axeblade cleaving air; the soft, terrible thud as it bit flesh, clove bone.

Demetrios uttered no death-cry. He fell in silence. It was a better death than his emperor's. Cleaner; braver. But no less absolute.

Three

⊕

T he Lombard had come back.

Theodora, freed from her convent to give John a proper claim to the throne, was a gentle soul as imperial ladies went. She was also the beauty of the family: tall and wheat-fair, with her father's clear blue eyes. Aspasia felt smaller, darker, and plainer than ever beside this loveliest of her sisters.

She refused to let the rest of it twist her vitals. Theodora's apparent contentment with her handsome, ruthless husband. The daughter in the cradle. The new swelling under the empress' girdle.

Aspasia had lost her own child a week to the day after its father died. It would have been a son. There would be no others, even if she wanted to marry again.

She had almost died. Yet that had been her salvation in the end. When the emperor's butchers left, she rose from her bed. She found the house steward cowering in the kitchen with the rest of the servants; she roused them to do what must be done for the one who was dead. Then she went to the palace. Not to take a bloody revenge. Not even to demand reparation. She was not thinking as clearly as that. She simply wanted to be where she was born.

Theophano was still, then, the Basilissa's daughter. She spoke for Aspasia; she was listened to. Aspasia bore her child in Theophano's chamber, and saw it die, and all but died herself. While she lay there, not quite dead and not quite alive, one Basilissa fell and the other took her place. Then it was Aspasia who spoke for Theophano, and Theodora listened. She was no fool: she made them swear to take no revenge against herself or her husband. Theophano swore without visible reluctance. For Aspasia it was harder. But she was royal and Byzantine, and she did not, when it came to the crux, want to die.

"My life is a better revenge," she said to Theophano. "He has to know that I am here, and that I am who I am, and that I seem to forgive him. He who never forgives or forgets the smallest slight, is hardly likely to find that a comfortable prospect. I'll outlast him, Phania. I'll spit on his grave."

Theophano said nothing. She had grown into her beauty; she looked, when not animated with speech, like the image of a saint. Aspasia knew how deceptive that serenity could be. Theophano too was biding her time, although for what, she did not confide even in Aspasia.

On one thing at least they were agreed. They would not at any cost let themselves be sent away to take the veil. The emperor would happily have packed them off; fortunately he had other and more pressing concerns, and Theodora was not hasty to subject her sister to an ordeal which she herself had so lately escaped. That was another of Theodora's virtues: she did not hold grudges.

And now at last, after three years' absence, the Lombard was back. He was not the leader of the embassy this time, but he was most certainly a part of it. Like his German king, he was nothing if not persistent.

"You might," Aspasia said, "move over a little."

Theophano obliged. There was room enough on the narrow bench for two, if one was as small as Aspasia. The view was excellent. Aspasia doubted that many even of the eunuchs knew of this anomaly in the wall, hardly big enough to be called a closet, with its mullioned window and its clear view down upon the Golden Hall. They were up above the ordered ranks of the court, and so placed that they could see both the emperor and the petitioners who faced him; they could hear every word, catch every expression.

Aspasia folded her arms on the ledge and rested her chin on them. However weary she might be of life and living, she never tired of the spectacle that glittered below her. They called it the Chrysotriclinium, the Golden Hall.

In a palace renowned for its splendor, it was supremely splendid. It was great enough to contain the full court of an empire, and it was all gold: golden walls, golden pillars, golden floor. It looked like an edifice of light, or like a house of God. God ruled here, the philosophers said, in and through the person of the sacred emperor.

Its focus was the throne itself in the domed curve of the apse under the image of Christ the King, on a great dais carpeted with cloth of gold. Three ranks of guards stood armed and glittering behind it: the inner rank of those who were most noble and most trusted, and the second rank of those who had yet to earn their master's fullest trust, and the third rank, the outer rank, of Varangians in scarlet and gold, their axes on their shoulders. Aspasia could not even now look at those axes without a cold clenching in her middle.

She made herself look away at the wonders that widened every newcomer's eye. A tree of gold rose glittering before the throne. On its boughs perched jeweled birds that spread their wings and sang. At the emperor's feet crouched golden lions. Every now and again they rose and lashed their tails and roared.

When they were silent, the air was full of music: the sonorous chords of the two great golden organs, or the brass blare of trumpets, or the chanting of the emperor's eunuchs, proclaiming his praises and the praises of Christ the King, for whom the right side of the broad throne was left empty; but full, said the priests, of his presence.

John Tzimisces looked the part of the emperor. Aspasia could grant him that. Shod in the crimson buskins, wrapped in silk and in cloth of gold, crowned with the great crown with its pendant pearls, he seemed above mere flesh and blood. His hair was hardly less bright than the gold that bound it; his beard was ruddy gold, thick and long and richly curling; his face between seemed carved of ivory. Only his hands marred the perfection of the semblance: they were short and thick and rough with use, a soldier's hands, more apt for a sword's hilt than for the frail rod of the scepter. The rest of him preserved the hieratic stillness of his office, but his fingers were restless, flexing on the rod, toying with it.

A stirring in the court, a rustle that spread from gate to throne, announced the coming of the embassy. Servants moved swiftly to draw the great purple curtain between throne and hall. Aspasia, above it, could see the emperor behind it: he slumped perceptibly, raising the crown to rub the brow beneath, leaning to exchange a word or two with the guardsman closest to him.

On the other side of the curtain the gates opened wide. The choir renewed its chanting: a hymn of greeting. The embassy entered, pacing slowly. Most of them looked faintly stunned, bedazzled by so much magnificence and acutely uncomfortable in imperial silk. Aspasia wondered how many had had to be separated by force from their own finery and compelled to accept the robes kept for just such occasions, like the vestments in a cathedral's sacristy.

She did not at first see Liutprand. He was not in the front rank. Someone else had that; someone whom she did not know.

"There," Theophano breathed behind her.

There, toward the middle, wearing a robe she knew. She had given it to him. It had held up rather better than its wearer. He was thinner than she remembered, grey-pallid under the olive darkness of his skin; the hair that showed under the hat was more grey than black. But he held himself erect and he walked without assistance, and his eyes gleamed as wickedly bright as they ever had. He was in no awe of all this spectacle. When the curtain drew back to reveal the emperor, his lips twitched. When the throne soared up toward the ceiling and hovered there, high above the gaping envoys, he seemed to bite back a smile.

The embassy advanced under the guidance of a stately eunuch. A high one indeed, Aspasia noted; one who did not stoop to conduct the lesser embassies. Nikephoros had not been so courteous.

At the foot of the emperor's column, the envoys went down in obeisance. Not all of them were pleased. Big blond Germans, those were, little inclined to bend the knee to any foreign king, still less this one who claimed to be their own emperor's equal; or, more intolerable yet, his master. But they were ambassadors, and they knew their place. They bowed as they were bidden to bow, down to the ground, three times. Then the one who led them must do it again, go down on his knees three times as he approached the throne. It came down as he came up to it, until the emperor's feet rested again on the footstool, and he looked down from a merely human eminence upon the man who knelt before him.

The Master of Ceremonies stepped forward, imperially haughty. The ambassador set a letter in his hands. He took his time in reading it, in silence broken only by the roaring of the lions. The envoy, to do him credit, did not even stiffen, although some of those who had accompanied him leaped like deer; one or two crossed themselves, backwards, in the Roman way. Liutprand said something in the ear of one of them. Aspasia could guess what it was. "Not magic," he would be saying. "Mechanism. Stiffen your backbone, boy. Can't you see they want us to gawp like yokels?"

She smiled to herself. She would be glad to speak to him again. She had missed his peculiarly acid wit.

The Master of Ceremonies finished his perusal of the letter. It was all a show: he had read it before, when the ambassador came for the first, formal greeting. This was the audience that mattered, the one in which they would consider the purpose of the embassy. The exchange of courtesies was relatively brief.

"Your majesty," said the ambassador, "Autokrator, Emperor of the East"—Bold, that, and not to the emperor's liking: he frowned—"I bring you greetings from my lord, Otto, King of the Germans, King of Lombardy and the Italies, Emperor of the West." Bolder still, to claim that particular title.

John chose for his own purposes to disregard the insolence. "We trust that our son the King of the Germans is in good health?"

"My lord the Emperor of the West," said the ambassador, "is in excellent health and spirits."

They smiled at one another, with a gleam of teeth. The Autokrator inclined his head. The pearls of his crown swayed and shimmered. "We are pleased to receive his gifts and his tribute."

"Your majesty," said the ambassador, "is gracious."

The ambassador was apt to his task: almost as apt as a Byzantine. He fenced gracefully, with flawless patience; he fell into no traps, not even the most subtle. It was John the soldier, John the field commander, who wearied first of the game. He leaned forward as far as his robes would allow, and set his scepter sword-fashion across his knees. "Your king has a request to make of us?"

"Indeed," said the ambassador, "your majesty. Our emperor proposes an alliance; a pact of mutual advantage. His majesty has a son, a prince of great promise, now come to manhood and well ready for the duties of a man and a king. It would please him greatly to fulfill those duties in a union with a princess of the East."

Bluntly enough spoken, now that he had come to it. John regarded the ambassador for a stretching moment, his face still, unreadable. "You ask that we should give a lady of our royal house to a king of the barbarians?"

"A king of the Romans, who will be an emperor. What better match for him who is lord of the West than one whose kinsman is lord of the East?"

"Does he hope," asked John, "to lay claim thereby to this throne on which I sit?"

That was blunt even for a soldier. The Master of Ceremonies was shocked. The ambassador allowed himself a smile. "My emperor is a practical man, your majesty. He has a son. You have, if not daughters, then kinswomen of marriageable age. We can offer the hand of alliance in certain matters which may concern you. The claims of Byzantium in Italy, for example . . ."

John's eyes gleamed. But he was emperor as well as soldier; he offered nothing and accepted nothing without careful consideration. "You seek a princess? Not simply a lady of breeding?"

"My prince is royal in all respects. Were he seeking a lady of lesser eminence, he would hardly have troubled your majesty with his suit."

"And yet," said John, "a princess of royal blood, raised in the Sacred Palace, is hardly a common commodity."

"Your majesty speaks truly," the ambassador said, "and with most refreshing frankness. Yet we are informed that there are ladies of the blood royal, of suitable age and of suitable purity to please our prince."

No widows, then. No aging maidens. No culls to mock a barbarian's presumption.

"Between the first flower of womanhood and—shall we say, twenty summers?" the ambassador said. "Our prince would not object to a lady somewhat older than himself; he is, after all, not yet sixteen years old, but well grown and strong, and certainly a man."

John turned the scepter in his hands. It was hard to tell under the beard, but it seemed that he was smiling. "Do you perhaps have someone in mind?"

The ambassador raised a brow. "Can your majesty propose a candidate?"

"Our majesty has not yet determined whether we will grant our son's petition."

"Yet if your majesty should," said the ambassador, "if you should grace us with your favor, would you perhaps present us with a list of possibilities?"

"We might," said the emperor. "We shall ponder it."

"Yes," said Theophano. "That means yes."

Aspasia would have agreed, but she was feeling contrary. "His sacred majesty is as coy as a maid, and somewhat more fickle."

"Not here." Theophano was calmly certain. "He needs what the westerners can give. He wants Italy back; he wants the Holy Land. The German thinks that he can gain a foothold in our empire by marrying his son to one of our princesses. The Autokrator means to gain a foothold in the west and make the German bow to him, and give up that overweening claim of his. Emperor of the West. Have you ever heard such insolence?"

"He who holds the prize," said Aspasia, "might be said to have the best claim to it. And he holds Italy."

"There is that." Theophano leaned past Aspasia, gazing

down into the hall. The ambassadors, dismissed, took their leave with suitable pomp. Her eyes followed them. "Suppose," she said slowly. "Just suppose . . ."

"Yes?" asked Aspasia.

Theophano did not answer at once. When she did, she went at it sidewise. "It's a pity you aren't ten years younger."

"Or prettier," Aspasia said. "Or able to bear children."

Theophano's arm went round her at that, holding tight for a moment, then letting go. "No; he wouldn't allow it, even then. You'd be too much like a rival. He'll choose someone with less of a claim to the succession: someone born outside of the Purple Chamber. Someone . . ."

Someone like Theophano.

Their eyes met.

"A barbarian," Aspasia said.

"A king," said Theophano. "An emperor who rules in Rome."

"Haughty; overweening."

"Royal."

"I'll wager he knows not a word of Greek."

"He can learn."

"Or his bride can learn German."

Theophano smiled. It was her mother's smile: deceptively, perilously gentle. "His bride," she said, "will be an empress."

Four

⊕

A properly brought up noblewoman ought in all things to be both demure and circumspect. Theophano knew that very well. Aspasia had taught her. But Theophano was also royal, and she had learned the craft of queenship in her mother's hard school.

She should have waited, attended the Basilissa, spoken a word here and there, let it be known by degrees that she wanted this that they all were whispering of. Others had begun to do just that. Some of the eunuchs and a handful of the more sporting noblemen had wagers on one or another of the Basilissa's sisters. There was even a small sum on Aspasia.

Theophano did not wait or intrigue or reckon odds. On the evening after the embassy's coming, when the emperor had retired to his privacy, she presented herself at his door.

Aspasia was with her. Theophano accepted the escort with equanimity and perhaps a certain degree of relief. She was bold as a good strategist should be, but she was not foolhardy; and the emperor's chamberlain was an old ally of Aspasia's.

Even for that he might have dismissed them out of hand, but he had been a soldier once, as eunuchs could be if they attracted the right sort of notice. He knew a bold stroke when he saw one. He would not smile at it, that would not have been proper, but he met Aspasia's glance, and his own had a spark in it. He inclined his head a precise degree and consented to bear their petition to the Autokrator.

The women sat in a dim and drafty antechamber and waited. Theophano was quiet and might have seemed serene, except for her fingers that worked in her skirt, pleating and smoothing, pleating and smoothing.

Aspasia did not even try to pretend. She sat for a little while, but the chair was hard, and her feet wanted to pace.

Theophano's voice was loud in the silence. "Do you think this is mad, then? Am I a fool, to want this?"

"Yes," said Aspasia.

Theophano knew her too well to be surprised. A smile flickered, vanished. "Then why are you helping me?"

Aspasia stopped, spun on her heel, faced Theophano. "Because I'm mad and a fool, too. Because this palace is a cage, and there is a door in the west, and maybe the key is in your hand. Not mine, it can't be, unless his sacred majesty is far more of an idiot than I ever took him for, but you—you can fly free."

"I could wait," said Theophano, "as the Basilissa did. Whatever these barbarians may claim, the one and true and Roman empire is here, and if I leave it I can never come back."

"You could wait," Aspasia said. "Do you want to?"

"No." Theophano regarded her hands, which had stilled in her lap. Her eyes came up and fixed on Aspasia's face. "You hate him, don't you?"

Aspasia's throat closed. She forced words through it. "Would it matter if I did?"

"I don't, you see," said Theophano. "There's not enough of him to hate. If he could care, or not care, one or the other, he would be worth something of my soul. But there's nothing to him. He wanted the crown, that was all. What got in his way, he got rid of." She drew a careful breath. "I am going to get in his way."

Aspasia did not speak. She hated him, and no matter that Theophano saw clearly how little a creature he was, once one took away the crown and the buskins. It was not the kind of hate that poured poison in a cup, or hired assassins to do what he had done to Demetrios. It was there, that was all. It made her want to trouble his peace now and then, when he might have forgotten who and what she was. She was going to outlast him; and she wanted him to know it.

Her expression was frightening Theophano. She smoothed it, although she could not smile.

It was that face which she turned upon the chamberlain, who entered with an air of mild bemusement. "Their sacred majesties will see you now," he said.

They waited, the Autokrator and the Basilissa, in one of the inner rooms. They sat together often of an evening, in the Autokrator's chambers or in the Basilissa's, with small attendance, conversing a little but most often silent. The Basilissa, from her years in the convent, knew all the colors of silence. The Autokrator seemed to find it restful. Or maybe, Aspasia thought, he was such a creature of habit that once he had begun to do a thing, he went on doing it forever after.

He seemed unperturbed by this intrusion upon his nightly custom. His greeting was courteous, with a leavening of his famous charm; he saw them seated, made comfortable, given wine sweetened with honey. The Basilissa smiled through it, her calm as perfect as Theophano's tried to be. "Sister," she said to Aspasia. "How good to see you. And niece. Have you been keeping well?"

"Very well, Basilissa," Theophano murmured.

The Basilissa smiled. The Autokrator nodded. Aspasia set her teeth and resolved to endure. This was Theophano's battle. Let Theophano be the one to fight it.

Bold as she had been in seeking this audience, now that she had it she was all courtier. She seemed prepared to spend the night in talking of nothing in particular, from the health of the Basilissa's chamberlain to the races in the Hippodrome. It was beautifully done. Surely the emperor thought that it was he who brought up the subject of the western barbarians and their embassy.

"And will you give them what they ask?" Theophano inquired coolly, as if she were not about to hazard everything on this one throw.

The emperor did not frown at her presumption. He was warm with wine and the sound of his own voice. "Do you think I should?"

"That is for your majesty to ordain," said Theophano.

His majesty laughed. "Certainly it is, and so I shall. But what would you do?"

Theophano lowered her eyes. Aspasia saw the glitter of them under the long lashes. "I, your majesty? If I were emperor?" He nodded, much amused. "I think . . . I would negotiate and deliberate and temporize, and drive a hard bargain; but give them what they ask."

"So? You would give them a princess of the blood?"

"I would give them what they ask for, no more and no less. A princess, but not one born to the purple; that would make them too proud. Young enough to be acceptable to the boy in Saxony, old enough to please the old lion who is his father. A maiden, I think; a widow, even one proved fertile, might prove awkward in her earlier alliances."

"Beautiful?"

"Unless I wished to give them insult, yes. I would give them at least one who was bearable to look at."

"All our princesses are bearable to look at," said the emperor. He sat back, stroking his beard. His eyes had narrowed slightly. "And whom would you choose, cousin? Would you perhaps choose yourself?"

Theophano raised her eyes. They were as limpid as a doe's. "Would you choose me, your majesty?"

"Should I?"

"Does your majesty wish me to answer that?"

The emperor smiled. "You look," he said, "exactly like your mother."

Aspasia went cold. But Theophano returned the emperor's smile. "Your majesty flatters me."

"Maybe," said the emperor. He was still amused, but it was a colder amusement, with a slight, perilous edge. "What would you do if you were married to this King of the Germans?"

"Be queen," said Theophano, simple as a child.

"Would you call yourself Empress of the Romans?"

"I might," said Theophano.

The emperor laughed. "You would, indeed. And would you send your armies against us?"

"Would you force me to do so, your majesty?"

"Who knows?" The emperor raised his cup and drank. "I see that you are more clever than any of us suspected. Do you think I'll let you go and maybe show yourself dangerous?"

"Will I be more dangerous in the wilds of Germany, your majesty, than in the Sacred Palace?"

The emperor lowered his cup. "You want to go."

Theophano did not deny it.

"You would let yourself be given to a barbarian? It's exile, you know, and lifelong. You'll never see the City again."

"Yes, majesty," said Theophano, soft and perfectly steady.

"Do you hate it so much?"

Her face changed not at all. "I love it with all my heart and soul."

They looked at one another. Aspasia, watching them, saw the understanding pass between them. John had killed to gain his throne. What Theophano would have to do, only God knew. But she would do it. She had what he had, what her mother had had: ambition as bright and hard as steel, and fully as deadly to cross.

He nodded slowly as if she had spoken. "A convent would hardly begin to quell you, would it? You'd be an abbess or nothing."

"I am nothing now," said Theophano.

"Nothing but what I command you to be," the emperor said. "I shall think on it. You have the advantage of the first stroke, at the very least; and courage to go with it. The German king might find you somewhat more than he bargained for."

Theophano bent her head as she rose. It was beautifully done: agreement, obeisance, withdrawal, in one graceful flowing movement.

Aspasia was a shadow in her wake. For a moment she thought that the emperor might call her back, but he said nothing. Even after she had passed the outer door she felt his eyes on her, wearing no expression that she could read.

The emperor did not mar his imperial dignity with haste. The days stretched, each seeming longer than the last. Others approached him, though only Theophano spoke for herself. The rest did it properly, through kin or trusted allies, some to the emperor, others to the Basilissa. Not all trusted to the power of argument.

"So far," said Aspasia, "the price is up to a prime team for the Hippodrome and an estate in Anatolia."

"Who is that?" Theophano asked.

"One of the Komnenoi."

"What, little Euterpe, with her harelip, poor thing?"

"Hardly," said Aspasia. "*She* has a sweet nature and a kind eye, if someone will stop to notice. No; it's her cousin. The one with the temper."

"The one whose husband left her within a month of the wedding and shut himself up in a monastery?"

"Where, he said, he need never again endure the whips and flails of a woman's tongue. Yes, that's the one: Irene. The family is desperate, I gather."

"I can imagine," said Theophano. "I remember Irene. God help the Germans if she's sent to be their queen."

"She won't be," Aspasia said. "She's not a princess. None of them is, except you."

"I'm not the only princess in the City," said Theophano. She turned back to the embroidery in her lap. With great care she chose a new color, threaded the needle, began the tracing of a vine about the half-fledged imperial eagle.

Aspasia tried to be as cool, to go back to her reading. There were more than the two of them in the chamber: the empress was there with most of her ladies, all of them either plying their needles or reading something appropriately edifying. As Aspasia paused, some of them prevailed on the empress to summon Alexios the eunuch, who had a voice of rare power and purity.

He had barely entered and begun to sing when a disturbance silenced him. It was the emperor's messenger. His majesty wished to speak with the Basilissa, and with the Lady Theophano.

Theophano rose slowly. Aspasia doubted that anyone else could see how the blood had flooded and then ebbed from her cheeks, or how her hands tried not to shake. This might be another matter. It might have nothing to do with the German marriage. It might be nothing at all.

Aspasia shook her head once, firmly. She would not let it be anything but what it was. And that, in a word, was victory.

Five

✦

The ambassadors from the west seemed well pleased
with the bargain they had made. They could hardly
quarrel with either Theophano's beauty or her birth,
although Aspasia heard one man mutter of tavernkeepers'
get. Germans, Aspasia gathered, were much preoccupied
with purity of lineage. But the bishop who spoke for them
all was an Italian, and he had a share of sense: enough to
know how fortunate he was in getting a tavernkeeper's
granddaughter. On the other side, after all, she was the
daughter of an emperor.

Liutprand was not among the ambassadors when the emperor presented Theophano for their inspection. Aspasia,
unnoticed in Theophano's shadow, looked for him but
could not find him. Nor could she speak to any of the westerners. She was kept apart from them as Theophano was, in
a wall of women and eunuchs: to be seen, admired, but
never touched or spoken to. That would come later, when
the negotiations were done and Theophano was given into

the envoys' keeping. Aspasia told herself that Liutprand's absence meant nothing. He might be occupied elsewhere. He might have chosen not to come out in such weather as this, pure Byzantine awfulness, a raw wind out of Scythia and a sluice of rain on top of it. Some of the westerners who had come looked wretchedly rheumy; even as she looked at them, one throttled a sneeze. Wise Liudo, to stay inside in the warm.

He had never missed an audience before. Had he quarreled with the bishop who led the embassy?

Aspasia determined to send him a message. He had not yet, after all, sent her any word of greeting; or perhaps he had, thinking her still a nobleman's wife in the City, and it had gone astray. He would want, she told herself, to know where she was.

But time that had stretched so endlessly long was suddenly, vanishingly short. There was everything to do, and scant days to do it in. The westerners, their bargain concluded, wished to sail as soon as the weather allowed. At first Aspasia had no opportunity to send a message, then there was no one who could take it. She was bound in the palace, gathering together a household fit for a queen. Theophano would take servants of all degrees, and waiting-women, and guards, though those would leave her in her new husband's hands and return to the City. And she would take Aspasia.

Theophano did not ask. She said, when the westerners had seen and accepted her and her path was fixed, "You should be sure to pack warm clothes for the voyage. And it's cold in Germania, they say; though maybe no colder than here."

Aspasia paused in what she was doing; what it was, she never afterward remembered. "What makes you think I'll go with you?"

"What makes you think you won't?"

"The Autokrator might not permit it."

"Was that what you were thinking of when you made sure he saw you with me and knew that you were part of this?"

"I was thinking of you," said Aspasia more sharply than she would have liked.

"Then you don't want to go."

There were no tears in the great dark eyes. It was Theophano's great failing as a court lady: she could not weep at will. But Aspasia saw the hurt in her.

"You want to stay here," said Theophano. "Where I can never come again. Where your husband's murderer sits the throne. Where any turn of that murderer's whim might mew you up in a cloister."

"Where I was born," said Aspasia. "Where I have every intention of outlasting his so-sacred majesty."

"Alone?"

Aspasia shrugged, though her heart was cold. "Maybe I'll marry again. Maybe I won't need to. The Basilissa will look after me."

"Who will look after me?" asked Theophano.

Aspasia stiffened. "That was not kind, Phania."

"I don't mean to be kind. I want you with me. We've been together since I was a child. I owe you my place here—and yes, this new life I'm going to, far as it is, but with a throne in it. The Basilissa may be fond of you; she is your sister, after all. But what if she dies or is deposed? What then, Aspasia? Where I go might be a land of barbarians, but I will never abandon you." Theophano took Aspasia's hands in hers, a rare gesture now, since she had grown into royal dignity. "Think of it, Aspasia. A whole new world, new people, new ways. I've seen how it's been for you since Demetrios died. You've been living half a life, hid away in the empress' shadow. Won't you come out in the sun again?"

"I am in the sun," said Aspasia. "I am the Basilissa's sister and servant. I live in the heart of the world."

"I hear you in the nights," said Theophano, "walking the

floors. Tell me these walls don't close in on you like the bars of a cage. Tell me you don't see yourself as an emptied vessel, cracked and flung aside. Don't you want to be whole?"

"I can't," Aspasia said. "The doctors are sure of that."

"There is more to life than breeding," said this child who existed to breed kings. She let Aspasia go. "I want you with me. The Basilissa will send you if I ask. The Autokrator will be glad to see you go."

"Then you give me no choice?" Aspasia meant to sound angry, but it came out wry instead.

"You can stay, of course. And end, soon or late, in a convent. Probably soon. The emperor finds you an uncomfortable presence."

He could hardly be more uncomfortable than the truth as Theophano spoke it. Aspasia could see quite as clearly as Theophano. She knew how thin this line was that she walked, and how close it was to vanishing. John Tzimisces would never give her to any man as a wife, barren or no. It would be the convent for her, the walls and the veil, and life turning endlessly inward, until all that was Aspasia was gone, and only prayer was left. The pious would tell her that that was sanctity. She preferred to call it dissolution, and to escape it by any means she might.

Even if that was to leave the City, and follow Theophano, and become a barbarian?

No, she thought. A barbarian she would never be. But to go out into the world . . .

She had thought of it. She could hardly have done otherwise, with Theophano before her, exactly and perfectly right for this western queenship, and herself too old, too scarred, too inarguably royal. But she was beloved of Theophano, and certain to be asked for precisely this.

She had thought, but she had not let herself fix on it. Part was dread of leaving all that she had known, and sailing into the dark. Another, much greater part was desire. Yes, she wanted to go. She wanted it so badly that it caught her breath in her throat. She had never wanted anything as much as that. It terrified her. It was not proper or reasonable or Byzantine. It was the old blood speaking: the blood of Basil the Macedonian, who rose from stable lad to emperor. Maybe he came of an older blood than anyone knew. Had not the great Alexander been King of Macedon?

"If the emperor knows how badly I want this," Aspasia said, "he'll have me snatched away by night and locked in a nun's cell."

Theophano's smile was sudden, brilliant, and swiftly, utterly masked. "Then he shall know how strenuously you resist me, and how much you would prefer to remain here, even without your long companion."

"Clever child," said Aspasia. Her hands were fists. With an effort of will she unclenched them. Freed, they were cold and shaking. Fear, yes. But gladness, too. She had mounted to the precipice. Now at last she gathered courage to leap. And in the leap was sheer, white exultation.

In the midst of it she had no time for a missing ambassador. He was not in any of the lesser meetings, where the envoys were permitted to acquaint themselves with their would-be queen. In one of them at last, when acquaintance had deepened sufficiently that an attendant on the princess could exchange a word or two with one of the westerners, Aspasia learned that no quarrel kept Liutprand away. He was ill. Not so much now, the man said, seeing her expression, but he was being kept abed. She would have asked more, but the man was called away, and she had duties that would not wait.

She would see him when they sailed, surely. That would be soon: tomorrow was the banquet and the ceremonial of farewell, and the morning after, wind and sky permitting, they would embark. There was no need to hunt him down, with so much else weighing on her.

But she was stubborn, and it was not like Liudo to keep

so long abed with so much to do and see and quarrel with. Since no one would go in her name, she went herself, leaving the empress' palace to its genteel uproar. There were things she should not leave, but she thrust them on the least hysterical of Theophano's chosen women and made herself forget them. In plain dark mantle and veil she looked like a servant. She walked out of the palace as easily as if she had been invisible.

Beyond the great bronze gates she faltered to a stop. The sun was shining and a keen wind blowing, whipping tears from her eyes. The City roared and teemed before her. The road was full of people, animals, carts and wagons and litters. Sights and sounds and scents nearly struck her down. She had not passed these gates since Demetrios was killed, nor seen aught of the City but what royalty ever saw from its walls and towers. She had forgotten how solid it was; how inescapably real.

She clutched her veil about her before the wind caught it and snatched it away. She could not make herself move forward. The City would take her; it would devour her. She would go back, find someone, send him with her message.

And why was she here, if not because she had failed to do just that? She scraped together every scrap of courage she had, and took a deep breath. It was not far to the house where the westerners were staying. Down toward the Middle Way, through the Forum of Constantine, into a narrow serpent of a street with a cistern at its head, and past the cistern a house like all great houses in this city: bleak windowless walls, iron gate, every evidence of unwelcome; but within, splendor. This was not the drafty barn in which Nikephoros had barracked Liutprand's earlier embassy. This was a palace, a house of favored guests, enriched by the emperor's generosity.

The porter, like all in the house, was in the imperial service. He admitted Aspasia with courtesy as a messenger from the palace, and called another, younger servant to guide her. The boy was not garrulous. She could not tell if he liked or loathed the one she asked for; nor could she see in him any hint of Liutprand's condition. He was not keeping her from seeing the man: that, surely, was a good sign.

There was a servant on guard at the door to which Aspasia was led, a man whom she recognized from older days. He did not know her. But then he had never seen her in widow's garb, and her veil was drawn over her face. He had always been a dour man, with a dark, heavy, old-Roman face, and no liking to spare for anyone who was both female and Byzantine. He greeted her with knitted brows, and her guide with rough words in the bastard Latin of Italy. Aspasia knew enough of it to piece together his meaning. "What is this? Hasn't anyone been told that my lord is not to be disturbed?"

"This lady comes from the palace," said the servant in clipped and correct Greek. "She brings a message for the Bishop of Cremona."

"Then let her give it to me," Liutprand's watchdog said in Greek quite as clipped if not so correct. "My lord has little enough time left in this world, that he can squander it on trifles."

"What would you have him do with it? Put it away for later?" They both stared at Aspasia. She glared back. "He's dying, then?"

Liutprand's man stood stiffly, walled behind a black scowl. "Is it any business of yours?"

"It is if I choose to make it so." She drew herself to her full height. "Tell your master that the Princess Aspasia wishes to speak with him."

There was something to be said for the imperial manner. The Italian liked it not at all, but he bowed to it. He did as he was told.

He was not gone long. When he came back he looked even less happy than before. He let her in, keeping close behind her, as if she could be a danger to his master.

There were only two rooms, an inner and an outer. A pair of priests sat in the latter, one praying, one reading from a book. Both rose and bowed as Aspasia passed. Another priest waited in the inner room. It was small but pleasant, with a latticed window, and walls made beautiful with a mosaic of flowering vines. The priest seemed to fill it. Pure Lombard, he must have been, a great, fair-haired, blue-eyed barbarian who would not have looked at all amiss behind the shield of a Varangian guard.

Aspasia had taught herself not to shrink from the Varangians. They had given Demetrios a quick death; a merciful one, they might have said. But whenever she saw them, she could not help but remember the sound of their axes biting flesh.

This Lombard in his black robe, with his priestly tonsure, was no slayer of men. His eyes were gentle in the strong-boned ruddy face, his voice soft and mild. "My lady," he said in quite passable Greek. "It's a great honor that you deign to come in your own person."

"It's great nonsense," said another voice which she knew very well, although it was much thinned and weakened. It broke into a storm of coughing. The big fair priest was with him in an instant, bending over the bed, raising him as gently as a child, and holding him while he coughed himself into silence. No sooner had he done that when he spoke again, quieter this time, but not a whit less fierce. "What possessed you to come here? Don't you have enough to do in the palace?"

"I rejoice to see you, too, old friend," said Aspasia, smiling, though she wanted to weep. Thin and pale though Liutprand had been when she saw him in the Golden Hall, that was the picture of health beside this. There was color in his cheeks, to be sure, but it was the hectic flush of fever. His eyes glittered with it. His breath had a rattle and catch that she knew too well.

A chair appeared by the bed. She sat in it and took Liutprand's hand. It was as thin as a bird's claw, thin and cold, with no strength in it. "Was it polite of you," she asked him, "to send me no message, not even a word of greeting? I'd thought we were friends."

"We were," said Liutprand. "That's why."

"What, so you could indulge your vanity? I've seen fever before. You'll get over it soon enough, and get your looks back, too."

"I never had any to get back," Liutprand said, "even if I were going to live that long. I won't see Italy again. I'll be lucky to see the ship my body sails on."

"Nonsense," said Aspasia, though her throat was tight.

His eyes burned with more than the fever. "Stop it," he said, hardly more than a whisper. "Stop telling me lies. I always trusted you to tell the truth—a rarity in any woman, let alone a Byzantine. I'm dying and I know it. I hoped you wouldn't, till it was too late."

"Why, so that you wouldn't have to look at me again?"

"So that I wouldn't see you cry."

She was close to it, but temper burned the tears away. "You won't. I'm royal and Byzantine. And ready to strangle you. We could have had days to talk. Now there aren't any left."

He did not deny it. He looked as angry as she felt. "I don't suppose I can get rid of you."

"Not until I'm ready to be got rid of." She drew her brows together and sat more solidly in her chair, and kept her grip on his hand. He lacked the will or the strength to pull away.

There was a silence. Even with their tempers crackling in it and grief running long and slow beneath it, there was something almost companionable about it. However little Liutprand might want to admit it, he was glad of her presence.

"So," he said after a while. "Little Theophano will marry

my prince. They say she's grown into a beauty. Is she still as deceptively sweet as she used to be?"

"More," said Aspasia. "She wanted this; she set out to get it."

"Of course she did. We would never have asked for her by name, that would have been too obvious, but she was the one we came for."

Aspasia nodded. She had thought so since she knew that Liutprand was in the embassy.

"I heard," he said. "About your husband. Old Phokas got no more than he deserved. Your Demetrios shouldn't have waited to be sure of it."

Hard words. Cruel, if anyone else had spoken them. But Liutprand's compassion was not a virtue he ever wanted to admit. It was in his eyes, behind the anger. "No," said Aspasia. "He shouldn't have waited. He was a fool. He paid for it."

The thin fingers tightened in her own. "I'll tell him so when I see him," said Liutprand.

Aspasia wept, but she laughed. "You do that. He always liked you, you know, though you rather took him aback."

"Did I? I'd have thought he'd be used to it."

"One of us was enough," said Aspasia. She rose. His Lombard waited with impeccable patience, but she knew that she had stayed overlong. The burst of strength that had greeted her presence was fading fast. Liutprand's hand was cold in hers, life ebbing from it as she stood there. She throttled an urge to clutch at him. He could not go now. She had just found him again. All the things she had stored up in her memory, to tell him when he came back; all the books she had read, that he would want to know of; all the quick sword-thrusts of wit, and no one else as adept in stroke and counterstroke. How could he be dying? He was her friend, and only now was she sure of it.

He did not need to know how weak a creature she was. She smiled at him and stooped to kiss his brow. It was burning dry. "I'll come back tomorrow," she said. "May I have your blessing?"

He was not entirely deceived, but there was no strength left in him for argument. She bent her head. In a fading thread of voice he gave her the blessing.

She left quickly. Too quickly, maybe. It was that or burst out howling where he could hear. The sound of his coughing followed her, and voices raised, high and urgent. Almost she turned back. But what could she do? He would only hate her for lingering—or worse, for letting him see her cry.

She straightened her back and settled her veil. Proudly, as a princess should, she walked back to the palace.

Six

Aspasia could not keep her promise to Liutprand. By morning he was dead. She had known in her heart that he would be; and so, she was certain, had he.

His people mourned him, but the embassy went on as it must, as he had wished that it should, even writing it into his last testament. She could do no less than anyone else who had been his friend. She quelled the ever-rising tears with a scowl, and went where duty called her.

She passed the day in a fog. It was grey and it was empty, the color of grief. She spoke when there was need, even smiled. No one remarked that she seemed abstracted. Maybe she was a better dissembler than she knew.

When morning was past and the day's mass sung, Theophano readied for the banquet that would be her last in the court of Byzantium. She knew that Liutprand was dead, had shed a tear or two when she heard it, but like Aspasia she had no time to spare for grief. And maybe no room for it. The Lombard had been Aspasia's friend more than her own. There was a whole new world in front of her, and the old slipping away behind. Standing up for the first time in the robes of a princess who would be a queen, she could remember only what she was leaving and what she was going to, and amid the sorrow and the fear, the swelling excitement.

It moved Aspasia in spite of herself. She put on her usual somber gown, but it was her best one, of brocaded silk, sewn with silver thread and a shimmer of black pearls. Theophano's new maid put up her hair, not too elaborately, but handsomely as befit an emperor's daughter. Tonight, Aspasia would be that.

The emperor honored the western embassy: he feasted them in the best if not the largest of the halls, where nineteen couches flanked the great golden table, and the walls and pillars were hung with gold, and the very dishes on the tables were of gold. He sat in the center of the upper table where it met the lower like the bar of a tau cross, robed in purple over white, with the empress on his left hand and the chief of the ambassadors on his right. Theophano had the place of honor next to the empress on the women's side of the table; Aspasia sat beside her. No one ventured to protest, not even the lady who would have claimed the place. They remembered what Aspasia was.

Aspasia sat quietly, eating well enough: she could always eat, no matter how her heart ached. Liutprand would have been delighted to be here, to see his people seated next to the emperor himself, and no matter what he thought of the man. Nikephoros had granted the westerners no such grace. He had invited them, yes, but to a lesser hall, and seated them at the bottom of the lower table, with the petty tribesmen and the servants. To teach them a lesson, Demetrios had said. Their king rose far above himself, taking the title of Emperor of the West.

John was a milder man. He wanted what the westerners had to give; and maybe he wanted them to know what world it was that Theophano inhabited, to understand what sacrifice she made for their prince's sake.

Aspasia, born to the purple, saw it now as if she had become a stranger. So much gold, so much glitter in the light of the lamps. Course upon course served with the full ceremonial, intricate as high mass in Hagia Sophia. Servants like shadows, silent, impeccable, ubiquitous. Eunuchangels from the emperor's choir, and players on flute and harp, and dancers, and mummers who acted in mime the words of an old comedy. Very old. It was written when Athens was young.

Did they know Athens at all, these barbarians in the sunset countries? Rome, yes, that had mastered them once, but what Athens left was a rarer thing, an empire not of lands and laws but of the mind.

"Someone should teach them," said Aspasia, but softly, where none but herself could hear. One of the three vast bowls passed by her, wrought of gold so heavy that it hung on gilded ropes from the roof, with a servant to guide it on its track from guest to guest. More magic that was mechanism, clothed in extravagance that could only be imperial. Aspasia chose an orange from the heaped nuts and fruits, and waited while the servant prepared it for her. There would be no oranges in Germania. There would be—who knew what? Nothing as splendid as this place and this feast. Nothing in the world was as splendid as this.

The women about her twittered like birds. The men's voices, deeper, made Aspasia think of the sea. Tomorrow she would sail on it. For the first time since she was born, she would pass beyond the walls of the City.

She drew a sharp breath. Suddenly she wanted to be gone, away, free.

As long as state banquets were, guests were permitted to withdraw discreetly when need called them, and to return with equal discretion. Aspasia schooled herself to rise quietly, helped by a lull in the dancing, when others stirred and stood and sought the door. It was not that kind of relief which she needed. She paused in the passage, leaning against the wall, closing her eyes for a blissful moment.

When she opened them, one of the inevitable servants was there with a basin and a cloth. The water in the basin was scented with lemon. She let him bathe her brow and her throat, gravely dutiful, asking no questions and expecting none. When he was done he went away.

She knew she should go back. She walked slowly, more or less toward the garderobes. People passed, some in haste.

One, returning, paused. Aspasia recognized him after a moment, clouded as her brain was. Liutprand's priest. He looked wan and tired and sad, though he brightened a little at sight of Aspasia. "Lady," he said.

"Father," said Aspasia. "Did he tell you that you had to come?"

The priest almost smiled. "He ordered me. I sit in his place, unworthy though I am of it. I try to take joy in it. He would."

"And then he would go home and be merciless to it in a book."

The priest laughed, though he stopped quickly and looked startled. "He said that you understood him. There was no one else, he said, who saw him so clearly, and still forgave him for it."

"Like calls to like," said Aspasia.

"So he said," said the priest. He caught himself as if at a memory. "He left me something for you."

"His will? I have that: it came with his messenger."

"Not only that," the priest said. He hunted in his robes and drew out a packet wrapped and bound in silk. "He wanted you to have this. To remember him by, he said. 'The priests can pray,' he said to me, 'and the women can weep. Tell the emperor's daughter to remember me as I was, and spare me a smile now and then.' "

Liutprand's gift weighed heavy in Aspasia's hands. She

knew the shape and the heft of it even through the wrappings. He had given her his book.

His priest stood trying to smile, with tears running down his face. She patted him absently. It did not seem absurd that he was twice her size. "I loved him, too," she said.

"I . . . see . . . you did." He swallowed hard. "My name is Gaufrid. If you need anything—if the world seems too strange, where you and your princess go—you only have to ask."

He left hastily. Aspasia stared after him. She had, she realized, gained an ally. How strange these barbarians were; how quick to give of themselves. She would have to learn how they did it, if she was to live among them.

She shivered. Her arms tightened, clasping Liutprand's gift to her breast. Its solidity calmed her. For a moment she felt that he was there with his wicked tongue and his clear eye, and no patience at all. He was no saint, was Liutprand.

A good enough epitaph. She tucked his gift in her sleeve, and went back to the emperor's feast.

For all her reading and thinking and plain fretting, nothing had prepared Aspasia for the sheer strangeness of standing on a ship's deck. Even in the calm of the harbor, the timbers swayed and dipped; there was nothing solid under them, no earth to hold them steady, only the shifting, treacherous water. What it would be like when they ventured out into the wider reaches of the Middle Sea, she could only begin to imagine.

And yet she was not afraid. There were still walls here, city walls behind, the walls of Galata shore beyond, and down at the mouth of the Golden Horn, the towers of the chain standing guard against the world; but those would be past by nightfall, and only open sea in front of them. People who had ridden or sailed outside of the City had told her of the sky-fear, the terror of space without bound or limit, until the earth seemed to fall away, and one tottered on the brink of the void.

She wanted it. She stood on the ship, a shadow in Theophano's slender shadow. The City rose above and about her, but she was sundered from it. The captain bellowed orders in impenetrable Italian, and his crew cast off the lines that bound them to the land. The quay was ablur with faces, aroar with voices, many come to see the princess taken away into the west; but the ship was a world of its own.

One of Theophano's maids was sniveling audibly behind the screen of her veil. The others were merely and mutely miserable. Their eyes clung to the City: roofs and walls and terraces climbing up and up into the bitter-blue sky, hazed in the smoke of its myriad braziers and furnaces, wrapped in the ceaseless roar that was the life-pulse of the greatest city in the world.

Aspasia drank it in with fierce intensity. This she must remember. This she must keep. She would even weep for it: it was hers, she had been born in it, she would never come back to it. But she would not cling to it. All of it that mattered was within her. What rose above her was only earth and stone and human flesh, and a tomb outside the walls, that others must tend but she would never forget.

The wind was cold on her cheeks, stinging where the tears fell. The City blurred and ran and slowly poured away.

Theophano was very quiet. She stood unmoving down all the length of the Horn, under the looming towers, into the narrow straits of the Bosporus. There the current caught them, and running up the sails they caught the wind. On the left hand rose sheer crags and softer slopes just touched with the first green of spring; on the right, the walls of Constantinople that seemed to rise straight out of the sea. The domes of Hagia Sophia floated above them, insubstantial as moons. The Sacred Palace rose glittering in the circle of its walls, slipped past, sank.

When the last angle of the wall bent away from them and sought its own way inland, Theophano turned at last and let herself be led into the creaking dimness of the cabin. It was low and dark and smelled of tar and salt, but it had been furbished as befit a queen. The maids, bereft of their City, clung gratefully to the silks and brocades and the carved and inlaid furnishings; they took refuge in fluttering over their lady, who suffered them in silence.

It took them a very long time to settle. At last, rather desperately, Aspasia all but flung a book at one and needles and silks to the rest, and lit the lamp that hung swaying above their heads. With something familiar to hold on to they quieted somewhat, though Phoebe never quite stopped sniveling. At least, Aspasia thought, none of them was seasick. Yet. The Sea of Marmora, people said, was placid as seas went. So today it seemed to be, by heaven's good fortune. One or two of the women seemed somewhat pale, but grief would account for that; and they were quiet, which was all that mattered.

Theophano was too quiet. Aspasia watched her warily, making no pretense of handwork. Nor did Theophano. She seemed to listen to the reading—something harmlessly dull on the proper conduct of the wellborn lady. Her hands were motionless in her lap. Her face was as empty as an icon's. Her eyes, downcast, offered nothing for the reading.

This once had been an exuberant child. When had she changed?

When she became a woman. When she determined that she would be a queen. When—surely, when she saw what became of her mother, and knew what price one paid for power, and still knew that she wanted it for herself.

Maybe in the west she would learn to laugh again. Empresses in Byzantium did not, but German queens might. German men did; Aspasia heard them up above in the sun and the wind, deep and free. They were glad to see the last of that too-vast, too-potent, too-urbane city. They were going home.

Theophano heard them, too: she stiffened a little, and her lips tightened. Aspasia reached for her hand. It was icy cold.

"I think," Theophano murmured, "I wish . . ."

"To go back?"

Theophano shook her head once, sharply. "No. Not back. Not forward, either. Just to stay and be, and not have to face either, west or east." She laughed. There was no mirth in it. "I'm afraid, Aspasia."

"So am I," Aspasia said.

"You?" said Theophano. "You are never afraid of anything. I start at shadows. I was going to be so brave, Aspasia. I was going to take the world by storm, and be an empress, and set kings under my feet. Now I've started on it, and I want to dive under the blankets and never come out." She looked up, into Aspasia's face. Her eyes were not at all like a frightened deer's. They were almost angry. "What if I hate him, Aspasia?"

That was not comfortable to think of. "Maybe you'll find him pleasant. Maybe, if God is merciful, you'll come to love him."

"But what if I hate him? What if I hate everything about him, and his kingdom, and his people? What if I've sold myself for a title, and none of it is worth the price?" Theophano's fingers clenched on Aspasia's, sparking pain. "What if *he* hates *me*?"

"He won't," Aspasia said. "You'll make sure of that. You have your beauty and your dignity, and yes, your temper, too. You know how to be a wife and a queen; what else have we trained you for all these years? If you can't warm to him, then you'll school yourself to endure him, for the power he brings you. If he can't warm to you, then all we've done has been for nothing, and you are not the woman I took you for."

This time Theophano's laughter was truer, if somewhat

less steady. "Dear indomitable Aspasia. If the world won't go the way you would have it, then you'll make one that will. It's you who should be queen, and not I."

"No," Aspasia said. "You know that's not what I ever wanted."

"What do you want?" Theophano asked her.

Aspasia sat still. She was aware of the women about them, the lamp over them, the sway and surge of the sea under the ship, the voices of men and the crying of gulls. No part of it mattered more than any other. Slowly she said, "I never wanted much. To be good, yes, and to be a good Christian and a good woman and a worthy daughter to my father. Then when the time came, to be a good wife to my husband. I served my empress as I could; I took in charge the daughter she entrusted to me. I wanted that, and I was happy in it."

"But now?" Theophano asked. "Don't you want anything now?"

Aspasia was not to be pressed. She was thinking as she spoke, feeling out the limits of it. "Then God took it all away. All but you. And I looked up and saw that where I had only known a roof, was sky. What do I want now? To fly, Phania. To fly free."

"A queen is never free," said Theophano.

"Yes," Aspasia said.

"Would you leave me if I let you go?"

Aspasia looked down at the fingers wound in hers, and up into that face which she knew rather better than she knew her own. "Not as long as you need me," she said.

"Then you're not free at all."

"But I am," said Aspasia. "I can choose, you see. I choose to accept your compulsion. I choose to serve you. I choose to go where you go. Once we come there—who knows what will happen? Anything can happen, Phania. Anything at all."

Theophano was white with the terror of it, but a spark had kindled. For a moment she was the old, reckless, hoyden Phania, scenting adventure in the wind and reveling in it. "Anything," she echoed. *"Anything."*

Seven

Rome.

Even a child of Constantine's City, Byzantine born, bred to empire, could pause at the sound of that name. There was the empire born; there was the forge of holy Church in the blood of the martyrs; there the West had fallen, and barbarian chieftains set their feet on the necks of the Roman legions.

Rome: a patched and crumbling wall, a city of ruins and of empty places, a federacy of villages that reckoned themselves a city. They even had what they called a Senate, and factions that recalled dimly the factions of Constantinople, and quite as lively a bent toward insurrection as they had had in the heyday of the Republic.

The pope was no part of the Romans' city. His palace stood apart by the basilica of St. John on the Caelian Hill, in that city within the city called the Lateran. Between it and the habitations of worldly Romans stood only ruin and the green country, a tangled wasteland with here and there a field or a vineyard.

It was stranger than anything Aspasia had imagined, even after the long ride up from Bari on crumbling Roman roads through crumbling Roman towns, in the ruin of the empire. Bari was Byzantine even yet, and greeted Theophano as the daughter of an emperor. But the north of Italy was the barbarians', and Rome was theirs; and how truly Otto was emperor, was clear enough to see. In the contested lands between Bari and Rome his messengers waited, and guards in Saxon panoply, to whom the Byzantines surrendered their charge. Proud as the Byzantines were, strong as they had seemed to Aspasia's eyes, now they seemed a pitiful few. When they were gone there were no civilized people left except Theophano and Aspasia, and silent Helena, and tender Phoebe who was hardier than anyone might have expected. Maria lay ill in Bari—of homesickness, Aspasia judged, more than any other malady—and Anna her sister had begged leave to nurse her. Theophano gave it. Better two who were willing, she had said, than a dozen who were not. Phoebe was not precisely willing, but she seemed to have decided that it was worth the price to serve a queen. Helena never told anyone why she stayed. She was simply there, well-nigh a perfect servant, with her plain face and her impeccable manners.

Now Phoebe and Helena crowded with Theophano into the curtained litter. Aspasia, perched on a borrowed mule, rode rather more comfortably beside them. She had been practicing German with Father Gaufrid, whose mule she rode, but as the city drew closer, her capacity for study shrank. She gave it up before she could disgrace herself utterly, and fell with relief into sane and civilized Greek. "*That* is Rome?"

"That," said Gaufrid with saintly forbearance, "is Rome. Yes."

"But it's in ruins. And is that a farm? Who ever heard of a beanfield in a city?"

"Constantinople is very different," said Gaufrid.

She could never tell when he was chaffing her. His face was bland as always, his eyes limpid blue, turning from her to the sadly shrunken city. The country through which they had been passing, the campagna of old Rome, was green enough, but that green was marsh, breathing forth fever.

"There is no glory in it," Aspasia said. She felt betrayed.

Gaufrid busied himself with flicking flies from his mule's ears, as he always did when he was not minded to argue. "Wait," was all he said, "and see."

Aspasia sighed. The city crawled closer. In a little while she could see a flutter of pennons and a gather and stir of people. There was a gate behind them. Not the Lateran gate, Gaufrid said when she asked. That was farther eastward. This was the Porta Latina. Theophano would enter by it and be carried through the city to the pope's palace.

When they came closer, she would open the curtains that protected her from mud and dust and flies and prying stares. There was no sign of movement now, no eye at the crack. Aspasia glanced guiltily away. She should be there, lending Theophano her strength. But there was hardly room within for three, let alone four, and the sky was high and clear, and the air though full of marshy reeks was cleaner than the musty closeness of the litter. She coaxed the mule a little nearer, drew her veil a little more modestly over her face. The escort seemed to sit straighter on their mounts; their faces, hard foreign soldiers' faces, grew almost eager. That, she thought, must be how they looked when they went to battle.

Wall and gate were hung indeed with pennons, crimson and blue and gold, and the people before and beneath, whether mounted or afoot, glittered in their finery. Surely there were a thousand of them, raising a shout as the company came up the last of the road, a great, alien roar. A few of them moved forward: monks in somber black, prelates in green, white, scarlet, gold. The most splendid of them wore a tall cap like a helmet and rode a snow-white mule.

Gaufrid crossed himself. "His Holiness," he said reverently. "Pope John himself."

Aspasia was rather less awed. These bishops of Rome reckoned themselves princes among the princes of the Church. In Constantinople matters were regarded rather differently. This John was a very great prelate, yes, but Basil the Patriarch was fully his equal; as was John the emperor. And Aspasia was *porphyrogenita*.

Pope John seemed a kindly enough old man under the glitter of his rank. He got down from his mule with two stalwart monks to assist him and waited on foot in the middle of the road, until the escort drew up before him and, to a man, dismounted and knelt. Aspasia did likewise. The pope blessed them in sonorous Latin and signed the cross over them. Then he approached the litter.

The nearest of the guards had the presence of mind to rise and draw back the curtain. Theophano sat within, a veil over her face, her women crouched behind her. She looked like an icon. Her head bowed for the pope's blessing. He smiled at her and said in quite passable Greek, "You are most welcome in Rome, daughter. May God grant you many years among us."

Theophano murmured a reply. The pope withdrew. The escort began to move again, on foot still, leading their mounts.

Now that God had had His due, human royalty could make itself known. Aspasia knew that the Ottos, father and son, must be in that roaring throng of foreigners, and surely that was their banner, the dragon of Charles the Frank, who was called the Great, and atop its standard the golden eagle, aping the Eagles of the Roman legions. But there were too many of them, the sun too bright on their finery. She blinked away the dazzle.

There. A man on a red horse, a boy on a grey. Both were crowned. Both wore the purple, rich mantles over white tunics. The man rode a pace or two ahead. Every line of him from head to booted heel was hard and spare, every angle cut clean, honed like a sword. His close-cropped beard, foxred in youth, was salted with grey. Deep lines were carved in his face; his eyes were sunk in his skull. But they were bitterly keen, amber-gold like a falcon's, taking in all before him with one swift glance.

The boy had his ruddy hair, and the shape of the face was like enough, narrow, flat-cheeked, long-chinned. But the son's eyes were a less startling color, somewhere between grey and green, and his expression had no hardness in it. He looked in fact rather sullen, though to do him justice, it did not seem to be habitual. He was appallingly young.

Sixteen, they said. His cheeks showed the first beginnings of a beard. When he dismounted he showed himself small for a Saxon, smaller than his father, and slight. His voice when he spoke was deep enough, and not ill to listen to, even reciting stiff formal phrases. Theophano replied in Latin as careful as his. He seemed surprised at that. Had he expected her to know only Greek?

He would be astonished when he discovered that she was studying German. Even as it was, he lost somewhat of his sullenness. He was not so ill to look at, seen clear, without a scowl to mar him.

These westerners seemed determined to prove that they could wallow as blissfully in ceremony as any flock of Byzantines. There was a great deal of it, and more as they marched in procession through the city. Pope John led them with his army of priests. The Ottos, elder and younger, rode on either side of Theophano's litter. Their guards, swelled almost to an army, warded the way before and behind.

It was almost enough to make up for the greeting Rome gave them. People lined the streets, to be sure. Some cheered. But some jeered; and most simply watched them go by. This was no empire of their making, they seemed to say, and these were no emperors of theirs. Let the Germans shout their acclamations if they were minded. Rome would not so condescend.

One of the guards muttered where Aspasia could hear. "Barbarians." She almost laughed.

"Oh, now," his companion said. "They're downright civilized today. Look: they're not even throwing anything."

The guardsman spat. Aspasia did not know the Greek for what he said, but that it was eloquent, she could well guess. The other grinned and rode on, but his hand was never far from his sword.

When the German emperor was in Rome, he held court in the palace of the Lateran. It was fitting enough, people said. Everyone knew that the pope was Otto's creature.

"Better Otto's than the Roman whore's," someone said in Aspasia's hearing.

"Ah," said someone else with an air of reminiscence—fond, Aspasia was not sure she should call it. "It's been a duller world since Marozia and old Theodora went to their just reward."

"A warm one, I'm sure. This pope may be dull, and he may be a German puppet, but this we can say for him: he's not given to keeping his women in the papal palace."

"Amen," said the other, not quite mockingly.

It was all remarkably like home. The same tangle of intrigue; the same jostling for favor between prince of the Church and prince of the world. Even the palace sought to rival the Sacred Palace. It too had a Chalkê, a great gate of bronze beneath an image of Christ the King; it had a hall of nineteen couches, and a hall of the throne, and a myriad glittering passages, and chambers brilliant with mosaic-work, pavements of marble and fountains of porphyry and everywhere hangings of gold and silk.

It was like the City, and yet it was purely alien. Here the

big fair-bearded barbarians were not the emperor's servants, set to tasks which no civilized man would perform. They were the emperor's people, his lords and his trusted kin. The little dark Romans crept about the fringes and took the leavings of the emperor's table. Often they bit the hand that fed them.

There was no place in the palace for women, the late unlamented pope's proclivities notwithstanding. The royal ladies had perforce to lodge apart in a high and splendid house that was, for all of that, inescapably a convent.

Even Aspasia could appreciate the irony. She did not, except in nightmares, fear that they had been tricked—else the Empress Adelaide had fallen victim to it also.

She received them when they were brought in at last to rest and bathe before the feast of welcome. She seemed remarkably young for the mother of a grown son; and she had been a widow when she married Otto, rising from Queen of Lombardy to Queen of the Germans, and thence to Empress of the West. Aspasia saw where the younger Otto had come by his wide grey-green eyes, if not his smallness. Adelaide was a true barbarian. She towered over Theophano, who was not a small woman; her figure was magnificent. Juno, Aspasia thought, to the life. Even to the temperament.

Once the greetings were disposed of, she inspected Theophano with the air of a sergeant-at-arms. No one moved; no one ventured to speak. At length she pronounced her verdict. "Not perfection, but better than I'd hoped for. You take after your mother, I gather?"

Theophano kept her eyes lowered, her voice soft and sweet. "If your majesty pleases, they tell me I resemble my father."

"Romanos?"

Aspasia stiffened. This was an artist of the arched brow, the not-quite-smile. She dared to imply that Theophano was not her father's daughter, not the child of Aspasia's princely brother; that she was bastard seed. It was a great insult, a killing insult, had they been Germans and not royal Byzantines.

Theophano flickered not an eyelash. "Romanos, your majesty. I am not, alas, *porphyrogenita;* not the child of a ruling emperor. I am the child of his youth, when he was Caesar to his father, my grandfather, the Autokrator Constantine."

"Ah," said Adelaide, expressionless. If she was disconcerted by the litany of imperial names, she was determined not to show it. "Your age?"

Surely she knew it to a day. Theophano answered sweetly, "I am just eighteen, your majesty."

"Older than my Otto," said Adelaide. "That may or may not suit. We shall see." She turned on her heel. "Follow me."

Aspasia told herself that it was to be expected. An empress with a grown son had a twofold battle on her hands: to keep her power while her husband lived, and to keep her power over her son. Of course she would test this stranger who had been brought to supplant her. Theophano understood it very well. She was unfailingly meek, unfailingly gentle, unfailingly patient. Aspasia was immensely proud of her.

But Aspasia, who did not want to be a queen, did not need to practice a queen's restraint. She detested the Empress Adelaide as cordially as the empress seemed to detest Theophano. There was nothing logical about it. The empress, for her part, seemed oblivious to Aspasia. Phoebe spoke neither German nor Latin, and Helena never spoke at all; there was no one to tell Adelaide that she had an enemy, or to name that enemy for what she was. She was only the little dark maid, the shadow in the princess' shadow.

That suited Aspasia well enough. Theophano had ample occupation in learning the ways of this realm which she would rule. And more to the point, of the man whom she would marry.

They met again at the banquet, spoke the words of betrothal and shared a cup and a plate, but there was no occasion to speak other than formal words. Otto, seeing her for the first time without her veil, was quite gratifyingly smitten. Theophano showed nothing of what she thought.

They looked well together. They were nearly of a height; with his mantle laid aside, he showed more breadth of shoulder than one might have given him credit for. He would never be a big man, but he had substance enough.

Aspasia said so when at last they could be alone, she and Theophano, in the room that was a nun's cell, with the maids asleep without. Aspasia combed Theophano's hair slowly, to make the time stretch. Theophano eased into the strokes; little by little the tension left her. Aspasia was dismayed to see how much of it there was.

Theophano sighed. "He's so young," she said.

"He'll grow," said Aspasia.

"I know that." Theophano sounded almost impatient. "His face is spotty; that passes, too. And he's rather handsome. That's not what I meant. Look at his father."

"His father is sixty years old."

"His father is an emperor. He's a child. He wants to be a king. He doesn't quite know how to go about it. He's callow."

"So might his father have been at sixteen." Aspasia coaxed a tangle into smoothness. "Don't you like him?"

"Like . . ." Theophano set her chin on her fist. "I like him well enough. But is that enough to marry on?"

"It's better than most women get."

"Or most men," said Theophano. "He likes me, I think. He told me I'm beautiful. He was blushing like—"

"Like a boy," Aspasia finished for her. "Give him time, Phania. Of course he pales beside his father. His father is a great man; a great king. Think how many years he's had to hone himself in, how many wars he's fought, how many men he's mastered."

"Women, too," said Theophano. She shivered lightly. "I'm glad I've not been sent to marry him. You see what it did to Empress Adelaide."

"I do indeed," Aspasia said dryly.

Theophano shot her a glance. "She has to be like that. Like iron. Or he'd break her."

Aspasia shrugged. Lucky Phania, to be capable of Christian charity. Aloud she said, "Young Otto won't break you. He'll cherish you. And you can be the queen you were born to be."

"Yes," said Theophano slowly. Then, more firmly: "Yes. Of course I like him. He's clean, he's presentable, he's demonstrably intelligent. He can't help it if his father is—his father. If he will have me, then I will have him."

"That's well," said Aspasia, "seeing how far a walk it is to Constantinople."

Theophano laughed, startling them both. It was young laughter, but given time, it would grow. Aspasia almost wept to hear it. She did weep, for no reason at all, except that she was tired, and she had been knotted so tight for so long, and now, all at once, the knots began to loosen. She flung her arms about Theophano. Theophano, after a moment's startlement, completed the embrace, half laughing still, half crying too, but all sure of this that she had chosen.

Eight

Theophano was a prisoner of her own ambition. If she wished to be a queen, then like a queen she must have no time that was her own; it was all given over to learning the ways of her new kingdom and preparing for her wedding to the younger of its kings. The price for that was more than high enough in Aspasia's estimation: from first daylight to well after sunset she suffered the company and the instruction of the Empress Adelaide.

Aspasia, secure in anonymity, was only as much a captive as it suited her to be. It was delicious, that freedom. Now and then she paused to be guilty; but Theophano abetted her, asking only that she be there in the morning and again at night, and letting her choose what she would do between. Most often that was simply to wait on Theophano. Yet in the burgeoning of the Roman spring, when the world was washed clean with rain and the sun was mellow gold and even the miasmas of the fens seemed inclined to have mercy on the poor fools who breathed them, Aspasia found that she could not stay within walls. Wrapped in her plain mantle, she went where she pleased, and if anyone paused to consider her, he reckoned her a nun like any other.

The first day she tried her freedom, she found a place which no one else seemed to know of, and which she claimed for her own. It was within the compass of the Lateran, but barely; it must have been a garden once, and kept still an air of disheveled civilization. It had a fountain, reduced now to a moss-grown basin and a cracked fragment that might have been a nymph's foot, and near it, half-hidden in a thicket of brambles, a relic of pure heathendom. All that one could easily see of it was its head, much worn but still perceptible, with its mane of curls and its curly beard and the nubs of horns pricking from its brow. One had to brave the brambles to see the rest of it; and an eyeful it was. In Greece they would call it a satyr. It was endowed as satyrs invariably were, richly, exuberantly, and most shamelessly.

Aspasia could thank the wise God that she was a widow and a scholar; she had leisure to appreciate the artistry of the old pagan who had carved this monument to sylvan Pan. Once she stopped blushing, she fancied that she was welcome in the god's domain. He seemed to smile at her as he played on his crumbling pipes, and his garden offered a haven when she had had enough of the city and the court. It was close enough to Theophano's convent that Aspasia could slip away for an hour with a book and a bit of bread in a napkin, and slip back again before anyone missed her.

Today she had more need of the god's peace than usual. She should not in fact have gone out at all. Empress Adelaide was determined that the princess from Byzantium should be instructed in every intricacy of both German and papal protocol, and there was no persuading her that a daughter of the Autokrator of the Romans might not require so extensive a grounding as a lady of lesser lineage. Theophano needed all the patience she had ever cultivated, and most of Aspasia's with it. Aspasia was happy to give it to her, but then there was none left for herself. She snatched her book and made her escape. Only an hour, she promised herself. Only that. Then she would be as saintly as ever Theophano could school herself to be.

There was a curse on the day, surely. First a company of armed barbarians barred the way to the outer city, with a great deal of milling and shouting and proclaiming to all and sundry that the Margrave Unpronounceable of some unpronounceable domain had come to honor the king's wedding with his august presence. Then a procession of chanting monks barred the way to the basilica and looked fair to fill it with their celebration of an unpronounceable Latin saint. Aspasia, as a woman, even a woman who seemed a nun, was patently unwelcome among them. When she circled to evade them she lost herself for an endless time in an intricacy of passages, each the image of the last.

Her hour was well up before she found the passage she was looking for and came out in the green quiet. She stopped simply to breathe, and laid aside her veil, for the sun was warm. The rough edges of her temper began to smooth a little. In a day or two she might smile at her misadventures. She bent her head under the arching vines and made her way toward the garden and the fountain.

It was a peculiarity of Rome that where people lived, they lived in swarming throngs, as if the emptiness of the ruined city was too much for them; they could not endure it, but must crowd together in the smallest compass imaginable. That was so even in the tiny principality of the Lateran, and even in the garden there was often a hum and a murmur of voices, though no one ever found the little greensward or the statue of Pan. Today inevitably was a day of voices, louder and clearer than she remembered, and growing no less so as she advanced. It sounded like men talking, not loudly but with considerable liveliness—like, in fact, a disputation. Pope John and Emperor Otto were fond of scholarly arguments, and were given to inflicting them on gatherings of the court. There had been one just before Aspasia came to Rome, which people were still talking of: some infant prodigy from either Gaul or Spain, his provenance depending on who told it, who had demolished a great German master with a few well-turned phrases.

Clear as the voices were, maddening as the day had been, Aspasia was hardly surprised to find her haven occupied. Two men were in it, one sitting on the fountain's rim, the other pacing up and down and discoursing with impressive eloquence. The one by the fountain was unstartling, a monk in a habit notable only for its cleanliness. He was young though no boy, with a plain, blunt, thoroughly undistinguished face; while he listened to the other with nods and shakes of the head and an occasional word, he whittled at something small, complicated, and only vaguely distinguishable.

The other was astonishing. He was older than the monk, but how much older was difficult to tell: he moved so quickly and with such animation that the eye wanted to call him a boy. But a boy could not boast so beautiful a black beard or so rich a voice. No monk, that one, nor indeed anything Christian at all. From the curl of his slippered toes to the summit of his snow-white turban he was purely a son of the Prophet. His Latin was leavened with Arabic; his face was ruled by as noble a nose as ever clove its way out of Arabia; his long robe swirled as he spun, stabbing home one last, triumphant point.

The monk laid down his carving and applauded. "Bravo, Ismail!"

"Then you concede the point?" the infidel demanded.

"I concede the excellence of your argument," the monk replied. "As for the point, I hold it inarguable."

The infidel scowled terribly. "But I have just argued it."

"Surely," said the monk, laughing. He held up his handiwork. "Look, what do you think of this? I've a reckoning that with a bigger one I could teach astronomy. See, I'll mark the planets so, and so, and so, and when I turn this part here and shift this part there, even the dullest ox of a duke's son can see how the planets move."

The infidel's scowl blackened, but then it faded, and he laughed. It was remarkable how he could laugh: it was like the sun at midnight, so sudden as it was, and so beautifully brilliant. "Allah! All the splendor of my intellect, and what does it gain me? One grinning dog of an infidel, carving his endless contraptions."

The monk grinned happily. "But this one works. See. Wouldn't you like to know where Venus is when Mars is in his house?"

"I can know that by looking up at night." But the Muslim took the carving and sat on the grass beside the other, turban next to new-mown tonsure, and tried the workings of what was, Aspasia judged, an armillary sphere.

She could judge it very well. Without thinking at all, she had come out of concealment and stood almost over them. "May I see?" she heard herself ask.

The Muslim jumped like a cat. The monk raised bright eyes of no color in particular and regarded her with perfect calm. She might almost have said that he knew who she was. She did not know him at all, but Rome was full of monks, and this one was as undistinguished to look at as clearly he was remarkable in his craft. He rescued the sphere from the Muslim's slackening fingers and held it out to her.

It was wonderfully made, only a little larger than her cupped hands, but every piece carved with exacting precision. She tilted the ring that was for Venus and set it to turning. "She should go backward here," she said, touching the place with her finger.

"So she should," said the monk. "So she shall, when the sphere is finished."

He seemed happy to speak to her as someone who might know what she spoke of. The Muslim did not quite turn his back on her, but his expression was eloquent enough. The monks in the basilica had regarded her in much the same fashion.

The nerve of the man, she thought. Trespassing in her place, where her faith was queen, and daring, by heaven, to avert his eyes from her in scorn. Because she was angry and still startled that he should be here at all, she said what she thought. "I had heard," she said, "that women in Islam are not quite as low in the scale of things as vermin, if never as high as camels."

The monk laughed. The Muslim glared. At least he did it at her, and not at the ground between his feet. He had magnificent eyes. She told him so.

Dark though he was, his flush was clear to see. He seemed to have lost all his eloquence. "Or don't virtuous sons of the Prophet address themselves to females?" she asked him.

"Do virtuous daughters of the Prophet Isa," he asked the air just aft of her ear, "address themselves promiscuously to men not of their kin?"

"In their own country they may do as they please."

"Ah," he said. And after a pause: "This then is a province of your Byzantine emperor?"

She stared. "How did you know—"

He would not answer. The monk did, for charity. "Your Latin is excellent, my lady, but your accent is unmistakable. If, that is," he added, "one has such an ear as Ismail. I tell him he's wasted on Galen and Hippocrates. He should turn his hand to nobler arts."

"And what art is nobler than the art of medicine?" Aspasia wanted to know.

"Theology," said the monk. "But I was thinking of music. You should hear him sing. He never will, unless I threaten him. He says that singing is frivolous."

"Unless one sings hymns," Aspasia said.

"There are no hymns in Islam." Ismail's voice was cold. "Only holy Koran."

" 'There is no god but God, and Muhammad is the Prophet of God.' "

His eyes on her were wide and a little wild.

"Is my accent as bad as that?" she asked.

He blinked. The wildness faded a little. "I have . . . heard worse." Not warm, but not quite so cold, either. "Where in the world did you learn Arabic?"

"In Constantinople," she said. The memories wanted to flood and drown her. She held them at bay with words and will. "I know I learned it badly, but there was no one to teach me, most of the time. Only books." He did not say anything. "How in the world did a Muslim come to the court of the Roman pope?"

"As all men come: on ship, ahorse, afoot."

He was not about to say more than that. The monk said, "Ismail is a Moor, from Córdoba. We met in Vich, which is near Barcelona, and is a Christian city. He had a mind to see other lands than his own; he came with us when we came to the Holy Father. He cured the Holy Father of a flux, and the emperor of a malady of the eyes. Do you have something, maybe, that he can cure you of?"

"Can he cure the heartache?" Aspasia's tongue asked for her.

"For that," said the Moor, "there is no cure but time."

She bit her traitor tongue. This was outrageous, and it was making her as wild as she seemed to make this infidel. She raised her chin a fraction. "My name is Theophano," she said, "but they call me Aspasia."

"But—" said the Moor.

The monk said nothing.

"Oh," said Aspasia. "Everyone in the City is Theophano; it's a name we're all too fond of. The one you know, the princess, is my lady."

"I've seen you with her," said the monk. "My name is Gerbert, from Aurillac in Gaul. I serve his holiness the pope, and of late his majesty the emperor."

Aspasia's eyes narrowed. "It's you they all talk about. The child with the golden tongue."

"Not so much a child," he said, drawing himself up to his full height. It was not much, but it was a fair bit more than she had. "As for the golden tongue, I can't say it's that, but it moves quickly enough when it has to. It could use a little more honing in logic. Would you happen by any chance to be a logician?"

He asked it so plaintively, with such wide-eyed longing, that she could not help but laugh. "No, I can't say that I'm more than an apprentice in the art. Grammar always distracts me, and the lure of a new word."

"I'm always running after a new number," he said, "or a new contraption." He turned the one in his fingers, and shrugged a little wryly. "Ismail could teach me, but he won't. He says he's a wretched teacher. He isn't. He forgets, that's all. He stops teaching and starts practicing, and if the pupil is wise, he learns by splendid example."

"If he knows what to look for," said Ismail. He rose with the grace of one born in a chairless country, and bowed to them both. "If my brother will forgive me; if the lady will permit. I am expected where I should not tarry."

Gerbert said something fitting. Aspasia could not find anything to match it. The Moor left with dignity, which did not quite look like flight.

"Poor Ismail," said Gerbert. "He never knows what to make of Christian women."

"He seems to improvise well enough," Aspasia said.

Gerbert smiled. "Oh, but you see, you caught him all out of his reckoning. You startled him into saying what he thought. That's a dreadful thing to do to a Moor."

"I hope he survives the shame of it," she said.

"He may. I," said Gerbert, "will have to confess a sin. I enjoyed it much too much."

"I could see." She stood as Ismail had, but without the

grace. "I really do have somewhere that I should be. Do you come here very often?"

"Once in a great while," Gerbert said. "More often if there's someone interesting to talk to."

"Maybe there will be," said Aspasia.

She looked back once as she walked away. Gerbert was sitting where she had left him, knife back in hand, tongue between his teeth, perfecting the workings of his sphere.

Nine

N ow that Aspasia knew the monk from Gaul, she saw him nearly every day, waiting on pope or emperor or singing in one of the chapels or, once or twice, sitting in the garden under the eye of sylvan Pan. But the Moor she saw only once, and that but a glimpse, moving quickly away from her. She should not have cared what one lone arrogant infidel did with himself, but she found herself thinking of him at odd moments. Very odd, sometimes.

Once in a great while she still woke with tears on her face and a great knot in her belly, and knew that she had dreamed of Demetrios and of the child who had died. A day or two after the meeting in the garden she woke so, and lay in the dark, and stretched out her mind's hands for Demetrios' face. It came, but when she saw it clear, it was not his face at all. It was too narrow, and its nose was too sharp a curve, and its beard was too rich and black. She cried out—whether against it or after it, she never knew—and it was gone, and Theophano was there, reaching to comfort her. Always before she had refused that comfort, but tonight she clung. She could not stop crying. Theophano did not try to make her. She cried herself back to sleep, a sleep blessedly without dreams.

In the morning Aspasia was furious with herself. Theophano said nothing, which was like her forbearance. Aspasia did not dream of Demetrios again, but she could not get the infidel out of her mind. It was anger and good Christian indignation, and yes, she could admit it, fascination. Arab physicians were common enough in Constantinople. One had been her teacher for a while in Arabic and in medicine. That had been a eunuch, and this patently was not, but otherwise there was little to choose between them.

Except that Abd al-Rahim had been no more to her than a teacher and an occasional companion, and this one was becoming something altogether different. If she was not careful he would become an obsession. She wanted to see him again. She wanted to tell him what she thought of his arrogance. She wanted to make him see her as more than female, and infidel, and beneath his lordly contempt.

She did not talk of him to Gerbert. Gerbert talked of him, but too seldom. He had too much else to talk of. The wedding—he was full of it, as they all were. The pope and the emperor, his studies in Gaul and Spain and Rome, his abbey in Aurillac, the friends he had gathered and still gathered wherever he went. He had a gift for friendship, did Gerbert. And now he had a new friend, a monk from Rheims, who seemed at last to be the logician he had been looking for. This Gerann was a master of the school in the cathedral— for in Gaul no one studied except in abbeys or in cathedrals; there was nowhere else to go in that dark and barbarous country—and he wanted Gerbert to go back with him when he went, to teach him mathematics in return for what he knew of logic. "Not," said Gerbert, "that he has much of a head for numbers, but he does want to complete his education, and I want to complete mine. When I've seen my prince married to his princess, I'll set off for Rheims. The Holy Father has given me his leave, and the emperor has agreed to let me go."

He was almost handsome, he was so happy. Aspasia was glad for him. What else she felt, she did not let him see. She did not have his gift for friendship. She was more wary, less free with herself. But when she made a friend, as she had with Theophano, as she had with Liutprand, as now she had with Gerbert, she gave him everything that she had. It was a flaw, she knew that. There was no ease in her. It was all or nothing. And when her friends went away as people always did, whether to Rheims or to death, she had no skill in accepting it.

She set herself grimly to learn. Maybe it would teach her to accept other and deeper things: Demetrios, the child she had lost and the children she would never have. She still had Theophano, would always have her. That, Theophano had promised, and Theophano was a woman of her word.

The week before Easter it rained incessantly. That was not at all the wonted way of Rome in April, as if winter had got lost and come back out of its season. Everyone huddled round braziers, and those who had the blessing of a hypocaust had it stoked and rekindled.

The cloister to which the women were relegated was old enough to have a hypocaust, but the nuns would not use it. That was pagan comfort, and they were Christians. For their guests there were braziers, but those did little more than soften the edge of the damp.

"It's exactly like home," Aspasia said through chattering teeth as she struggled to light the recalcitrant coals. They were all wet to the skin despite the canopy which had tried to cover them on their procession to and from the pope's palace. Nothing but walls could keep out wind-slanted rain.

Theophano could not stop shivering long enough to answer. The other women got her out of her rain-sodden silks

and into soft warm wool and took down her hair. Aspasia,
even engrossed in fire-tending, shot her worried glances. She
had not looked well all day; she was paler now than she
should be, and she was too quiet.

Aspasia knew better than to ask her if she was ill. She
would never admit it. When the coals yielded at last to persuasion and consented to warm the air, Aspasia drew up a
chair as close as she dared, and made Theophano sit in it.
Theophano did not even try to resist. Aspasia laid a hand on
her brow. It was burning hot, but she was shivering.

Even as little time as she had spent in Rome, Aspasia
knew the Roman fevers. The marshes bred them. Romans
died of them in infancy or grew to a gnarled and indomitable old age. Foreigners simply died of them. It was a black
jest among the Germans, that if Roman brickbats did not
fell them, Roman fevers inevitably would.

Fear was not anything Aspasia would let herself submit
to. Theophano was going to be married on the Sunday after
Easter. The marriage meant too much to all of them, both
East and West. She must be well for it; she must be strong.
She must live to bear her callow young king the heirs he
needed.

Aspasia left her well wrapped in blankets, with Phoebe
coaxing her to take a little honeyed wine. She did not want
it, and was almost petulant about it. Aspasia stretched her
stride.

Brother Gerbert was in comfort in a room small enough,
with a brazier large enough, to be almost warm; and he had
a lamp to see by as he wrote letters for the emperor. He did
not seem to mind that Aspasia interrupted him, although
the others in the room, a pair of monks and a scribe from
the papal chancery, looked on her with considerable dis-
favor. She took no notice of them. "Can you find the Moor
for me?" she asked.

Gerbert's brows went up, but he was as wise as she had

hoped. He asked no questions. He put down his pen, covered his ink-bottle, tidied his place at the table, all in a swift smooth motion. He spoke only once, and that when they were striding together down the passage. "Your lady?" he asked.

"Fever," said Aspasia.

Gerbert strode a little faster.

Where they found the Moor, or what he was doing when they found him, Aspasia never afterward recalled. It seemed to take most of an age, but when they came back to the convent, there was still a wan grey light in the sky.

Sister Portress would have given them trouble. The monk she would have admitted, if he had not smiled and bowed and blessed them all and gone back to his warm room and his emperor's letter. The Moor in his turban, shivering nearly as convulsively as Theophano, was unconscionable. Aspasia made him conscionable. She simply walked through the gate and held it for him to pass, and listened to nothing that Sister Portress said.

The Moor held his tongue and followed Aspasia. Later she would wonder if he had ever seen the inside of a convent before. Now she cared only that he should see to Theophano.

Someone had fetched another physician, one of the local butchers from the look of him. Theophano was in bed, whiter and weaker than ever. The physician stood out of reach and out of clear sight and babbled in incomprehensible Italian. What he thought he was doing, Aspasia could not imagine.

The Moor stepped lithely past Aspasia and took in the room with a swift glance. He said nothing, but his nostrils flared. He looked like a horse brought to the race, all nerves and speed, focusing abruptly and absolutely on the contest before him.

He ejected the Italian so smoothly that the man could not

have known he was ousted until the door shut in his face. Helena went with him. Her silence was nearly as perceptible as his yattering, fading down the passage to the gate.

The Moor bent over Theophano. His voice was softer than Aspasia had imagined it could be, speaking Greek of remarkable if accented purity. He told her who he was. He called himself the emperor's physician. Aspasia had given little thought to what exactly he might be, or whom he served, if anyone, among the great ones in Rome. All she cared to know was that he was from Córdoba, and that he knew what he was doing.

In a moment he had Theophano's hand in his and her eyes on him in such trust as she had never given a stranger. His own eyes were warm and astonishingly kind. He looked like a different man.

He had no assistant. That was another question to ask, later. Aspasia found herself with his box of medicines, fetching and carrying as he commanded. He seemed unaware of her except as a pair of hands. They were good hands, she thought. They had had good training. They knew what he wanted, sometimes before he asked for it. It was like him to take them for granted, and never a word or a glance to show that she had done well.

But he was healing Theophano. He examined her with exquisite discretion, named her fever to her, smiled and said, "I know that scion of devils, and he knows me. This potion of mine will send him howling back to his master. See, it is bitter, but I mix it with honey, so, and mellow it with wine. Drink now, and ask your good angel to bless you."

Theophano drank as trustingly as a child. She even smiled—she, who had scowled her way through every ague and fever of her childhood. The Moor saw her tucked well in blankets, and bowed as to an eastern queen. "I shall return in the morning," he said, "if my lady will allow; and if God wills, your fever will be broken. Today is not the first of it, I judge?"

Theophano shook her head. Her eyelids were heavy already, but she reached out and clasped his hand. "Comes and goes," she said slowly, as if it was an effort to focus on the words. "Kept quiet. Not to worry—people—"

"But," said the Moor, "when the proper people worry, then they call me." He laid her hand gently on the coverlet. "Sleep well, my lady, and mend."

Theophano nodded. She might have said something else, but sleep took her before she could begin.

Aspasia concentrated on returning bottles and vials to their proper places in the box. She was aware that the Moor watched her. She half expected him to snatch the box out of her hands and do it himself. But he did not. He was a meticulous craftsman: each compartment was labeled in Arabic, each label matching its twin on bottle or vial.

The last bottle slid neatly into its allotted place. She did not close the lid. He had instruments still to put in. She held out the box.

He took it politely, which surprised her. His voice was brusque enough. "The preparation which I gave her, give her three drops at middle night, no more, in a measure of honey mixed with wine. I shall attend her in the morning. If she wakes and has discomfort, rub her breast and throat with this salve, and wrap them well in soft cloths. Let her breathe of it if she will. It will ease her."

Aspasia inclined her head.

He returned the last instrument to the box, shut it with a small, distinct click.

"She will be well?" Aspasia asked him. It was not her will doing the asking; it was her tongue, and her fear for Theophano.

A thin line appeared between the Moor's brows, but he said mildly enough, "That is with God. She is young and her health is good; I shall do all that I can. Among us all, yes, I think she will be well."

"She has to be," said Aspasia. "She will be queen."

"As God wills," the Moor said.

There were nuns without, looking ready to expostulate but thinking better of it. Aspasia cared only that none of them was Empress Adelaide. She sent one of them to find a servant with a torch. It was well that she was obeyed.

The Moor would not have waited. Aspasia guided him down to the gate and let him look out into black dark and the hiss of rain. He was shivering again, even in the shelter of the gate.

"I would offer you hospitality," Aspasia said, "if you would take it from Christians."

"Would the Christians permit you to offer it?"

That was irony. Aspasia lifted her chin. "If I commanded, they would."

"No," he said, "lady. I have my own house not far from here." She must have looked surprised. His brows went up a fraction. "What, did you think I sprang out of the ground?"

"I thought you lived in the palace."

"When the emperor travels, I travel with him. Here, I have my house."

She nodded slowly. "One needs a place that is one's own. It's a blessing when one can have it."

"A blessing indeed, for the Roman Church as for me. The good fathers like little to see a son of the Prophet in the heart of their faith."

"What is a son of the Prophet doing here of all places in the world?"

For a moment Aspasia thought that he would walk away from her, even in the dark and the rain. Then he said, "I give healing where there is healing to be given."

"Surely there is healing to be given in Córdoba."

His face wore no expression at all. "There are physicians by the score in Córdoba. Here, of those who know the art and are not charlatans, there are but a precious few."

"And you."

"And I." He darted a glance at her, dark under the dark brows. "And you, lady? Are you but a princess' servant?"

"She calls me friend."

"And kinswoman?"

"Do we look like kin?"

"In face," he said, "no. In other ways, utterly. It seems to trouble her little that you were born higher than she."

"How—" Aspasia shut her mouth sharply.

He had heard her. He almost smiled. "Is it a secret?"

"No," said Aspasia. "Yes. I don't want— How did you know?"

"You have an air about you. You lift a brow; the world obeys."

"I do not!"

He laughed, which startled her speechless. "You are doing it now," he said, "my lady Theophano Porphyrogenita."

When she had her wits back, the servant had come with the torch and a scowl, and borne him away.

She loathed him. She despised him. She could not for the life of her forget him.

Ten

Theophano, watched over by the physician from Córdoba, recovered well and quickly from her sickness.
By morning the fever had broken, and by the morning after that she was out of bed and preparing to attend the
Easter mass.

The Moor was not entirely pleased with that, but even his
authority could not stand against the necessities of empire.
He asked Theophano's leave to remain near her for a day or
two—to hover, she called it. She gave him rather more than
he had asked for. She asked the emperor to make him her
physician. The emperor, well warmed with wine and well
captivated by Theophano's smile, granted her what she
asked.

"Now you can hover to your heart's content," she said to
the Moor when she came from the palace.

He seemed not in the least surprised. "Now will your
highness do as I bid her and go to bed?"

She went, but that was hardly obedience: it was late and

she had no duties until morning. She took the dose he gave her, hardly grimacing at the taste; she smiled. As if he could not help it, he smiled back. "You are going to be a great and terrible queen," he said to her.

"So I intend to be," she said.

The night before her wedding, Theophano was allowed at last to seek an hour's solitude. She was supposed to pray. She had confessed her sins; she had heard mass. She had had her last lesson with the empress and her women. Now she was left to herself, and at her asking, to Aspasia.

On Easter day the rain had stopped, only to begin anew the morning after. But now at last it was gone. The sun, setting, shone through the high narrow windows of the nuns' chapel. The nuns were in bed already, for they had to rise in the deep night for their night office. They left behind a deep quiet, a memory of incense, an echo of their voices chanting compline, high and piercingly sweet.

Aspasia prayed a little, but mostly she watched Theophano. So long, they had been together. All of Theophano's life, most of Aspasia's. Aspasia could remember her newborn, a small crimson creature who even then had had an empress' strength of will.

She looked like a child, kneeling on the cold stone, erect and rather stiff, hands clasped in front of her, eyes shut. Now and then her lips moved. Her cheeks, innocent of paint, were pale, but she did not look ill. Only abstracted, and perhaps a little afraid.

Her eyes opened. She sank back on her heels. She drew a deep breath, let it out slowly. "Tomorrow," she said, "there will be no turning back."

"Was there ever?" Aspasia asked.

Theophano kept her eyes on the altar and on the painted Christ above it. "Tomorrow I can no longer refuse to face the truth. What all of this is. What . . ." She let her voice fade. After a moment she went on. "Her majesty was blunt.

If I had any doubts as to what will be expected of me, I can have none now."

It took Aspasia a moment to understand. When she did, she almost laughed. "What, didn't I teach you well enough to suit her majesty?"

"Nothing suits her majesty. Except her son. Him she dotes on. She told me that if I failed to satisfy him, I would be derelict in my duty."

"You won't fail," said Aspasia.

Theophano frowned a very little. "She as much as told me that a maiden could not begin to please a man. Then she made very certain that I am a maiden, so that no one can reject me." A flush touched her cheek. Not shame, Aspasia thought. Anger.

And no wonder. "It's the way of these things," Aspasia said, trying to soothe her.

"Did they do it to you, too?"

Aspasia felt the heat rise in her face. "They did it to me. The family's honor resided in me, after all, as it does in every woman."

"Did they laugh at you? Did his mother glare and hope that you would fail?"

"His mother," said Aspasia, "told me to my face that I might be the emperor's daughter, but I was scarcely fit to fasten her son's shoes."

"That is exactly what she said to me," said Theophano. She looked less angry now, more like herself. "Aspasia," she said. "What I'm supposed to do. What if—what if I can't?"

Ah, thought Aspasia. There it was. Sometimes it never came out at all; and that was not well for the bride or the marriage. She spoke as firmly as she could, without seeming to protest too much. "You can, Phania. Even if you loathe him. Because you must."

"I don't loathe him," said Theophano quickly. "I don't even dislike him. You know that."

"Then you have nothing to be afraid of."

"But what if I don't like him enough? What if he doesn't like me?"

"The way he looks at you," said Aspasia, "I don't think you have any need to fear that."

"But," said Theophano. "When we're alone. When—when there's nowhere to go. He's younger than I am, Aspasia. What if he doesn't know what to do?"

"He knows," Aspasia said, praying that she told the truth. From all that she had heard, his mother and his father between them kept him as closely as a girl. He had the look: half hungry, half terrified. Boys who knew women might still know the hunger, but the terror was a little less.

If the emperor had any sense at all, he would see to it that tonight of all nights his son took tutelage of a woman wise in the body's arts. One maiden was enough for a wedding night.

Theophano seemed to accept Aspasia's assurance. She lowered her eyes, perhaps prayed a little more, perhaps pondered what she would say next. When she spoke, her voice was almost too soft to hear. "Is it too terrible, Aspasia?"

"No," Aspasia said. "It's not terrible at all. Even the first time. There's pain; there's blood. You have to be ready for that. But when it's past and you've stopped being afraid of it, there's nothing better in the world."

"Nothing at all?"

"Well," said Aspasia. She looked at the Christ over the altar and the Virgin beside him, and crossed herself carefully. "No. In the world, nothing. If there's love between the two of you, and honest liking, and hope of children to come from it, it's as close as a human body can come to what heaven is."

"That's not what the empress said," said Theophano.

"That's not what anyone says. It's heretical."

"But true," said Theophano. "You make me believe that."

"I want you to. It's not anything that just happens,

Phania. You have to make it happen. You have the choice: to make it purgatory or to make it heaven. Why should you suffer unless you must?"

"They say it's good for the soul."

"The soul isn't what has to bear and beget children. If God had meant it to be as sinful as the priests say it is," said Aspasia, "then why did He put such pleasure in it?"

"That was the devil," said Theophano. "Or so they say." She smiled; she was close to laughing. "I'd rather be a heretic like you."

"Hush," said Aspasia. "Be brave, and be glad. That will be more than enough."

Theophano threw her arms about her and clasped her tight. "For you I'll do it."

"And for your Otto."

"For Otto, too," said Theophano after only an instant's pause. "I'll make him love me. I'll teach myself to love him."

"Then your children will be strong and beautiful, and your kingdom will prosper."

"God willing," said Theophano.

God was kind to the King of the Germans and to his eastern bride. For their wedding gift He gave them the full beauty of spring, warmth and sunlight and an exultation of birdsong. Even sour, cynical Rome forgot itself for an hour and cheered the procession, pelting it with flowers.

There was glory in it. Aspasia, in the midst of it, knew it as a dazzle of colors, gold and crimson, blue and purple and scarlet and green, furs and silks, emeralds, rubies, opals, and diamonds. Theophano was all gold, her long hair free as befit a bride, veiled in golden silk and crowned with flowers. She rode a milk-white mare caparisoned with gold and crimson; a youth in crimson and gold walked at its head, and maidens in white walked behind and before her, singing in high pure voices.

Aspasia was no maiden, but Theophano would not have her elsewhere but there. She rode at Theophano's back, out of mourning at last, in gold and crimson like the princess she was. She did not pretend to be unconscious of it. Even Theophano had been surprised to see her. "Aspasia," she had said in honest delight. "You're beautiful."

Not beautiful, no. But handsome; that, she could admit to. Theophano was the beauty. Aspasia was content to be her shadow, to arrange her train when she mounted at the convent's gate, to ride at her side through the ruins and the teeming towns that were Rome. They rounded the Caelian Hill and passed the vast hollowed drum that men called the Colosseum, and the broken Forum, and the heights of the Palatine and the Capitoline. They passed over the Tiber past the castle called Sant'Angelo, and left Rome's walls behind them and entered Pope Leo's city, the citadel of the Vatican where was Saint Peter's basilica.

Saint John of the Lateran was the Holy Father's church, head and center of the western world, but Saint Peter of the Vatican was its heart. There Charlemagne was crowned and called Emperor of the Romans. There Otto was crowned after him, and Otto his son had been crowned in his turn. Now the young king would take a bride out of Byzantium and make her Empress of the Romans.

Here was almost a proper city: a city of pilgrims. They thronged it now, lining the broad processional way, filling the square. The emperor's guards held them back from the basilica itself, warding the broad steps.

At the door the emperors waited, father and son, as they had waited at the gates of Rome. Here as there, the pope stood with them in the army of his acolytes.

They wore the purple in the manner of Byzantium. Aspasia would not forgive them for claiming it. She could admit that they looked well in it. Otto the younger did not look so young now, with all the world to be the center of, and Theophano to be his bride.

She left the white mare, dismounting with grace and dignity. Aspasia was there to set her robes in order, to smooth her hair and settle her veil and to offer her a smile. She smiled in reply. There was no tremor in her; no hint of fear, now that she had come to it. Aspasia's throat tightened. Now she understood why mothers wept at weddings. It was not grief; it was pride, and joy too keen to bear.

She swallowed hard and willed the tears away. A large solemn personage came forward to claim Theophano's hand: the Byzantine ambassador, speaking for her father who was dead and her emperor who had given her to the barbarian king. With ample orotundity of phrase he gave her into the pope's care. The pope, smiling, accepted her. He led her to her betrothed; he took the veil from her and blessed it; he laid her hand in Otto's.

By that in its simplicity, they were wedded. The rest of it, the mass and the prayers and the chanting, the blessing and the vows, was for the people's sake, to give them a proof that they would remember. Theophano passed through it all with flawless serenity, her voice when she spoke the vows clear and unshaken. Otto stumbled a little, but he seemed to gain strength from her calm. His voice at the end rang out with something very like exuberance.

When all the words were said, Otto took the crown from the pope's hands. He blinked a little as the jewels flashed and flared. Theophano knelt at his feet, head bowed. As the crown came down, her head came up. Gold met gold. *Empress,* the choir proclaimed her. *Empress of the Romans.*

The pope spoke the last blessing. He joined their hands for the last time, gave them leave to seal the union. Otto's face was scarlet, but he approached her manfully and kissed her with remarkable competence. At that, the younger lords abandoned solemnity. Their roar drowned out the choir and pursued the king and his new queen out of the basilica into the dazzle of sunlight, in the sight of Rome and the world.

* * *

Aspasia was not prepared for the full reality of a wedding among the barbarians. It tried to be properly civilized, but there was no stopping the young men once they had begun. Nor did she need a better command of German than she had, to know what they were saying and singing. She could trace the path of it in Otto's blushes.

Theophano mercifully did not have Aspasia's gift for languages, and she had enough to occupy her with Empress Adelaide beside her, watching her every move. Her manners were exquisite, as Aspasia could well judge: Aspasia had taught her. She did not try to touch Otto. He, in his confusion, did not try to touch her. His ears were a glorious shade of crimson. He managed, for all of that, to laugh at some of the sallies, and even to try one or two of his own.

The feast dragged itself into eternity. The wine flowed freely. Germans drank, Aspasia thought, like Macedonians. Even the women. She made sure that Theophano's cup was kept full, but also that it held measurably more water than wine. She could not unfortunately do the same for Otto, but when she looked, she saw that his father had him in hand.

Her eyes met the emperor's. At first he seemed not to know her; then he started, and his glance sharpened. She allowed herself the flicker of a smile. The corner of his mouth twitched infinitesimally. They erred who said there was no humor in him. It was rare and it tended toward the sardonic, but there was ample for the purpose.

There was something more than irony in him now. Her breath came short suddenly. It had been too long since anyone looked at her so. As more than a shadow; more even than a princess. As a woman, and desirable.

Someone spoke to him. He looked away. If he looked back, she did not know it. Would not. She engrossed herself in serving her lady.

They put the young couple to bed with due solemnity and more than due hilarity. Aspasia could happily have throttled the young asses who saw Theophano all but naked in her shift, and stripped poor Otto of his and flung him bodily into bed beside her. They would have stayed even to see the marriage consummated, if the emperor had not driven them out with a battlefield bellow.

Aspasia was caught up in the retreat. More than half of her would have resisted it, but she had a little sense left. Phania was stronger than she knew. If she could not calm her skittish colt of a husband, coax him to make a man of himself, and make him take pleasure in it, Aspasia would be profoundly disappointed.

Aspasia made her way out of the pope's palace. So must it have been when John Octavian was pope: full of drunken laughter. Once or twice she tangled with men who wanted something other than wine. One proved amenable to reason; the other, to a knee in the groin. That one tore her gown not quite past repair. He would receive an accounting in the morning.

Ruffled, scowling, but uncowed, she found the passage to the convent. Halfway down it she paused. The air was soft. There was a moon, nearly full, bright enough almost to read by, and a splendor of stars. Somewhere, someone was singing. The words were in no tongue she knew, but the tune was sweet and plaintive, like the nightingale's lament.

Her hand slackened on her gown. The rent opened, baring her shoulder. The breeze caressed it. Her mind's eye saw Otto in the light of the clustered lamps, thin and spotty in his nakedness, but well enough made for all of that, and quite adequately a man.

She turned abruptly. The way was strange in the dark, but the moon guided her. She lost herself only once, and found her way back, and took the turning she had missed.

The fountain bubbled softly in its basin. The moon danced on it. Sylvan Pan played his silent pipes. His eyes laughed, welcoming her. She sat at his feet and turned her face to the stars. What she did was mad, she knew it very well. She would be richly fortunate if she took nothing worse than a chill. A fever could seize her, or a night demon, or if God turned His face away, an incubus.

She did not care. She had lived long and well enough. She had had a husband whom she loved. The child she had raised, though not born of her body, was wedded and bedded and crowned a queen. She was alone in a strange country, widowed and empty, a barren seed. What did it matter what became of her now?

That was what it was to be free. It was a kind of damnation, and yet with it a kind of salvation.

She lay back on the grass, not caring what the dew did to her gown. She stretched out her arms and breathed deep of grass and dew and starlight. Her mind knew too well that she was a woman on the verge of middle age. But her body knew only that she was a woman.

When the moon bred a shadow, she was not surprised at all. She crossed herself, for safety. The shadow only grew the more solid. It was clothed in something that glimmered; it was crowned with white.

Turbaned. Even then she did not move. Could not, maybe, though half her breast was bare and she could not have been more shameless if she had tried. Maybe he did not see her, there in the statue's shadow.

He came to stand over her. "There are quicker ways to kill yourself," he said.

Moon and madness fled: the moon behind a cloud, her madness in cold clarity. She sat up, clutching her gown together. He bent. His hands were strong and warm. He set her on her feet as easily as if she had been a child, and held her there. The moon, emboldened, slipped from behind its veil. She saw his brows drawn together over the glitter of his eyes. "Why do you always glare at me?" she asked.

He tilted her chin up, bent his head. She swayed and almost fell. But a kiss was the farthest thing from his mind. "Not wine," he said. "What, then?"

"Moonlight," she said.

He did not scoff at her. That was astonishing.

Her gown had slipped off her shoulder again. She heard the hiss of his breath, saw the swirl of his outer robe as he took it off and wrapped her in it. It was warm; it had a faint scent, like cinnamon. "Who did this to you?"

His voice was edged with iron. She shivered. She would not want to be the one it cut. "No one who matters," she answered him.

"Rape matters," he said.

"So it does," she said. "So he would, if he had done it. I doubt he'll be thinking of it again for a day or six. I kneed him somewhat harder than was strictly necessary. I don't," she said, "take kindly to being pawed over."

He stared at her.

She laughed. It was nothing that she meant to do, but the moon was in her, and he was so perfectly nonplussed. "Did you think I was defenseless?" she asked him.

"No," he said. He sounded like himself again, stiff and haughty. He turned her without quite touching her, back toward the convent. "If my lady will permit, I will escort her to her gate."

"And if my lady does not permit?"

"My lady will," he said.

She considered temper. She felt the damp of the dew that had soaked through her wrappings of silk and linen, and breathed air aseethe with fever-demons. Even the moon had wrapped itself in cloud and would not come out.

She could read omens as well as any astrologer. She held out her hand, imperious. "Escort me to my gate," she said.

Eleven

The Emperor of the East traveled widely enough in his wars, but his heart and center was in the City. If he changed his habitation it was only to cross the Bosporus to the summer palace, or to move from palace to palace within the City itself.

The Emperor of the Germans had no place truly to call his heart and center. Saxony, yes, that was his ancestral domain; Rome, that gave him what power he had over more than the Germans; Aachen, that had been Charlemagne's capital. But even Charlemagne had been a peripatetic emperor. His *palatium,* his royal focus, his court and clerks and the apparatus of his kingship, was a thing of bags and coffers, the kingdom of a wanderer.

That, Aspasia thought, was the legacy of the tribes. In some respects it was the most barbaric thing about these Germans, that they wandered and never truly settled. It was little wonder that the Romans would not accept them, when they would not remain to make themselves master but must always be newly returned or soon to depart. Romans had dwelt in the same place since Romulus was king. Even when they went away, they did so only to come back, and if they could, to leave their bones in Roman earth. Otto the elder and Otto the younger were no part of them.

It was no surprise to the Romans, and should not have been to the Byzantines, that when young Otto was wedded and bedded, his father ordained a long royal progress through the cities of Italy and in time over the Alps into Germany. There was logic enough in it, Aspasia conceded. Theophano should know what lands she was queen of. These people, being barbarians, had a need to see as to be seen, to know who their lords were and to be assured that there was a power over them.

"Otherwise," said Gerbert, "they forget and turn rebel."

He was riding with them, he and Gerann the logician, since the kings' way into Germany for a long while was his into Gaul. Aspasia was delighted to have his company. Gaufrid the Lombard would be leaving them in Cremona; after that she would have no friend with her but Theophano, and Theophano had a husband and a kingdom to manage.

She seemed to be prospering. As early as this was, but a month after her wedding, she showed no sign yet of having conceived an heir; but it was not for lack of trying. Otto had the look of a man well pleased with his wife. Theophano looked, if not besotted with him, then certainly content. They rode now side by side, Theophano in her litter, Otto on his grey stallion. As Aspasia watched, he leaned from the saddle, took Theophano's hand and kissed it. That was bold even for a barbarian, but the Germans seemed delighted. Some bellowed for more.

Otto did not blush as easily now as he had before his wedding, but at that he went scarlet. The Germans only grinned the wider.

Aspasia found that she was smiling. It was difficult to

disapprove as sternly as she ought. It was difficult in fact to remember that she was a proper royal Byzantine. The moon had stayed in her since that night in the garden; it had thawed something in her that had been frozen since Demetrios died. She wore black still, most days, because it was practical and she had grown used to it, but somehow and another she had gained a gown or two to rival her mended crimson.

She left her mule for a while to walk with Gerbert. The Lombard and the logician were hot at it, disputing the relative merits of faith and reason. There were other people listening, riding or walking on the Roman road under the blue Italian sky. By evening they would be in Cremona, and Gaufrid would leave them; and Aspasia would ask leave to visit Liutprand's grave. If she got back on her mule again and rode a little aside from the line of their march, she could see the city before them and the open country between, green and richly watered. After the bare dun hills of Tuscany and the lofty crags of Italy's spine, it seemed all the richer and softer: a gentle country to have sprouted so thorny a shoot as Liutprand.

Someone new came up beside them, mounted on a bay horse. The horse was fiery and did not take kindly to walking pace, but the rider bore its fretting easily. He did not dismount. Ismail the Moor never walked if he could help it.

Gerbert greeted him happily. He smiled in return. Aspasia studied the road in front of her feet. She was coming to a decision about him, and it was not the one she wanted at all. There was too much of the moon in it, and not enough of logic or reason or plain common sense. What it came to was very simple. She wanted him in her bed.

He did not want her at all. That was painfully clear to see. He neither sought her company nor avoided it. When he was called on in his professional capacity and she was there, he took it for granted that she would assist him. She learned a great deal from him, but as he had said to Gerbert, he was not a teacher. He had no patience. He never stopped for explanations. He did what he did, and one followed him or one did not. It did not matter to him.

No patience? Aspasia thought. No. He had a world's worth of it, but only for the sick. With them he was infinitely gentle. He always told them as much of what was wrong with them as he judged that they could bear. He never lied to them.

She could almost wish that she would get sick, simply to have his attention undivided. But fevers had never had much power over her, even the Roman fevers. A night in the garden that would have killed any other woman left her as healthy as ever. If anything, too healthy. She could have done without her body's remembering, late and out of season, that a man's touch was sweet.

There were other men who would have been glad to oblige her. Some of the Germans liked a little dark woman in a crimson gown. Not all of them were as direct about it as the man who had torn the gown. A few even treated her like a lady.

Her taste did not run to big yellow-haired men. It never had, even before the Varangian axes. It wanted dark and slender, and a beautiful beard.

Dark and slender wanted nothing female that she knew of. In Rome he had women servants. Aspasia had seen one of them once, slipping out of his house on an errand. He had brought none of them with him. Only a pair of servants, male both and older than himself, and a boy to look after the horses. The boy could hardly be doing woman's duty at night: he had a harelip, and he was somewhat simple.

She blushed under her veil. Such thoughts to have on the open road in Christian company. She would have to look for a confessor. Gerbert, maybe. He was more than a monk now: Pope John had made him a priest before he left Rome.

* * *

It was a while before she had occasion to talk to him. Cremona was behind them, and Liutprand asleep in the cathedral's crypt, more peaceful now than he had ever been alive. They had come to Pavia, which was Empress Adelaide's city, and for which alone Aspasia would have disliked it.

Like Cremona it lay in the wide green valley at the meeting of two rivers: Ticino that flowed out of Lago Maggiore, and broad slow winding Po. It was a royal city, both palace and fortress. From its towers one could look north and west and see the loom of mountains.

Aspasia shivered in the sun. All too soon they would be riding over them, ascending the steep passes into the wilds of Germania.

Gerbert sat with perfect calm upon the parapet, oblivious to the dizzy drop below. As usual he was making something, a cat's-cradle of beads and string this time, which would be an abacus. Aspasia had been reading to him from Cicero, but it was hard to keep her mind on old scandals when she had one of her own to distract her. She closed the book and let it fall to her lap, and watched Gerbert's square clever fingers.

There was nothing elegant about Gerbert. He was a farmer's son, he had told her. "My great-grandfather was a stablehand," she had told him.

She reminded him of it now, to take her mind off a certain narrow dark face.

He strung a last bead, coaxed the string into its proper hole in the frame. "Mine was a swineherd," he said, "but he never became an emperor."

"Maybe you will," said Aspasia.

"Pope, more likely," he said. "If it could be likely at all. I'll be a schoolmaster: that's as much as any peasant should aspire to."

"I wonder," Aspasia said, but softly. He did not seem to hear her. He was playing with his abacus, making patterns that were numbers, persuading them to shift and change and grow.

"Gerbert," said Aspasia.

He looked up.

"Gerbert," she said, "I think I may need a confessor."

He waited for her to go on. She thought that maybe she should dislike that silence, but it was oddly comfortable. It did not ask anything. It simply was, for her to fill or not, as she chose.

"Or maybe I don't," she said. "I don't know. My body says that it needs something more than spiritual comfort. Am I living in sin, do you think?"

"Have you done more than think about it?"

"No," she said. "Not yet."

"Has he asked you?"

"He doesn't even know I'm alive."

Gerbert raised his brows. "He must be blind."

"I'm that obvious?" she cried.

"You're that captivating." He said it perfectly candidly.

"Not to him."

"Are you sure of that?"

"You don't know who it is, do you?" she demanded.

"Not unless it's Ismail."

Her mouth was open. She shut it. "I am obvious."

"Well," said Gerbert. "No. But he is."

"Yes. He obviously doesn't care if I live or die."

"You are forgetting," Gerbert said, "that Ismail is a Moor."

"No," said Aspasia. "Not for a moment."

Gerbert shook his head. "Of course he's an infidel. That's not what I meant. He knows what you are. He thinks himself so far beneath you that he can never dream of aspiring to you."

"Is that why he looks so far down his nose at me?"

"He has his pride," said Gerbert. "Would you rather he groveled?"

"No!" Aspasia snapped.

"Well then." Gerbert tried another flashing, clicking calculation. He smiled at the pattern it made. "He was a man of substance in his own country. He never talks about it, but I think he's kin to the caliph."

"Then he's not beneath me at all."

"Not in birth. But exile can do strange things to a man's mind."

"He is an exile, then," said Aspasia. "He's not here because he wants to be."

"He wants it well enough, though he didn't choose what sent him here."

"What was it?"

"I don't know," said Gerbert. "Nothing shameful, I don't think, except to a man as proud as he is. I think he made a mistake. Said something he shouldn't, to someone unwise. Or stayed a friend to someone who wasn't in favor. You know courts. You know what they can do to an honest man."

"I know," Aspasia said. "Does he . . ." She stopped. But she had to ask. "Does he have a wife in Córdoba?"

"It wouldn't matter to him," said Gerbert. "Muslims can have four wives."

"Christians can't," said Aspasia. "Does he?"

"Yes," Gerbert said.

There. That settled it. Ismail was a married man. Aspasia would confess the sin of wanting him, and accept absolution and a good stiff penance, and cure herself of him.

Except that it was never so simple. "Only one?" she asked.

"That I know of," said Gerbert. "He's odd for a Muslim. He's continent. He says he doesn't like bought love. I tell him he'd make an admirable Christian."

"Maybe he will yet."

"One can always hope." Gerbert spun a bead, frowning a

little. "He's not really married, you know. By Christian lights."

"Are you encouraging me to compound a sin of the flesh?"

"I'm not a very good confessor, am I?" said Gerbert. "It's the peasant in me. My mother used to make marriages for the whole village. She never could see the use in Christian chastity. Except for priests. Priests have their duty, she told me, and so do ordinary people. And for the latter, that is to be fruitful and multiply."

"I can't," said Aspasia, very low.

He heard her. He put down his abacus, came and held her. She did not mean to cry. It made her angry, but the anger only made the tears flow faster. "I don't *want* this!" she cried.

A good confessor would have dried her tears and set her on her feet and told her kindly but firmly to pray for guidance. Gerbert let her cry herself out. Then he said, "I think you do."

"It's a sin."

"God can judge that. I'm only human."

She pulled away, scrubbing at her cheeks. "You are a dreadful confessor."

"I am," said Gerbert. "I'm trying to learn. Do you want me to say what I should say, or do you want me to be honest?"

She said something she had heard one of the guardsmen say. It was German, and therefore, she told herself, not quite as shocking as plain Greek.

Gerbert gave it a moment's silence. Then he said, "Yes. That does express it rather well."

She tried to scowl, but laughter kept breaking through. Gerbert always did this to her. "You may be an honest man," she said, "but you'll never make a saint."

"At least," said Gerbert, "I'm in good company."

Twelve

The Alps were a wall across the world. They went up and up, cleaving to heaven. Snow crowned them. But the passes were open, and free of more than snow. The emperor saw to that.

Aspasia knew of it because she knew how to listen. There were armed men in plenty to guard the great crawling beast that was the court and the empire, but an army of them had gone off westward with a charge which, from the look in his eye, the emperor had high hopes of.

"Saracens," said Gerbert. "They have a lair in these mountains; they come out in packs and fall on anyone who passes."

Ismail was with them, keeping close watch on Theophano in the cold high air. He had had to give up his horse as the road steepened; he would not stoop to a mule, however surefooted such a beast might be. He did not look pleased to hear Gerbert, but neither did he seem angry.

"The emperor will rid us of them," Gerbert said, "God

willing. They've been a scourge on every train that comes down out of Gaul or Germania, and every one that goes up. More every year, and richer pickings. It's become a fine highroad, this."

In more ways than one, Aspasia thought, keeping her eyes rigidly ahead. She did not want to look back and see how very far away the lowlands were, and how very steep and narrow the way they had come. It was almost too much for the wagons. The big thick-bodied horses and the patient oxen heaved and strained under the crack of the whip. In the steeper places, servants got behind and braced. Sometimes one failed or fell. If he was lucky, the others held without him, and he recovered to find his place again.

She did not want to think what it would be like when they went down. They had been climbing forever against the breast of heaven, where the wind was high and cold and the air caught at the lungs, and nothing was safe or sane or human. She was born of cities; towers were as high as she had ever cared to climb.

"Regrets, my lady?"

It was Ismail who asked that, with a glint that might not be mockery. As if he understood her.

She felt her cheeks grow warm under the sting of the wind. "Adventure," she said, "is not all it is proclaimed to be."

"This is hardly adventure," he said. "Adventure is a howling gale and blinding snow and a pack of human wolves falling on us from above. This is a stroll in the sun."

"To a man of your vast experience," she said acidly, "so it might be."

He smiled his brief, startling smile. "Is that truly why you came? For the adventure?"

"Maybe I was commanded."

"Not you, I think."

She thought of staying angry. It was hard, up here above the eagles. She laughed instead, rather to her own surprise.

"No, I commanded myself. It was that or the convent, you see."

"You had no desire to devote yourself to God?"

"God," she said, thinking that what he meant by that Name was not what she meant. Perhaps. She looked ahead at the train of men and baggage; she looked at the mountains and the sky. "God is everywhere that is. I tried to worship Him in the cloister's walls. While there were books to read, prayers to say, offices to sing, I told myself that I was happy. But it never changed. Day by day, hour by hour, the same ordered round, till I felt my feet carving furrows in the earth. To a saint, that might be God. To me it was the donkey on the threshing floor."

He was listening. It was remarkable how he could walk and watch her, and not stumble or fall back. He did not say anything.

She did not know why she needed to explain, only that she did. "I have no art," she said, "in mortifying the flesh. It's a terrible sin. Mortal: because I know it and I can't properly repent it. Whenever I try, whenever I think that, yes, now I can do it, now I can give it up, now I can be God's holy servant, a horror comes on me, and I run out under the sky."

"Perhaps you should have been born a man," said the Moor.

"No," Aspasia said. Impatiently, not angrily. "Why would I want that, when I can be what I am and do what I do? Even," she said, "this."

He said nothing. No doubt she had offended him. Moors were worse than men of the City when it came to the pride of their sex.

She shrugged to herself. Even to seduce him she would not apologize for telling the truth. It was a great failing in a seductress; but she could not help it. He would have to love her as she was, or not at all.

* * *

They came out of the mountains at last, and never a Saracen to harry them. Those were hunted out as the emperor had willed, and slain to the last man. The mountains were clean, the passes free of brigands.

Gerbert left them where the road bent round Lake Constance past St. Gall and Reichenau. He was going westward to Rheims. They were going north and east into the heart of Germania.

It would not have been proper for Aspasia to seek him out, but he came to her when the train was gathering to begin its morning's journey. His eyes were bright, and not with tears. "I'm going home," he said.

"I thought home was in the Auvergne: your abbey with the difficult name."

"Aurillac," he said. "Well, yes. But it's Francia, do you see? It's my own country. I'd forgotten how much I love it."

"One does," she said, rather low.

He laid a hand on her arm. "There. Maybe you'll go home too, someday. When your adventures are over."

"Maybe," she said.

There was a pause. His mule, ignored, stretched to nibble a bit of grass to which Aspasia's mule had already laid claim. Aspasia's mule did its best to lay the other's face open. Aspasia hauled it back and cursed it roundly.

Gerbert stepped forward suddenly and embraced her the way they did in Gaul, kissing her on both cheeks as if she had been his kin. By the time she had the wits to stiffen, he had let her go and sketched a blessing over her. "We'll meet again," he said.

The road was oddly empty without him in it. Ismail was there—often, when she thought about it—but his was not a comfortable presence. She was not even sure that she could call it friendly. He never spoke unless she spoke to him. He made it clear that he was there because it was close to Theophano.

She needed his arts seldom enough, God be thanked. She liked the mountains even less than Aspasia did, and with more reason: the litter was bad enough but the wagon was worse, and it was unthinkable that an empress should walk. Empress Adelaide did, but she was born in this country. Theophano was a Byzantine, and she knew what was proper.

And yet for all of that she was in excellent health, and the more so as they left the mountains and wound down into the forests of Germania. It was summer, and even the somber woodlands seemed to know it, dark spruce touched with fugitive gold. The scent of them was like nothing Aspasia had imagined, deep and green and wild, giving way as the mountains eased into a rolling lowland, to forests of beech and oak, and undulations of fen, and the sudden brightness of rivers.

She had thought to find it wild, and it was; she had known from talking to people that it was more settled than she might have expected, villages and towns set still far apart but growing as the empire grew. What she had not expected was to find it beautiful.

Italy was conquered land. This was land of the emperor's own blood, and it welcomed him with all its heart. He seemed almost light of mood as they rode now on Roman roads, now on tracks through the wildwood, stopping for the night in abbey or castle, walled town or forest holding. The weight of kingship on him never lifted, but it was less a burden here. Here he was welcome. Here he belonged.

Aspasia should not have been as pleased as she was to find Empress Adelaide out of her element. *The Lombard queen,* people called her. They bowed to her, they accepted her, but she was not one of theirs.

Nor yet was Theophano, but she meant to alter that. Somewhat of the dazzle was off her; she was talking to Aspasia again in the evenings instead of hastening through her toilet before her husband came. He still came, that was true, and he seemed as eager as ever, but she was getting her senses back.

"I've been cruel to you," she said one night. They were in a German town with a guttural German name, a square of wooden houses in a wooden wall, with a little stone church and a very pretty carved Virgin in it, which the empresses had gone to admire. The carver had been there, blushing and tongue-tied, and Theophano had been gracious to him in her halting new German. Everyone had been delighted with her.

Now Aspasia was combing out her long beautiful hair, and she was indulging herself in the pleasure of it, but thinking, too, and saying, "I've taken no notice of you at all. How can you stand me?"

"Easily," said Aspasia, coaxing a knot into smoothness. "You've been undemanding. It's restful."

"Am I—" Theophano stopped, half turned, caught the glint in Aspasia's eye. Her own narrowed dangerously, then cleared. "That's another thing I've forgotten. How it feels to laugh."

"What, you never laugh with your emperor?"

Theophano blushed. "You know what I mean. Laughter from—with—a friend. He doesn't understand all the things a woman can laugh at. Unless he begins it, it baffles him or offends him. He wants to lead, you see. He hates to follow."

"I know," Aspasia said.

"It irks him to no end," said Theophano, "that he has the title, he has a crown, people bow and scrape, and yet he's never truly the emperor. Always his father is before him. Standing over him. Guiding his every motion. Did you hear what his father did in St. Gall?"

Aspasia had; but she let Theophano tell it.

"They were in the chapel," Theophano said, "on Ascension Day, and his majesty stood alone in the nave, and he had a rod in his hand. He dropped it, to see what the monks would do: whether they would abandon their discipline and come running to see what it was, or whether they would go on about their duties. They did the latter, of course: the discipline is strong at St. Gall. But my lord heard about it afterwards, and he said to me, 'It's a wonder he could let his rod go, when he holds his kingdom so tight.' "

Aspasia set down the comb and divided Theophano's hair for plaiting. Theophano stirred with some of her old, childish restlessness. "I know why he does it. He had to fight to win his kingdom, and he had to fight to keep it. His first son, who was born to the English princess—he loved him as much as he can love anything. And Liudolf turned rebel because he saw his father married again to the Lombard queen, and he was afraid that her son would supplant him. That was settled in the end, and Liudolf was the heir even after my Otto was born. But Italy killed Liudolf with its fevers. Then the emperor decided that he would raise a son with no cause to turn against him, and no opportunity to begin."

"Which means a son kept under his thumb and not let out for even a moment." Aspasia nodded as she wove the first shining plait. "It's hard for a boychild, and the harder for that he fancies himself a man. He's been a crowned emperor—how long? Since he was twelve years old? Of course he'd want more than a crown to wear on feastdays and a place next to his father." She paused. "You aren't afraid he'll do as his brother did, are you?"

"No," Theophano said, if slowly. "No, that isn't in him. He chafes, but he's no open rebel. Liudolf was angry, everyone remembers that. Otto is only restless."

"Maybe the emperor could be persuaded to give him something to do," said Aspasia. "A castle to look after. A duchy to rule. Wasn't Liudolf a duke even while he was the heir?"

"Otto is an emperor," said Theophano, "even while he is the heir."

"So are your brothers emperors in Byzantium, but it's

John who wears the buskins and sits the throne. So was my
father emperor, until he outlasted all his rivals and took his
proper place."

"So you see," said Theophano. "It's a very Byzantine
tangle."

"They mirror us in everything," Aspasia said. "Did you
notice that the women have taken to doing their hair the
way you do?"

"I notice," said Theophano. "Some of them look very
well. Do you know what I've been thinking of? We could
send to the City. As rare as silk is here, and spices—what I
wouldn't give for a cup of wine with cinnamon, and mace—
you know how I love mace. We could have a properly civilized court, if we had silk and spices."

"Only silk and spices?" Aspasia mocked her, but gently.

"And good manners," Theophano said, "and people who
speak Greek. There's so much that we can do. They're ripe
for it. The old ones, they scowl and mutter in their beards,
but the young ones are wild to be civilized."

"They do take well to it, don't they?" said Aspasia. In the
pauses between the words she could hear them singing in the
hall, gorging and quaffing as their ancestors had done for
time out of mind. And those were noblemen. The kerns in
the fields were as shaggy as animals and well-nigh as mute,
though they could carve wood in wondrous wise and paint it
so that it seemed to breathe like a living thing. So must they
have done before Charles of the Franks made them Christian, carved their idols and tilled their fields and lived as best
they might in the wilderness that was the world.

Theophano's hair was plaited, a nightrobe laid across her
shoulders. She never wore paint to allure her husband; God
knew she did not need it, with that ivory skin and those
great eyes, and those lips so red and full and so deceptively
soft. They curved into a smile, sweet as a child's. She hugged
Aspasia to her and set a kiss on one unsuspecting hand.

"I'm always thinking of you," she said, "even when I seem to have forgotten."

"I know," said Aspasia.

"You know everything," said Theophano, almost laughing.

Aspasia heard it first: Otto's step nearing the door. Theophano did not forsake her smile, but she stilled, alert. Aspasia bowed, half lightly, half in honest obeisance, and made herself scarce.

It was good to have Phania back. It was not exactly the same, of course it could not be: they were older, and this was a new country, and she was queen. But Aspasia was pleased with what she had.

Theophano held audience every day, even on days when her husband was off hunting or disporting himself with the young men. She heard disputes, and judged them rather well in Aspasia's estimation. People would come in muttering about the foreign woman and leave, if not smiling, then allowing as to how the king had got himself a clever wife.

She undertook to be wise rather than pleasing, a bit of policy that she had learned from her mother. But being Phania, she could not help but be charming, and the more so, the ruder everyone else was undertaking to be. Some people of course called her a slippery Byzantine, sneered at her in corners and smiled at her in court, but the world was full of fools. As long as none of them was murderous, Aspasia took no notice of them.

No one seemed to hate the queen, foreigner though she was. Those who did not love her, who wondered aloud why no woman of the Saxons was good enough for their king, still managed to endure her. She made sure of it with gifts and favors where those would be accepted with grace, and careful diplomacy where they would not. She had a gift for that, for knowing what would offend and what would appease a difficult servant, whether it be lord or kern, priest or man of the world.

Aspasia was inordinately proud of her. Yet Aspasia, being Aspasia, could never be entirely content. She should have stopped her foolishness of wanting the Moor. That was a dream of Roman moonlight and Roman license. This was Germany, where she was waiting-woman to the queen. She had ample to occupy her: not only attending Theophano but learning German and teaching Greek and discovering this country that was not all one and the same. Distinctions of places and people might seem minuscule to her outland eyes, but to the people they mattered. She had determined to learn what they knew.

She should have come to her senses, and she had not even begun. In Rome where the land bred little dark people, Ismail had been foreign enough. Here he was as exotic as the phoenix.

As summer's heat mounted, Germans sweated and stank in their wool and leather and linen, or stripped it off and went half-naked. Inevitably then, as fair as their skins were, they burned and sloughed and burned again, and were miserable. This was never their season; they were made for winter's cold. But Ismail was in his element. The warmer it grew, the happier he seemed, although he was heard to observe that the heat could advantageously be drier. He was ready with salves for those who came to him scarlet and wretched from the sun, and he looked after scythe-cuts and beestings and sore eyes, and once a fishhook in a boy's foot. There were no fevers. Germans in their own country were as robust as they looked. It was Italy that killed them.

Aspasia did not know exactly when she became his assistant. It was nothing they decided on. She knew enough of medicine to begin, and she was interested in what he did, quite apart from what else she wanted of him. He went out in the mornings wherever they were, and let it be known that he was a physician. Often people were waiting, having heard of him already. Then others would come, and he would tend them until noon, when he went away to say his infidel prayer. Aspasia took to going out when she had finished Theophano's morning toilet, and lending a hand where she could.

She did not realize that she had done it regularly until one morning, a day or two after they came to the king's city of Magdeburg, she did not go. Theophano needed something, and then there was a set-to with Empress Adelaide over a necklace that the younger Otto had given Theophano, which the empress maintained had never been his to give; and when they had fought that battle to a standstill, it was almost noon and Aspasia had duties that could not wait. The next morning she went out guiltily early, and Ismail scowled more blackly than he usually did, although he did not say anything. He was short with her all that morning, and she was short in return.

The morning after that, she almost did not go. Theophano had a rare hour to sit and be read to while she did her needlework. Not that Aspasia minded reading and needlework, but the sun was shining and there was a soft breeze blowing, and the palace was quiet with all the men gone hunting. She fancied that she could hear the voices of the villagers outside, flocking round the strange man with the terrible frown and the healer's hands. She thrust the book into Phoebe's hands and made her escape.

It was a gloriously guilty delight to come out of the castle with its reek of crowded humanity and walk down the rutted track. German towns were surprisingly clean places. The dogs did what they did, likewise the horses, and middens were middens, but people tried to keep order and cleanliness, particularly where the emperor was. It was part of their pride.

This was one of the emperor's own towns, a city indeed as cities went here, in which they were to stay until the summer ended: Magdeburg on the marches of Saxony, with its broad brown river and its shining new cathedral. Inasmuch as Otto had a capital, it was here, enclosed in walls, with the forest cut back so that there were wide rolling meadows all about the town and running along the river. It was raw still with newness, but there was a liveliness in it, an air of youth that looks ahead joyfully to its prime. It made Aspasia think of one of the young Germans, a boy just come to manhood, eager to try his hand at both love and war.

For there would be war. The emperor was gathering forces to settle the marches, to strengthen them against the tribes from the east. His armies ranged eastward now; he would follow them, then lead them as he always had, and his son would go with him as he always had, while the women waited and worried and looked after the realm.

This morning at least war seemed far away. The men were hunting as they loved to do. Ismail was down in the town performing his acts of Muslim charity, with a canon or two from the cathedral looking on and disapproving. None of them ever did more than that. One had tried when Ismail first came, had driven him off with curses. That afternoon the archbishop had had a visitor from the palace, and in the morning when Ismail came to the square he was not prevented. Maybe at first he tended fewer people than needed him, but after a while they learned to trust him. He was the royal physician, after all. The most that anyone did was ask a canon for a blessing once Ismail had done what he could. Ismail did not care. His province was their bodies' healing; the canons were welcome to their souls.

"Don't you ever suffer the urge to convert them to Islam?" Aspasia asked him this morning, when the last sufferer had limped off for his blessing.

Ismail shrugged as eloquently as a Moor could. It was like a fragment of a dance. He was not looking at her, which was merciful: she could hardly tear her eyes from him. "What I could wish," he said, "is one thing. What is practicable is quite another. I serve a Christian king in a Christian country. It would hardly be a courtesy to turn his subjects to Islam."

"I thought it was an obligation."

"Not strictly," he said. "Prayer, and almsgiving, and fasting in Ramadan, and pilgrimage to Mecca, and the profession of faith: those are what we call the pillars of Islam. One does what one can. Here I fast and pray and give alms of my art. Someday I'll make the pilgrimage."

"And war? Isn't that holy, too, in Islam?"

"I am not a man of war," he said.

He did not look remarkably peaceful, either. The sun was some time yet from noon, but no one else came to ask for healing. He began to walk.

Aspasia walked with him. She cared little where they went. "It seems," she said, "not easy, but simple, to be a Muslim. One is what one is. One does what one is told. And that is that."

"Isn't that what it is to be a Christian?"

"Christians have theologians and canon lawyers."

"Why," he said, "so do we."

"And priests? And bishops? And contending orders of monks? And Patriarchs in the east and a pope in the west, and schisms and heresies enough to fill whole vaults of hell?"

"Schisms," he said, "yes. And heresies. There are Sunnites, who bow to Baghdad, where their false and usurping caliph is; there are Shiites, who have a caliph in Cairo; and there are we, who have our own in Córdoba, and he is the true caliph, but we are called rebels everywhere but in al-Andalus."

"In Spain?"

"Al-Andalus."

"Al-Andalus," she said, liking the feel of it on her tongue. "But no priests. You don't have those."

"Every man is a priest as you would think of it. We have muezzins to call us to prayer, and men to lead it, and someone wise and learned, or someone powerful, to give the Friday sermon. But anyone can lead the prayer or give the sermon, if he has wisdom and daring enough. There's no rite to ordain us, beyond what makes every man a Muslim."

Her cheeks went hot again. She knew what that was. It was hard to keep from thinking of it. She had never seen— she wondered—

She had stopped; he had gone on ahead of her. He would leave her. She wanted that; she did not. She hastened to catch him.

He seemed not to have noticed her absence. They had come round to the royal stables. With most of the horses gone, and the kennels all but emptied of hounds, they were unwontedly quiet. He went easily across the yard. Aspasia walked more gingerly. She was having doubts again. He rode his horse every day. She knew that. What was she dangling at his tail for? She should be in the palace, waiting on Theophano.

He was already inside. She picked up her skirts and went in.

It was dark after the bright sunlight, and odorous, but not unpleasantly so: horses, sweet hay, a milky richness that was barley. As her eyes focused she saw Ismail's white turban far down the passage.

He was in the stall when she came to it. She stood outside, ready, almost, to bolt. The stall was narrow and he at its farthest extent, bent over a hoof, muttering in Arabic. The mare curved her neck about to regard Aspasia with a bright dark eye. There was an almost human spark of mockery in it. The beast knew very well what she was doing there. Among its kind, it seemed to say, it was the stallion who trailed after the oblivious mare.

Ismail set down the hoof and freed the lead from its ring. A word, still, absently, in Arabic, sent Aspasia scurrying back. The mare came out with dignity, albeit tail first. She was a beautiful creature, a ruddier brown than her master, with a black mane as long as a woman's, and a black waterfall of tail. A bay, Aspasia reminded herself. That was her color. She had a star on her forehead, and one white foot. Her eye dared Aspasia to retreat now that she was in reach of the great square teeth. She stepped closer still and laid her hand on the mare's neck. It was warm silk, arching under her touch.

"I had never thought," said Ismail, "that princesses of Byzantium were folk for horses."

"We aren't," said Aspasia. She stroked the long sleek neck. "You've seen me ride a mule. You know how much art I have."

His lip did not curl, which was admirable of him. "You have more than you think. You sit well, for one untutored. And you think of the beast before yourself. It's a pity you couldn't have been born a Muslim."

"And a man?"

He did not answer that. Did his cheek darken? It was too dim to see.

Now he would escape her: would call for a groom and demand his saddle and ride away from her. Except that he did none of those things. He led the mare out of the stable into the dazzle of the morning and set about ministering to her with his own hands. She accepted his service as graciously as any royal lady. He gave it with remarkable dignity, as if every nobleman played serving-man to his horse. Maybe, in al-Andalus, he did.

"Did you bring her from Córdoba?" Aspasia asked after a while.

Ismail looked up from picking a hoof. "She comes from Arabia," he said. "But yes, I brought her from Córdoba."

He said the name with no bitterness that she could discern. But she could not see his eyes: he had bent again to the hoof.

She was stroking the mare's neck again. There was a surprising degree of pleasure in it. Aspasia's mule, which had been Gaufrid's until he insisted that she take the gift of it, liked to have its neck scratched, but its coat was much harsher than this. Aspasia smoothed the long mane and began idly to plait a strand. "I had heard that such horses went only to princes. There were some in the stables in Constantinople. They were for the emperor, or the emperor's favorites."

"She was payment," he said. "For a debt."

"A great one, then," said Aspasia.

"A child's life." He set down the last hoof, set to work on the mare's tail with brush and comb.

"And you brought her all this way."

"I had heard," he said, "of Frankish horses."

Aspasia thought about them. Not that she could judge; but none that she had seen matched this mare for either beauty or fire. From the depth of his scorn, she supposed that there was more to it than that.

He came round to the mare's head. Aspasia had plaited a row of narrow braids. He raised a brow. He did not frown, which surprised her. "My sister liked to weave roses into the plaits," he said. "If I protested, she laughed. 'Zuleika knows,' she would say. 'See how she looks at us. She likes to be beautiful.'"

Aspasia drew a slow breath. "You have a sister?"

"Three. That was Maryam. The others were married long since, but she was the youngest; she was still at home. She was to marry a young man whom I knew."

"And did she?"

He smoothed one of the mare's plaits. His eyes were too dark to read. "He discovered a prior obligation. But another came forward, and he was suitable, if not so young. She has two sons now. I'm told that she is happy."

"A woman can be," Aspasia said. "It takes very little. Her husband's respect; her family's peace. Children whom she can love."

There should have been nothing in her voice to betray

her, but he reached out almost as if he were not aware of it, and touched her cheek. "Gerbert told me," he said.

"Gerbert is an irrepressible busybody."

A smile lost itself in his beard. His hand drew back. Aspasia caught it.

She did not do anything with it, simply held it. It was long and rather thin, with fine tapering fingers. It curved nicely about her smaller, rounder hand. "Gerbert told me," she said, "that you have a wife. And sons?"

"One," he said, "of each."

"He told me that it would not matter to you. Because you can have four, and as many concubines as you like."

"He told me that it would matter to you. Because Byzantines count even the dead."

"Only if there are more than three," she said. "And it can only be one at a time."

"Tidy enough now," he said. "But on Judgment Day, what then?"

"Rank confusion." She looked down at their linked hands. "I can't make it matter enough. Which sets me in mortal sin. Again. For . . . wanting . . . at all. For wanting an infidel. For wanting an infidel with a wife and a son."

His fingers tightened. She could not yet look at his face. "I am not wanton. I never was. I was a good daughter, a good wife. I was modest as a lady should be; I never cast eyes on a man who was not my husband. What need? I loved him. And he died, and our child died, and I was empty. What came to fill me again . . . it was a devil, maybe. Looking for a heart to dwell in; fixing it on the most unsuitable of men."

"If that is a devil," he said, "then that devil has a wife, and she has set up housekeeping in my heart. Though I would rather call it love."

"The priests would tell you that love is the Archenemy himself."

"Your priests are some of them good men. But some," he said, "are appalling."

"So my devil would have me think." She ran a finger along the back of his hand, finding it softer than she had expected, like silk over the narrow bones. "I can't make this seem a sin."

"Among us it is not."

How could he keep his voice so steady? She raised her eyes at last. His own were darker than ever.

She stopped thinking at all. She freed her hand, caught his face, pulled it down and kissed him.

He neither tensed nor pulled away. It was she who drew back, but he caught her.

The first kiss had been quick, with more of defiance than of passion. The second was longer and deeper and much more thorough. No raw boy, this, to snatch when he could savor.

A boy or a poet would have said something when they had finished; preferably something passionate. Ismail did not. He touched her cheek again with one light finger, tracing the curve of it, so simple and so tender that she almost wept. Then he went back to tending his mare.

Thirteen

✠

Becoming Ismail's lover was remarkably like becoming his assistant. One day it seemed that he did not know or care if she was male or female or as sexless as a post; the next, there was no mistaking what he thought of her.

Not that he said anything. Ismail was never a man for stating the obvious. The day after the kiss in the stableyard, Aspasia went to salve burns and stitch up cuts, and he was as he always was, sharp, short, and anything but patient. She should have known better than to expect anything else. But she was a fool, and it had taken most of her courage to face him. She stayed as long as she was needed, and not a moment more. Then she went away and cried in solitude, and threw everything that she could throw, until both her tears and her temper were exhausted.

The next day he came for her. It was raining, which meant that he would have set up an awning and gone on with his tending of the sick, but Aspasia would not wait on him. She had an empress for that, and it was time she remembered it.

Theophano had not been well when she woke. It was nothing, she insisted. She would not let anyone call Ismail, and Aspasia was too deep in her temper to protest. By midmorning the indisposition seemed to have passed. Theophano spent an hour with her husband, whom idleness made petulant, then yielded to her women's persuasion and rested in her chamber. Phoebe, who had a voice like a ringdove, read to her until she fell asleep.

Aspasia was wide awake and thoroughly cross-grained. She decided that it was time she turned out her own small cubicle, vast concession in this crowded palace, but one which Theophano had insisted on and Aspasia had not been fool enough to refuse. Her bedding needed changing; the bed needed airing; there was a wine-stain on her best gown; and never mind that there were servants who could see to it. It was thoroughly satisfying to strip the bedclothes and fling them all together at the waiting servant; to seize the featherbed and heave it up and over.

Suddenly it was as light as one of the feathers in it, lowering in narrow brown hands, with a narrow brown face above them, and narrowed black eyes. Aspasia found that her mouth was open. She shut it with a snap.

The servant was gone. God willing, she had not been there when he came. It was a rich scandal for the servants' hall, that he should be here in her chamber, and both of them all alone. He could be flogged for it or worse.

"Is that why they exiled you?" she asked. "Because you were given to invading women's chambers?"

His lips went thin. He considered, transparently, dropping the featherbed and walking away.

It was she who let the mattress go and walked around it and stood in the door, arms folded tight against her. He would have to walk over her to escape.

He let the bed fall. It sighed into its frame. He turned. "It was not for my exploits with women that I was sent away," he said, "but rather for the lack of them."

"You refused someone? Like Potiphar's wife?"

He knew who that was. She should not have been surprised. "Rather precisely like her," he said. "Except that I never gave in meekly, and there was no miracle to save me. I said much that I should not have said. As much as my life was worth. That was my sin, madam. I told a prince what I thought of him, which at that moment was very little indeed."

"Did he hurt you?"

"A day or six in his prison. Nothing that wouldn't mend. Then a choice, because a brother prince spoke for me. Death then and there, or exile. I took the coward's portion." He stood very straight, head up. Again as in the garden of the Lateran, she saw the boy under the years and the learning and the beautiful beard: a thin, intense, beak-nosed child, all sharp edges and touchy pride. *Now you know me,* his eyes said. *Now you can cast me out.*

She shook her head once, hard. "It was never cowardice to choose to live, and live an exile. You came here and turned your back on your own people for a penance. Didn't you?"

"I was going to Egypt," he said. "I shall still, when they have no need of me here."

Which would be never, as he could not help but know, unless he was blinder than she thought. All of aching, barbarous, vermin-ridden Europe needed the arts he had. In Córdoba, he had said once, were scores of men his match or greater. So too in Egypt and anywhere under Islam.

"If you ever converted to Christianity," she said, "the Church would call you a saint. You have everything that a saint needs."

"Except purity of the flesh."

"Saints are tempted more sorely than ordinary mortals. You haven't fallen yet, that I can see."

"My coming here does not constitute a fall?"

She glared at him. "I am the one who has fallen. You, I'm sure, only came to drag me off to the town. How many sore eyes today?"

"Six. And I ran out of salve. And there was no one to help me with the mixing." He stopped. His glare was quite as fierce as her own. "How do you expect to become a physician if you practice it only when it pleases you?"

"I don't," she said. "I'm not your apprentice."

His mouth twisted. "No. You are not. You are a lady, and royal. You do nothing but what gives you pleasure."

That was painfully close to the mark. "Maybe I do," she said, stiff and haughty. "Maybe I don't like to be taken for granted. Maybe I want you to notice that I exist apart from a pair of hands and a willing body."

He stared at her as if he had never seen her before. "You want," he said. "You want me to—what? Sing love-songs under your window?"

"You might tell me that you know I exist."

"How in God's name could I not?"

Did she have to beat him to get him to see? She planted herself in front of him; she seized the front of his robe and knotted her fists in it; she pulled him down, eye to blazing eye. "Ismail ibn Suleiman, do you love me?"

"My lady Theophano Porphyrogenita," he said, "I do. I love you. Do you want it in rhyming couplets?"

He was the most maddening man alive. Telling her what she wanted most in the world to hear, and meaning it with all of him that she could see, and still edging it with mockery.

She did not kiss him. That would have been too easy. She thrust him back and set her fists on her hips. "I would prefer it in occasional glances or a kind word when I do something right. I do sometimes. Don't I?"

"More often than not," he said. "But you will never make a physician if your teacher does nothing but coddle you."

"I don't want—" she began. But that was not true. She did want it; and not only because it was he who taught it. It had become a joy in itself. She tossed her head. "So I want it. Can't I have it, and you too?"

"Not in the same place."

The breath ran out of her. She could have cried. She laughed instead, or maybe it was a howl of rage. "Oh, by God's sweet Mother! I don't know whether to love you or kill you."

"Love me," he said. "Killing is a lesser sin, maybe, as your priests would see it; but it's untidy."

This time her laughter was real. It carried her toward him, right into his arms.

One of them, somewhere in the midst of it, dropped the curtain over the door. In the dimness, lit by the lone slitted window, it was easier to be wanton: to let her garments fall, all of them, and coax him out of his own. He was more modest than she—startling in one who knew down to the bone what a woman's body was like. But it was his own that he was shy of. He was too thin; she would have to do something about that. She liked the way his shoulders fit, and the way the black hair curled on his chest, and the way it ran down his belly to the dark soft center of his navel. He did not want her to undo the cord of his drawers. What the nether part of him wanted was obvious even under the voluminous linen.

His skin was fine and tasted of cinnamon. He was tender about the ribs. She threatened him with that until he let her loose his drawers. Half of him was anger and half of him was mirth, and all of him was blushing furiously.

He did not have anything to be ashamed of. "What did you do at home?" she asked him. "Meet in the dark and couple in your shirt?"

His blush deepened. He was all but helpless with it. She had a little mercy, and turned her eyes to his face. "I told you I was a coward," he said.

"Only half of you." She laid her body against his. It was not bliss. They did not fit yet. There were angles, and elbows. She felt as if there ought to be more of him; he ought to tower, even lying down. That made her want to cry suddenly, which made her angry. She could not even sin properly.

They struggled, a knot of awkward angles, limbs that ought not to be there, she half resisting, he half refusing, until one of them began to laugh. The other caught it irresistibly. They clung, giggling like children. One would wind down, then recall it anew, and go off again.

And then all at once they fit. Her elbows were where they belonged. He was no smaller than he ought to be. She looked at his face under her own, and it bore only the shadow of Demetrios'. The shadow seemed to smile. It melted, and there was only Ismail, dark eyes still sparking with laughter, but growing soft.

Later she would suspect that God or the devil had protected them. No one came looking for Aspasia. No servant walked in to tidy the room. If anyone passed, she did not pause. They might have been alone on a mountaintop.

Aspasia would happily have lain till nightfall, cradled in his arms. But even lovers were slaves to time. She dragged herself up. He did not try to hold her. He sat up himself, watching as she washed in the basin, blushing a little even yet when her glance slid toward him. While she dressed, he bathed himself fastidiously from head to foot.

He would not let her help him dress. It was not fitting, he said, stiff as only Ismail could be. They could have quarreled. She bit her tongue, let him have his pride. He put it on with his many garments, wound it tightly with his turban, until he seemed to stand in armor, a masterpiece of lordly indifference.

But she knew him now. She set a kiss in the palm of his hand for him to take with him: a bit of whimsy which he tolerated admirably. His farewell was more decorous. He kissed her on the lips and said, "I never take you for granted. I never shall."

Sins of the flesh did not, Aspasia knew perfectly well, brand a woman on the forehead for the world to see. Yet surely people knew that something had changed. She listened for their whispers; she watched for their glances. They were too clever, or she was a fool. She saw nothing, heard nothing. Even Theophano acted no differently toward Aspasia than she always had.

But then she had ample distraction. Her morning's indisposition appeared again the next morning, and the next. By the fourth morning Aspasia was certain. Other signs were there, which she had eyes to see. By spring there would, God willing, be a new heir to the western throne.

Theophano's was not a demanding pregnancy nor, past the first few weeks' illness, a difficult one. Once her husband knew that he was to be a father, he all but smothered her with gifts, praises, tender attentions. He would even have given up the summer's campaign to hover at her side, but his father was having none of that. War was man's province, as birthing was woman's. He went reluctantly, with many glances backward; to console his lady for his absence, he gave her a brace of waiting-maids, plump fair Saxon girls whom Aspasia had to train, Helena being too silent and Phoebe too gentle.

They were good enough girls, if not remarkably intelligent. Aspasia could leave them to their own devices for a little while in the morning and go to her lessons with the Moor: those were public and of long standing, and accepted. More private pleasures were harder to come by, but love was nothing if not ingenious.

Ismail kept his promise. He did not take her for granted. He was no more patient and no more polite, and where people could see, he never touched her and seldom looked at her, but plainly he knew that she existed. When they were private together, he showed her how very well he knew it.

She was growing more in love with him rather than less, the longer she knew him. In an odd, prickly, temper-sparking way, they fit one another. A quarrel with him, though it could send her off to rage at the moon, was profoundly invigorating. Yet he could be quiet, even gentle, when he wanted to be. That was when they would lie together for as long as prudence would allow, not speaking, not moving, unless perhaps he stroked her hair or she played with his beard.

Some of the younger men were going back to an older fashion: shaving their faces, or all but the upper lip. She reminded him of it once as summer stretched into a mellow autumn.

"Are you asking me to do it, too?" he asked her.

They had found a place to tryst in: a house in the town, the owner of which was away most afternoons. The room under the roof was surprisingly cool if one opened the shutter and let the wind blow through, and Frau Bertrada kept it aired and clean. There was always a jar of wine waiting, and bread, and sometimes a bit of cheese in a cloth; today there were apples, small but sweet. Frau Bertrada approved of them, Aspasia suspected, though God knew why. Maybe it was Ismail's salves she approved of, and the boil he had lanced for her great barrel of a husband.

She dragged her mind back to what Ismail was saying. "Do you want me to shave my beard?" he asked.

"Would you?"

He went stiff, but he said, "I was thinking of cutting it. To be cooler."

"No!" Her vehemence made him jump. "Don't you touch it. It's beautiful as it is."

"It's hot," he said, scratching at it.

"Then I'll cut my hair," she said, "and we'll both be comfortable."

"No!"

Her tone exactly. She laughed; after a moment he laughed with her.

"A bargain," she said. "You keep your beard, I keep my hair."

"But," he said, "mayn't I shorten it even a little?"

She eyed it measuringly. "A little. A finger's length. No more."

She cut it for him to make sure that he kept to his bargain. She did not try to shorten her hair. It was her one beauty. She was vain of it. Someday no doubt she would atone for that, but amid so many sins, one more could hardly matter.

"No sin," he said when she told him what she was thinking. "Nor is this that we do. In Islam it is marriage: where there is free consent and fidelity. In Christendom, at root, is it any different? I see how the common people marry. They live together and share what is theirs, and if there is a priest near enough he blesses them, but if not, it makes no matter. Intent is enough."

"I know," she said. "My heart tells me; as fast as guilt rises, it sinks down again. I love you, and I want no other man but you. If I could marry you in the world's eyes I would. But I can't. It's one of the reasons why I love you, you know. That you don't try to tell me otherwise."

"Why? It would be a lie."

"Yes."

He sat cross-legged in the middle of the bed, looking like a boy with his beard cut short, watching her comb and braid her hair. She swooped suddenly, comb and half-done braids and all, and kissed him until he warmed all over again. Not a boy, no. A boy could never have lasted as long as he did, or given her so much pleasure. She did not tell him about the thread of silver that she had found in her cutting. He was young yet. Barely forty. Just come into his prime, and likely to live long, with her to look after him.

She paused, too briefly for him to notice. Lifelong. That

was what she meant this to be. What he meant, she knew. He reckoned her a part of him. Like his wife in Córdoba. Whom she had never seen; whom she prayed God she would never see.

He did not know why she clung suddenly with such passion, but he was willing to indulge it. She saved the tears for later, when he would not see. They were not tears of grief, unless it was grief to be so happy.

Fourteen

Theophano's daughter was born at winter's end in the palace at Magdeburg where she had first made her presence felt. They named her Mathilda, for the elder Otto's mother. She was small and somewhat frail, but soon enough she seemed to rally.

"She knows what she is," Aspasia said, bending over the cradle to touch the small downy head.

Her mother, curled in the bed and looking hardly old enough to be a bride, smiled sleepily. "Of course she does. It's in the blood. Otto is not too disappointed. She's not the son he wanted, but she's a good enough beginning."

"And she is his," said Aspasia. "He's singing it all over Magdeburg. The people love him for it. Kings and kingship are out of their reckoning, but new fatherhood they understand."

Theophano yawned, but her eyes were wide awake under the long lashes. "You've come to know the people well, haven't you? Everyone knows how you study with Master

Ismail. He told me yesterday that you were the best pupil he's had."

Aspasia felt the blush rising. Theophano would take it for the embarrassment of praise. "Did he say that? All he ever does is snap at me."

"That's his way," said Theophano.

"He's always kind to you."

"Only when I need him," she said. She stretched, winced. She was still a little torn from the baby. "He says I'm not to think of trying for a son till after Pentecost. Otto will be wild."

Aspasia doubted that. Kings could find consolation enough when their queens were indisposed. Although, she admitted, Otto was a pious boy, and he came of a strong-willed family. He might after all be faithful.

Or, if not faithful, then firmly under his mother's thumb. Empress Adelaide had remained in Italy when the emperors left it, to rule as regent and to build what power she could. But before winter closed the passes, she left her regency to another and came north. She wished, she said, to see her grandson when he was born; and, Aspasia knew, to regain the power over her son that his marriage had robbed her of. Theophano, caught up first in the miseries of pregnancy, then in the labor of bearing and raising a child, could not rule her husband as she was used to do. That she had delivered a mere daughter only deepened the empress' pleasure. All the more opportunity to turn Otto away from her.

Theophano did not need to be told what her husband's mother intended. Through what was left of Lent, she bided her time. On Palm Sunday the emperor held court in Magdeburg with the full and formal rite. Theophano kept to her chamber. The next day, Holy Monday, the court prepared to move to Quedlinburg for the Easter Court. Theophano's wagon waited with the others, and Theophano appeared when it was time to go, wrapped and swathed against the briskness of March in Saxony and leaning palely on Helena's arm. The nurse walked behind with the baby.

Theophano would hear no protests, even from her husband. "No, no," she said. "I want to see the Easter Court. It's to be so splendid; I'm sure it will be good for me."

"But," said Otto, "if you strain yourself too soon—"

She smiled wanly but with entrancing sweetness. "Please, my love. It's so wearisome here without you. Won't you let me go with you?"

His mother glared frostily, but he never saw. He lifted Theophano into her wagon with his own hands and saw her settled to his satisfaction before he called for his horse to ride beside her. He did not see the light in Theophano's eye. Empress Adelaide did not need to. This was women's war; and Theophano had won a victory.

It was a skirmish only, the empress' eye said. The war was barely begun.

Theophano was hardly as fragile as she endeavored to look, or Aspasia would never have let her take the road. It was the baby whom Aspasia fretted over; but Ismail had no sympathy, and he was the royal physician. "All infants look puny for the first month or two," he said, "and I have this one under my eye. Better for her to travel where her mother is than to be left in the care of servants."

And, he did not say, of what passed for physicians in this benighted country. Aspasia sighed and held her peace.

Magdeburg was a lowland city, a river city, a bastion against the tribes of the east. Quedlinburg was a city of the mountains. They were not the white pinnacles of the Alps, but neither were they to be sneered at, steep jagged slopes riddled with caves and crannies. There was a great abbey there, of which the emperor's daughter was abbess, and a castle that was half fortress, half palace. Within its strong walls was splendor: antique marbles, eastern silks, gilding of silver and gold. The hall that had been a war-chieftain's banqueting hall was still discernibly that, but over it the emperor had cast a glamour of imperial dignity.

Here even more than in Magdeburg he seemed in his element. He was in a rare good humor: the wife he had taken such pains to obtain for his son was proved fertile if not yet of sons; the wife he had won for himself in Italy, and with her the kingship of that fractious country, sat at his side in exemplary amity; the marches of the east were secure, his own country serene about him, and his empire for once at peace. Now for the high festival of Easter he had his kin about him, his allies and his friends, and with them a great press of embassies from all the world.

All of it, Aspasia thought as she stood in comfortable obscurity that cool Easter day, with the glories of the high mass past and the high feast still to come. They were all on the dais together, four thrones with the emperor's midmost, his son beside him on his right hand, their empresses on the flanks, crowned with gold. Otto the elder wore the great state crown with its cross of pearl and diamond and its studding of gems, his son one somewhat lesser and without the cross. All of them wore the purple, but not, Aspasia noticed, the crimson buskins that in Byzantium, more truly even than the crown, proclaimed the emperor. Otto the elder's shoes were purple, and sewn with pearls and gold.

He would never look less than severe, but there was a light in his eye. Well there might be with such a prospect as he had before him: all the lords of his native realm with their ladies and their children, great lords and ladies of the Church with his daughter the abbess prominent among them, and advancing one by one with gifts and homage and words of praise and pleading, envoys from every corner of the world. Rome, Benevento, the Rus, the Magyar tribes, the Bulgars, Bohemia, Poland, the mark of the Danes, the Saracens of Africa; even haughty Byzantium acknowledged the power of this western upstart. If the ambassador was somewhat ambiguous in the direction of his obeisance, if it seemed to turn ever so slightly in the direction of Theophano, then that was only just, and it altered nothing. Otto, whom men were calling the Great, was become great indeed. It was but prudence to acknowledge it and him.

There were one or two men in the embassy whom Aspasia knew: kin or the friends of kin. Later she would send for them, when the formalities were over and there was time for lesser matters. It was a hunger in her suddenly, to hear the news of the City, to see new faces and hear new voices, but with the lineaments and the accents of home. The strength of her longing startled her. It was all she could do to stand still and keep her face expressionless and be a proper waiting-woman.

Her eye, flinching away from the pain, settled on the first German face it came to. It lingered there, with no thought of hers behind it. Only slowly did a name fit itself to the blur of fair hair, sunburned fair skin, jeweled but very German tunic. He was older than Otto the younger, a year or two past twenty; taller and much more prepossessing to look at, although like many of the fair Germans he had only the merest transparent wisp of down on his lip. That, she was sure, was why so many of them shaved their faces. It seemed better to them to look beardless altogether than to betray how little they had.

This one did not need a beard to look like a man. It was in everything he was: head high, shoulders up and back to show their handsome width, big hand resting oh so lightly at his belt where a sword would hang if this were not the emperor's court. There was a certain tilt to his chin, a suggestion of flare about the nostrils, that spoke not only of mettle but of challenge.

Cousin Henry, young Otto called him, half in youthful awe, half in condescension. Henry, Duke of Bavaria, who if his father had had his way would have been King of the Germans. That elder Henry, brother to Otto the elder, was long and safely dead; and not, amazingly, at his brother's command. They had hated one another from childhood, people whispered, because Otto was king and Henry was not.

Henry's son and namesake was to all appearances a loyal servant of his uncle the emperor. Otto the elder treated him no more brusquely than his own son. Otto the younger admired him transparently, envied his manly beauty, and made certain that he knew who wore the crown. Henry bowed and smiled and did homage as propriety commanded, but he was never servile. In his duchy, Aspasia had heard, he ruled like a king. Rumor had it that there was a chest in his private chamber in Merseburg, and in it were robes of state, and every one was royal purple; and when he could be private he took them out and held them in the light and swore vows that he would wear them one day, when his uncle and his cousin were disposed of.

He was a pretty picture, standing just on the edge of a shaft of light in scarlet tunic and saffron braies and cloak of pure deep green. There was a woman next to him, but not plump young Gisela with her wheat-colored braids, who was his wife. This was an older woman, gowned and veiled as severely as a nun: Judith, lady regent of Bavaria. She bore a remarkable resemblance to her son, even to the air of royalty unjustly constrained. She leaned on Henry's arm and watched the procession of embassies with a calm cold eye. She bided her time, and cared little who saw it.

Aspasia's glance crossed the emperor's. He was amused. His empire was steady in his hand, and he knew it. It pleased him to see his kin here, his brother's son in the place that was proper to him, and his own son high and proud on a throne the equal of his own. This was the world as it should be. This was all that he had prayed for and fought for and won.

What he would win next, no doubt he already knew. He was scrupulous in his courtesy to the Byzantines. He presented his son's wife with evident pride; he let it be known that she was delivered of a daughter. He made it clear that he expected the next inevitably to be a son: an emperor for the Romans. "For now that Italy and Germania are secure," he said, "we may safely reckon them one realm. Gaul will follow. Then, who knows? Westward to Hispania, eastward to new and wider lands; the tribes subdued and brought to the faith of our Lord, the hammer of Islam broken, the west of the world secure under a single ruler. Charles the Great dreamed of it. We shall make it a living truth."

The court sent up a roar of approbation. The Byzantines were more restrained. They bowed, they murmured, they withdrew. They could not have been unduly surprised. It was clear enough what this barbarian was doing, even without his boasting of it.

Aspasia, swaying in the surge of sound, began to wonder if it was more than a boast. If it could be done—if he lived long enough, was strong enough, left it to a son who could carry on where he had begun—maybe truly it could be. Rome renewed. The world united. Christ at its head, and on its throne—why not an heir of Saxon chieftains? The other half of him, the mother-half, would be true Roman. He could hold the world in his hands.

Aspasia was exalted with it, dizzy, a little wild. The wine at dinner only made it stronger. She went out as soon as she prudently could and found Ismail where he had said he would be, grinding powders in the smaller of his two rooms in the town, with a pair of braziers to make the space summer-warm. He did not drink wine, and he did not eat with infidels, although he relaxed his prohibition for the infidel who was his lover. She brought him a napkinful of tidbits that he would eat: dried apples, raisins, a loaf of fine white bread.

He acknowledged her with a preoccupied nod. In a less antic mood she would have sat quietly by until he finished.

Today she could not sit still. She slid up behind him and circled him with her arms, working her hands into the recesses of his robe. His back was narrow and warm and familiar, his scent of spices overlaid with the sharpness of herbs. She paid no attention at all to his sudden, outraged stiffness, but nibbled the back of his neck. He flung down the pestle and snarled. "Woman! Have you no respect?"

"None at all," she said.

He spun in the circle of her arms, beard bristling. She laughed and kissed him.

"Drunkenness," he said, "is an abomination in the eyes of God."

"I only had a cup," she said, "and half of that was water. You should have been there, Ismail. The whole world was. Saracens, even, from Italy and Africa. They had their own table and their own cook, but they ate with the rest of us. It was gracious of them."

"I never pretended to grace," he said. His voice was rough, but his beard had stopped looking so angry. She smoothed it carefully, pausing to trace the thin line of his mouth. It did not want to soften, but she was determined.

"I'll help you with your mixing," she said, "if you'll kiss me first."

"I know where that will lead," he growled. But he kissed her, and she made certain that it did not lead where he had feared. Not immediately or directly. They mixed the salves and the medicines, working side by side, quickly but without haste. Haste was for children.

"I'd hate to be eighteen again," she said as she sealed the last jar and labeled it in both Greek and Arabic.

"Eighteen? Why eighteen?"

She shrugged. He was done; so, with a final flourish, was she. She wiped the pen and covered the ink-bottle and put them away. "I have a birthday in the autumn. I'll be twenty-nine. I should be lamenting lost youth. Lost beauty, too, except that I never had any to lose."

He snorted. He sounded uncannily like his mare. "Your judgment is hardly sound in such matters."

"What, the date of my birthday?"

He never had patience with silliness; and she had taxed him to the limit already. "Beauty is a perishable commodity," he said, "and much too highly valued. Youth may be worth regretting. I for one am glad to be free of it. All the humours in a roil. Spots and anxieties, and searching in every mirror for signs that at last one is a man. I much prefer the placidity of age."

She laughed aloud. "Oh, you are a doddering ancient!" She had his turban off. There was a little more grey in his hair than there had been last year, and maybe it had retreated a very little more from brow and crown, but there was plenty of it still. In the summer he shaved it to the skull. In winter he let it grow for what warmth it could give. "What a beautiful child you must have been," she said, "with your black ringlets and those great eyes."

He glared. "I looked like a half-fledged hawk. All beak and bones."

"Beautiful," she said. "I never was. A whole family of golden queens, and then came I, like a brown mouse. I think that's why they let me marry. By the time they got over the shock of my attracting a husband, it was done, and there was nothing anyone could do about it."

"They were blind," he said.

"It's useful to be a mouse. One can do as one pleases, and no one sees."

"That's not a mouse," he said. "That's a small grey cat."

She grinned at him. "Yes," she said. "A cat who likes to make herself small and seem a mouse. But sometimes she stretches, and flexes her claws, so"—freeing him from his robe—"and uncoils her long supple tail, and shows her white cat-teeth."

She nipped him. He pulled her to him. He never stayed angry, even when she provoked him unmercifully. She loved to hear him laugh; it was a game to trick him into it, and temper could do it. It made him forget himself and all his carefully nurtured dignity.

She linked her arms behind his neck and let him bear most of her weight. He was stronger than he looked. He held her easily, not laughing, not yet; not even smiling. "If you were my wife," he said, "you would never dare to mock me so."

"Wouldn't I?" She let her head fall back but kept her eyes on his face. "You'd have to beat me every day. Twice a day on Sundays. Even then I'd be barely docile."

"I never beat my mare. Why should I beat my woman? I'd tame you by sheer weight of my authority."

"What did you tell me about your mare? You let her think that she is taming you; that when she is obedient, it's to her own will."

"Do you think that you are taming me?"

"Would I tell you if I were?"

The smile broke out then. She smiled back in pure delight. "You are outrageous," he said.

She nodded happily.

"A creature infinitely various and perfectly exasperating."

"Fascinating," she said.

"Exasperating." He set a kiss on the point of her chin and swept her up in his arms. He had to pause. He was strong and she was small, but there was enough of her to matter. He got a solid grip on her and, grunting only slightly, carried her to his bed.

Between that and what followed after, it took him a while to get his breath back. She was up by then and regretting the bells that called the city to vespers. He lay where she had left him, still modest after all their sinning, or maybe he was cold: he pulled the blankets to his chin. She would be glad when summer came, and she could in conscience keep him from covering himself.

His kiss was warm enough and would have been pleased to linger. She turned her back on the temptation.

Maybe it was the last of the wine; maybe it was over-surety, for they had never been caught. She came out of the house in which Ismail was staying, full into the arms of a man who was striding past. It knocked the breath out of her. She would have fallen, but he caught her and held her upright, muttering something that might have been an apology.

Words very like them were on the tip of her tongue, frozen there. Henry of Bavaria, all alone without even a boy to carry his cloak, stood in the narrow twisting street and stared into her face as if he recognized it. She prayed devoutly that he would not. Her mantle was dark, but under it, like an idiot, she had kept her finery. Ismail had not even noticed.

Henry, damn him, did. His face shifted in an eyeblink from blank irritation to extraordinarily well-feigned pleasure. "Lady Aspasia! A thousand pardons. I was charging like a bull on my own errand, and I never saw you. Are you well? Did I hurt you?"

She shook her head. He was still holding her. He was very large and very German, looming over her in the evening light. She did not mean to start shaking.

He could not like a decent barbarian go on his way and leave her to her bruises. He had to escort her solicitously to the well at the street's head, sit her on its rim, and hover. Was there a cold gleam of mockery in his eye? Or was it something else, and not cold at all?

Some Germans liked a little dark woman in a crimson gown. Easy enough thought to think in the safety of the palace. A little dark woman in crimson, alone in the town at vespers, coming from her lover's arms—could he smell it on her? See it in her, that she was a sinner?

If he asked her where she had been, she would tell him the truth: that she had gone to the young empress' physician seeking one of his remedies; hinting of matters dark and secret, women's matters. No lie in that. Let him ask, then let him go. She was late.

He did not ask. She could not escape without touching him. He regarded her frankly, as if he liked what there was to see. "You are a handsome woman," he said. He tilted her chin up with a finger. She set her teeth. If he kissed her, by God, she would bite him.

"Very handsome," he said, smiling what was no doubt a charming smile. "Is it true what they tell me? Are you really old Constantine's daughter?"

She nodded. It let her escape his hand.

His smile widened, ingenuous as a boy's. "And they sent you here? What were they thinking of?"

"Getting rid of me," she said.

He laughed. "Yes, John wouldn't want you where he could see you, would he? Considering how he got his crown."

"He married my sister," she said, "who is quite as royal as I am, and considerably better to look at."

"One of your blonde Greeks. Yes, I've heard of her. I fancy a dark Greek better."

She could see very well where this was going. She stood, although it set her uncomfortably close to him. He smelled of wine and sweat and man. She braced her hands on his chest and pushed. He stepped back more in surprise than for any strength of hers.

His hands rose to clasp her wrists. She eluded him. "My empress is waiting," she said with all the dignity that she could muster. "Good day, my lord duke." She fled, not looking back, though the skin crawled between her shoulder blades.

Fifteen

⬧

After the Easter Court the emperor went on to Merseburg with Duke Henry in his train. Otto the younger chose to remain in Quedlinburg with Theophano, and for a miracle his father allowed it. Empress Adelaide, presented with such a dilemma, chose to follow her husband; or perhaps her husband settled it by commanding her.

"He's the one man who can ever rule her," Otto said, half awed, half resentful. But he was free of both of them, and he was like a boy on holiday. Even the ostensible cause of his liberation barely darkened his mood.

Mathilda was ailing. From the first she had been rather a colicky baby, but now she cried constantly, fretfully, until they banished her with her nurse to a far corner of the palace so that her mother could sleep. There did not seem to be anything desperately wrong with her. She ate, and mostly she kept it down. She grew thin, but she was growing taller, and babies were often like that, like soft clay: thickening, then stretching, then thickening again. But she cried, and

nothing quieted her except Ismail's holding her and talking
to her in Arabic until she fell asleep.

It was not that he was tender or soothing. He was neither.
He held her capably and gently enough, but he was not a
man to go all soft in front of a baby. He read to her from his
books of medicine, and quite appalling some of it was; it
was a mercy that no one but Aspasia understood. If she had
been a little less worried, she would have laughed to see him
in the small cramped chamber with the painted walls,
wrapped and swathed against the cool of spring in the
mountains, with the baby on one arm and the book in his
hand, reciting in a dry soft voice the components of a cure
for leprosy.

"I would be happier," he said to Aspasia, "if I knew what
she was trying to tell me."

"Maybe she only wants you there, and no one else," said
Aspasia.

He shook his head, impatient. "Life at its best is damnably fragile. Life in infancy is a candle in a windstorm." With
great care he freed the child's hand from its swaddlings. It
curled at once about his finger. He let it, but turned it to the
light. "Look, there. That tinge of blue. I don't like it. It may
be something she will get over. It may, God forbid, be something she will not. And I don't *know*."

It was a cry of agony, disguised as temper. Aspasia could
not touch him. The nurse was there, watching, knowing
nothing of Arabic.

"We can only wait," Aspasia said, "and see."

He glared. "Platitudes."

The baby stirred, fretting. He went back to reading from
his book.

Aspasia had to leave them to attend her empress. Theophano knew that the child was ill. She did not know enough
to worry unduly. Ismail was there, after all, and Aspasia
when he had to rest. She had a husband to look after, for
once without his father or mother to interfere. When either

of them saw Mathilda, she was asleep or quiet and looking no more frail than she ever did.

They would have to know. But not yet. Maybe not ever, if Ismail's fears proved groundless.

It seemed after a while that Mathilda got better. She stopped fretting so constantly. She did not put on flesh, but she seemed to be nursing well enough. Ismail allowed himself to relax his vigilance, enough to go back to tending the rest of his charges.

The last of the winter's snow melted and ran in bright streams to the lowlands. The roads that had been quagmires began by degrees to dry. Otto went hunting and brought back meat for the pot: birds, coneys, deer fed on the new grass, once even a boar. Theophano began to count the days until they could start making a son.

"I want it," she said to Aspasia in some surprise. "Not just for the heir it will bring. For . . . the rest of it."

Aspasia smiled.

"It's horribly sinful, of course," said Theophano. "But since a queen can hardly afford to be a virgin, and a chaste marriage is hardly the way to provide her husband with heirs, then maybe, don't you think, it might be permissible to enjoy it?"

Aspasia laughed aloud.

There was a hint of a frown between Theophano's brows, but she smiled a little, unwillingly. "*You* have always been a perfect pagan. Is it your name that shaped you, or were you born that way?"

"I was a terror in my cradle," said Aspasia.

"You look so happy," Theophano said, studying her. "I've noticed that. I'm the blissful bride, the triumphant mother, and you go about as merry as a lark. Even in the dead of winter, when everyone else was blue with cold and cursing heaven, you never stopped smiling."

"Oh, come," Aspasia said, keeping her voice light,

though her heart had gone cold. "I was quite as snappish as anyone else."

Theophano shook her head, calmly obstinate. "Not quite, Aspasia. What is your secret? Have you been closeted with my physician, brewing up the elixir of life?"

Aspasia was not cold, suddenly. She was burning hot. She looked about desperately for a diversion. Helena was out. Phoebe was dozing. There was no book within reach. Theophano's hair did not need looking after. She was ready for her husband when he came back from the hunt, perfect as an icon and well-nigh as serene.

"Why, aunt," said Aspasia's gentle, cruel niece, "you're blushing. Don't tell me you have. Or is it something even more outrageous? Have they told you that Cousin Henry has been asking about you?"

"That child," said Aspasia with more venom than she had intended. "He has visions of a *porphyrogenita* in his bed. And never mind that she is old, ugly, and barren. What would that matter, if it gave him a throne?"

"You are not either old or ugly," said Theophano. "As to the other, are you certain? Have you asked Ismail?"

At least Aspasia was not blushing now. She was cold instead, and not on Ismail's account. "I am certain."

"You asked him?"

"I asked him!"

Theophano let the echoes die. "I'm sorry," she said. She reached out and took Aspasia's hand, folding it in her own. "I thought—I confess I hoped—maybe that was what it was. That the doctors were wrong in the City."

"Oh, no," said Aspasia. "They weren't wrong." She paused. "Are you saying that you thought I was pregnant?"

It was Theophano's turn to blush.

"I could hardly carry a bastard," Aspasia said, "and sing like a lark. Whose did you think it was? Cousin Henry's?"

"No," said Theophano at once. "Oh, no. Oh, Aspasia,

you must be hating me. That I should think, because you had such a light on you, that you had found someone to love you."

Aspasia shut her mouth with a snap.

"For me it would be a sin, you see," said Theophano. "For you it would be salvation. I know how you loved Demetrios—better now maybe than I ever could. I saw how you mourned him. Then suddenly you were glad again. Can you forgive me for thinking that I knew why?"

Aspasia glanced at Phoebe, who seemed to be sound asleep. There was no one else near. She drew a breath. It would be bliss to share this secret at last: to share it with Phania, who would understand, who knew and deeply admired Ismail. She should have done it long ago.

"I forgive you," she said.

Clamor overrode the rest of it. Dogs barking; hoofs clattering; men's voices raised, proclaiming their victory in the hunt. Theophano half rose to her feet, anticipation lighting her face. She turned back quickly enough, focused on Aspasia, but her smile was not looking for revelation.

Nor would Aspasia give it. The moment had passed. Soon enough Otto came in, flushed and proud, to tell the tale of the stag he had killed, and then it was time to go down to dinner. Aspasia's secret was her own still; and Ismail's.

Ascension Day passed, and May came in with its crown of flowers. The Germans, Aspasia reflected, had a strong streak of the pagan in them still. When they were not as exuberantly ascetic as any desert saint, they were decking their halls with greenery for the solstice festival which they took care to call Christmas, or, now, running wild in the greenwood. They sang hymns to the Blessed Virgin, but there was another behind her, Freyja of the flowers, who made the earth bear fruit.

The flowers were barely wilted when Otto and Theo-

phano left Quedlinburg for Memleben. If it had been up to
Ismail, Theophano at least would not have gone; for she
would not go without her daughter. But Theophano would
not surrender her husband to his mother's power, and he
had no choice in the matter. His father had summoned him.
He could not refuse.

It was dismaying to see how quickly Otto regained his old
sullenness. Even the prospect of going back under his father's eye was enough to take the light out of his face.

"We shall have to do something about this," Theophano
said before they left, while she oversaw the packing and
stowing. "Now that my husband is a man with a family, he
should have estates of his own."

Aspasia nodded. She knew what Theophano was leaving
unsaid. It was time young Otto became a ruler in more than
name. Theophano, imperial Byzantine that she was, would
see to it.

They had an easy enough passage to Memleben, for
mountain roads in the spring. Even more than Quedlinburg,
Memleben was a mountain fortress; its veneer of imperial
dignity was thin indeed. It stood on a crag, gaunt and for-
bidding, and frowned at them through a mist of rain.

Ismail greeted it with a wordless growl. Even Theophano
seemed somewhat dismayed. The emperor's father had died
in that castle; it did not look to have been made more comfortable since.

It was barely ready for them. The emperor had not yet
arrived. The hall was swept and there was a fire on the
hearth, but the private rooms were damply cold. Ismail,
who had not stopped snarling since they mounted the track
to the gate, saw the queen's chamber readied, aired as much
as it could be, and warmed with his own precious brazier.
Only when Mathilda was established there in her cradle,
wrapped in furs, would he draw a breath without a growl
in it.

Theophano was contrite but unswayed. They could

hardly go back to Quedlinburg in the rain. "You may stay here if you like," she said to him.

He looked so scandalized that Aspasia had to bite her lips to keep from laughing. His glare spared a part of itself for her. "You have your royal kinswoman," he said, "who by now should know enough to look after a weakling child. If you have need of me, I shall be with the clerks."

Theophano could hardly argue with him. He bowed with full Arab formality, as he almost never did, and took his stiff-backed leave.

"Dear heaven," said Theophano when he was gone. "He's furious." She was almost laughing. "What a terrifying teacher he must be!"

"He is not," said Aspasia, "the sweetest-tempered of men." She flexed her cold-numbed fingers and warmed them over the brazier. "Will my lady rest a while, or will she show herself in the hall?"

Theophano frowned. Aspasia's use of her title was as eloquent of disapproval as Ismail's obeisance. She would have been within her rights to rebuke the insolence. She sighed instead, and said, "The hall, of course. I'll wear the gown lined with vair, and the blue slippers."

When she went to preside over the hall, Aspasia remained behind with the baby and the nurse. The baby was asleep, the nurse nearly so. Aspasia lit an extra lamp and sat beside it, and buried herself in a book.

The next day the emperor came. The sun, in deference to his imperial majesty, saw fit to drive the rain away. Grim Memleben was almost pleasant in the clear light. Rooms that had been dank and dark now seemed merely cool, and shafts of sunlight clove the upper reaches of the hall.

Otto the younger and his queen received their elders with becoming grace, although Otto would not smile. Aspasia, watching, wondered if he hated his father. Certainly there was no tenderness between them. They were rigidly proper always, when she was there to see. Empress Adelaide was more demonstrative: she embraced her son and kissed him, making much of his soft new beard, as if he had not had it when she left him a month ago. To Theophano she was scrupulously polite; they embraced as kinswomen, exchanged decorous kisses, smiled with clenched-teeth amity.

The empress was the same as she always was. The emperor had changed. At first Aspasia could not have told precisely why. His beard was no greyer, his carriage no less erect; his eye was as keen as it ever was. Yet he was no longer a man in vigorous middle age. He had grown old.

Grief, perhaps. Hermann Billung was dead at Ascensiontide, one of the oldest and certainly the truest of the emperor's friends, who had held Saxony in the emperor's absence, and whose strong arm had kept the tribes out of the eastern marches. Aspasia could guess what the death of such a friend could do to a man. The emperor had outlived all his enemies; now he was outliving his friends. He would be feeling his mortality: for the first time perhaps recalling that he himself was past sixty, a warrior still and indomitably when warriors counted themselves fortunate to see the farther side of forty.

Aspasia did not pity the emperor. He was not a man to invite compassion. But she could understand him, a little. He had been so high and proud at Easter. Now he must feel as if he had seen the summit of his life; the rest of it went only downward into a lonely dotage.

Yes, she thought. Lonely. His empress had given him an empire and a son, but she was not a woman for warm companionship. His son was chafing at the bit. His courtiers were courtiers. They served him in the main because he was the emperor. His warriors were all young and all in awe of him. None of them remembered him as aught but emperor.

After a month out of his power, it was strange to be in it again. Otto was quenched and silent. Theophano was determinedly unaffected. She fell with the rest of them into the emperor's way of doing things, but she did it with the air of one who obliges an honored host. She did not, like her husband, rise long before dawn to hear nocturns because his father did, then sit with him through matins and come back to rest because the emperor rested. She did accompany Otto to morning mass, and she stood with the two emperors while they gave the customary alms; she shared their breakfast, which was as frugal as a monk's, rough bread and much-watered wine taken after prayer.

Aspasia waited on her at dinner. Theophano wanted her, and Ismail was with the baby, who at least had not taken a turn for the worse. The hall was full of light, sunlight and lamplight both, and the fire in the center burning with a sweet pungent scent. There was a great deal of laughter and singing. A troupe of mountebanks had come in that morning to ply their trade under the emperor's eye. He could be severe in his piety, but he loved what passed for playacting in this part of the world: broad caricature, coarse jests, and much tumbling about. His priests were expected to disapprove, and did, although some gave it up and laughed with the rest.

The emperor was unusually free with his mirth. Almost antic, Aspasia thought, as he might have been when he was a boy. He showered the players with silver, to their manifest delight, and sang along with them when they gave him a rousing chorus.

Even she was laughing, half startled at herself. Such low humor, but so irresistible. The Saracen on a stick with his great hooked nose—he reminded her inescapably of Ismail, down to his choleric temper. The wife in all her veils, beating him roundly about the head and berating him for falling in love with his camel, made her hide behind her own veil and give herself up to mirth.

When she came out, the emperor's eye was on her. She could not help it. She arched a brow. He laughed and beckoned.

Everyone was intent on the mummers. No one noticed

the little dark waiting-woman as she slid quietly from behind the young empress to stand by the old emperor. He smiled at her. "You look well," he said.

It was not unlike him to notice a servant. Aspasia had been noticed before; she was not unduly taken aback. "My lord is kind," she said.

He snorted. "Come now. I know how blunt your tongue can be when the mood takes it. Do you like our mountebanks?"

"I shouldn't," she said, "but I do."

That made him laugh. His gaiety was almost feverish, she thought. She had reached without willing it to touch his wrist; she stopped, reclaimed her hand before it brushed flesh. This was not the time to play physician. He would almost certainly misconstrue it.

He leaned back in his tall chair, letting his eyes rest on her face. He did not make any secret of his pleasure.

She could have moved then and made something of it. The knowledge did not discomfit her as once it might have. Kings made their own laws: as much at least as imperial princesses.

She kept her hands decorously folded in front of her. He laughed again. "So prim and so much a lady! Madam, you will civilize us in spite of ourselves."

"It was for that purpose that I came," she said.

"Truly?" He was almost serious. "Do you think it can be done, my lady? Can we make a new Rome, here among the barbarians?"

"We can try."

"So we have," he said. "Your kinswoman is the beginning of it. He chose better than he knew, that emperor of yours. Better for us—if not perhaps for his own people."

"His sacred majesty knew what he was doing," said Aspasia. Or he thought he knew. He was no match for Theophano. This emperor might be. It would interest her to see.

A new turn of the jest distracted him. Aspasia crept back

to her place. He did not seem to miss her. In a little while the mountebanks were done, and with them the emperor's dinner. He would rest again briefly until vespers.

Aspasia did not always attend vespers. If she did not have duties, she tried to be with Ismail. Tonight in the emperor's presence she elected to be virtuous. The candles, the chanting, the Latin words, lulled her into a kind of peace. She almost did not miss the opulence of the Greek rite with its statelier chant and its procession of icons.

What startled her out of her half-dream, she did not know. She was next to Theophano in the chapel, across from the emperors. Otto the younger for once was taken out of himself: his faith was the best part of him, and the strongest. Otto the elder knelt beside him, erect as always. There was something about his face . . .

She started forward, forgetful of anything but that damp grey mask. He swayed. Someone caught him. Not his son: Otto was still rapt in prayer. People nearby began to stir. A temporary faintness, they would be thinking.

Aspasia reached him just as the stir began to spread. She closed it out of her mind. His face was worse than grey. One hand clawed at his breast. His breath came too hard, too fast.

They laid him down, tried to straighten him. Bodies pressed in. Aspasia snapped at someone large; he pushed them back. She sent someone for Ismail. He was as obedient as the other. She ventured the utmost: she knelt beside the emperor and began to examine him. No one stopped her. Stunned, all of them. Unbelieving. How could the emperor be ill? He was the emperor.

"A priest," he said. He had to breathe twice before he could go on, but his voice was quiet. "Fetch me a priest."

Aspasia looked down at his head in her lap. He knew where he was. He knew very well what was happening to him. There was no fear in him. He even smiled.

The priest came. The press parted to let him by. He was

an old man whose eyes had seen much. He did not need to be a physician to know when a man was dying. His calm was a near match to the emperor's as he began the last rites.

The first murmured words struck those round about like a fall of Greek fire. A wail went up, but was cut off. Someone had the sense to herd the others out, not without difficulty. A fair number stayed: those who were highest, or whose tonsures gave them immunity.

Aspasia's eye caught one face among the rest. Henry of Bavaria was watching as they all were, with fixed intensity. But he was not watching the dying emperor. He was watching the emperor's heir. His expression reminded her, in its peculiar intensity, of a cat contemplating catching and killing its dinner.

Ismail came in even as the priest sealed the emperor with the last blessing. There was a ripple among the watchers: a turban in the holy place, an infidel defiling it with his presence. He seemed oblivious. A glance told him all that he needed to know. He took the priest's place, which was not relinquished willingly, but he did nothing that anyone could object to. His presence set the seal on it, somehow.

When he withdrew, he took Aspasia with him. She did not need to be told why. The German emperor should die among Germans. His son was beside him now, dry-eyed, looking white and shocked. His empress swept in with great ado, saw what there was to see, and stopped, swaying. Aspasia wondered if she would faint. But she was made of sterner stuff. She roused them all from their stillness. "Must he lie on the floor like a dog? You, you, you—take him, yes, up. Take him to his bed."

They took him where they were bidden, and laid him in his own bed. He was still alive, but it would not be long. He did not speak. As he passed Aspasia, she marked how serene his face was. He looked like a carving on a tomb.

* * *

Otto of Saxony, King of the Germans, Emperor of Italy and Germany, Holy Roman Emperor, died in his bed even as the last light went out of the sky. He went tranquilly and without evident regret. His life was ended, and ended well. He trusted his God to look after the world which he had left.

Otto the younger of Saxony, King of the Germans, Emperor at last and in truth of Italy and Germany, opened his eyes on a world bereft of his father's shadow, and knew what it was to be free.

At first he was only stunned. He stood mute while his mother saw to what must be done: the sending of messengers, the preparing of the body for transport to Magdeburg where the emperor had wished to be buried, the setting in order of the cortege. He went with it still numbed and all but speechless, going where he was sent, doing as he was told.

Yet slowly he began to come to himself: the self he had been in Quedlinburg. He remembered that he was emperor. The one and only emperor now.

Or perhaps not. One man begged to differ. He kept his head down through the old emperor's funeral rites, but Aspasia saw the glitter of his eyes, and knew what it meant. She had seen it in Byzantium, in other men, lords and princes who were set high but who yearned to rise higher. Now that great Otto was dead, Henry of Bavaria had in mind to claim his throne.

He was keeping quiet, but he was making no great secret of his ambitions. Otto shrugged them off. "Henry was always covetous," he said in Aspasia's hearing, "but he's got a little sense. He knows better than to reach for what he'll never grasp."

Aspasia wished that she could believe him. But she was royal Byzantine. She knew a powerful ambition when it blazed in her face.

On the day great Otto was buried, when lesser Otto had been crowned and set on the throne, there was a high feast in Magdeburg to celebrate the passing of one emperor and the accession of another. The somber grandeur of its beginning gave way to drunken joy as the wine went round. The new emperor led the revels, drinking deep and long to his father's memory, but longer and deeper still to his own freedom.

When Theophano rose to withdraw from the hall, he rose with her, leaning tipsily on her. If she was dismayed, she did not show it. "Rome," he said to her, but loud enough for the whole hall to hear. "New Rome. We'll make it, you and I, and our sons after us."

She blushed scarlet under the paint that Aspasia had applied so carefully, so many hours before.

Otto laughed and kissed her soundly. "Come, let's begin!" He swept her up in his arms, grunting for she was a substantial armful of woman, and carried her off in a roar of ribald mirth.

Aspasia was caught completely off guard. She had been thinking about slipping away, but she could not properly do it till her lady left. That was supposed to be in decorous procession, leaving the emperor and the rest of the men to their carouse.

Theophano was already gone by the time Aspasia worked her way free of the hall. Ismail would be furious. He had expressly forbidden them to begin trying for a son, not so soon after a difficult birth. But Otto was clearly in no mood to listen to common sense. Mathilda was ill again. The old emperor was dead. The royal line hung by a thread.

She sighed and surrendered to the inevitability of a shut and barred door. They did only what royalty must do, as royalty must do it. As a physician in training she deplored that, but as a royal Byzantine she understood it all too well.

She turned from the door, meaning to seek her own bed in the queens' chamber. But she was waylaid.

Duke Henry waited for her at the turning. It was not an

accident that he was there, nor did he try to pretend that it was. He leaned against the wall in his coat of scarlet silk that clashed abominably with her own beloved crimson, and propped his foot on the opposite wall, barring her way.

She stopped perforce. She was not afraid of him, no more than she had ever been, which was perhaps absurd: he was much larger than she, and he had no scruples at all. "Sir," she said, clear and cold, "let me by."

"Eventually," he said. He folded his arms and regarded her. There was a torch just above his head. Its light gave his hair the sheen of beaten gold. She wondered what he was seeing of her besides a shadow and a scowl.

Whatever he saw, it did not seem to disgust him. He smiled. "You look well tonight," he said.

"I look tired tonight," said Aspasia tartly. "What do you want? Can't it wait till morning?"

"No," said Henry. He paused. "What would you do if I carried you away to a place I know of, called in a priest and married you before the sun came up?"

"I'd sink your own knife in your ribs," Aspasia said. She meant it. She was not afraid, no, not even yet. The passage was open behind her. She doubted that she could outrun him, but if she screamed, a guard must surely come running.

He must have read the thought in her face—and the more shame to her for being so easy to read. He laughed and shook his head. "There aren't any guards back there. I paid them off. They're getting drunk on the king's wine."

Maybe he was lying. Maybe he was not. She poised to leap, but she held her ground. "You don't look like a man who's mad with passion."

"Looks can deceive," said Henry.

"Not yours." Aspasia eyed him narrowly. "Let's not discuss your wife, shall we? Let's pretend you were free to carry me off and marry me—by force, since you won't get me any other way. What is it you're hoping to gain from it? Not a throne, surely. You've got a blood claim to that without any help from me."

"But a royal lady," he said, "a Byzantine lady, an emperor's daughter, born to the purple—what an ally for a king to have!"

"What an enemy for him to make," she said.

He kept on smiling as if he had expected her to say just that. "I can't believe you have no ambition."

"What, because all Byzantines are endlessly scheming to make themselves kings?"

"And queens." He straightened. He was much taller than she, and much broader. "Think of it, madam. A throne of your own, an empire to rule as you please. Haven't you ever wanted that?"

"No," said Aspasia. "What makes you think you'll get one for yourself?"

His lip curled. "You know yonder weed of a boy, and you can ask me that? Look at him! When he wasn't dangling at his mother's skirts, he was trailing at his father's. He's never had a thought to call his own."

"He might surprise you," Aspasia said.

"Of course he won't," said Henry. "He's a poppet on a stick. His mother jerks him this way, his empress jerks him that. He'll follow whichever of them pulls harder. And while he wobbles back and forth, I'll claim the throne that should have been mine."

"That's rebellion," said Aspasia.

"What, will you cry the alarm?"

Aspasia stood in his shadow, under the glitter of his eyes. He was looming over her, but she refused to be cowed. She considered his question carefully, and no matter how impatient he might decide to be. At length she said, "No. I don't think I will. He won't listen, and my lady won't want to hear."

"Then you do like me a little," he said. "Enough to let me do as I will."

"Enough to let you hang yourself without any help from me."

Henry heard that no more clearly than Otto had heard her warning about Henry. "I'll remember your forbearance," he said, "when I'm King of the Germans."

"That will be never," said Aspasia.

But he was gone. How so big a man could move so fast or be so silent, she did not know. He left behind him a scent of wine and wool, and a fierce, hot smell that might be blood, or it might be ambition.

King of the Germans, she thought. Not Emperor of the Romans. Otto the younger might have no greatness in him, but he at least aimed high, toward Rome itself. Henry might dream like a foolish boy of seducing a princess from Byzantium, but he asked no more of her than to be a queen of a small and still half-barbarous country.

If he had dreamed of the new Rome . . . if there had been no Ismail . . .

No, she thought. Deplorable it might be, and distressing in one of her breeding, but she did not want to sit a throne. Particularly not at the side of Henry of Bavaria, who clearly was going to vex Otto's peace with a rebellion.

She went to her bed at last and lay long awake. She surprised herself by weeping a little, perhaps for herself and for her lost ambition; perhaps for great Otto who was dead, and for his son who was going to have to fight for his throne. Perhaps even for Henry, who in another world might have been King of the Germans—but not, in the narrowness of his vision, Emperor of the Romans.

The younger Otto was a lesser man than his father, and too well he knew it. But he at least could see beyond his own native fields and forests. He, like his father before him, like royal Byzantium, saw the old place, the high place. He saw Rome that had been; that, if God willed, would be again.

"That's why," she said to the dark before dawn. "That's

what I came for. Not to rule, or to be a queen. To build the new Rome."

Henry would never understand that. Otto, weakling and women's puppet and shadow of his father though he might be, not only understood. He meant to accomplish it.

II

EMPRESS OF THE ROMANS

Germany

978-980

Sixteen

O tto had grown.

    Truly, thought Aspasia from her place in his empress' shadow at the height of Easter Court in Quedlinburg. The callow, often sullen boy who had wanted so badly to be an emperor, now was a man, if a young one: smallish and rather slight, but making up for it with the strength of his presence. He had an air about him, an ease under the crown, as of one born to wear it.

As Otto had grown, his long rival, the scourge of his kingship, seemed to have have shrunk. He knelt at Otto's feet in the posture of a penitent, but with resistance in every line of him.

Henry, once Duke of Bavaria, who would have been King of the Germans, knew well what recompense was due his sins. It did nothing to abate his arrogance. "Yes," he said, clear enough for all to hear. "Yes, I rebelled against my emperor—my lawful emperor, I will not call him. For if there is any law in this, that law would favor me, son of the son of a ruling king, and not this son of an upstart."

The court did not erupt. Otto had forbidden it, and Otto's friends made sure of it. But there was a growl in the air. Five years Henry had fought for a throne that was never his to claim; two of those years in open war, rending the kingdom asunder so that he might call himself a king.

Now he was captured, his allies in shackles behind him: the three Henrys all together, Henry the instigator and Henry of Carinthia and Henry, Bishop of Augsburg, with Boleslav of Bohemia rejoicing in a name that, however barbarian, at least was his alone. He had little enough else to be glad of. All of them would do well to keep their heads on their shoulders for what they had done against their rightful lord.

Aspasia had no pity to spare for them. Barbarians, the lot of them—and Henry most of all. A Byzantine would have known how to dispose of an inconvenient emperor; and that was not with this nonsense of war.

Henry would have made her a part of his rebellion, but she had refused. He did not seem to see her now, nor to know that she stood in her lady's shadow. Maybe he had forgotten her. Maybe he was too angry at them all to single out the woman who had known five years since that he would come to this.

Theophano shifted very slightly on her cushions. Her face was serene under the diadem. Her body in its silks showed but little of her pregnancy.

She did not glance at Aspasia. Nor did she move again. Aspasia eased by degrees. None of Theophano's pregnancies had been excessively difficult; with this, the fourth, she seemed as much at ease as a bearing woman could be. But one never knew. Only daughters had come of the last three: frail Mathilda who had died in the summer after great Otto's death, Sophia who was as robust as her sister had been feeble, small Adelaide with her wheat-fair hair. This one, please God, would be a son.

Henry, whom people had begun to call the Quarreller, was speaking again, emboldened by the silence. "I surrender to your compulsion, cousin, and to nothing else. Will you give me back my dukedom?"

Among the nobles nearest the emperor, one held himself erect and tremblingly still. That too was Otto, another of the royal cousins, Duke of Bavaria since Henry was driven out of it. He looked little like his namesake, a tall, thin young man with a rather unfortunate lack of chin, which his fair beard did little to hide. The man beside him whispered something; his lips twitched, tight and brief.

The emperor regarded his quarrelsome cousin. His expression was somber, almost grim. He looked very much like his father.

Henry stiffened. A little of the high color left his face. He jerked up his chin, a quick, nervous gesture.

"No," said Otto quietly, but not too low to be heard. "I will not give you back the dukedom. You lost all right to it when you reached for my crown."

"Yours by what right?" demanded Henry.

Otto shook his head slightly. "You never give up, do you?" He did not wait for an answer to that. "We name you rebel and traitor. We pronounce you guilty of sedition."

Henry's jaw was tight. His allies stood rigid in their chains. The bishop's eyes were shut, his face running with sweat. Only Boleslav seemed at ease. Maybe he did not understand Otto's meticulous court German. Maybe he did not care. He had bargained with Otto already and gained what he could from it: his freedom once this image of a trial was over, on condition that he departed from Germany and did not again rise up in arms against the German king.

He had nothing to be afraid of except the humiliation of standing there, defeated and in chains. For the others it was worse. Otto had refused to speak with any of them. "I do not bargain with rebels," he had said. "What I will do, I will do."

He looked down on them from his throne, enjoying perhaps the power he had over them; or perhaps not. His hands on the arms of the tall chair were somewhat pale about the knuckles. He said, "We judge you. We bid you recall that our office partakes of mercy as of justice, as we recall that you are our kin and were once our friends, born of the noblest stock of the Germans. For your crimes against the crown you should die. For that you are our kin, and kinslaying is the blackest of sins, we forbear to exact the ultimate penalty. You, my lord of the church, we hand over to your brethren for judgment, to be tried and condemned as they decree. You whose realms were in this world, who sought to raise yourselves higher than God and your birth allowed, we sentence as our clemency ordains. Henry, once of Carinthia; Henry, once of Bavaria, cousin and self-proclaimed enemy of our kingship: you have proved beyond doubt that you cannot dwell at peace in this realm. Therefore this realm will not have you. Go; be banished. Set foot never again in our dominion, lest indeed we put you to death."

The bishop opened his eyes. There was no relief in them. He could see the faces of the prelates about the emperor, and they promised none of Otto's gentleness.

His allies greeted their sentence with rigid composure. Aspasia, looking at the Quarreller, saw the cold glint of laughter in his eye. He bowed his head, but there was nothing humble in it. "We thank you," he said, "for your extraordinary clemency."

Softness, his tone said. *Stupidity.*

Otto smiled slightly. "Do you think so, cousin? Then you are welcome. Though you may not thank me when I add the rest of it. You are banished indeed, but not upon your own devices. My lord the Bishop of Utrecht has generously offered to provide you with lodging in his see under his august protection, until such time as I see fit to relieve him of his charge."

Aspasia almost laughed. Henry was thunderstruck. The court, after a moment of incredulous silence, burst out in applause and cheers.

It would have been sensible to dispose of him. But Otto's was a very Byzantine solution. It averted the sin of kin-murder and thus the threat of blood feud, but it removed also the threat of new rebellion. Henry had escaped from prison before, that was true: he had broken out of Ingelheim to raise this last and most potent of his rebellions. But Utrecht was strong and its bishop impeccably loyal to the emperor. This time, God willing, Henry would stay where he was put.

"He will," said Theophano. Her voice was flat: a promise.

Aspasia barely paused in taking down the heavy plaits. "Did you put his majesty up to it?"

Theophano sighed and arched her back, stretching the ache out of it. "Does it matter which of us it was?"

"No," said Aspasia.

Theophano half-turned, frowning a little. Aspasia smiled. After a moment Theophano laughed, not too long, not too light, but genuine enough. "In fact," said Theophano, "I would have had him execute the ringleader at the least. But he wouldn't. 'My father was never a kinslayer,' he said. 'No more will I be.'"

"Odd," mused Aspasia, "how much more he values his father now that the old man is gone."

"Isn't it always so?" Theophano inspected her face in the mirror. Aspasia saw it reflected, palely beautiful, and her own a shadow on its rim.

Theophano set the mirror down. Her ears were quicker than Aspasia's: it was a moment before Aspasia heard the voices without.

They were restrained, somewhat. But they were not the sounds of amity.

Theophano sat unmoving even when the quarrellers burst in upon her. Otto led them. His crown was off, his state robes laid aside for the plain tunic he preferred in private; his face was nearly as red as his hair. He halted in the middle of the room and rounded on his pursuer. "No. No, no, no! Do you understand? No!"

Empress Adelaide paid no heed at all to their sudden audience. She was taller than her son, and broader. She loomed over him. "Do you defy your mother?"

Otto swayed with the blow, but rallied. "You may be my mother. I am the emperor."

"By whose right?"

Henry's words, flung full in Otto's face. He went white.

Theophano rose. She did it slowly, as queens learned to do in Byzantium, to draw all eyes to them. It was wasted: these had eyes only for one another. But she had more weapons in her arsenal. She said, "Good evening, my lord, my lady."

Otto started like a deer. Adelaide turned the force of her wrath upon Theophano. "Good indeed, for you who have beguiled my son's wits clean out of his head."

Theophano raised a brow. "And how, madam, have I done that?"

"She has not!" Otto looked ready to do murder. "If there is any beguilement here, it is never my lady's doing. *You* would beguile me clean off my throne, and set my cousin in it."

Adelaide went cold suddenly. "Perhaps he deserves it. What have you done that is worthy of your father?"

Whatever might be between them, Otto was her son. He too went cold, cold and still. "You are speaking treason."

"I am speaking truth," she said. "This empire is not your so-beloved Byzantium. We have no dynasties here. The throne belongs to the one best fit to hold it."

Otto laughed. It was shrill, with an edge of hysteria. "What did my cousin pay you to turn traitor to your own son? Or was it simple and poisonous jealousy, because my wife is also my empress, and her counsel is worth taking?"

A flush stained Adelaide's cheeks, deep and ugly. "You will not do as I ask?"

"I will not put away my empress, however many daughters she gives me. Nor will I be your puppet, to dance to your tune. Even," said Otto, "if you are my mother."

Theophano heard them with impressive composure. She could not but know what Adelaide had been urging on her son: she had ears of her own, and eyes in hidden places. She knew also, inevitably, that the empress mother had spoken openly for the rebels, bidding her son restore the Quarreller to his duchy. Maybe Adelaide truly believed that the kingdom would never otherwise be at peace. Certainly her dislike of Theophano had grown to something very like hate, hate born of bitter jealousy, for Theophano took no counsel but her own, and she was teaching Otto to do the same.

Theophano spoke now, softly. "A mother may strive with her son's wife for mastery of her son. That is natural, and one may think inevitable. But to betray her son to his enemies—that is ill done."

"I have not—" Adelaide began.

Theophano cut her off. "We know that you have. Unless you reckon it an act of loyalty to go openly to the rebels and offer them such aid as you can give?"

"I acted out of loyalty to my husband who is dead. My son who lives—my son allied with the son of a traitor, gave him Bavaria in place of the one to whom it belonged—"

"The one who had lost it for rebellion against his liege lord." Theophano regarded her with wide dark eyes, the image of innocent incredulity. "You hated Prince Liudolf so much? He was your stepson, the Englishwoman's cub, and truly he turned rebel against his father. But his father forgave him. If he had not died, he would have been emperor.

You would displace your own son, because he dared dwell in amity with Liudolf's son?"

"Not mere amity alone gave that puppy the duchy of Bavaria." Adelaide's voice was venomous. Aspasia, looking at her, thought of the name she bore for piety, and the long and meticulous roll of her good works. They were a truth of her, perhaps. This was another. Sour jealousy and long rankling, and no love at all for the woman who had taught her son to think for himself. It had all come together in this travesty of a war.

"That puppy," said Otto with less venom but hardly less vehemence, "is loyal to the crown. He could be emperor in very truth, eldest son of the eldest son of Otto the emperor. He accepts that God did not will it; he serves me as duke and servant and friend. That one you are so fond of, son of a youngest son, inheritor of an endless and fruitless quarrel—did you hope that he might prove biddable? He might, I grant it. But his mother, by all accounts, is a worse harpy than you."

Adelaide drew a sharp breath. "You dare—"

"*You* dare overmuch," Otto said. There was a chair behind him. He sat in it. The straightness of his back, the haughty angle of his head, made it a throne. "Because you are my mother, I suffered your indiscretions. See? I do not call them treason. You see what came of them. God is with me, madam. Will you take issue with God's will?"

"God never willed that you rob your true kinsman of what is his, and give it to the son of a rebel."

Otto smiled very thinly. "My true kinsman, as you call him, is not merely a rebel's son; he is a rebel himself, and incorrigible." He shook his head. "Give it up, Mother. You backed the wrong side; you lost. I'll not change my mind."

"No mind of yours," said Adelaide, "while this foreigner sits and simpers and weaves her nets."

Theophano spoke very gently. "You never approved of your husband's insistence on a Byzantine bride for your son. Wise: for a Byzantine would know too well what an empress is, and yield too little to your authority."

"And pour poison in his ears." Adelaide turned on her almost with pleasure: a pleasure long awaited and too often forgone. "He was a loving son before you set him against me."

"Perhaps I had no need to. Perhaps he was weary already of your meddling."

"Meddling?" Adelaide swelled with wrath. "Meddling? When I was empress and mother, and he but an infant in a crown?"

"More than an infant," said Theophano, "even then. Now he is a man; and for that he would not stay in swaddling bands, you cast him off and took refuge with his enemies. I call you a poor mother, madam, and a worse queen; and a laughable traitor."

Adelaide struck her, a hard, ringing blow that rocked her head on her neck.

Aspasia leaped unthinking, with no thought in her but rage.

A hand brought her up short. Theophano shook her head. The mark of the blow rose already on her cheek, blood-red. The rest was bloodless, white as stripped bone. "No, Aspasia. If she needs killing, then I shall do it, or my lord." He sat motionless, appalled. She smiled at him. It was a sweet smile, like a child's. "I think," she said, "that her erstwhile majesty is weary of all this tumult. Wars, insurrections, the to-ings and fro-ings of your court—surely, my lord, we should free her to seek her soul's peace? For see, she is distraught; she speaks without thought, acts without discretion, strikes without restraint. In solitude or in the company of the daughters of God, perhaps she may find comfort."

Adelaide had gone too far in striking Theophano. She had wits enough to know it.

She did not try to defend herself. That was royally done.

A pity, thought Aspasia, that she could not have mastered herself sooner.

"Yes," said Otto, taking his tone from Theophano. "She is much beset with the cares and quarrels of our kingdom. A time of rest may heal her: in a house of God, if she is minded; or in a house of men, if that is her will. If only it be out of this kingdom which has so vexed her."

Little as Aspasia loved the old empress, she knew a moment's compunction. Otto had always been gentle with his mother; submissive, one might have thought. It made him the harder now.

He should have done it long ago. Aspasia hardened heart and mind: not difficult, when it came to it. Adelaide was never one to weep or plead.

Adelaide drew herself erect. "Very well," she said. "You will do what you will do. I will go where I will not trouble you."

"Where?" A mistake, that; but Otto was new yet to his manhood.

His mother forbore to seize the advantage. She hoped, maybe, that he would weaken further; she knew that he had gone beyond any compulsion of hers. "Home," she said. "Burgundy. My brother sees me too seldom, he says. No doubt he will welcome me."

Otto nodded, slight and stiff.

"I shall not," said Adelaide, "undertake a new rebellion against you. On that you have my word."

Otto's cheeks darkened. But he said composedly enough, "I accept it. Will you leave soon?"

She blinked rapidly. So, Aspasia thought. She had been playing weakness on weakness; and Otto had not given way. She was fast in her own trap, with her pride like a noose about her neck. "Tomorrow," she said. Her voice was flat.

"So soon?" He stopped himself. "Yes. Tomorrow."

She inclined her head. Then she bowed, sinking down in the pool of her skirts. She did not offer either embrace or kiss. Otto did not seek them. Emperor he had wished to be; emperor, then, he was.

Seventeen

Theophano was grimly satisfied. "Now we shall have a proper peace," she said.

She had had to wait for Otto to leave to say what was on her mind. He had not lingered long. He would not do his husbandly duty while she was carrying the child, and her mood was too little in keeping with his to give him any comfort. It was a terrible thing for a man to sunder himself from his mother.

Theophano could not—perhaps would not—share his grief. She contemplated a kingdom free of the empress mother and allowed herself a smile: a brief one, with a hint of the sword's edge. "Otto will do well now that he's free to think for himself."

"And you free to think for him."

Theophano arched a brow. "Are you judging us?"

"No," said Aspasia. "I think it's well that her majesty is leaving. She wants too much that should be yours."

"Just so," said Theophano. She sat for Aspasia to finish

what the quarrel had interrupted: the taking out of the last plait, the long slow brushing which was her one purely animal pleasure. Aspasia, falling into the rhythm of it, was almost startled when Theophano spoke again. "What do you think of Duke Charles?"

"Should I think anything?" Aspasia asked.

"You always do, whether you should or not."

Aspasia laughed a little. "Well then. He's rather nice to look at. He's good on the field, people say."

"And you? What do you say?"

"That I wonder if he's worth a quarrel with the King of the Franks for our taking him in when he'd turned rebel, and worse than that, giving him a dukedom. He's Lothair's own Quarreller, by all accounts."

"So he is," said Theophano. "But he serves us well. He seems the sort of man to remember to whom he owes his debts."

"I wonder how he'll pay them," Aspasia said.

"Faithfully, I think," said Theophano, "if we treat him with honor. I rather like him. He's very charming when he wants to be."

"Everyone wants to be charming where you are." Aspasia set a kiss on the parting of Theophano's hair.

Theophano smiled over her shoulder. "It's not only I," she said. "When you're away, he looks for you. Sometimes he goes so far as to ask."

Aspasia stifled a sigh. "He's new here. He can't have had time to learn."

"I think he knows," said Theophano. "He's very clever, and I think rather smitten; though maybe he's shy of showing it. Today when you were elsewhere he asked what your prospects might be."

"Dismal," said Aspasia. Truly: and was this another Duke Henry, dreaming of a royal Byzantine bride?

"No," Theophano said. "I don't think so. He's not the only one who's courted you, nor the only one now who makes bold to hint at it. You're not an impossible bargain, you know. Otto and I would dower you splendidly; and a man who's had his heirs already, wouldn't need you to get more."

Aspasia's head began to throb, heavy and slow. They had had this conversation before. But not for a long while; long enough for her to hope that she had heard the last of it. "You know I don't want to marry again."

"Do you honestly?" asked Theophano. "You have no calling to the veil, I know that, and I'd never ask it of you. But when I see you all alone, with no one to stand beside you—"

Aspasia set her teeth. She had never told Theophano of Henry's suit, useless thing that it had been; nor, much more to the point, had she confessed to her long sinning with Ismail. At first she had been too great a coward; then the proper moment never seemed to come. Nor had it come now. Soon, she told herself. When the kingdom was quiet. When Theophano would have time to understand.

"I am content," said Aspasia, keeping her voice quiet.

"Can you know that?" Theophano asked. "Maybe you don't want to be a duchess. Do you want to live out your days as a servant?"

"I'm much more than that," said Aspasia. "Let be, Phania. I'm happy in what I have. Happier—yes, even happier than I was in the City." She had not said it aloud before, or thought it, that she knew of. Yet it was true. "This is where I was meant to be: here, with you, making an empire out of this wilderness."

Theophano shook her head. "I never cease to marvel at you. This is what I chose, but you've made it more your own than I ever will. That's why I thought you might want to marry here. To put the seal on it."

"I have that," said Aspasia. "I have you."

Theophano turned with impulsiveness that had become all too rare, and clasped her close. "Of course I'd never keep you far from me. Even if you change your mind and want to be a duchess."

"I'll remember that," said Aspasia.

She remembered it as she slipped through the streets to Ismail's lodging. Dark though it was, with only starlight to light her way and no servant to guard her, she was not afraid. Foolhardy, maybe. Ismail would say so when she came to him. But she had never suffered worse than a fondling or a beery kiss, even when anyone thought her worth troubling with. Tonight she doubted that she was seen at all. She was quick and very quiet, and she knew every step of the way.

There was a light at the head of the stair, a glimmer beneath the door. Aspasia slipped the latch as she had many a night before, and let herself into the room.

Ismail sat at the table as he often did, close to the lamp that burned sweet-scented oil from his own country. He had been reading earlier: the book lay by his hand. His other hand supported his brow. He seemed asleep.

His shoulders were taut, no rest in them at all. Aspasia set fingers to the worst of the knots.

Very slowly he began to ease. He drew a long breath. She held her tongue. He had moods like this, sometimes; more often when he was ill or getting over illness—as all that winter he had been.

There was no fever in him now. He breathed easily. He had not coughed in days. Aspasia was almost ready to stop worrying about him.

He straightened, lowering his hand. "Before you can ask," he said, "I ate dinner. All of it. And took my medicine."

"But you didn't go to bed," she said. And when he rounded on her: "Now, then. I'm only twitting you."

He glowered. "And who is the physician here?"

"I am." She settled in his lap, not pleased to mark how

bony it was, but loving the warmth and the nearness of him. Her arms circled his neck. He was not too angry to allow it. She smiled. "I think we can reckon you recovered."

"Inasmuch as I can ever be in this pestilential country."

"That's Italy," she said. She smoothed his ruffled beard. "It was a bad winter. It's over. We've got peace now, and warmer weather. Maybe it will be warm enough for you."

"Nothing will be warm enough for me."

He was in a mood, indeed. She had to remind herself how much she had worried when for a whole week together he had been too sick to be prickly; too sick to do anything but lie and be ministered to. When he snapped at her one morning after the fever broke, she had cried for joy, because then she knew that he would get better.

He had been snapping ever since, wearing her patience to a shred. "It's a pity I'm not your mother," she said, "or I'd give you a good hard spanking."

He stiffened.

"You've been feeling very sorry for yourself," she said. "Maybe it's time you started thinking about something else."

He set her on her feet when he stood, which was courteous of him. He could have spilled her out of his lap. "If you're tired of me, why do you keep haunting me?"

"Habit," she said. She sat on the bed and tucked up her feet. "Her majesty is trying to marry me off again. Should I let her?"

"Who wants you?"

He did not mean it that way. She knew it very well. But she was tired. She had been nursing him all winter; he had given her not a word of thanks. "You'd be surprised," she said, drawling it. "Duke Henry is banished, but there's Duke Charles. And Margrave Hedbald. And milord of Schönberg. And—"

"So marry," he said. "Marry them all."

"I can't. I'm not a Muslim."

He glared. She glared back. "You really have been un-
bearable," she said. "Won't you come to bed and work off a
little of your spleen?"

Contrition was not a Muslim virtue. He came to bed, but
he came angrily, taking off his clothes with meticulous, furious precision. He was shockingly gaunt.

He lay down stiffly, leaving it to her to cover him with the
blankets and the bearskin that Otto had given him when
Sophia was born. She dropped her own garments and slid in
beside him. Now, she knew, she should smooth it over; coax
him, calm him, convince him that she had not meant it. She
was a good liar. Had she not lied to everyone for years, escaping even gossip?

She was tired. How tired, she had not even known. That
knot in her, that edge of temper: she knew what it meant.
Investigation proved it. Early again. She tended to it, sim-
mering.

He was not strict in his religion when it came to a
woman's courses. He did not cast her out of his bed or turn
his back on her, though temper might well have invited it.

She laid her head on his breast. After a while his arms
folded about her. "You've been thinking about Córdoba
again," she said.

He did not answer. She did not look up, to read his face.
She could feel it in him, in the way he breathed, in the way
he held her.

"Someday you'll go back," she said.

"Someday I'll be too old for the journey."

"Forty-five is not old."

"I was five-and-thirty when I went away. How old must I
be before they let me come home?"

Her heart clenched at the word. This was not home to her,
either, but she had made it so. He never had. Not even she
was enough for that. Home was Córdoba, and voices speaking Arabic, and the cry of the muezzin in the still hot air.

"I was young," he said. "Now my youth is gone."

"You weren't a boy when I met you. It's part of why I loved you."

His head shook. "Even middle age is slipping away from me. My body aches where old bones ache. It counts a new grey hair every day."

"You've been sick, that's all. You'll be well by summer."

"Will my hair grow black again?"

She looked up then. He had exactly six grey hairs on his head, and a dozen more in his beard. She told him so. "Shall I pluck them out?" she asked.

He scowled. It was somewhat less formidable than a glare. "Woman, have you no respect?"

"I can't recall that I ever did."

"Nor shall you ever learn it." He closed his eyes. "What did I do to deserve you?"

"A multitude of sins," she said. She laid her head back over his heart. Was he a little warmer than he should be?

Blanket and bearskins, that was all; and temper. After a moment he began to stroke her hair. He was calming, perhaps in spite of himself. Maybe he was tired, too. The last time, he had shouted himself into a coughing fit, and she would not have come back for a week, except that she could not trust him to look after himself. She had settled for not speaking to him for two days. Restful, he had called that.

Just when she thought that he had fallen asleep, he started to talk. Softly; almost as if to himself. "I had a letter," he said, "this morning. One of the priests brought it with the post from Rome. That was where they thought I was: with the pope. They were careful not to disapprove."

She did not say anything.

His fingers plaited and unplaited a strand of her hair. "I'm not welcome back. Old rancor is strongest, they say, and my enemy would have my privates set in silver if she could. That's what my kinsman wrote to me. He seemed appropriately concerned."

"Well might he be," said Aspasia. "He could lose his own estates for helping you."

"So he told me. Mine are safe, he says. My friends have seen to that; and my wife." Aspasia had learned to hear that word without flinching. Almost. "Her family has influence enough, and she has her own talent for persuasion. If I'm ever to go back, I'll have a home to go back to."

"You're fortunate."

"Exile's fortune," he said. "When I was sick I dreamed that I was home. Then I woke and I wept, because it was only a dream."

"I dream of my City sometimes," said Aspasia.

"And your husband?"

"No," she said.

He was silent for a while. His fingers had stilled, woven in her hair. Then he said, "My sister Laila is dead."

As simple as that; as baldly said. With equal simplicity she said, "I'm sorry."

"She died bearing a child. The child was stillborn. Her husband grieved for her. He gave her a splendid funeral. He endowed a mosque in her name, near the garden she loved. Prayers were said on my behalf, and a gift given, though that was hardly prudent."

"It was well done."

"I loved her," he said. "She was so young when I left her; she wanted to weep, but she was determined to be brave. 'I'll wait for you to come back,' she said. Now only her bones will wait for me."

He wept hard, once he had begun. Years of it, and all the more bitter for that it had been so long. Aspasia held him, saying nothing, simply being there. Maybe he would hate her for it: it would be like his temper. But she would not stop for that.

There were tears in her own eyes. Exhaustion; a shadow of his grief. She let them spill over. It was almost a luxury; almost a pleasure, to let go.

For once he did not snap at her for dripping on him. She was wetter than he. His nose was running: ultimate indignity. She fetched a cloth to dry them both. He did not snatch it, nor did he try to hide his weakness from her. He looked her levelly in the face and said, "I shall never go back to Córdoba."

"Until they call you back."

"I shall be dead then. I shall die here. That is what God has written for me."

She shook her head, but she was past desire to argue with him. She lay down again. He was asleep soon enough. She lay awake nightlong, as if she could surprise his death if it came, and drive it away.

Eighteen

After Easter Court the emperor led the caravan of court and *palatium* to the city he was fondest of, Charlemagne's city in the duchy of Lorraine: handsome, half-Roman, half-barbarian Aachen. Water-loving Rome had come to its hot springs and built a city about them. Water-loving Charles had made it the heart of his realm. The eagle of empire spread its wings eastward from the summit of the chapel's dome, granting the imperium to the Saxon kings.

This country was, by Otto's grant, Duke Charles' new-won domain. His grace the duke seemed to take the honor to heart: he was much out and about, making himself known to his people, and waiting on the emperor when it was most politic. If it troubled him that the descendant of a Saxon chief held the throne which could have been his own, he did not see fit to confess it. Aspasia heard him once, answering a drunken sally. "So I am Charles, and he was Charles, and he was emperor where I am duke and vassal;

and the people whom he conquered have conquered in his name. Things change. The world changes. I'm well suited where I am."

Clever with his tongue, that one. Maybe he noticed that Aspasia was listening. He got a laugh: Otto's court was trained to that kind of quickness. "And here you are," someone said, "lord of Lower Lotharingia. A pity my lord Lothair can't rule his own namesake."

Charles showed a gleam of teeth. "Yes indeed, it is a pity. My poor brother; throne and crown and all that he has, and he can't be Duke of Lorraine too."

"Not for lack of trying," the other observed. "He's got an army in the field, did you hear? He's threatening to cross the border."

"Let him threaten," Charles said. "We'll drive him off."

Bravado, thought Aspasia, going on about her business. They were all mocking the King of the West Franks, who was not pleased that the King of the East Franks should have taken in his scapegrace brother. That too went back to Charlemagne. Great he might have been, even a Byzantine could grant him that, but he had been a fool in his legacies to his sons. He should have learned from great Alexander, or from Rome that, divided in two, lost the West and came perilously close to losing the East. An empire divided, soon became no empire at all.

Lothair would have liked to see the empire restored and himself at the head of it. The Saxons had gone beyond wishing and into doing; and now there was Theophano, who was teaching her husband to be an emperor in truth.

The air was freer about the court with the empress mother gone from it. She was well on the road to Burgundy, with a guard of honor to make certain that she stayed on it. If she had hoped that her son would weaken at the last and call her back, she was disappointed. Theophano made sure of that.

Otto, once freed of her, seemed to walk more lightly. The trouble with the Franks only made him eager.

"War is a drug," Theophano said. "All men succumb to it. Even in the City—do you remember how it was when the fighting season came round? Especially under Nikephoros. All the boys were afire to go out and kill something."

"They do outgrow it," said Aspasia. "Some of them."

Theophano shook her head, unsmiling. They were in the royal baths, the two of them and the gaggle of royal women, filling the great steaming halls with chatter and laughter. Theophano loved to lie in the tepidarium for an hour at a time. It was the best way to feel light, she said, when one was pregnant.

Aspasia, gowned and veiled and somewhat regretful, for the pool looked enticing, bent to kiss the smooth brow. That won the shadow of a smile. "Give my regards to Master Ismail," Theophano said.

"Always," said Aspasia. It was part of the world now, and unquestioned, that in the hours between terce and noon, if no other duty pressed, Aspasia should serve as the physician's assistant. Lately she had had patients of her own, who were gladder of a woman than of a heathen; most in the court, a few in the towns as her name grew.

Today there were plenty of both. Every season had its fevers, and this spring had been an ill one for them. Then there was the dandy who wanted a potion to thicken his hair, and the pair of giggling girls in search of a charm to lure a lover, and a long line of sore eyes and running noses and bruises and splinters and one pair of young idiots who had gone at one another with knives. Aspasia sewed them up and sent them off, and sat for a while, just to be still.

In every city, as soon as he came to it, Ismail made sure of a room for a clinic and a room to sleep in, for Theophano could never persuade him to accept her charity. In Aachen both rooms were near the palace, one behind the other, in a house that, the landlady insisted, had belonged to the great

Roland who died at Roncesvalles. "Not," she always added, "that I'm saying anything against the Moors, as your lordship well knows."

His lordship cared for little but that the rooms were clean, well aired and well lit, and easy for people to come to. His servants lodged in the kitchen with the landlady's own servants, and his horseboy lived and ate and slept in the emperor's stable with the horses. It was as satisfactory an arrangement as one could find, although Aspasia would have welcomed a door between the rooms, and a landlady less given to appearing at odd hours with odd bits of news or dainties. The outer room had a door, but it did not lock or even latch very well. To keep his store of medicines safe, Ismail locked them in the chest that went with him wherever he traveled, and made his bed on top of it.

A poor situation altogether for clandestine sinning. Aspasia should have been resigned to it. It had been worse in crowded castles and on the road. It was seldom better.

She could risk no more than a touch and a kiss, which he was too preoccupied to return. He looked well enough. The journey had not brought back his fever. He seemed to have cured himself with free air and saddle-leather; but he still tired more easily than he liked, and today had worn down even Aspasia.

"Do you know what I would like to do?" she asked suddenly.

He did not answer, but she knew that he was listening: he had paused in grinding herbs for a salve.

"I'd like to go out," she said. "It doesn't matter where. Just out, where I can breathe."

"So go," he said.

"Alone?"

"You always do."

"When was the last time you took Zuleika out?"

That brought his head up. "Let me finish this," he said.

They had their ride, Aspasia jogging on her level-headed

mule, Ismail riding his dancing, curvetting mare, and the elder of his servants in silent attendance. Wilhelm knew, of course. Servants did. But he was discreet, or Ismail would never have kept him. He held his peace, did his duties, and was unfailingly polite to Aspasia.

Riding with Ismail was seldom occasion for dalliance. When he was on his mare he belonged to her. He was very single-minded: physician, horseman, courtier, lover. One at a time. No doubt that, even more than Aspasia's clever deceptions, had kept their secret as long as this.

"Do you love me all of the time?" she asked him suddenly, after they had ridden, as they walked from the stable. The servant was gone, discreetly. There was no one much about, and she was speaking Arabic.

He kept on walking with his quick, fluid stride. "When would I not love you?"

"When you're doing something else."

He stopped then and turned. She was several paces back, watching him. "Is that logical?" he wanted to know.

"You're so complete, you see. When you're a doctor, you're all doctor. When you're riding, that's all there is in the world. I can't be like that. I'm always thinking of six things at once."

"Woman's logic," he said. "Scatterbrained."

"So," said Aspasia. "Do you?"

He had to trace it back, frowning. But he was more amused than not. She thought he found her interesting. He never said so. Neither did he seem to tire of her. "Am I supposed to think of you every moment of every day?"

"No. Just love me."

He shook his head. "All this time and you doubt it?"

"One likes to be reminded."

His sudden smile warmed her. "Incalculable is the mind of a woman."

She laughed and held out her hand. After a moment he took it. There was no one to see. He kissed her fingertips.

Warm lips, rough-silken brush of beard. She shivered, though it was warm there between stable and palace, with the sun shining through the colonnade, and somewhere a child singing.

She was dizzy. Maybe she had a touch of fever. "I know a place," she said, a little breathless. One of the dozen parts of her observed that it was hardly safe at this time of day, with everyone going in and out. The rest of her did not care. They had been reckless before. The first time—that had been downright mad, madder than what she was thinking of now.

Yes, she was starting a fever. She would brew a tisane, afterwards. Quickly, trying not to giggle, she told him where to go. He was catching the mood of it. He would never giggle, that was far beneath him, but the glint in his eye was wicked enough. He nodded, kissed her lightly, put on his dignity again and went where she had directed.

She went the other way, the longer way, eluding suspicion. People greeted her. Some wanted to talk. She hinted at duties. God was with her: they let her go.

The baths were empty as she had hoped. The empress and her women were gone. Charlemagne had been mad, for a Frank: he had loved to be clean. His descendants were less certain of the virtues of the bath. Aspasia had heard the springs of Aachen called a devil's cauldron, as if hell's fire and not mother earth's had begotten them.

Ismail, bless him, had bought off the attendant, who was known to have a fondness for a certain wineshop and a certain young woman therein. He was in the water when she came, sitting where Theophano always sat, properly and blissfully warm, with the water lapping his chest. He was not wearing his drawers. Aspasia grinned at that, dropped her clothes where they fell, and paused, letting him look his fill. He was not as shy as he had used to be. But then, neither was she.

"I like it when you look at me," she said. "It makes me feel worth looking at."

"You are that," said Ismail. He leaned his head back against the curb of the pool. His teeth were white in his beard. He had lost one in the winter, on the side. She was sorry for that; but he was still beautiful when he smiled.

The water had taken all the tautness out of him, but not the desire. That was as eager as ever.

She lowered herself beside him. His arm drew her round into his lap. There was only one way to fit herself so, and he knew it very well.

They took their time. He had a winter's sickness to get over, and she was a little weaker than she had expected. Yes, most certainly a fever. A quick one, she hoped. She had no time for a slow one.

It was strange in the water. Like a dream: slow and warm and rather noisy. The attendant would have known exactly what it was, if he had not taken himself off to the wineshop. Maybe he was giving the potgirl a tumble. Aspasia laughed against Ismail's shoulder, flicked her tongue to the water beaded there, traced a line to his ear. His hand was doing delightful things along her spine. "I love you," she said in his ear in Arabic.

He said the same in her ear, in Greek. Then she to him in Saxon; and he to her in Latin.

That was their game. Their password, she liked to call it. To tell the truth in all the languages they knew.

It was a wonder to be both clean and sated. Aspasia even found a store of the unguent which Theophano favored, lightly scented with orange and citron, to rub into his skin as he rubbed it into hers. There was a pure pleasure in being stroked as if one were a cat, all drowsy bliss in front of the fire. He almost fell asleep. Poor man, he was convalescent still, and she had worn him out.

He roused quickly enough to her kiss. He was quicker to dress than she: single-minded again and turning to something new. But when she started toward the door he took her hand, not saying anything, not needing to. *Not yet,* the gesture said. *Be part of me for yet a while.*

As far as the door; a little farther. Their hands did not want to draw apart. She paused, barring his way. His outer robe was a little awry. She straightened it. His eyes smiled down at her. She laid her palm briefly against his cheek, then stepped back.

He stood absolutely still. She was dizzy again. It had been worse than mad to spend so long in the bath with fever on her. But it had been so sweet.

She turned carefully, to keep her head from spinning off her shoulders.

She froze.

Someone was watching them. A shadow to her blurred sight, a shape half in sun, half in dark, farther down the colonnade.

If one was brazen enough, one could seem innocent. Aspasia finished the step she had begun, and another after it, and another. What could any observer say but that the empress' physician and the empress' waiting-woman had been seen together near the baths? The two of them were often in one another's company, and no scandal attached to them.

Aspasia's feet faltered before her head caught up with them. The shape was a woman, and veiled, and dreadfully familiar. "Phania," she said. "Lady. I didn't know you."

Theophano did not raise her veil. Her voice was soft and cool. "So I gathered."

Aspasia glanced back before she thought. Ismail stood where she had left him, just beyond the door of the bath, as straight as one of the pillars, and as still.

Theophano was like an image of him, dark-robed to his white. Aspasia laughed, because she could not think of anything else to do. It was a feeble sound. It died young. "I've a bit of fever, I think."

"A very particular kind of fever," said Theophano in that still voice.

"Well," said Aspasia. "Maybe that, too." There was a silence. Her dizziness was gone, at least. Shock could do that. It should not have been Theophano who found them out. It was supposed to be someone else, who took the tale to her, and won her anger until she summoned Aspasia for the truth of it, and Aspasia told her—whatever Aspasia decided to tell her. Truth or lie, or anywhere between. Truth, Aspasia could hope. Secrets rotted fast if they were kept out of the light.

Maybe Theophano had not seen it after all. Maybe it was another thing that stilled her so, that made her so silent. It was unwonted for her to walk out of her apartments when she was so heavy with a child; unheard of for her to do it without attendance.

"Were you looking for me?" Aspasia asked her. "Has something happened?"

Theophano shrugged, a minute gesture, but eloquent. "I was looking for you. As to what has happened . . . maybe you know better than I."

Again Aspasia glanced back at Ismail. He was directly behind her. She had not heard him come. He bowed low in Arab fashion. There was nothing abject in it. "I greet your majesty," he said.

Theophano raised her veil slowly, as if she grudged its dimming of her vision. Her face was white and set. "Do you think," she asked, "that you have a right to anything that is mine?"

"No," he said, "majesty. What is not yours and never has been yours, except of its free will: that has a right to anything that I am."

That gave her pause. But there was very little that could conquer Theophano. "I give you leave to go," she said.

He might have resisted. Aspasia laid a hand on his arm. "Go. I'll take no harm."

He did not believe that. But her will, with Theophano's,

was more than he could withstand. He turned stiffly and went.

Which left the two of them. "I had not known him to be so biddable," Theophano observed.

"I call it wisdom," said Aspasia.

"Do you?" Theophano turned as Ismail had, with somewhat more grace. She expected Aspasia to follow. Aspasia chose to oblige her.

They got through dinner, one of the interminable state banquets. They got through the nonsense afterward. Otto was in it, and Duke Charles, and a bishop or six, and someone with a message which had the rest in a flutter. Aspasia's head by then was very light, as if to counter the weight of her heart. King Lothair was coming, it seemed, with fire and sword. Otto looked as if he would welcome a fight, but the others called the news empty wind. Lothair would not have crossed another king's borders, even to get his hands on his brother. Charles himself said so, with appropriate scorn.

Theophano retired early. It was expected of her, in her condition. It was expected that Aspasia accompany her.

There was ample ritual in putting the queen to bed. Theophano went through it as she always did, with dignity, but with warmth too, for which her women loved her. She did not single out Aspasia nor mark her with coldness. Aspasia supposed she should be grateful. It was not kindness. It was prudence, and avoidance of a scandal.

Theophano was angry. Aspasia knew her well enough for that. Angry clear down to the bone.

The coward in Aspasia begged to her make her escape with the rest of the women. Theophano could hardly call her back. By morning the storm might have blown over, or calmed enough to go on with.

Aspasia could have been so sensible with a stranger. Even with a friend. With Theophano, no.

They faced one another. Theophano sat up in bed, propped with pillows. With her hair in braids on her shoulders and her bulk half-obscured by the coverlets, she looked like a child.

She even sounded like one. "Why?" she asked.

"Because I love him."

"That little snappish man?"

Aspasia had her temper in hand. Just. "He's quite big enough for me."

Theophano folded her hands over the dome of her belly. "How long?"

There. The worst of it. Aspasia swallowed past the knot in her throat. "Since we met in Italy."

The dark eyes widened. So: Aspasia had surprised her. "You were very clever. And very, very discreet."

"Lucky," said Aspasia. "That's all."

"Possibly," said Theophano. "Does anyone know?"

"A servant or two. Some of the common folk, I think. Gerbert in Rheims: he knew about us before we did." Aspasia paused. "I'll ask you not to punish anyone but me."

"Do you expect punishment?"

"I've sinned. I can't say I repent it. Someday I may. Then I'll do penance."

"What I can't understand," said Theophano, "is why. Oh, not why you did it—that's clear enough to any woman with eyes in her head. But why that one? An infidel. An unbaptized man."

It truly horrified her to think of that. Aspasia should have expected it. She had learned long ago that she did not think as other people thought, or see as they saw. To a Christian as good as Aspasia should have been, an unbaptized man was a terrible, pitiful thing, born and raised without hope of salvation, condemned to die unshriven. Heaven was barred to him.

To Ismail, whose Allah was more truly part of him than

Aspasia's God had ever been to her. Who performed the rites of his religion as best he could, not form alone but substance too, with devotion as perfect as a saint's. In whose Paradise love was welcome as it never was in the Christian heaven.

Aspasia stopped herself before she said any of it. Heresy, all of it, and appalling; it assured her of damnation. And she was so far down in it that she could not even care.

She spoke carefully, measuring each word before she let it go. "Who knows why any being loves another? That he should be what he is, that is God's will and God's making. But for that, he leaves nothing to be desired."

"Height," said Theophano. "Beauty. Sweetness of temper."

"None of which is a virtue of mine."

Theophano shook her head. "He is impossible. You must give him up. Duke Charles will take you; he need never know how you have beguiled your widowhood. Thank God you have no children. A brood of little Moors would be difficult to explain away."

Aspasia stared at her. Cold, she was that, and hard. One had to be, to be an empress. But to be so cold and so hard—"Phania. Have you forgotten who I am? Can't you—won't you—understand?"

There was no understanding in those dark eyes, and no yielding, either. "I will dismiss him. That would be best. He can go back to the pope, or wherever he pleases. He has served me well. I grant him that. He will have my commendation and such help as I can give."

"No," Aspasia said. "You can't send him away."

Theophano arched her brows. "Is it your place to tell me what I can or cannot do?"

"If you dismiss him, then I go with him. That is a promise, your majesty."

"I forbid you."

"You may forbid. You may even lock me in prison. It matters nothing. I am married to that man in the eyes of God. Where he goes, I go. Where he stays, I stay. You will have both of us or none. That is the choice you are given."

There was a silence. Aspasia discovered that she was trembling. She could not stop it. Still less could she take back what she had said.

Something was broken. At first she thought it might be her heart. It was that; but not only that.

They had been growing apart, she and Theophano. She had known it for a long while; known too that her secret had little to do with it. Theophano, in growing out of childhood, had grown away from the one who, more than the woman who bore her, was mother to her. That was nature, and natural. One acknowledged it, one mourned it a little, one allowed oneself to be glad, for one's youngling was an empress, fit consort for an emperor.

She was still Aspasia's youngling, her all-but-daughter. And Aspasia had told her to her face that before Aspasia was a mother she was a woman; and it was as a woman that she chose. Worse than that: she chose an infidel.

Maybe if she had told Theophano when it began, before it became a set and settled thing, she could have hoped to be forgiven. Now there was only the cold choice and the colder truth.

"I will not marry," said Aspasia, "unless I marry Ismail. I will not stay unless I stay with him."

Theophano was as still as she had been in the colonnade, when she saw what there was to see, and knew it for what it was. Had she berated herself for blindness? "Go," she said. Her voice was perfectly calm. "I will summon you when I am ready to judge you."

Judge. Yes, she would do that. She did it now, betrayed child and Christian queen: the same judgment for both, and the same condemnation.

Aspasia paused. Theophano's eyes were closed, dismissing her.

"So be it," said Aspasia. Not as coldly as she might have hoped, perhaps, but implacably enough.

Nineteen

I don't know why I'm surprised," Aspasia said. "She's quite as merciless as I am, and almost as unscrupulous. And she's a better Christian than I can ever hope to be."

"What, do you think she'll forgive you?"

Aspasia spun to face Ismail. "Only God can forgive such sins as mine."

He raised himself on his elbow. He was in his bed, because she had made him lie there; but she could not be still. She measured the few paces' worth of the room, turned on her heel, came back. He regarded her levelly—coldly, one might have thought. "So it comes to that."

"No," said Aspasia. "I'll buy myself a bishop. Or a pope, who knows? I'll get my absolution."

Ismail could hardly be shocked. He had lived in sight of the papal curia. But his brows drew together. "I should never have let you leave me out of it."

"It was the wisest thing I could have done. She's angry with me. You have no part in it."

"Don't I?" He shook his head. "She has the right of it. This is impossible. It drives both of us to lying and conniving; now it has set you at odds with your empress."

"The worst she can do is send me out of her sight."

"Exile," said Ismail. "You don't want that."

"There is no exile while I have you."

He shook his head again. "I am not what you want. You'll see that when you come to yourself." He sat up. "I'll go away. That will be best. You know enough of my art to look after her majesty. She may not forgive you at first, but she will need you. Need will teach her to love you again. You'll live well enough without me."

"No," said Aspasia fiercely. "*No.* I chose you in front of my empress. I won't undo the choosing."

"You will," he said. He was as stubborn as she was. "As long as I stay, she will remember what I am and what I have done, and what she cannot accept."

"She will learn," said Aspasia.

"Not that lady," said Ismail. "Some things, yes, she accepts with truest Christian charity. But not this. Not me. My hands on her, making her whole—those, she endures, because there is no one else who can do it. My hands on you . . . she will never forgive or forget."

"I will teach her," Aspasia said.

His lips set in a thin line. He did not care that Aspasia had raised Theophano from a baby; that she knew her empress as no one else did. He knew what he knew. That was enough.

She wanted to hit him. His eyes dared her to try. She knotted her fists behind her back and willed herself to be calm, to say steadily, "Maybe I have pushed her too far. It is possible. I'll not deny it. Still less will I go crawling to her because my impossible lover has deserted me. What honor will I have then? How will I hold up my head?"

"You can always hold up your head." In her furious silence he drew the blankets about him. "It is best that I go.

You would see that, if temper did not blind you. Your place is here, with your lady who needs you. Mine is wherever there are ills to be healed."

"I won't let you go," said Aspasia. "I will not."

"Is that love, then? To bind me with a collar and a chain?"

"Am I no more than that to you?"

Her pain touched him, she knew it. But he was long practiced in enduring it. "You know what you are to me," he said. "If I could marry you before the world, give you wealth and honor, take you home to Córdoba—then I would take your counsel, and gladly. But I can do none of those things. I can cherish your honor, that is all, and guard your good name; and that I can only do by leaving you."

"I'll lock you up," Aspasia said. "I'll keep you prisoner till you come to your senses."

She was talking wildly. She knew it in some dim part of her. In all this tumult she had forgotten the fever. It had not, alas, forgotten her.

She chose quite consciously and quite in accordance with her body's wishes. To sway; to catch herself just after he saw. But her knees had a will of their own. They buckled without warning.

She bruised her elbow going down. Damn him for not being there to catch her. Damn herself for letting him think it a pretense—when she had never in her life pretended to anything like a swoon. She had feigned other things in plenty, most of them reprehensible, but woman-weakness, never. She had been proud of it; boasted of it once or twice. Thrice. When she had had a plenitude of wine or of loving or of sickness. Sickness like this one, a swift, wildfire fever, burning her to ashes.

It was sharp but short. Likewise Ismail's fear for her. He was the last man in the world to be overawed by a bit of fever.

But while she had it, she held him. She asked no more of it. He tended her with the gentleness that he granted any sick creature, with maybe a little more for that she was herself.

Theophano did not come or send word. It was prudent, for the child's sake. But Aspasia wept a little now and then, because she was weak, and because what she had done could not be undone. Mended maybe, with time and care, but it would never be what it was before.

Maybe now Theophano understood what it had done to her husband to send his mother into exile. Or maybe she did not. Aspasia did not know her, had never known her, not truly.

Did anyone know anyone at all? Even Ismail. He went about his duties as he always had. He tended Aspasia. He slept on the floor in the outer room, wrapped in blankets: as decorous as if he had never been her lover. Who would question it? Who had, when it was he in the bed and Aspasia watching over him? He was the foreigner, the infidel, untouched and untouchable.

They were not quite sure that he was human. Human was Christian, and chosen for salvation.

On the third day of her fever, Aspasia decided that she had had enough. She was weak and shaking still; when she sat up, her head swam. She took no notice. Weakness fed on itself. She would starve it to death.

Ismail was out, called to look after a lordling who had put out his eye, it seemed, with his own sword. Ismail had been scrupulously polite to the lordling's messenger, and nasty to Aspasia. She did not mind. It meant that he reckoned her recovered, or close enough; though he commanded her to stay put until he came back. He was muttering in Arabic as he left, pungent observations on the nature of idiots, idiocy, and edged weapons.

She dressed slowly, with pauses for dizziness. They were the clothes she had worn when she came there, but clean and smelling of sun. She knew where the comb was, and the little bronze mirror. She looked ghastly enough to frighten babies. Paint she could have had, if she had had the strength to grind and mix it. She thought of it, sighed. No. She would need all she had, to go where she wanted to go.

She might have been wise to wait a day, until the last of the fever had spent itself. But she had begun; she would go on.

She took her time about it. She rested often. People greeted her, some with surprise, as if they had missed her. Only one or two made bold to ask where she had been. She smiled but said nothing.

The city was restless. Nervous. Through the ringing in her ears she thought she heard people arguing. "The King of the Franks is coming, I tell you. I had it from a peddler. He's crossed the border and he's marching on Aachen."

"Rumors," other people said. "Nonsense. If the Franks are coming, why isn't our king getting ready to stop them?"

That silenced most of them, but a few were stubborn. "I know what I heard. My cousin, he lives near Liège, he was supposed to come for our Hedda's wedding, and where is he? You tell me that."

"Where do cousins get to when they've got all that way to come? It's nonsense, I'm telling you. There's no Frank here but his grace the duke."

His grace the duke would be incitement enough to his majesty the King of the West Franks. Aspasia did not shake her head, it made her too dizzy. She made her way past the palace gate, where the guard favored her with a grin and a deep bow, and turned as she had often turned, toward the queen's apartments.

Theophano was not in them. It was the hour for audience, which Aspasia had known and planned for. She changed her dress, putting on one more suitable for appearance in court, and painted her face with care. One of the maids was pleased to help with her hair; one of the silent ones, who spoke only when spoken to. Her stolidity was comforting.

Armored in woman's armor, with her pride keeping her on her feet, Aspasia took her place among the empress' women. There were glances, and some were sharp; but most of those in the hall had ample occupation elsewhere. The men in front of the emperor had the unmistakable look of townsmen with a dispute, but someone else had usurped their place: a weary, dusty, panting man who reeked of sweat and horses. "They are coming," he said. "My lords, your majesty, believe me when I say it: the Franks are coming to Aachen. They were right behind me. They almost shot my horse out from under me."

"It's dead in the stableyard, sire," said the guard who stood behind the messenger. "Arrowshot. God knows how it came this far."

"But how—" Otto was less surprised than bemused. "Franks indeed, you say? Not another pack of rebels?"

"I saw their flag, majesty. What's it they call the red one, the one that looks like fire burning?"

"The oriflamme," said Otto slowly, as if he needed to taste each syllable. "The banner of Saint Denis. Then it's the king himself. Plundering?"

"Not much," the messenger said. "They're just marching straight on. It's Aachen they're wanting. 'Take that for the noble Duke Charles,' they yelled when they shot at me, 'and his so-noble lord.' "

Otto rose. There was no fear in him that Aspasia could see. He looked almost as if he would laugh. "Oh, what a fool I've been!" He put off his crown carefully, setting it in the hands of his chamberlain. The mantle of state hindered him, dragging at him. He freed himself of it, impatiently. "We are invaded. Up, my lords. To arms. To arms!"

A confused roar came back. Otto's voice soared over it. He was down off the dais, in among his court, driving them in front of him. Women scattered, shrilling. Priests fled.

Theophano sat unmoving on her throne. Most of her women squealed and ran like the others. A few stayed, frozen maybe with fear, or refusing to believe what they had scoffed at for so long. Franks in Otto's kingdom. King making war on king.

Aspasia bent to the empress' ear. "Far be it from me to speak of defeat, my lady, but this is sudden, and ill done. Will you stay and chance a siege? Or will you go where your baby may be safe?"

Theophano neither stirred nor glanced at her. "If they come," she said, "I shall go. See to it."

Forgiveness, it was not. An empress used what she must use. Even if it soiled her hand.

Aspasia bowed to it. She did not say that she was close to collapse, or that Ismail would have her hide when he knew. No, she would not speak of Ismail.

The women were like hens at threat of a fox: all flapping panic and no good to anyone. Aspasia slapped one, shook another, snapped at a third. Once they were aware of her they left off their nonsense. She got them going where she needed them to go. They would never love her for it, but love was an irrelevance. "The empress needs you," she said. "Now go!"

They all needed a miracle. Otto had troops in the city, his own honor guard and the levies of those lords who were with him. But his army, the real might of his kingdom, was scattered all over it, tending its fields and recovering from the Quarreller's rebellion or warding the eastern marches against the Magyars and the Slavs. The western marches, even this contested duchy of Lorraine, had never needed an army to defend it.

New messengers came in as the day waned. Lothair had picked up his pace. By morning he would be at the gates. He had an army with him, thousands strong. Otto with his hundreds could not hope to face them.

The young idiots would have been happy to try. Otto,

though young, had lost his idiocy long ago. Emperors did. His bishops and his older lords gave him the counsel of prudence. Duke Charles gave him more. "I know Lothair," said Lothair's brother. "He'll outnumber you impossibly, and he'll crush you if he can. But he's easy to distract. Throw him a bone; he'll stop to gnaw it, and then he'll go away."

Otto looked around at the walls of Charlemagne's palace. The last of the light stained them as if with blood. "A bone indeed," he said, "and great enough for a mastiff. Pray Saint Vitus he chokes on it."

The confusion was indescribable. Half of Aachen, in terror of the enemy, wanted to join in the retreat. Every petty lordling and freeholder had his own orders, which he bawled at the top of his lungs. The streets were clogged with people and animals, carts and barrows, a whirl and tangle of torches in the deepening night. Anyone who had anything of value seemed determined to take it with him, no matter its size or unwieldiness.

Aspasia had the women in some semblance of order through sheer, merciless refusal to hear any word but obedience. Those who could ride, she set on mules or horses. Baggage was what each could carry. There was no time for fripperies, no room for anything but essentials: food, medicines, weapons.

Theophano, of all people, gave her the most trouble. She would not ride in her litter. "It's too slow," she said. "Too likely to be captured. That mule of yours that has such soft paces: she can move if she has to. I'll ride her."

"You are eight months pregnant," said Aspasia, word by gritted word.

"And healthy," Theophano said, "and in urgent need of haste. If Lothair has a hostage—if that hostage gives birth to my lord Otto's heir—"

"Better a live heir than a dead one."

"I will ride," said Theophano.

If there had not been that barrier between them, that cold distance, perhaps Aspasia could have swayed her. But what was done was done. The empress would ride. "And God help all of us," said Aspasia.

They mounted in a milling, shrilling, clattering crowd. Someone dropped a torch; it fell in straw and set it alight. No one had the wits to do anything but shriek, until a guard doused the flames in the oldest way in the world. The shrieks went up an octave. He grinned and swaggered back to his horse.

Aspasia set her teeth and fixed her mind on getting Theophano settled. None of the guards had the least idea of how to handle a pregnant woman. Theophano was not helping: she could ride if she had to, but she was ill-balanced now, unwieldy. The mule, thank heaven, was imperturbable. She would carry her awkward burden, and she would let Aspasia cling to her stirrup. Aspasia refused to consider what that meant for herself. She had to walk, there were no mounts left to carry her. Therefore she would walk. It was as simple as that.

At last they were moving. At a crawl, it was true, but it was movement.

The gate Aspasia had decided on was a small one, little more than a postern, and not much used. It would not admit a litter. That much she was willing to grant Theophano: the empress' stubbornness gave them a chance at a quicker escape. Otto, apprised of it, had sent word back that he would take the same way once he had settled what needed settling.

He was angry, the messenger said: his face was as red as the Frankish king's banner. But he was in control of himself. He would join his empress when he could. He sent her his blessing.

She sent her own in return, as composed as if she were not teetering on the back of a mule, and gave the word to advance.

The way to the postern was choked with people, but the guards beat a path through them. The gate itself was all but deserted. Everyone had gathered at one or another of the greater gates and left this one as Aspasia had hoped, nearly empty.

They rode through it in something like an orderly file. Guards first, for safety; then the empress; then her women. Narrow as the gate was, Aspasia dropped back, waiting for the mounted ones to go through. She was glad of the rest: though she knew soon enough that she should not have stopped. Her knees were determined to buckle.

A shadow loomed in front of her. It bobbed and danced in the torchlight. It seemed to have a hand separate from the rest of it, hovering in front of her face. "Get up," it said in a familiar voice.

She blinked. Ismail glared. His mare snorted and tossed her head. He thrust out a foot to go with his hand. "Mount," he commanded her.

Somehow she scrambled up behind him. The mare was not much higher than she was used to but considerably more lively; and less than delighted with the extra burden. Aspasia locked her arms about Ismail's waist and clung. The mare sprang through the gate.

Maybe she slid out of awareness for a while. When she looked about her, Aachen was well behind them, a shadow and a glimmer and a memory of tumult. There was a moon, which was well: they had put out their torches by Theophano's order, to pass more secretly. The road was clear enough under their feet. They stumbled only a little. They were almost quiet.

Ismail's mare seemed to have resigned herself to indignity. Her walk was dancing-light but she refrained from curvetting, and she had stopped flinging her head about. Her stride was surprisingly smooth. She seemed to flow past the shadows that were servants on foot, women on mules and disgruntled packhorses. She slowed as she drew near the empress.

Aspasia had not meant to be defiant. Yet she was that, and no help for it: riding pillion behind her lover, too weak of wit and knee to get off and walk. He took the place he always took when he traveled with the empress: at her right hand, alert to her every nuance.

Cold displeasure was not a concern of his. Her pregnancy was, and her insistence on taking the saddle. "You could have chosen a better time to study horsemanship," he said.

Theophano shot him a glance, a flash in the moonlight. "And when would I have greater need of it?"

"Necessity as a teacher is much overrated." He reached with breathtaking and quite characteristic boldness and felt her brow. "You're going to regret your stubbornness."

"Doesn't one always?"

There was a barb in that. Ismail took no notice. "I have my medicines. You have your prayers. Between us we may get you through this undamaged."

"So I trust," said Theophano.

Twenty

They struggled as far as they could, pressing mercilessly. But by the first glimmer of dawn they were still a bare third of the way to Cologne.

It was Theophano who called a halt. The riders, most of whom were seldom if ever in the saddle, were in pain. The foot-travelers were flagging badly. Some of them, seeing that there was no pursuit, had dropped back, perhaps to follow later, perhaps to take their chances in Aachen.

They had no tent: there had been no time to find one. There was food, Aspasia had seen to that, and water enough, even if there had not been a stream in the wood in which they camped. They dared a fire: they needed its comfort. "And," said Theophano, "every bandit in the countryside will have gone to ground for fear of the Franks."

She had kept up her spirits. She needed to be helped from the mule, but that was soreness only, she insisted. They made her a bed of branches and spread cloaks and blankets over it, and persuaded her to lie on it, but she would not rest while there was so much to look after. People needed to see her there, awake and in command of herself. It gave them courage.

Aspasia glanced at Ismail. He shrugged. What could anyone do? Theophano would not let him examine her. It was too public, she said. He could hardly throw her down and strip her. He watched her narrowly, alert for any sign of trouble. Aspasia would have to be content with that.

She was well-nigh done herself. She could hardly keep awake for the breakfast which the cooks, laboring nobly, seemed to produce out of air. When it came her turn to dip into the pot, she could eat only a mouthful or two. She went back to the cloak that she had spread on the ground near Theophano, and wrapped herself in it.

When she opened her eyes again, she did not know where she was. The sun was high, dazzling her. Voices shouted; metal clashed.

She started up. The Franks—dear God, the Franks had come.

Someone cried out somewhere past the camp's edge. "Hold, you fools! It's the emperor!"

It was. He was bone-tired, blood-stained—"Not my own," he said, sharply impatient—and in a rare and splendid temper. His face in the sunlight was crimson.

"The duke was right," he said when they had got him seated with a cup in his hand. A wolf-grin nearby was Charles himself, pausing between drafts from the wineskin. "Lothair took the bone we tossed him." Otto's voice rose. "He is sacking my city!"

"Hush," said Theophano. "Hush, my lord."

"He plays me for a fool!" Otto cried. "He laughed as he broke down the gate. He mocked us all."

"Let him mock, sire," Charles said. "He'll not be so happy now, with the trap empty and the quarry gone. You'll live to make him pay."

"So we shall." That was Theophano, sweet and implacable. "Our fortune and his folly that he lacked the wits to follow us. We shall teach him to regret it."

Otto nodded. His eyes glittered. His rage was no less, but
he was calmer. He took the food that was given him, ate it
hungrily. Soon after that, when his priests had offered up a
prayer, he slept.

Lothair had indeed taken the bone that was Aachen. He did
not pursue the emperor to Cologne. When they were all safe
within the walls, with the Rhine at their backs, word came
that the Franks were retreating. The sack of Charlemagne's
city was prize enough for any war. Otto, the message said,
had had his lesson. Lothair, having taught it, would return
to his own country.

"A lesson," said Otto, "indeed. A lesson in war." And he
ordered up his levies.

There was no dissuading him from it. An emperor could
not take such insolence from any king, even a king who was
not his vassal. Lothair had invaded Otto's domain, sacked
his city, made a mockery of his name. Otto would give him
measure for measure.

Theophano had no mind to stop him. She had not lost the
baby, but it was no thanks to Lothair. A fortnight after she
came to Cologne she bore another daughter: early but alive,
and seemingly as robust as her surviving sisters.

Otto was not unduly cast down. As soon as he was allowed, he went in to see his lady. He had a gift for her as he
always did when she lay in childbed. "It's not much," he
said, "but I'll have something better when I come back from
Francia."

Theophano smiled. It had not been a difficult birth when
it came down to it, but she was coming back somewhat
more slowly than she might. Still, for Otto she would put on
her bravest face. If he knew that most of it was paint, he did
not admit to it. He kissed her tenderly and bent to look at

the small red mewling thing which lay in her lap. "Beautiful," he said, as he had with every one.

"The next one will be a son," said Theophano.

"That lies with God," he said. He lifted the bundle of blankets and baby in arms grown capable with practice, and smiled into the small wrinkled face.

"Her name is Mathilda," said Theophano.

His eyes widened slightly, but he did not protest the choice. "A good name," he said.

"A queen's name," said Theophano.

Mathilda worked a hand free and grasped at air. Her father offered her his finger. She wrapped her whole hand around it. "Mathilda," he said, his voice warm and full of pride. "Mathilda."

The room was much larger when he had left it, with all the press of people who had followed him in, and half of Theophano's women gone with him. Theophano sighed. Her face seemed to thin, almost to fall in upon itself.

Aspasia helped her to lie flat. There had been no word of Aspasia's leaving her. Aspasia had been midwife to this second Mathilda, with Ismail there but forbearing to interfere. It was part of her training, he said. Theophano had been in no condition to object to their ministrations. Egregious sinners they might be, but they stood between herself and the dark.

"I wouldn't have thought you'd give her that name," said Aspasia, once Theophano was settled.

Theophano turned her head on the pillow. "He wanted a German name for her. It's less ugly than any other I could think of."

Aspasia smoothed the coverlets with care. "I hope it brings her good fortune."

"She should have been a son," said Theophano. She shifted restlessly, shaking off Aspasia's hand that came to help.

"My mother had six of us before she had your father. But she had him. Trust God to do the same for you."

"I am sick," said Theophano, "and tired of breeding daughters. I want a son. I want him with every part of me."

She was not in a mood to be reasonable. It was better than coldness, Aspasia supposed. "Then you will have to try again," she said. "When we give you leave, you can begin."

"If my husband comes back alive." Theophano shut her eyes. "Never mind. I'm tired; I hurt. I forget myself."

"One needs to do that sometimes."

Theophano's eyes opened. They were level on Aspasia. They remembered. They did not forgive. "But for the two of you I would be dead."

"Perhaps," said Aspasia.

The empress' brows drew together, strong and strikingly dark beneath her bright hair. "I wish . . ." She shook her head. "Wishing wins nothing. Go, let me rest."

Aspasia bowed. There was nothing else that she could do. Maybe it would do Theophano good to be alone, to think on sin and forgiveness and on accepting what she could not alter.

Ismail was in the stable. Here in Cologne it was like a cavern, a great stone vault full of clamor. The clatter of hoofs, the neighing of horses, the shouts of men, mingled in deafening cacophony. Otto was getting ready to ride, not direct to the war but back to Aachen, where his army would muster with the sacked and looted city to rouse it to a proper rage.

Ismail was in the midst of it, a turbaned head among the bare or hatted or helmeted ones, overseeing the saddling of his mare. He was not delighted to see Aspasia.

She was not delighted to see which saddle he had, and what was loaded on it. "Where are you going?" she demanded of him.

"Aachen." He set his own hands to the saddlebags, securing them properly.

"You are not," said Aspasia.

He took the reins from the stableboy, who ran off to help another man with his horse. The mare, strangely, was calm, as if this tumult was her native element. Ismail smoothed the mane on her neck and murmured in her ear. She blew into his palm. He walked with her toward the gate.

Aspasia trotted in their wake. Ismail had been acting oddly since he came to Cologne: almost shrinking from her. Trying, damn him, to do what he had threatened before her fever bound him. She could not feign another. There was no time, even if he could have been deceived. "What about the empress?" she half-shouted, stretching to come level with him.

"The empress will be heartily glad to see the last of me."

Aspasia got a grip on his sleeve and pulled him to a halt. "She will not! What if she gets childbed fever? Who will take care of her?"

"You will." He freed himself with maddening ease and went on, dodging flying hoofs and flying men.

Aspasia caught him again outside. It was hardly less peaceful there, but the noise was smaller under the sky, and this time she held the mare instead of the man. "You can't go."

"I have to."

"All the way to Paris, if it comes to that?"

"If it comes to that." He bit off the words. "The army needs all the hands it can find. Armies always do. And I can fight if I must."

"You can't go," she said again. Her voice was not too desperate. She was glad of that. "You can't just up and leave."

"I can do whatever I have to do." He pried her fingers from the bridle, not gently, but not brutally, either. "You need to be free of me."

"And you of me?"

His head shook, a bare flicker, as if he could not stop himself. "Allah keep you."

He was up before she could stop him, in the saddle laden with his medicines and his box of instruments: every one of which she also had, by his gift or her own obtaining. She could do anything here that he could do.

She looked about wildly. A horse—if she had a horse—

A trumpet sang. The emperor had come out. What had been tumult became pandemonium. She had to flee or be trampled.

Ismail was gone, lost amid the uproar. She could not even curse him. He would not have heard it.

Twenty-One

A spasia could have told Ismail how little good it did to sacrifice himself. Theophano was not interested in sacrifice. She saw the sin and the stain and Aspasia's refusal to repent it. That he was not there mattered nothing. If anything, it only proved Aspasia's obduracy.

It did, she admitted, ease the threat of further discovery. Her bed was hardly solitary, the castle was too small for that, but her bedmate was Theophano. A cool, distant, steadily recovering Theophano, who had ample occupation as Otto's regent in his absence. The more hale she became, the more duties she took on herself, the less warmth she had for Aspasia.

Aspasia had always thought of herself as sufficient unto herself. She was a philosopher of sorts and a physician of necessity. But she had never been completely alone. As a child she had had her father, who in spite of his imperial duties had always had a moment to spare for her. As a young woman she had had Demetrios, and at nearly the same time,

Theophano. Then when Demetrios was lost she had had Ismail.

Now she had none of them. Mathilda, whose mother took no pleasure in her sex, was too young to care for more than the nurse's breast. Sophia and small Adelaide were in Quedlinburg, safe from all these wars and alarms. Aspasia was alone, and she hated it.

She had ample occupation. There were always the sick and the halt, and there were duties in plenty for the empress' kinswoman. In this world of women and children and old men, she could be a great power if she chose. Even without the will for it, she had the skill and the strength, and often no choice but to use them. Ennui was not her trouble. Time was anything but heavy on her hands.

It was empty, all of it. What use to be a queen, or a queen's right hand, if she had no one with whom to share it?

She tried to turn to God. She went to the cathedral. She heard mass, and stayed after it as the silence fell and the incense faded and the shadows came down, filling the great empty space. God was there. The bishop had said so from the very altar.

Aspasia could not see or hear Him. The stain on her soul was too black. It blinded her to Him. Perhaps, if she confessed it . . .

A canon agreed to hear her confession. Maybe he knew who she was. Maybe he did not. He put on the stole and waited, his face falling into lines of what no doubt a pious person would call holiness. To her it looked like vacuity. What could she say to him? "Father, I have sinned these five years, sinned knowingly and mortally and joyfully with a heathen Moor. I would do it again in a moment if he came back to me. I cannot and will not repent it."

She mumbled something: plain sins, a lie, a trespass, a blasphemous word. Empty sins, which she repented honestly enough. He mumbled in return, blessing, absolution, a token of penance. Her soul was maybe a shade less black than it had been when she began. She still could not see God anywhere. That surely could not be He, whispering deep within her, bidding her keep the vow she had made to Theophano. *Where he goes, I go.* No, that could not be God. Quite His opposite.

She lay in bed, awake. Theophano breathed softly beside her. One of the maids was snoring. Mathilda whimpered in the nurse's arms, fell silent as the nurse gave her the nipple.

Softly Aspasia slipped from the bed. No one stirred. The nightlamp burned low, but it granted enough light to show her her shift and her gown, laid across the bed's foot, and her shoes set in a line with the others'.

She had not thought of what she would do until she did it. If they had not all been heavy sleepers, even Mathilda, she could not have accomplished it. With a bag in her hand, half full of necessities, she crept out of the room.

It was close to dawn. The cooks were up, baking bread. Aspasia coaxed a loaf out of a sleepy scullion. She added a cheese to it, and a pair of sausages, and wrapped them all in a cloth. No one asked her what it was for. People would suppose that the empress' kinswoman had her reasons.

The guardroom was less amenable. She had to wield her rank there. She got the man she wanted: a scarred and grizzled veteran whom the captain was not delighted to lose. The man himself at least seemed willing, and he saw to the saddling of her mule and a horse and their provisioning with water and feed. "You never know," he said when she raised a brow.

Aspasia nodded. That was why she had chosen him.

He helped her into the saddle, mounted himself. As softly as they might, they rode out of the stableyard.

Aspasia was a connoisseur of postern gates. This one came out damnably near the midden, and reeked of it. The mule snorted in disgust. Aspasia kicked her into a trot. A voice called from the wall.

It was not a human voice. It was a cock crowing.

There was precious little light to celebrate. The sky was heavy, pregnant with rain that never quite fell.

Very soon Aspasia was going to regret this. It was insanity. A woman alone, with one lone man to guard her, jogging down the road to Aachen. Ismail would not be there. The emperor's army was gathered and gone, bringing fire and sword into the north of Francia.

But maybe—

The rain began at midday. It was soft at first, hardly more than a mist. As the day waned, the rain fell harder. It soaked through the heavy wool of Aspasia's cloak. It turned the road to mire.

She did not turn back. There was nothing that she could do in Cologne that another could not do as well. No one needed her or wanted her. Aachen, poor raped city, might welcome her.

She was a little out of her head. Not with fever, that was past, but the mood that had been on her when Demetrios died was on her again. She did not want to die, she was not as far gone as that. If she could be somewhere and someone else; if she could escape from herself . . .

The road's misery was the price of her escape—her abdication, conscience might call it. She had left a message with the captain, to be delivered no earlier than noon. By now Theophano knew where she was. It was too late, she hoped, for pursuit to catch her.

Maybe the rain was a blessing. It would slow any force that came after her; and it would have driven the wolves of the road, four-legged and two-legged, into shelter. They met no one but a drenched and shivering penitent making his slow way on his knees to the royal city, and a company of mountebanks in a cart, who wanted to know if the empress was still in Cologne. Aachen was in sad straits, they said. The Franks had sacked it thoroughly, and then the emperor had stripped it of the little that was left. "He'll have some rebuilding to do when he gets back," said the woman who seemed to speak for them all, as she whipped up the galled and ribby horse. It laid back its ears and lurched toward Cologne.

Aspasia pressed a little harder after that. Her mule was not happy, but the beast was tough even for one of its kind. She promised it a dry bed when at last they stopped, and sweet barley, and all the hay it could eat. It flicked a long ear as if to ask why anyone should have to travel so far for such delights. She patted its neck in apology and huddled deeper into her cloak.

They came to Aachen as the light was fading. The mule's head was down, its ears drooping with exhaustion. The horse could barely keep pace with it. The riders were wet to the skin and racked with shivering. Aspasia suspected that her lips were blue. Heinrich's were.

There was a guard on the gate. The gate itself was broken, but someone had patched it: Otto's men, maybe, before they left for their war. The city stank of sodden smoke. Doors were broken, walls torn down. Here and there where fire had been, the skeleton of a house stood stark against the sky.

Heinrich touched Aspasia's arm. "Look, lady," he said. "Look at that." His voice was thick with more than damp.

Aspasia looked where he pointed. The chapel's dome seemed untouched, the eagle on it still, wings spread wide, glaring across its broken dominion.

Glaring westward, toward the kingdom of the Franks.

Lothair's men had done it, a last mockery before they went back to Francia. "His majesty will turn it round when he comes back," said the steward of the palace, who had greeted Aspasia with surprise but without excessive displeasure. "So he promised us. And will her majesty be coming, lady, since she sent you on ahead of her?"

"Not yet," Aspasia answered. The Franks had got into

the palace—they would have done that first, she was certain—but they seemed to have been stopped before they quite stripped the queen's chambers. The hangings were slashed or taken, and the rugs had suffered from blood and mud and worse things, and Theophano's beautiful silks were all gone. But Aspasia's own box had taken no worse than an axe-blow to the lid. Her clothes were in it, dry and whole and fragrant with herbs.

She wore the most presentable of them to dine with the guardians of the city, the day after she came there: her crimson gown and her veil with its border of golden eagles, and the heavy golden collar which had lain at the bottom under the plainest of her gowns. She was rather more splendid than the feast which she sat to. Provisions had come in at the emperor's direction, but they tended more toward necessities than luxuries. The wine was dreadful. She reminded herself to inspect the cellars, to see what could be salvaged.

She had not meant to take on herself the ruling of the city. But they all knew her rank here, and there had never quite been time to explain that she had come, not as the empress' emissary, but as a coward and a runaway. They seemed to ascribe her arrival, all but alone and in nothing resembling royal state, to an excess of modesty.

She sighed to herself. Was this God laughing at her? Ismail was not in Aachen, of course he was not. He had gone with the army. All that was here was more of what she had fled. And if she ran away from it, where would she go? Even she was not fool enough to follow the emperor.

She put on her court smile. "We shall of course inform her majesty of what you have done here," she said, "and when she is able, she will come."

They were pleased with that. Relieved; glad to have royalty to lean on when they had thought themselves abandoned.

* * *

The first thing that Aspasia commanded, once she had seen what there was to see, was the restoration of the eagle to its proper direction. She was not usurping Otto's prerogative, she did not think. The insult rankled too deep; the Byzantine in her rebelled. She sent a crew of intrepid climbers to the summit of the dome, and they coaxed and cursed and wrestled the great gilded bird back round from west to east, and bolted it in place. The next crowned trickster who took it into his head to shift it about again, would have to contend with iron bars.

She was scrupulous. She sent word to Cologne, formal and precise, of every order she had given and every step that she had taken. "I pay for it," she said, "on promise of your majesty's fulfillment, as the treasury of the city has departed with the enemy."

Bold, that. Theophano might send back an order for her to be clapped in chains.

What came back was not an order, but the empress herself.

She came in with her train which, if one had not known what it was before Lothair took Aachen, one might have reckoned splendid. She herself rode at its head in the litter which Aspasia had sent from Aachen, and although she was veiled, she had had the curtains drawn back. People cheered as she went by; she inclined her regal head and blessed them over and over as she rocked and swayed through the streets.

Aspasia heard it, a swell of sound drawing inexorably closer, while she waited at the palace gate. Everyone else had gone down to the city's gate. So should she have done, but she could not make herself go. The message had come a bare handful of hours before, and no word of it was for her. They had had time to prepare the palace for the empress, to air the rooms that had been shut, to set the cooks to preparing the feast. There was better wine now, and more provisions. Aspasia had made sure of that.

Now the empress was coming. People were singing, some

in German, some in Latin, a hymn of welcome. They were heart-glad to have their empress back again.

Aspasia did not want her at all. She would demand a reckoning that Aspasia had no desire to pay.

The procession advanced toward the palace, a triple stream, the court in the center and the people on either side of it, singing and shouting. Aspasia, alone at the gate, watched it come. Theophano had seen her: the veil turned toward her once, and held, before it bent again upon the crowd.

In front of the gate the procession halted. Theophano descended, graceful as she could never help but be. She paused for one last long moment to let her people look at her. Then on the arm of her chamberlain she entered the palace.

Beyond the refuge of ritual was a place of stillness. They came to it slowly. Theophano had elected to endow Aspasia's insolence with an air of legitimacy. She paid where she was asked to pay. She approved what she was asked to approve. She altered little except what her presence must inevitably alter. She said in front of the court and the city, with a fair semblance of warmth, "You have done well. None could have done better."

Aspasia did not wait on her in the evenings. The rooms that Ismail had used when he was in Aachen were whole and hardly touched, and the landlady was pleased to have Aspasia in them. Aspasia retreated there where his memory lingered, and slept where he had slept. It was brave of her, she thought. She had never been able to reenter the house where Demetrios had died.

There was no death here. That was the difference. The medicines that he had had to leave behind were still there, most of them, only a little scattered and trampled. She could work with them. She took measures to replenish what was missing, and when she could, ground the powders and brewed the elixirs for which people came begging. She did not ask to be paid, but people had their pride.

She was contemplating one such payment in mild dismay, one warm fallow-gold evening, when the summons came. The piglet had escaped its tether and made itself comfortable in the middle of her bed. It was clean, as piglets went. But her bed was hardly where she wanted it.

The empress' messenger was thoroughly startled to receive an armful of squealing piglet. "For your trouble," said Aspasia. "Go, tell her I'll come. I've somewhat to settle first."

What she had to settle was the piglet, but that was disposed of. Her mind was less simple a matter. She dressed carefully, painted her face, smoothed her hair as much as she might with no maid to help her.

Her majesty waited in a chamber which served for private audiences. Aspasia had expected that. She had expected the wine and the cakes, the careful formalities, the courtesies accorded a noble stranger. All of that was as she herself would have done it.

She had not expected to be so calm. Something was healing after all. She was learning how to be solitary. Hard work could do that, and time.

Theophano set her cup aside. She had barely touched what was in it. She folded her hands in her lap and looked at Aspasia. One could have called it bold, that stare, if it had not been so dreaming-soft. "I meant what I said of you," she said, "when I came here. You have done well."

"Even without your knowledge or consent?"

"You have always done what it pleases you to do. It pleased you to make this city whole again. I can hardly quarrel with that."

Theophano's voice was quiet, her face serene. Aspasia rid herself of her own half-empty cup and sat back in the high carved chair. "I didn't know what I was going to do until I did it."

"Your heart knew."

"I suppose," said Aspasia. She paused. Theophano said nothing. "I came here because Ismail had been here. I stayed because I could see no profit in following him further. He believed that we should honor your wishes. He was always a better servant than I."

Theophano neither tensed nor frowned at Ismail's name. She said, "You were never born to be a servant."

"God knows what I was born for. Not peace, I know that. And never sainthood."

"Nor queenship, either," said Theophano, "although you have the art of it when you are minded to try."

"No," said Aspasia. "Not queenship. I can see what needs to be done, and see that people do it. I don't take joy in it."

"What does give you joy?"

Aspasia had not expected the question. She looked at Theophano. Theophano gazed back, dark and soft. Slowly Aspasia said, "I like to play at doctoring. I like to mend what's broken; to heal what's sick. I like to read when I can, and think, and pretend that I'm a philosopher."

"Is there nothing that you love?"

"No thing," said Aspasia.

Theophano lowered her eyes. Her face was still again, like something carved in marble. "He left you."

"He is stronger than I," Aspasia said.

"He is wise," said Theophano.

"You understand," said Aspasia, "that this changes little. I will not marry again unless I marry him. Nor will I sin again, unless it be with him. You have my oath on that."

"I never took you for a wanton."

"No," Aspasia said.

The color rose in Theophano's cheeks. "Even with him. If he had been a Christian—if there had been any way at all—"

"It's done," said Aspasia. She was tired; tired of all of it.

"He's gone. I'm sorry I gave you pain. I'll give you no more. Whatever you want of me, ask, and you may have it."

"Is there anything that you would ask for?"

Ismail, Aspasia would have said if she had been a fool. She shook her head. "Nothing, except your forbearance. I never stopped loving you simply because I loved him."

Theophano was not ready to speak of that. Perhaps she never would be. She shook her head, slight and taut. "What is past is past. We have a world in front of us, and time. I should like to know that you will be part of it."

Aspasia could not speak. This was not what she needed, this stiffness, this groping for civility.

She rose suddenly, not thinking, not with her mind. She knelt at Theophano's feet and laid her hands on the empress' knees. Theophano regarded her with an unreadable expression. "My lady," she said. "Theophano. May we begin again? I'm a wretched servant, but such as I am, I give myself to you."

"I accept you," said Theophano. She took Aspasia's hands. Her own were cold, but warming as Aspasia gripped them. She drew Aspasia up and kissed her. It was a kiss of— not peace. But truce, and the beginning of acceptance.

Aspasia would have left then, but Theophano was not done with her. "I have been thinking," the empress said. "It's not fitting that you should be no more than my waiting-woman. You should have somewhat of your own: rank in this kingdom, and respect, and to be thoroughly worldly about it, an income." She overrode Aspasia's protest. "I know you have what you earn from your doctoring. That's little better than trade; if you didn't take such pleasure in it I'd call it indecent. No, Aspasia. I mean for you to have a proper position. Before I came from Cologne I settled your name on an estate. It's not large but it's prosperous, and it's only three hours' ride from Magdeburg."

"But—" said Aspasia.

"Anything, you said," Theophano reminded her. "Anything I asked, you would do. I ask you to take this gift. You've always cared too little for your own honor. It's time someone looked after it for you."

"But what would I do with an estate?"

"Manage it, of course. Look after its people. Do what needs doing."

"Are you sending me away?" Aspasia said it very low, almost a whisper.

Theophano heard her. "I am doing what I do with any other person of rank in this kingdom. I am giving you lands to administer in the emperor's name. You will have your duties to the court and the emperor and to me. You are still—if you wish—my servant."

Aspasia bent her head. She was no better than a child, fearing to be sent away when all Theophano wanted was to honor her. And never mind that she did not want the honor. Theophano would have known that very well. It was like her, to mingle reward and punishment, and make a gift of it.

"If I may serve you still," Aspasia said, "then I take what you give. Gladly—no, not yet. But I shall teach myself to be pleased with it."

Theophano smiled faintly. "Sometimes you sound exactly like Liutprand."

"It's my way of keeping his memory alive," said Aspasia. A smile tugged at her own lips. She did not want it, but it would not go away. She bowed, for the empress, and let the smile escape, for Theophano. It was like a candle in a dark place: faint and feeble, but bright enough for the purpose.

Twenty-Two

✦

The name of the holding was Frauenwald. It was a little over three hours on muleback from Magdeburg, a deep green valley between tall ridges, with a little river running through it. There was an oakwood at one end, where pigs grew fat on acorns. The rest was cleared land sown with oats and barley and rye and a little wheat, and pasturage for cattle and horses, and an orchard in a wall of withies that managed sometimes to keep out the deer.

Near the valley's heart, where the river bent round in a long slow curve, was the manor house. A palisade walled it, with a gate on the south side and another on the west, opposite the river, that looked out upon the orchard. It was larger than a farmstead, less formidable than a castle. The house within the palisade was built of wood with a steep pitched roof thatched with barley straw. There were two barns, each almost as big as the house, and a clutter of smaller buildings: storehouses, houses for the serfs and the servants, loomhouse, dairy, smithy, and over against the wall the odd wall-less roofs that covered the hay and the corn in season.

Aspasia settled in slowly, feeling her way from day to day. It was all strange, and its people spoke a dialect which she had to struggle to understand, thicker and slower than court Saxon. The house at first seemed dark and odd with its great wooden beams and its central hearth that vented its smoke more inside than through the smokehole in the roof, and windows only in the rooms at either end. Her own sleeping place was oddest of all, a steep-ceiled loft with the most intricately carved bedstead she had ever seen, and carved beams, and a carved chest, and carving even in the shutter over the window; and color everywhere, white and blue and red and green and even gold, like a page from a Hibernian Gospel.

"The old master," said Gerda, whose husband was the bailiff. "He was an odd one, and he loved colors. He got the boys to do the carving, and brought in his cousin who was a monk at Fulda to do the painting, and told them to do their worst. And so they did."

"I . . . think I like it," Aspasia said, blinking at the splendor of it.

Gerda did not smile. She was reserving judgment, which was her privilege: her husband carried the title, but everyone knew where the power lay. But her manner thawed perceptibly.

Where Gerda led, the rest followed. The free folk were big, fair or ruddy Saxons. The slaves were Slav or Magyar, smaller and darker and considerably dirtier until Aspasia had the bathhouse built and commanded that everyone use it. She was not loved for that. *Foreigner,* they all said in tones that said *Witch* and *Lunatic.* But she was mistress, and she was not above hauling a screeching, struggling rebel to the bathhouse and pitching him bodily into the tub. She had her way, however preposterous it might be.

Aspasia came to Frauenwald at midsummer. She left

again toward autumn to wait on Theophano in Quedlinburg. When she came back, she had a companion.

Princess Sophia was five years old that autumn, and precocious. It had not been Aspasia's intention to bring her away from the safety of Quedlinburg. But Sophia had had her own opinion in the matter. When Aspasia prepared to go back to what—somewhat to her surprise—she found herself calling home, Sophia announced that she was going, too. "I want to see your house," she said. "And your dirty boys. And your painted room."

Aspasia cursed herself for telling tales that a quick-witted child could remember. "You'll see it," she said, "someday. Not now."

"Now," said Sophia. She looked remarkably like her grandfather, and she had her grandfather's strength of will. "I am a princess. You have to do as I say."

"I do not," said Aspasia. "I am a princess, too, and I say that you will stay here. When you're older, if your mother gives you permission, you may come and visit me."

"I'll ask her now," said Sophia.

Whereupon, intrepidly, she did. Theophano, in the midst of overseeing the transfer of the court to Aachen, paused to hear her daughter. "I want to go," said Sophia. "Aunt Aspasia will look after me and give me all my lessons. I promise I'll behave myself."

Theophano looked from her daughter to her aunt. "Does Aunt Aspasia want you?"

"Aunt Aspasia," said Aspasia, "wonders whether she is fit to look after a princess royal."

"Did you say the same thing when you were presented with me?"

Aspasia drew a careful breath. "I was not the same woman then that I am now."

Theophano understood. She nodded very slightly. "Everyone changes," she said. "It's the world's way. Will you take her if I give her leave?"

"As I took you?" Aspasia asked, level and low.

"For a little while. Until I come to Magdeburg."

Aspasia bent her head. She was not forgiven, then. Not completely. "For a little while," she said.

Therefore she came back with Sophia and a handful of the empress' own guards and a maid fit for a princess, for Aspasia had none. They descended on Frauenwald like a flock of bright birds. Sophia in her silken gown was as splendid as a peacock, more splendid than Aspasia had ever tried to be, and royally imperious.

Gerda adored her. The lesser folk worshipped the ground she walked on. The children followed her in a goggling crowd, obedient to her slightest whim. She was appallingly spoiled.

Aspasia resolved not to be hasty. The child was a princess, and a Saxon princess at that. Until her mother gave birth to a son, she was her father's best hope of an heir. She was a very intelligent child. She was bound to know what she was worth.

Aspasia was neither her nurse nor her tutor. That privilege was reserved for a better Christian. Sophia was a guest, that was all. And one did not tan the hide of one's guest, however richly she deserved it.

"I like your house," Sophia said in the middle of the harvest, when even Aspasia went out and helped to bind the sheaves, though she had so little skill in it that the children outstripped her. Sophia, of course, did not do anything. She was too lofty for that. She sat under an awning and watched, and sulked because her devoted followers had to work in the fields instead of wait on her.

Aspasia took a moment's rest under the awning, all sweaty and scratchy as she was, with bits of straw in her hair and down her back. One of the boys brought cool water from the river. She smiled at him. He smiled back, but he was more interested in Sophia.

"I like your house," said Sophia, "and your painted

room. Your boys aren't as dirty as you said they were. Except today." She looked critically at young Rolf. Her nose wrinkled. "He smells," she said. "Tell him to go away."

He did not need to be told. His shoulders drooped. He crept away.

"That was not kind," Aspasia said.

"You smell, too," said Sophia. "You look like a common person. You're not a princess at all."

Aspasia stood. Sophia regarded her without apprehension. Why should she be afraid? She did not know what she had said.

That was well for her. If she had known, Aspasia would have slapped her silly.

Aspasia went back to the field. After a while Sophia's maid took her away, God knew where and Aspasia hardly cared.

They got the harvest in before the skies decided to open and drench everything: a miracle, and worth a feast. They had roast ox and new cheese and onions out of the garden, and barley cakes and a whole cask of ale, and apples stewed with a precious bit of cinnamon, that no one here had ever tasted the like of. Even the slaves got their bellies full; the dogs had all the bones they could gnaw, and the pigs feasted on the leavings.

In bed alone, for Sophia had the room under Aspasia's, less splendid in itself but furbished handsomely enough with rugs and hangings from Byzantium, Aspasia pondered the training of princesses. She had no mandate to train this one. And yet, having given the child over to her even for a month, could Theophano have expected that Aspasia would forbear to civilize her?

God knew she needed it. Aspasia would not say that Sophia was badly brought up. Unwisely, maybe. Incompletely. Will as strong as that, coupled with quickness of wit, needed a rare degree of domestication.

She stretched out, eyes tracing the intricate carving of the beam over her head. It was a dragon, she had ascertained not long since, mating with a sea serpent. The dragon was crimson, the serpent a pure and brilliant blue with a golden eye. Waves curled under them; clouds curled above, full of birds and winged beasts that transmuted into the branches of a tree, curving and twisting round the beam until it met the slant of the roof. She liked to imagine that the sea serpent was laughing at her. It seemed thoroughly delighted to be where it was, coiled in an inextricable tangle with the white-fanged, green-winged dragon.

Green was a holy color in Islam. Aspasia, on impulse that she almost immediately regretted, had had the doors painted green. Rolf, the boy whom Sophia had slighted so crushingly, was carving the lintel above the south door. It would be a plowman with oxen, he had said, and a woman on a mule, and something else that he had not decided on yet.

Aspasia rolled onto her face. She still woke up groping for the body that should have been beside her, narrow, wiry, not remarkably larger than her own. No word had come from him. For all she knew, he had not gone with the army at all, but had turned his face toward Rome or farther: toward Egypt, where he had always wanted to go.

It was over. She said it aloud, to give it substance. "He's gone," she said. "It's past. Ended. Finished. I had five years more of it than I had any right to."

Five years too long. She could not forget him in a moment, or even in a season. He had left her honor with her, and Theophano was coming slowly to forgive her. Sophia was proof of it. The empress would never have given her eldest daughter into the care of the egregious sinner that Aspasia had been.

"Damn him for being right," muttered Aspasia. "Damn him for being at all. If he hadn't—if I hadn't—"

She lay on her side. The shutter was open. It was a dangerous thing to let the moonlight in, and the demons that rode the night. They were weaker by far here than they were in Rome. Cleaner, maybe. Wilder. The breeze that crept past her face had a scent of mown hay and autumn flowers. She would get a rosebush, maybe, for the kitchen garden. There were beautiful roses in Aachen; the Franks had not touched them. She would have to ask for cuttings.

It was not as if Ismail had been all of life to her. He had been very little of it, in truth. A few stolen nights. More than a few days of learning what he had to teach. Most of what she was, was nothing to do with him.

How much of a body was the heart?

She rose abruptly. She was naked but the air was warm, only a slight edge of autumn in it. She leaned against the windowframe. The moon washed all the color out of her. If it could have washed thought as well, and grief, she would have been glad.

"This is what I have," she said, looking out over the shapes of light and shadow that were her manor, and the loom of the wall, and the moon-silvered fields beyond it. "This is what I am. This is what I shall always be." Mistress of this place. Servant of an empress and of her emperor. Teacher, maybe, since she could not help it. All of that she was born to, or had been brought to. It should be enough.

She turned her back on the moon. Tomorrow she would lay down the law for Sophia. Her highness would not like it, but liking was not what a teacher strove for. Or, for that matter, a mother.

Sophia stayed longer than Aspasia had expected. The empress was delayed: the army was coming back. Rumor was confused as to whether it came in victory or in defeat. Otto had swept through the north of Francia, driven Lothair back, plundered and taken lands and castles that owed fealty to a mere and secular king, but sparing in his piety the holy cities of Rheims and Soissons. Then he had come to the royal city, to Paris that had been Lutetia of the Romans, and with his lines of supply drawn thin to breaking, had turned back. Lothair, bold now that his enemy was in retreat, ran hard on Otto's heels, even caught him at one of the river crossings. But he was safe, with no more loss than a quantity of baggage and a porter or two; and Lothair had drawn off, forbearing to press the advantage.

"He doesn't want Germania, and Otto doesn't want Francia," said the messenger, drinking Frauenwald's own brown ale and taking his ease at Aspasia's table. "So honor's satisfied, more or less, and they'll think about coming to terms." He drained his cup and wiped his mouth on his sleeve, nodding approval as Aspasia filled it up again. "That's good ale, that is. You ever thought of sending a barrel or two out, to see what it'd fetch?"

"We don't have enough for that," Aspasia said. "Maybe in a year or two, when we've got another field cleared."

"You do that," the messenger said. He was at ease with her. She wore homespun wool here, because it was better to work in, and she kept no state, nor wanted any.

She had not managed to get Sophia into wool, but the child was sitting where she was put, and she had only begun to wriggle. Aspasia leveled an eye on her. She tensed to be defiant; was astonished when Aspasia nodded. "Yes, Sophia? Did you have something you wanted to ask?"

Sophia blinked. Aspasia swallowed a smile. Keep them off balance, was her inevitable rule. It was working not too badly with this one. Sophia thought before she burst out in questions; the question she asked was only a little haughty. "Have you come to take me back?"

"Well," said the empress' messenger, sitting straighter, plainly remembering that this was a princess. "Well, highness, her majesty did say—"

"I don't want to," Sophia said. "I want to stay here."

Aspasia would have wagered silver that Sophia could not wait to go back to her nurses. Sophia shot her a glance. Imp: she knew what Aspasia was thinking. "I want to stay," she said. "I want to see what Rolf decides to put in his picture."

"You can see that when you come again," Aspasia said.

"I don't want to come back. I want to stay."

Her voice was rising. Aspasia stood. Sophia checked, briefly. Aspasia took a deep breath and swept her up, silks, howls, and all, and carried her off.

The howls stopped almost as soon as they had begun. Aspasia kept going. People got out of the way. This had become a common spectacle. Most of them had even stopped muttering about it.

Aspasia dropped Sophia on the bed she shared with her maid. She floundered in it, struggling to sit up. Her face was scarlet, but her glare was somewhat short of murderous. She was learning; she was definitely learning.

Aspasia set her hands on her hips. "Well, madam?"

"I want to stay," said Sophia, not quite as defiantly as before. She tried a trembling lip and a brimming eye. Aspasia was impervious.

"I do," Sophia said. "I don't want to go to Magdeburg."

"We can't always have what we want," said Aspasia.

"Why?"

"Because God made the world so."

"Tell God to make it different."

Aspasia did not know whether to laugh or be appalled. This was not Theophano or even great Otto. This was herself to the life, heresies and all. "God made it the way He wanted it, and us to live in it. Even you," Aspasia said before Sophia could ask. "Even a princess."

"I don't want to be a princess. I want to stay here."

Aspasia sat on the bed. "I can see that," she said. "But you are a princess, and your people need you. Don't you want to see your father when he comes back from the war?"

"He can come here," said Sophia.

Aspasia drew her brows together. "What did I tell you about arguing?"

"I'm not—" Sophia stopped. Her eyes lowered. In a very small voice she said, "I wish I didn't have to go."

"That's better," said Aspasia. "Your father will be proud of you. You've grown up since he saw you last. You're learning to be a proper princess."

"Just learning?"

"Well," said Aspasia. "It takes time."

Sophia edged toward her. Not to touch, she was not ready for that yet, but she said, "I wish you could be my teacher all the time."

"Maybe someday," Aspasia said. "If you behave yourself with the nurses your mother chooses for you, and study all your lessons."

"That's hard," said Sophia.

Aspasia nodded. "If it were easy it wouldn't be worth doing."

Sophia looked as if she would have argued with that but thought better of it. After a moment, with careful politeness, she asked, "May I please go out now?"

"You may," said Aspasia, as careful as she, and as polite.

Twenty-Three

⊕

Aspasia did not go with Sophia to Magdeburg. No summons had come that named Aspasia by name; she chose not to assume that she was expected. She did not want to see the army come back. If Ismail was not with it, that would be pain. If he was, that would in its way be worse.

She stayed in Frauenwald, looking after the house and the holding, overseeing the fall sowing, readying for the winter. There was peace in it, and something remarkably like contentment. That would not last, she knew, but it was no trouble to her. She was like a winter wood, drawing its silence about it, but pregnant with promise of spring.

What she was gravid with, she did not know. Sophia left a space that wanted filling. There would be no child of her own in it. Maybe she would go to Magdeburg after all and ply the physician's trade, and wait on the empress, and be a part of the empire again.

But it was quiet here, and she lacked the will to move. She

let the quiet fill her. There was healing in it, the smoothing of wounds to scars that in time would shrink and fade.

The army came back into Germany after the feast of St. Gall. Aspasia had word of it from a rider passing through. The empress had met her emperor in Aachen and heard a mass of victory, though rumor had it that Lothair too had praised God for his enemy's defeat. Now they were coming eastward into Saxony.

On the feast of All Souls, everyone in Frauenwald who could be spared walked the path through the oak forest to the next valley and to the village there, and the little abbey. The abbot sang the mass in his sweet old voice, and his dozen monks and novices sang the responses, filling the wooden chapel with their chanting. There was a stone chapel begun, little more than a row of stakes and a prayer. It would be beautiful when it was done, the abbot said. It would have a marble paving on the floor, and windows of colored glass, and a relic of the True Cross that the Archbishop of Magdeburg had sent with his blessing. "You see," said Abbot Heribert, "how it is spring here; a spring of the heart, even when the world seems to turn toward winter. Old Rome is dead, but we shall bring it back again, more splendid than before."

He meant his abbey, which was growing from wood into lasting stone, and his Church, which was remembering its virtue after a long siege of broken faith and libertine popes. Earthly Rome was nothing that he troubled to think of. But to Aspasia, who was nothing if not a woman of the world, his words were like a cock's crowing. She was not ready to wake, not yet, but her sleep was lighter, and her dreams had changed. She was remembering what she had spoken of with Theophano in the City long ago; of emperors and empires, and making Rome anew.

It was still only remembrance. She went back to Frauenwald, walking in the company of her own people—for they had become that in her mind as, she suspected, in their own.

There were cows to milk, animals to feed, dinner to lay on the long table in the hall. That was real and solid and present. Dreams were for the night still, and for the dark before dawn.

After All Souls the sun went into hiding. It never quite rained. Mist filled the valley, turning it to a grey nothingness. Aspasia guested a lordling with his whole rowdy retinue one dank night, because they had lost their way in the fog and did not trust their wits to find Magdeburg. They drank most of a month's supply of ale, and ate an ox and a pair of sheep. She was glad that it had been a good year, or the manor would go hungry come spring.

His lordship was an acquaintance of hers from court. He had been in the war and was not at all shy about telling of it, particularly after he had got into her reserve of wine.

"And then we came to Paris," he said late in the proceedings, when the ox was but a stripped carcass and the sheep's remains had gone to feed the servants. "We'd sacked his Frankish majesty's pet palace, not far from there, but we left his pet archbishoprics alone—our king is a pious king, even when he's at war. And there we were on the hill they call Mars Hill, or something like it . . ."

"Montmartre," said Aspasia helpfully.

He nodded. "Something like that. We were getting hungry: we'd got plenty of loot, but food was running short, with no good way to get it in across the whole of Francia. We were about ready to go home. It's not right, you know, kings fighting kings. Fighting's for barbarians, and for lords who want more than they've got."

He stopped to drink from his cup. Aspasia waited politely, not touching her own cup. She did not remark on his conception of war. It was quite enlightened; almost civilized.

"Not that I don't like to fight," he said as if to defend

himself. "Fighting, plain and simple—that's the spice in life. But not when it's king against king."

She nodded. "And so you camped on Montmartre."

"We camped," he said. "The walls were black with Franks. The gates were shut and bolted. They had their oil boiling and their sand heating up. They were all set for a siege. And we got the word from the emperor. It was a good word, once we thought about it." He grinned to himself, remembering.

"We got up on the hill in ranks like in a battle, and when the signal came, every single one of us sang out together: '*Alleluia!*' I swear to you, the earth shook. God knows, Paris did. We gave them the whole trope, with the cantors holding and holding and holding, louder and louder and louder, and then—we stopped. We went down off the hill and rode away."

"Just like that?" Aspasia asked.

"Just like that." He shook his head. "I've never heard anything like it. Never will again, I don't think. You should have seen the Franks. Jawbones on the ground; every last one of them; and quaking in their boots. I think they thought we'd call up a host of angels and slaughter them all."

"It was better, the way you did it," said Aspasia.

"I suppose," he said. "They got over it fast enough. We had to fight our way back. If you ask me, I'd call the whole thing a draw. Lothair in Aachen, us on Montmartre: we came out about even."

"Ah," said Aspasia, "but he only turned the eagle around. You gave him the purest holy mockery, that he'll never in his life forget."

"Didn't we?" said his lordship, grinning again and looking round for more wine.

He left in the morning, not too eagerly. Aspasia thought she could see why: one of Gerda's daughters had a flushed and sated look about her. It was hardly for Aspasia to object, though she hoped the girl had got no more out of it than a night's pleasure.

The fog that had let up for milord Bruno's departure closed in again by noon, a blind grey wall of it. The eaves dripped mournfully. The women tried their hand at spinning and weaving, but the loomhouse was too dark, the air too thick; the thread would not spin evenly, nor could they trust the weaving. They retreated to the hall, where the men already were, mending tools and harness and spinning tales.

The women settled by the fire with bolts of cloth already woven, some that they had made and some that Aspasia had brought from her own stores. The fine linen was a marvel, but the length of silk struck them speechless. They all had to finger it. One or two of the men condescended to wander over and stare, then wander back. The children came to see what everyone was looking at. "You may touch it," Aspasia said, "but only if you wash your hands."

That got rid of most of them. They went back to their tumbling and playing, with one or two of the older children to keep them out of the fire. Aspasia, with Gerda and another bold soul, set to cutting the silk, then to stitching it. It was a gown she had in mind to wear at Christmas Court: plum-colored, with a pattern of flowers. She would embroider the edges, she thought. Maybe with eagles; maybe with something less obvious.

One of the girlchildren was tenacious. She sat on her haunches and watched, but did not venture to touch. After a long while she ventured a question. "Yes," Aspasia answered. "This is silk. It comes from Byzantium."

"What is it made of?" Gerda's daughter asked, plump rose-gold Mechthild who had so enchanted milord Bruno. She ventured a touch, eyes round with wonder. "How in the world do they spin thread so fine?"

"That's a great secret," Aspasia said. "But since you are

my own people and know how to keep your counsel, I'll tell you. No human creature spins it. It's the work of a worm."

"No," said Mechthild.

"Truth," Aspasia said. "It's a little worm, a moth's child, that spins a bed to lie in. That bed is the silk."

None of them believed her. Mechthild might have taxed her further, but Gerda's grim glance forbade. Mechthild bent her head over her sewing, cheeks bright scarlet. It was a long while before she said another word.

Aspasia shrugged to herself. She never forgot what she was. They did, often, until some strangeness reminded them. It was not grief enough to linger over. She kept on setting the careful tiny stitches in the silk, glancing now and then at the women about her, or the men in their own circle farther down the hall, or the children running everywhere. Quiet it was not, but there was peace in it. The fire burned almost clean for once, and clean straw on the floor carried a scent of sunlight under the damp. Wood, smoke, humanity, an overlay of dog and a whiff of cat, mingled in a pungency that was more pleasant than not. Aspasia breathed it in, breathed it out again. It would be time soon to think about dinner.

People came and went now and then. The hall was not a privy: on that Aspasia was adamant, and even the dogs had learned to respect her.

There was a sudden flurry. Rolf got a pup by the scruff of its neck and hauled it struggling toward the door. The glance he shot Aspasia was guiltier than the pup's. She bit her lip to keep from smiling. Rolf's voice came back, faint but clear. "*Not* in the hall. *No.*" What the pup said was inaudible.

She came to the end of a seam, bound it off. Johann the bailiff shifted in his seat, clearing his throat. The men began to rise, their minds no doubt on the milking and the feeding. Some of the children had arranged to disappear. They would be the ones with duties in kitchen or barn, and hope against hope of being overlooked in the confusion.

The door flew open. Rolf flew in. His eyes were wild. His tongue seemed to have forgotten its office. "S-s-some-some-thing—something—"

Aspasia reached him first. She was smaller than these Saxons, and quicker. She got him by the shoulders and shook him. "What is it? Wolves? Invasion? Devils?"

"Devils!" cried Rolf. "At the gate—pounding—wanting to be let in—"

And where, Aspasia wondered, had Stefan got to, who was supposed to be manning the gate? She snatched a wrap from one of the benches and a torch from the wall. It was almost burned down, but it would have to do.

People followed her. Gerda; Mechthild. Rolf, though quaking with terror: she had made him remember his pride. Not Johann. He would tell her afterward that someone had to guard the house. If there was an afterward. One or two of the men, and Gerda, had had the presence of mind to take up weapons: a cudgel, a rake, a pruning hook.

They were a grim army who advanced on the gate. It was solidly shut. Stefan stood on the wall as if to hold it against all comers, and glared out and down. "No!" he bellowed as Aspasia came up. "Not without—

"Oh," he said much more mildly. "Mistress. I was telling these heathen devils—"

Devils, thought Aspasia. Indeed. Stefan was a Slav, a captive in war; he had been as far as her City. He knew what he meant, as Rolf, poor yokel, had not.

She looked down. A dark face looked up under a dark hood: dark eyes, dark arch of nose, dark beard bristling with temper. No such face had ever been born in Saxony.

Her voice seemed to come from far away. "Let them in," she said.

"But—" said Stefan.

"But," said Rolf, "these are devils!"

"Only one," said Aspasia, "and that one I know." She spoke louder. Too loud, maybe. "Let them in, I said."

There were half a dozen of them. Servants. A pair of men-at-arms. But Aspasia was aware of only one.

They had the full rite of hospitality, with bath and dry clothes and ample provender. Aspasia remembered little of what she thought or felt, except the prick of anxiety. What ever would she give him to drink? He did not drink wine or ale. There was water from the well, milk from the cows. Maybe, if the cider had not gone hard . . .

It was sweet still; only the hint of a bite. He drank it. He let his cup be filled again.

She could not speak to him. She had the house to look after. Never mind that Gerda was quite able to do it. Aspasia was everywhere, overseeing everything.

Except Ismail.

Nobody thought it strange. They were all appalled by him. "You *know* him?" Mechthild asked, shivering a little. "What is he?"

"The empress' physician," Aspasia answered. The girl shied. Aspasia had snapped at her, not even meaning to.

Mechthild rallied at once. "He looks like a devil," she said.

"He is a Moor," Aspasia said, not quite in a snarl. She flung fresh loaves onto a platter and thrust it at Mechthild. "He comes from Spain. He has saved the empress' life more times than I can count. Mine, too."

Mechthild's eyes were round. A little later, Aspasia saw her talking to Rolf, and both of them gaping at Ismail.

He was used to being goggled at. Everyone did it, wherever he went. He sat by himself at one end of the table, with his own servant waiting on him and driving off rivals. In that place, among these people, in a clean white robe and a clean turban, he was perfectly improbable.

Her place was empty. She was derelict in her duty as people saw it here. If it had been Córdoba or Constantinople, where men and women did not dine together . . .

He would not say anything. He ate delicately, with his beautiful Arab manners. He spoke when he was spoken to, in his Arab-accented Saxon. He never once turned to look at her as she went about the hall, fussing and fretting and getting in the way.

There was no help for it. She had to sit. She had no appetite for anything except the wine. Of course it went straight to her head. Or it was his presence that did it. He was not supposed to be here. He could not be here. She would open her eyes and it would be morning, and she would have dreamed it all.

Everyone finished eating. It was proper for Aspasia to stay in her place and talk to the guest while the others cleared the tables and put them away. Ismail's traveling companions were comfortable: they seemed to have found common cause with some of the men, and the girls were interested in the soldiers, one of whom was not ill to look at, and the other of whom had a handsome set of scars. Got in the war, he said. No, not the new one; the one before that.

His voice filled the silence. Once the table was out of the way, Ismail sat as close to the hearth as he could safely manage. "This weather," he said, "would make a sea-devil weep."

"German weather," said Aspasia. "They say England is worse."

"Impossible." He spread his narrow hands to the flames, turning them, warming them.

"Did the empress send you?"

He did not flinch or start, or even glance at her. "She didn't forbid me."

"Did you see her?"

He nodded. "She's well."

"She didn't seem to need me. Or I'd have stayed." He was

silent. "All she had to do was send a message and I'd come. I didn't abandon her."

Aspasia was babbling. She knotted her hands in her lap and shut her mouth tight.

He sat back in his chair. He looked perfectly, damnably calm. It was the fire that made his eyes glitter.

"Why did you come?" Aspasia asked. Demanded. Hating herself for it.

"Where else would I go?"

"Egypt."

His head shook just visibly.

"Rome, then. Aachen. Magdeburg."

"You were in none of those places."

He said it in Arabic. His language, that they had made their love-language in this country where no one else knew more than a word of it.

She answered in Saxon. "What happened to my honor?"

"It is yours to keep," he said, still in Arabic. "If you send me away, I will go."

If . . .

"It was you who left," she said in Arabic. "Not I."

"I thought that I could be strong. I was a fool."

"Yes."

He looked at her. It was the first time since he came from the gate. She went hot and cold, and hot again.

"If you tell me to go," he said, "I will go."

"And if I tell you to stay?"

His cheeks were darker than nature could account for. "Her majesty said . . . whatever you do, short of treason to the crown, this place is yours. She won't take it away from you."

Aspasia was finding it hard to breathe. "Do you think that matters?"

"Not to your decision," he said, "no. To your peace of mind, maybe."

"There's no peace where you are."

"Then I will go," said Ismail.

She rose. She was suddenly, completely furious. "Don't say that. *Don't* say it. Ever again. Do you hear me?"

"I hear you," he said. "I won't leave you again. Unless—until—you command it."

"Then you'll never leave me at all."

"*Inshallah,*" said Ismail.

Twenty-Four

It was spring for Aspasia that fall and winter in Frauen-wald with Ismail, and after that at Christmas Court. Theophano said nothing when Aspasia rode into Magdeburg with Ismail, grey mule and Arab mare side by side in accustomed amity. Nor did Aspasia introduce the subject. The silence was eloquent enough; and Ismail's presence, unquestioned, in the empress' train.

Theophano was pregnant again. Aspasia would not have called her happy in it. But hopeful—she was that; and besieging heaven with prayers for a son. Her husband prayed with her more often than not. He had come back from Francia with a headful of new ambitions, foremost of them a journey to Italy. "It's time," he said, "that I looked after the rest of my empire. The Franks will keep to their place. My rebels are secure behind stout bars. The east has defenders enough. I'll cross the Alps come summer and remind the Italians that they have an emperor."

His Germans did not like to hear him say that. They

wanted him for themselves. "As if," said Theophano, "they could have the whole of him, and an empire, too."

That empire needed an heir. An heir could hold the title in one realm while his father ruled the other. Otto would not do to his son what his father had done to him in keeping all the power in his own hands and leaving none for his son.

"And why," Sophia wanted to know, "can't I be the heir?"

She attached herself to Aspasia at Christmas Court, determined to have her aunt to herself and refusing to be put off. Her mother suffered it. It made for peace, which was a valuable commodity, particularly where Sophia was.

Aspasia could not say that she minded. Ismail had bought a house in the city near the quarter of the Jews; seeing Aspasia in her manor, he said, had made him think that he should have a holding of his own. She was there in the nights as much as she could be, but the days were Theophano's, and increasingly Sophia's.

When Sophia asked her question, Aspasia was giving her a lesson in Latin and, incidentally, in conduct proper to a princess.

"Well," Sophia demanded when an answer was not immediately forthcoming. "Why can't I?"

"Because you're a princess," said Aspasia, "and not a prince."

"Why does that make a difference? I'm bigger than any of the boys, and stronger. Smarter, too. I could be a king. I'd be good at it."

No doubt she would be. Of all the kin and progeny of great Otto, she was most like her grandfather, and with her mother's Byzantine complexity on top of it. Aspasia despaired of convincing that imperious intelligence that a woman's body condemned her inescapably to a woman's place. "A woman can't be a king," she said. "It's the way God made the world."

"Why?"

"A woman is weak," said Aspasia. "She can't fight in battle as a man can. She can't rule as a man rules, by the force of his presence."

"That's not true," said Sophia. "Mother does it all the time. She doesn't fight, but then she doesn't have to. She has soldiers who can do it for her."

"A king should do his own fighting."

Sophia frowned. "Then that's all a king is? Somebody who fights wars?"

God forbid that this child ever learned the art of dialectic. She would be unstoppable. "Men rule," said Aspasia. "Women help them. God made them so."

"Did God tell you that?" Sophia asked.

"God told the bishops, and the bishops tell us. We have to do as they say."

"Why?"

"Because they'll punish us if we don't."

"Dear God," Aspasia said to Ismail in the warm haven of his bed. "That child would drive an angel to murder."

"She does have a rather appalling command of logic," he said.

Aspasia sighed deeply. "It is logic, isn't it? Of a particularly ghastly kind. It accepts no authority but itself. And it makes a dreadful sense. If a king isn't only a soldier, and if a woman's wits can match a man's, then why can't a woman be a king? Women do it, as she knows all too well: rulers in their husbands' absence, regents for their young sons, even queens in their own right, as we've had a time or two in Byzantium."

"So you agree with her."

"It's not that I agree," Aspasia said. "It's that there's no good argument against her. In a perfect world, in a perfect state, maybe she could be a ruling queen. In this one, her people would never allow it. They want—need—a man."

"There's your argument," said Ismail. "Not logic but necessity."

Aspasia raised herself on her elbow, glowering at him. "You of course are not about to deny that women are possessed of intelligence."

"Some women," he said. A mighty concession for a son of the Prophet.

Aspasia was in no mood to indulge him. "Most men don't have the wits God gave a gnat. They're bigger, that's all. Bullies."

His brows arched. "Indeed?"

"Not all of them. Most. Most women are idiots. And Sophia, drat the child—Sophia knows it. What in the world will we do with her?"

"I thought she was to go to Gandersheim and be an abbess. That should give her scope for her ambitions. Won't she be level with a bishop, then, and mistress of her own house?"

"God help the house," said Aspasia. She paused. "Yes, that's what her mother wants for her. I can't say I'd argue with it. They're not cloistered at Gandersheim. She'd be free to live as she pleased. Though whether that is at all a good thing . . ."

"Time will tell," Ismail said.

"I suppose we can pray," said Aspasia.

After Christmas Court Aspasia went back to Frauenwald. Ismail stayed a while with Theophano, assuring himself that she was well, then followed Aspasia home. Frauenwald was growing accustomed to him. They had stopped calling him a devil.

As winter passed and spring brought in the new green, Rolf set to work finishing the carving over the door. The woman on the mule was done, and the plowman with his oxen, and the oak tree that shaded them and the barley that grew under their feet. Now he gave them a companion: a horse and a rider. The horse was a delicate deerlike creature caught in a caracole, and the rider wore a turban above the fierce arch of his nose. He was Ismail to the life.

At the gate of summer, Aspasia left her house and her people and went to wait on her empress. There was another high court, another treaty made and sealed: this one with Lothair of the Franks, who had had the winter to think, and who agreed that king should not cross swords with king. He came to Otto in his own person, sacrificing his pride to do it, and proposed a resolution. Otto won Lorraine beyond dispute. Lothair won Otto's aid against his enemies in Francia, whoever and wherever they might be.

Otto accepted the bargain. He had the better part of it, and he knew it.

He conducted himself well. He demanded no more than his due, and he treated the Frankish king with unfailing courtesy. Aspasia was as proud of him as if she had brought him up herself.

Lothair went home, if not cheerfully, then without undue displeasure. His brother Charles, whose presence there had begun the war, remained in Otto's following.

"A good end to a bitter fight," Otto said, at ease with his empress and his friends in his reborn city of Aachen. Theophano had come to take the baths as she had the year before, because they eased her in her pregnancy. He was pleased to be with her, with no campaigns to beset him and no invasion appearing out of air.

Aspasia reflected that they had done well together. Otto had always been the fonder of the two, the freer with his affections. Maybe what he felt for Theophano was love, or something close to it.

Theophano did not share it. She liked him, Aspasia could see that. She had pleasure in the marriage bed. But what Aspasia had had with Demetrios, what she had tenfold with

Ismail, had not fallen to Theophano's portion. She was empress to an emperor. She was not, with it, a lover to a lover.

It was a good marriage, as marriages went. They shared what they had. They ruled together. They were in agreement in most things.

Not, unfortunately, in all. It came to a head when Aspasia was there, at the beginning of a siege of summer heat, wretchedly hot and wretchedly early: the scarce end of May. Theophano might have avoided it if she had been less hideously uncomfortable. Tempers were short as it was. It was too hot to ride, too hot to hunt, too miserably hot to sit in a steaming hall, sweltering in royal splendor, settling the affairs of an empire.

Aspasia, with Ismail for reinforcement, had forbidden Theophano to do any such thing. Otto had no escape. He came in from the hall, still in his robes, to find Theophano prostrate on a couch. Ismail had offered an expedient from the Arab countries: a fan as broad as the couch was long, dipped in water and hung from the ceiling, with servants to wield it. It was cooler, everyone conceded. But even with that, Theophano was anything but comfortable. Her thin linen shift clung to her swollen body. She plucked at it with rare irritability, wincing as the baby kicked.

"Soon," Aspasia soothed her.

Theophano frowned. The arrival of her husband interrupted her answer, if answer there would have been.

She was polite to him. She even smiled, if thinly, as he kissed her forehead. "Are you well?" he asked her.

"I am well," she answered with a hint of an edge.

Aspasia would have got rid of a lesser intruder. This one she had to endure, and hope that he did not linger.

He wanted to talk about affairs of state. He did not seem to notice that Theophano replied in monosyllables. He was full, again, of his Italian expedition. "In the autumn," he said, "when the baby is old enough to travel, we'll go south.

I've sent word to Pavia and Ravenna and Rome. They'll be ready and waiting for us.''

"With brickbats?" Theophano inquired.

He blinked, then he laughed. "I hope not. Even in Rome. You'll have to help me civilize them."

"I don't think that's possible."

"Anything is possible if we have you. Germany is in love with you. Italy will fall at your feet."

"Will it?"

"Incontestably." He glanced up at the fan and down at his robes. A servant hastened to help him.

When he was in his shirt, wet as that was and plastered to his body, he sighed and stretched. "Ah, that's bliss. Where did you get this marvel of a fan?"

"Master Ismail showed us how to make it," said Theophano. She shifted, uncomfortable. One of the maids fussed with the cushions. Theophano waved her away.

Otto ran his hands through his hair. It was thinning already; his beard was growing thicker as if to counter it, redder than his hair, almost fire-colored. He smoothed it in long loving strokes, plainly proud of it. "I've been thinking," he said, "that when we go to Italy we should pause in Burgundy. We'll pass through it, after all. It's only courteous to call on its king."

Theophano's eyes narrowed. "Only its king?"

Maybe he was not as oblivious to her mood as he seemed. Aspasia tended to forget that he was almost as clever as his empress. He was less devious, to be sure. But he was no innocent.

He kept on stroking his beard. "And maybe my mother," he said.

"She betrayed you."

"She made a mistake. I don't think she'll make it again."

"Can you be sure of that?"

"How can I know unless I test her?"

Theophano closed her eyes. Maybe it was weariness.

Maybe she wanted to hide the glitter of anger. "You are the emperor. You will do as you will do."

"So," said Otto. "And maybe we need her. She is still, after all, Queen of Lombardy."

"Queen," said Theophano, "yes. That first. Only then is she a mother."

"Is it not so with all of you?"

Her breath hissed, but her face was still. "I am your queen. She belongs to none but herself."

"Then we shall teach her to belong to me." Otto took Theophano's hands. They lay limply in his own, neither refusing nor inviting his touch. "My lady, I know you've never liked her. She's a hard woman to like, let alone to love. But she wields power that we can use."

"Unless she succeeds in using you."

"Not if you can help it."

Theophano opened her eyes. "You ask much of me."

"Because I know you have it to give."

There was a pause. Theophano's lips tightened, eased. She drew a slow breath. "If you are wrong in this, you could lose everything you've fought for."

"But if I am right," he said, "I gain more than I ever had before. She holds the key to Italy, as she held it for my father. We'd be mad to throw her away."

"Or to leave her lying about for someone else to use." Theophano sighed. "Necessity is a great tyrant."

"Only if you let it rule you."

"Wise prince," said Theophano, not entirely in mockery.

He kissed her hands and laid them gently in her lap. "No wiser than you, my lady. You would have come to it in time. See how quickly you saw it when I set it in front of you."

"Did you give me a choice?" she asked.

"You'll be glad," he said. "Someday."

She did not see fit to argue with him.

Twenty-Five

⊕

The summer's heat went on and on. Otto, in search of an imagined dream of coolness, took his court on a long wandering progress through the north of Germania. It was if anything more beastly than in Aachen.

Aspasia could not even take refuge in Frauenwald. Theophano was drawing close to her time, and she was more swollen and miserable than ever, and the more unreasonable for it. She would not stay in abbey or castle until her child was born. She was empress. She would ride with her emperor.

Otto was no help at all. He wanted her with him; needed her. He heard Aspasia, he heard Ismail, he heard every persuasion they could bring to bear. He looked at Theophano and remembered not a word of it.

"A little longer," he said. "She's a good month still from bearing. In a fortnight we'll stop. We'll be in Utrecht then. We'll stay there till the baby is born."

"Essen is closer," said Aspasia.

"Essen is a refuge in the wilderness. Utrecht is a city, with a proper palace. When we come there," said the emperor, "we'll stay as long as we need."

Aspasia bit back the angry words. Otto was smiling, but there was steel behind it. He bowed slightly in the saddle, dismissing her.

When the court was on the march, Theophano rode in the center of it. She had the sense now at least to stay in her litter. The curtains were up to catch what breeze there was: not remarkably much even in this relatively open country, a scattering of trees amid marshy meadows, and a stream at every turning.

She half-lay, half-sat amid the cushions, seeming no more wretched than she ever was. Her maids had a waterskin and a supply of cloths to sponge her with. People came and went with trifles for her to settle. She was always more patient than the emperor, particularly in small things.

Ismail rode behind the litter, looking even fiercer than usual. He hardly glanced at Aspasia as she turned her mule in beside him. "Wasted effort," he said.

"I had to try." Aspasia glared at the back of Theophano's head. It lurched and swayed with the motion of the litter. "He says he'll stop at Utrecht."

"She won't last that long," said Ismail.

"Don't you think I know it?" Aspasia was almost shouting. She shut her mouth with a snap. Much more softly she said, "Maybe she'll go into labor in Essen."

She did not. Aspasia did not like the look of her at all. But she refused to stay with the monks.

"Do you want to lose your baby?" Aspasia demanded of her.

She shook her head. "I won't. It's the heat, that's all. I'm perfectly well except for that."

That and the dropsy, and a flush in her face that was like

fever but was the blood seething high with all that she was doing to herself.

"You are an idiot," said Aspasia. "Are you trying to kill yourself to keep from having another daughter? What if it's a son? What if he dies?"

Theophano crossed herself, but her face was stony. "I will not lose this baby. I will bear it—him—in Utrecht."

That was all that she would say. Otto came a little while after, and she made herself charming for him, defying Aspasia with every word and glance. He was blindly enchanted and utterly in awe of her, vast as she was and—to him—monumentally beautiful.

When he went to hear the monks sing compline, Theophano heaved herself out of her chair and made her way across the little rough garden. She was supposed to walk as much as she could: it would help the baby.

The monks would not come to the guesthouse while there were women in it. The lay servants, such as they were, were at compline or gone about their business. If Aspasia listened she could hear the monks chanting, now in solo, now in chorus.

Theophano walked up and down doggedly. Aspasia sat on a bench and watched her. There was a whisper of breeze. The weather had been threatening to break for days now: clouds on the horizon, thunder rumbling away to the west, toward Utrecht.

Maybe tonight, she thought. Maybe tomorrow.

Theophano paused. Aspasia half-rose. Theophano went on. Slowly Aspasia sank down. She was all on edge.

She was no good to herself, still less to Theophano, while she was in this state. She breathed deep. If she could not gain a surrender, then she would settle for a truce. For tonight.

She was calm when Theophano came back to her. The empress sat gratefully on the bench and let Aspasia sponge her brow and breast with the cool cloth that had been waiting for her. "Do you know what I mind the most?" she asked.

She sounded like her usual self. Truce, then, on both sides. Aspasia dipped the cloth in the basin of water and herbs and wrung it out. "No, what?"

"My vanity. Looking at myself and seeing this shapeless mass."

"You aren't vain," said Aspasia. "Nor ugly either. A different kind of beauty, that's all."

"If this is beauty, then cows are the soul of loveliness."

"They do have beautiful eyes."

Theophano shut her own. "And they call me ox-eyed." She sighed. "I'll be glad when it's over. Completely over. All of it."

Her husband's bed, she meant. Aspasia said nothing. She had never felt blessed before. But to be barren, to have no hope of bearing children—that was also to have no fear of it. A night's pleasure was all too brief for what could come out of it: nine months' mounting misery, with agony at the end of it, and even death.

A man was brave when he went into battle. A woman when she went into childbed—brave was a feeble word for what she was.

Theophano took Aspasia's hand. "I know," she said. "You're afraid for me. Don't be. I'm well; the baby will be well. You'll see."

That, thought Aspasia, was how women could do it. Bright lies and careful blindness, and immovable obstinacy.

They left Essen in the morning under a sky that even so early was like hammered brass. They went as quickly as they could before the day's heat closed down. Theophano was determined to be well. It was all Aspasia could do to keep her off a horse. She did walk for a while. Aspasia, who had told her that walking was useful, could hardly give it the lie now. Within the hour, mercifully, Theophano consented to be helped into her litter.

She looked a little better, maybe. Certainly she looked no worse.

Toward noon the trees began to thicken. There was forest ahead. Their lodging that night, if fortune favored them, would be a little castle by a stream that flowed into the Rhine. Aspasia did not remember its name or the name of its lord. People here spoke even more uncouth German than they did in Saxony. It had strange words in it here and there. Viking words, people said, though there had been no raids here in a year or five. Otto had taken care of that.

Theophano was quiet. She seemed to be dozing. Aspasia watched her with increasing uneasiness. She was flushed with heat, but under it she seemed paler than Aspasia remembered. Too pale. Her fingers flexed in her lap, flexed and eased.

Ismail nudged his mare up beside the litter. He reached, laid a hand on the swell of her belly. Her eyes flew open. There was no sleep in them at all.

He lifted the light coverlet which she had drawn up over her knees—in this heat, when even the priests had so far forsaken modesty to as to ride or walk in their shirts or, brazenly, in their breeches. Theophano resisted him. He took no notice of her. His glance took in the spreading stain, and all that it implied. Her water had broken. The baby was coming.

"When?" he demanded.

She kept her head up, but her voice was low. "Just now. Within the hour."

"You fool." His eye found Aspasia. "Go. Tell his majesty to stop the march."

"There is no need—" Theophano began.

"Be quiet," said Ismail.

That shocked her. She obeyed him.

* * *

There was no good place there to halt, but people who knew this country promised one a mile or two farther on. Otto would have pressed the pace. Ismail snapped him too into submission.

It was, Aspasia reckoned, three miles or better before they came to a clearing broad enough for the empress' tent. Most of the court went on at Ismail's urging to inflict themselves on his lordship of the river and to send back what help they could. Otto stayed, with a strong guard and a priest or two and such of the women as might prove useful.

Ismail was as calm as he always was in a crisis. He would have denied that this was one. Women did it every day.

But not empresses, Aspasia was inclined to remind him. Not in a tent in the woods, with thunder rumbling overhead and the emperor fidgeting without. "If I could only *do* anything," Aspasia heard him say.

"Go away," Ismail said with rude mercy. "Pray. Rest if you can. We'll fetch you when we need you."

Otto must have gone away. Ismail came into the tent, looking rather pleased with himself. There were only a handful of women there, level-headed all, and cleverhanded. Aspasia had insisted on that.

He went so far as to smile. "It occurs to me," he said, "that this could be much worse. No hordes of milling courtiers. No cackle and stink. We'll be able to breathe."

Theophano laughed, startling the rest of them. "So you'll forgive me for being so stubborn?"

"That," said Ismail, "no." But he was not scowling at her. He looked her over carefully, nodded. "You'll do. Thank God, you're no delicate flower of womanhood."

"Macedonian stock," she said. "It's sturdy. I'm built for this."

It was still a terrible, wonderful thing. Every woman who came to the birthing stool looked death full in the face.

Aspasia, who had never borne a child alive, fought the long fight with her. The sun made its slow way westward.

The night came down. The emperor came and fidgeted and was driven out.

"One would think," muttered Aspasia, "that this was the first instead of the fifth."

"Men," said Theophano before another pang took her and robbed her of breath for anything else.

"There has to be an easier way," she said much later.

Ismail looked up from examining her. "If you find one, be sure to tell the rest of us."

She laughed: a catch of breath. She was exhausted and wringing wet. Aspasia sponged her down. Brave child. She was always light of heart and tongue just when one might have expected her to be sobbing and shrieking. She did not shriek. She shouted when she had to, to take her mind off the pain.

"I think I want to walk," she said.

They helped her up. She doubled over almost at once, but she would not lie down, nor crouch on the stool. "Walk," she gasped. "Walk!"

They walked, round and round the tent.

Thunder rumbled now and again. Aspasia noticed it in the quiet. No breath of air stirred the tent's sides or crept in through the flap. The maid whose duty it was to wield the fan had fallen asleep. Aspasia nudged her awake. She started guiltily and plied the fan with exemplary vigor.

Theophano lay on the cot for a while to rest. "I hope," she said, "that this is the last time I get myself into this predicament."

"Let's get you out of it and see," said Aspasia.

Ismail said nothing. He did not seem perturbed. Everything was as it should be, as far as Aspasia could see. But one never knew. It was so early for the child; please God, not too early for it to live.

The thunder was louder. Closer.

Something hissed. Suddenly it was raining: hard, black,

warm rain. It rattled on the tent roof. The scent worked its
way inward, rich and wet; but none of the rain itself. The
oiled leather kept it out.

Theophano breathed deep. It seemed to make her
stronger. She struggled up, wanting to walk again.

The rain fell. She walked. Thunder boomed full overhead.
Lightning dazzled them all.

They would take it for an omen out there. Poor Otto, afflicted with signs and portents, and no heir to show for it.

The pangs were harder now, and closer together. Aspasia
looked up, to find Ismail looking back. Soon. His face was
set, as pale as it could ever be. His beard was in a tangle. She
reached without thinking, to smooth it.

Theophano clamped a hand on her arm. Stopping her.
Bearing down. Yelling with the effort of it.

A thin voice echoed her: half born and howling lustily, as
if to claim the world without a moment lost.

Aspasia had it, wet and struggling, all but escaping. She
got a solid grip. It leaped into her hands.

"What? What is it?"

Aspasia hardly knew the voice, as raw as it was, away on
the far side of agony. She lifted the wriggling, wailing thing,
so small to have cost so much.

She laughed.

Ismail grinned back, white in his dark face.

Theophano crouched between them, gasping, beginning
to be angry. "It's another daughter. Oh, God, another
blessed girl. Another—damned—"

"Your majesty," Aspasia said, laying the baby in her
arms where she could see. "God give you great fortune. You
have a son."

They named him Otto. It was somewhat too much of a good
thing, maybe, but it had an ample precedent. His father was
beside himself with joy. The kingdom—his kingdom one
day, if God willed—rang from end to end with shouts of ju-

bilation. Daughters were worth a mass and a prayer. A son was worth a festival.

Theophano was richly and ripely content. Her duty, please God, was done, and she was none the worse for it. The son she had got out of it on that night of rain and wilderness seemed strong enough, if somewhat small. Puny, his eldest sister said. Sophia was not delighted to have a brother, even if there had been any chance in the world of her becoming king.

She would have to be dealt with. Theophano spoke of it after Otto's christening, when the tide of celebration had at last begun to ebb. They had baptized him for safety's sake, that night in Ketil forest, with rainwater and prayer amid a troop of grinning guardsmen. He had his name and a proper sacring in the font of Mainz at the hands of half a dozen bishops, with most of Germania crowded into the cathedral and the city.

Now he could settle to the task of growing into a king. "And his sister," said Theophano, "will have to learn to accept it."

"Acceptance is never easy," Aspasia said.

Theophano raised a brow.

Aspasia engrossed herself in young Otto who, replete with his nurse's milk, had fallen asleep in her lap. He liked her, the nurse said. He did tend to stop crying when she held him, though maybe that was coincidence.

She smoothed the fuzz of hair on his skull. It had been dark when he was born; most of it had fallen out since, leaving him ignominiously bald. He would be fair when he was older, or redheaded. She thought that his eyes would be dark. They were blue now, bright and endlessly alert. He was lively even when he was asleep.

"You're fond of him," Theophano said.

Aspasia glanced at her. "I'm fond of all your children."

"This one is different."

"He's a boy."

"Better?"

"Of course not," Aspasia said quite as tartly as Sophia would have if she had been there.

"And yet," said Theophano, "you never held the others as you hold him."

"None of the others was Otto." Aspasia rocked him. She realized that she was smiling. She often was, these days. Like a blissful idiot.

"He should have been yours," Theophano said.

"Then he wouldn't have been Prince of Germania." Aspasia shook her head. "No. He belongs to you. I'm glad to borrow him now and then, when it's your pleasure."

"Would you do more than borrow him?"

Aspasia stilled. "How do you mean?"

"Raise him for me. Teach him what he needs to know."

She meant it. Or she was lying more subtly than Aspasia had ever known she could. Aspasia met her eyes. "Am I fit?"

"No one else can do it as well."

It was not exactly an answer. "There is," said Aspasia, "a matter of sin and repentance. Or lack thereof."

Theophano drew a careful breath. "Ismail is part of you." That did not come easily at all, or happily, but as a truth which she could not escape. "The sin that is on you—it stains only you. If he were, if he could be, a Christian . . ."

"But he is not."

"No." Theophano's hands were knotted in her lap. She unknotted them finger by finger. "Someday, maybe . . ." Aspasia did not speak to affirm or deny it.

Theophano faced her fully. "Teach my son," she said.

It was the greatest gift that anyone could give; and the greatest terror. Aspasia looked at the infant sleeping in her lap. His mother had been much the same when she was newborn.

What was there with these empresses, that they trusted her with their children?

The elder Theophano had never been amenable to questions. The younger one would tell her to stop belaboring the obvious. Was it not enough that they trusted her?

Aspasia sat and rocked and allowed herself to smile. It was all the answer she gave; all the answer she needed.

III

EMPRESS MOTHER

Germany and Italy

983-984

Twenty-Six

✦

It was Christmas in Aachen, snow fallen in the night, the noonday sun blinding bright upon it: a splendid setting for the coronation of a king. The third of the Ottos, three years old, had taken the throne of Germany. He was to be the seal of his father's faith to the people of Germany, the elder Otto's promise that they would be looked after even as he occupied himself in Italy. There he undertook to rule and secure the greater empire, faded and shrunken but still wanly proud, the Empire of the Romans.

But even as the youngest Otto was set on his throne, word came from Rome: the emperor was dead of a fever. Italy had killed him as it had killed so many others. The heir, just now risen to the eminence of a king, found himself not only king but emperor, lord of Italy as of Germany.

A king's death was not like any other man's. Grief, yes, there was that, but beyond it a dull shock, as if the earth had shifted underfoot. Fear came soon enough, and watchfulness, and mistrust even of one's kin. Especially of one's kin; and all the more if they were royal.

Snow-clad, banner-brilliant Aachen was nothing like Memleben in the spring where great Otto had died, and Otto the younger had been little enough like his iron-browed father, but death made them equals: kings alike and dead alike, and mighty in their absence. But Memleben had seen a grown man, if a young one, move to take his father's place. Aachen had a child so small that he still on occasion wanted the breast.

"No throne as weak as one held by a child," Aspasia heard people say as she struggled through the milling chaos of Charlemagne's chapel. For once her smallness was an advantage. She could slip under arms, through vanishing gaps between bodies. She was trampled on, but not too badly. Worse was not being able to see over all the heads, to be sure that Otto was still where the bishops had left him, seated high in the upper chapel on the throne of Charlemagne. If he took it into his head to come down—if he tripped and fell—

The devil's own malice thwarted and slowed her, but she was stubborn and, when she had to be, ruthless. For a miracle there was no one on the stair to the upper chapel. She picked up her skirts, stiff and heavy though they were, and ran.

Otto was still there. He had had enough of being dignified: he knelt on the cushioned seat, leaning on the arm, and watched open-mouthed the tumult that roared and seethed below. The diadem, the only one of all the king's trappings that had been made to his measure, had slipped over his brow. His mantle was askew.

Aspasia stopped to breathe. Now that she knew he was safe, her heart was pounding fit to leap out of her breast. With every scrap of discipline she had, she composed her face. She smoothed her crumpled skirts, straightened her shoulders, climbed the six steps. She did not look down. That would make her dizzy, and not only with the height.

Otto turned as she reached the uppermost step. He looked as if he could not decide whether to smile or to frown. "Look," he said. "Look down. Why are they making so much noise?"

"For you," said Aspasia. He looked dubious. She held out her hands. He hesitated, but after a moment he grinned and jumped.

She was braced for it, or he would have sent them both tumbling down the steps. He was not a large child, but solid enough, and lively. He had his mother's restless intelligence and her great dark eyes, although his slightness was his father's, and his ruddy-gold hair, and his longish narrow face. Once he had greeted Aspasia with proper thoroughness, he wriggled until she let him down. She kept a grip on his hand, which he allowed, although he strained back toward the throne and the spectacle below.

"Come," she said. "It's time to go home."

His chin set. He clamped his mouth tight on a word that would, he knew very well, gain him one of Aspasia's scathing rebukes.

"Home," she said, quiet but firm.

With dragging reluctance he obeyed her. She took him down the back way, where his sisters and their attendants also must have gone. There was no sign of them anywhere in the chapel. The roar had abated a little. Someone was taking charge of it: a strong voice raised, commanding quiet, calm, a hearing for her majesty.

Aspasia was as reluctant as Otto to leave so fascinating a spectacle, but she knew where her duty lay. Theophano would take the reins of empire as she had been trained to do. The youngest of the Ottos, whose empire it was, was Aspasia's charge. As Aspasia led him down the dim torchlit passage, the roar of the crowd faded. Theophano's voice was too light and sweet to carry far, but her herald more than made up for it. She was heard, and heard in something close to silence.

Otto tugged at Aspasia's hand. She realized that she had stopped. Foolish: she could not make out the words here, however hard she tried. She looked down into the wide dark eyes. "Is my father dead?" he asked her.

She had never held with lying to children, even for their comfort's sake. The prick of tears in her eyes was surprising, and unwelcome. She nodded.

"Then I'm the king," he said.

She blinked. Sometimes he startled her with what he understood. "Yes," she said. "You are the king."

He thought about that. His brow puckered. "Did he die because I'm king?"

Aspasia's throat was tight. "No, love. He didn't die because you became king today. He had a fever, away in Italy."

"Will I have to go to Italy? Will I have a fever?"

A chill ran down her back. She crossed herself. "Right now you will go to your room and have a honeycake and tell Gudrun what it's like to be a king."

For a moment she feared that he was not to be distracted. He started to speak, stopped, nodded slowly. He was quiet as she led him away, back to his nurse and his honeycake.

Someone else was there beside the nurse, making short work of her storm of weeping. Ismail turned with barely concealed irritation. His face cleared as he saw who it was. "Thank God," he said, "that someone has a grain of sense."

"Of course I do," said Aspasia. She wanted to leap on him as Otto had leaped on her. But even if it could have been proper, he would not have welcomed it. She fixed the nurse with a hard stare. "Gudrun. What is this?"

Gudrun made a visible effort to compose herself. "Nothing, lady," she said with commendable calm, although she had to sniff at the end of it. The emperor had not been either the ruler or the general that his father had been, but he had had a gift of his own. His people liked him. Gudrun's grief was honest, which could hardly be said of the nobles in the chapel.

For the child's sake she mastered it. She took Otto in hand. Aspasia, seeing him well looked after, sent for the guard. He came in his own good time, looking as shocked as Gudrun. "Watch the door," said Aspasia. "I'll send men to relieve you. Until I do, don't move. Do you understand me?"

The man nodded. She left him puzzled but alert, and no doubt glad of something to take his mind off his grief.

Ismail went with Aspasia, not asking leave, not caring whether she minded that he took the guardsman's place at her back. In strict truth she did not. Ten years together had made them like two halves of the same almond. He would be thinking exactly as she did, and not wasting effort in holding her back.

She glanced at him as they strode through the rumbling, seething palace. He was not quite the same man whom she had first seen in Rome, in the pope's garden. There was grey in his beard now, and the hair under the turban was flecked with it. The lines were set a little deeper in his face: the long grooves that framed his mouth, the shorter one between his brows. He was still slender and quick, high-strung as one of his own horses.

"You think he'll try something," he said as they crossed an empty courtyard.

A flock of starlings chattered and quarreled over something in the snow. A bit of bread, Aspasia saw, peering through the tangle of wings and yellow beaks. They looked exactly like the nobles in the chapel.

"Cousin Henry will try something," Aspasia said. "This is what he's been praying for, and what his father prayed for before him."

"He's in prison still," Ismail pointed out. "Five years'

worth, and no end granted to it. His jailers won't let him out now, surely?"

It was hard to tell sometimes when Ismail was arguing purely for the sake of argument, and when he believed what he said. Aspasia stopped and faced him. "Who knows what his jailers will do? The emperor is dead. His heir is a three-year-old child. His mother is well loved, and anyone with eyes can see that she is capable, but can we trust these Germans to name her regent as they ought?"

"It will go as God wills," said Ismail. "Do you think there was more than God's hand in the emperor's death?"

"I don't think Cousin Henry poisoned his cousin," said Aspasia. "German hate is hotter than that, and cruder. Italy killed my lord Otto."

Ismail glared at the starlings. "I should have been there."

She swallowed the words that came flooding. "You are my lady's physician," she said.

"Yes." His face did not soften. "God wills as He wills. Our lady is going to have to be stronger than she has ever been."

Aspasia nodded. Her throat was tight again. Her voice was strangled. "His Germans have been unhappy, with him spending all his energies in Italy, and last year so terrible a defeat." Ismail said nothing. They were Saracens who had won that victory, Muslims out of Sicily and northern Africa, driving the German emperor from the south of Italy. "He tried," she said. "He gave them his son to be their king. But Italy was too strong for him. It's a pity he couldn't have waited. A year, even. Half a year. But this—"

"This is what is." He drew his mantle closer about him, ruffling like an angry hawk. "Shall we go wherever you were going? Or are you waiting for us to freeze?"

"I am going to strengthen the guard on my prince's rooms," she said, moving forward with dignity. "And to wait on my lady empress."

"Empress mother, now," he said.

She set her teeth. "Empress mother," she said. Making herself say it, once, for the truth's sake.

The empress mother came in from the chapel with all the pomp she was capable of, and a face like a marble mask. Matters were in hand. Messengers were sent, masses ordered, the people comforted. Just so was it done in Byzantium: promptly, firmly, and with dignity. The empire must know that there was an emperor still, however small, however new to his throne.

The hall was spread for the feast which would have celebrated the crowning of the new king. Some of the servants had begun to clear it away. Theophano stopped them. "We will dine," she said, "in memory of our lord who is dead."

The word, spoken in German, fell heavy amid the banners and the greenery. Aspasia wondered if anyone saw as she did how much it cost Theophano to say it. But it had to be said.

"He is dead," she said. "Proof comes with the Holy Father's legate, but those who run before are certain of it. My heart knows it. Let us dine now," she said, "and remember Otto of the Germans, who was Emperor of the Romans."

Twenty-Seven

The emperor who was dead lay in his tomb in the gate of St. Peter's, away in Rome. The emperor who was living waited in Aachen for the lords of his realm to name his regent. They were long days about it. Sometimes the shouting came even as far as the nursery. There was a broken head or two for Ismail to tend, but mercifully no bloodshed.

Half of them wanted Theophano. Half contended for Henry, no longer of Bavaria, held in prison in Utrecht for rebellion against the crown. Rebel and intransigent he might be, and Quarreller as they called him, but he was the child king's closest kinsman.

"Five years locked in the same four walls might have taught him the error of his ways," said Ismail.

So far the years had brought them: they had a house to go to, where they could be by themselves if they chose, and no one would whisper scandal. He huddled as close to the fire as prudence would let him, with his new book in his lap. It had come in from Baghdad, and purported to reveal all the latest advances in medicine. Aspasia, leaning over his shoulder, had yet to find anything that she did not already know, or know for false.

She folded her arms more comfortably about his neck and set her chin on his shoulder. He reached absently to run a finger down her cheek. "I don't believe," she said, "that anyone would be such a fool as to give Otto into Cousin Henry's hands. Unless it's Henry they want for king; for that's what they'll have, if he gets his claws on our princeling."

"There is the law of the Germans," he said, "which ordains that the regency be given to the nearest grown male of the blood royal. What he does with it is hardly the issue. A regency of empresses is a Byzantine thing, and foreign, and little to be trusted: much like our lady Theophano."

Aspasia nipped his ear sharply. "See who talks of foreigners! Can't you ever stop arguing all sides of a question?"

"No."

She came round into his lap, book and all. He cradled her comfortably. There was a wicked light in his eye. She encouraged it, but she said, "Phania is the only sensible choice. She's been empress in rather more than name since great Otto died; she knows what to do in this empire, and how to do it. What can Henry set against that? His blood and his sex, and a reputation for treason."

"To some of the lords, blood and gender may be enough, and treason is hardly that if the council chooses to ignore it. His majesty chose an ill time to die, with the east like tinder waiting for the spark, and the south overrun, and Italy more restless than ever. The empire needs a regent who can lead his armies to war."

"There are warleaders enough," said Aspasia, "and Phania knows how to rule them."

"Her majesty is a woman," said Ismail.

Aspasia sat bolt upright. He grunted. She had caught him

with an elbow. She glowered at him. "Do you know what I think? I think that all this talk of womanly weakness is just that. Empty wind. A man's lie, for a man's vanity."

"What, will you take up a sword and go to war?"

"No more than a priest would," she said. "Why should it matter that Phania is a woman? She's worth ten of Cousin Henry, both in and out of council."

"So she is," he said. "But men are vain, as you say, and Christian men have even less sense than most. If they would but yield to nature as God meant, without all this idiocy of virgins and martyrs—"

She stopped him with her lips on his. When she drew back he grimaced. She shook her head, not quite smiling. "Alas for my soul: I almost believe you."

"Your soul would be perfectly safe if you accepted Islam."

He did not speak with the zeal of a proselyte. He knew better. She looked into his face and thought how dark it was, and how fierce and how foreign, and how much beloved. "All this time," she said, "and I've never tired of you. Do you know how strange that is?"

"Most strange," he said, "and rare. Passion fades, they say. I say it when the young women come to me with their big bellies, and the boys who filled those bellies are long and uncatchably gone."

"Maybe that's what kills it," she said. "Children."

She said it almost lightly. The pain was old now, and long since beaten into submission. She had made the best of it. There were Theophano's children to look after. Children enough for both of them, Theophano liked to say.

Aspasia clasped Ismail to her with sudden intensity. "I won't ever stop loving you," she said. "Not though I live to be a hundred, and every tooth drops from my head, and I look the veriest crone. Will you love me then? Even as ugly as I'll be?"

"I shall hardly be better," he said, "at a hundred and

eleven." He smiled his rare white smile. "I shall love you all my life. And when we die, if God is merciful, we shall wake with one another in Paradise, and spend all of eternity together."

"Squabbling happily," she said, "with occasional moments of peace for variety."

"And passion," he said, "as often as we wish, for as long as we desire, forever and ever."

He showed her what he meant. She was delighted to be instructed. Thinking, when she could think, that there was something to be said for the Muslims' heaven. It was so much less work to get to, and so much less dull when one got to it. Which was heretical and sinful, and would damn her certainly, and she did not care. Muslim she would never be, but a pagan she was surely, and she was glad of it.

The lords of Germany ended their council at last, and named the Empress Theophano regent for the child king. It was no more than they ought to have done. Theophano, who had never admitted to doubt that they would do it, summoned Aspasia to attend her in the evening between vespers and compline.

It was snowing again, with a bitter wind blowing, seeking out every crack and cranny of the palace, defying any hearth or brazier to conquer it. Her chamber did the best it could with hangings on the walls and rugs on the floor and furs heaped upon her chair. She sat in the midst of them, her face cleansed of paint and her hair in two simple braids, watching as Aspasia came into the circle of firelight.

Aspasia did obeisance as was proper. Theophano drew her up and kissed her and made her sit in a chair but little lower than her own. There were furs on it, thick and warm. Aspasia burrowed into them.

"You look like a bright-eyed bird," said Theophano. She had won a great victory; it shone out of her, even through grief that was both deep and lasting. She beckoned. A small flaxen-haired maid brought wine steaming in a silver pitcher, and cups of chased silver.

Aspasia's had eagles on it. She traced one with her finger, shying a little for the cup was hot. "I'll never be fond of German winters," she said, "except as exercises in penitence."

"They are that," Theophano said. She sipped her own wine slowly, savoring it. "But think how clear they make the mind; how welcome even a little warmth is, how glad we are when spring comes. Life is all the sweeter then for the winter's bitterness."

Aspasia nodded. She could still blush a little, thinking of other warmth than that of spring.

Theophano watched her over the rim of the cup, melting-eyed, which meant that she was plotting something. Aspasia endured her scrutiny in silence. The scars were old that had been open wounds once. Theophano seemed to accept what she could not change; or at the least, to endure it in silence.

Now she was empress regent, and her power was as nearly absolute as any woman's could be. She might choose to act at last upon old jealousies. She could claim Aspasia wholly for herself in her son's name, and wield force of arms to assure it.

It was in her, that ruthlessness. She could not have lacked it and been the empress that she was. And yet, Aspasia dared to think, she was still bright-eyed hoyden Phania who loved her aunt best of any woman in the world.

Theophano set down her cup and drew the furs closer about her. Time and childbearing had darkened her hair; it was no longer wheat-gold but the color of oakwood in sunlight, a subtler sheen but no less beautiful. "I am minded," she said, "to send you away."

Aspasia stilled. Her heart was cold. "So. After all these years I'm to pay for my sins."

"Those," said Theophano, "no. It's not exile I'm speaking of. You know that I stand regent for my son in his minority. I've been advised that I would do well to give him into the care of a safer guardian than I could be, traveling endlessly about the kingdoms as an empress must, and caught up in the cares of their rule. A churchman, I think, can look after him and guard him, and educate him in proper piety."

There was no regret in Theophano's voice or face, no sign of grief that she must surrender her child so young into the hands of strangers. She was empress; she knew that her children were not hers to keep, only to wield for the empire's sake. Aspasia, who had no need to harden herself, clenched deep within. But her mind was as clear as it ever was. "You'll send me with him?"

"You," said Theophano, "and Master Ismail."

She could hardly have failed to see the light that kindled in Aspasia's face. She chose not to remark upon it.

Aspasia could not let it have its way. "Is that wise, my lady? One of us, yes, whom you can trust—but two of us will deprive you of anyone competent to tend you when you are sick."

"I shall pray that God keeps me in good health," said Theophano.

Aspasia opened her mouth to protest, closed it again. After a moment she asked, "Whom have you chosen to guard his majesty?"

"Archbishop Willigis would gladly do so," answered Theophano, "but I need him with me. The council suggests Warin of Cologne."

Aspasia considered what she knew of the man. He was not an impossible choice. He was younger than some, and well educated as such things were reckoned here; no scandal attached itself to his name. His see of Cologne was in the west of Germania, well away from the turmoils of the east.

"I am certain," said Theophano, "that his excellency will carry out his charge with all due zeal. But I should like my child to know more of his world than what is here in the west. Who better to teach him than you? Master Ismail will look after his body as you see to the welfare of his mind and heart."

Which left the soul to Archbishop Warin: hardly a small charge. Aspasia did not need to ponder what she would do. "You won't keep Ismail with you?"

Theophano shook her head firmly. "This child has to grow to be a man. I intend to do all that I may to make sure of it."

Aspasia could hardly argue with such logic. She bowed her head. "I shall do as my empress commands."

"Only for that?"

Aspasia looked up. For an instant it was Phania and not Theophano who sat there, neither child nor woman but something of both.

"And for you," said Aspasia, "as you know very well. And for our Otto. I'll keep him safe for you."

"God grant," said Theophano.

Twenty-Eight

The devil was loose.

Henry the Quarreller had escaped from his prison. He had gathered an army; he was marching on Aachen. Most of the council's naysayers had gone to meet him.

Aachen was in greater ferment now than when word came of the emperor's death. Theophano had no time to think, barely time to sleep or eat. If she did any of them, it was because Aspasia compelled her.

"Cologne," she said. "More than ever, we need Cologne, its walls and its army. We'll go that far together. Then when Otto is secure, I'll leave him to you and Archbishop Warin, and turn southward." She lifted her chin a little. "We need Empress Adelaide. She has Italy, with all the strength that it can bring to bear."

And all the rancor that she bore her son's wife. They had had their reconciliation, with the second Otto between them to assure that they did it. Then, wise man, he had given his mother the regency of Italy and kept her there, with rank enough and power enough to seal her loyalty.

Now Theophano must make firm that loyalty and use it in her son's name, and no matter that it was bitter to contemplate. She knew what was royal and what was necessary; none better.

Aspasia nodded. "Still," she said, "how wise is it? If you leave Germany now, you leave your place open to any who can seize it."

"How wise is it for me to send a messenger?" Theophano shot back, unwontedly sharp. "There are things that only I can say, bargains only I can make. And I have to be certain that Italy is ours."

Their eyes met. They remembered, both, how Adelaide had favored Henry's cause once.

"Not now," said Theophano. "God willing. That was before her son had an heir. Before we could offer her a share in ruling this empire."

"You'll do that?"

"I will do whatever I must."

"Then take Otto with you," said Aspasia.

"And lose Germany altogether?" Theophano closed her eyes. Her face was drawn and hollow. She had aged, Aspasia thought. Her husband's death had taken the last of her youth. She was still beautiful, but not as a young woman is, all curves and softness. Grief, care, queenship, had pared her to the bone.

She raised her hands to her face, let them fall. Her eyes opened. "Otto remains in Germany," she said, "where he is properly king. You will guard him. As shall I, until we come to Cologne."

There was no altering Theophano's mind once it was made up. Aspasia was losing her touch, or Theophano had grown too wise to fall victim to fine Byzantine manipulation. They rode to Cologne in the midst of an army, on guard day and night, and still Theophano was bent on leaving her son and going on to Pavia. No matter that he was in danger. No matter at all that the passes of the Alps were deep in winter's snows. She would go. There was no more to be said.

Aspasia had grown accustomed to the wildness that was Germania: the deep woods, the Roman roads, the rivers, the towns and cities set amid their circles of cleared land. It was not a dark country, and all the less so in winter, with snow-light even at night. Cologne within its walls, huddled on the banks of its wide and dreaming river, seemed as dark and odorous as a kennel; or a prison.

For the first time in her life she understood people who shuddered at the thought of cities. She envied Theophano, who lingered a bare few days, then took horse—breeched under her gown, riding astride, no time for the decency of a litter—and rode for Pavia. The city closed in about those who were left, and winter with it, a hard, killing cold without the blessing of snow.

Otto, thank God, kept his health, which was not always as robust as Aspasia would have liked. He did not pine unduly after his mother. He missed his sisters more. They were in Quedlinburg, with Abbess Mathilda to look after them.

Adelaide and young Mathilda were too small to care, but Sophia had been vocal in her objections. Her father had liked to laugh and say that she should have been born a boy. She agreed wholeheartedly. She had yet, at the advanced age of eight, to understand why her infant brother should be king, and not she who was so much older, stronger, and more manifestly fit.

It would be the convent for her, Theophano had long since decided. In the west, not all holy women need be nuns, bound forever to the cloister. Some might take the vows of the canoness, to chastity and obedience but not to poverty; to live within the walls of a convent but to be free to travel beyond them with one's servants and one's household and all that made one worthy in the world. It was hardly a life

for a saint, but for a princess there was much to be said for
it. Aspasia might even now and then have been tempted, if
she had not had Ismail.

She had taken to walking the walls of the city. It was the
only way she could breathe, the only time she could trust
herself away from Otto. Archbishop Warin was unfailingly
polite, but she knew that he thought her a fool.

"A broody hen," Ismail corrected her with infuriating
precision.

She bared her teeth at him. "And who is only here because his majesty is?"

His majesty, bundled in furs until he looked like a bear-
cub, tugged at his nurse's hand, begging her to walk faster.
One of the guardsmen laughed suddenly and swept him
onto a burly shoulder, to his delight.

Aspasia found that her snarl had melted into a smile. Ismail was incapable of it. All that she could see of him was
the tip of his nose, rubbed raw by the wind, and the end of
his beard. The rest of him was lost in a vast mantle of black
wool and bearskin. "You should go in," she said. "He's safe
enough up here; I won't keep him out long."

The bearskin growled in most lifelike fashion. She
laughed, startling herself. How long had it been since she
did any such thing?

Otto rode his guardsman like a horse, and very well too,
as he had seen the men do.

"When this is over," Aspasia said, "we'll have to gather a
troop of fosterlings. Children learn better when they're in
company; and a king should have friends who've known
him from his childhood, whom he can trust."

"You expect this ever to be over?" Ismail paused in an
angle of the wall, where a tower cut off the wind, and the sun
offered a feeble likeness of warmth. They could see the river,
broad and black and edged with ice, and an expanse of
wind-scoured field, and an outrider of forest.

Aspasia stood a little closer to him. She could not do what

she wanted, which was to slip under his mantle and warm him with her body. Later. Someday. There was no place for them here, with every cranny full of soldiers, and the bishop's servants everywhere one looked. "Everything ends," she said. "Even German winter."

"Yes, and what will that end see?"

It was the cold that made his mood so black. And, maybe, want of her. She was as given as the next woman to flattering herself unduly.

Otto rode toward her on his grinning mount. He leaped down into her arms, and for once did not want to slide the rest of the way to the ground. His cheeks were scarlet; his eyes sparkled. "Look!" he said. "Out there. Men on horses. I'm going to have a horse. Otric said so."

Aspasia had smiled and said something appropriately indulgent, before it struck her. She turned with him in her arms. Men indeed, and horses, riding out of the wood, spreading over the open spaces. Sunlight, grown suddenly bitter, flashed on helmet and spearpoint. The wind caught the brightness of banners. Above them all rose the dragon of the Franks and the eagle of the empire.

For a witless instant she thought that Theophano, a bare fortnight gone, had come back with all Italy behind her. But that was no woman under the banner. Armored, helmeted, still he was not to be mistaken. Henry the Quarreller had brought his quarrel to Cologne.

Aspasia did not see why everyone was so shocked. Of course Henry had come here. Henry was many things, few of which had anything to do with virtue, but he had never been an idiot. He could see what was perfectly obvious to anyone with eyes. There was Germany, which he wanted. There was Otto, mewed up in Cologne, with his mother fled away to Italy. Otto, crowned king of the Germans, Germania in the flesh. Who held him, held the empire.

Aspasia had heard of sieges; read of them, often. She had

not known what it would be like to live in one. Starvation was far away yet, and they had been shut up in the city since they came there, but to look out past the walls and see the army camped beyond them with its engines drawn up—that was different.

They began the dance with a herald's voice bellowing his master's terms. Those were simple enough. The city held the imperial regalia and the child who was entitled to them. Henry—they called him Duke Henry, as if Bavaria were still his by right—would take them. If they were given him promptly, he would spare the city. If they were not, he would sack it.

Cologne returned no answer. Archbishop Warin was in the cathedral saying mass. The emperor was in the nursery where it was warm, being read to sleep. Like his sister who had died, he loved to hear the sound of Arabic; it could soothe him when nothing else would.

The army, ignored, settled into its encampment. They set up their engines. In the morning they began to hurl stones at the walls. Archers stood on the walls, but there was little to shoot at: the camp was just out of range, the engines warded with shields. Aspasia would have welcomed a jar or two of Greek fire. Lacking that, they could do little more than wait, and endure the crashing of stone on stone, and wish for a good swift battle.

The life of the city went on much as it always had. After the first day or two, one grew accustomed to the sound of falling stones. Otto could not go up on the walls again, rare target that he would be, but there was city enough for him to play in, and his presence seemed to cheer the people who saw him.

He was happy enough. Aspasia determined to be content with that; and prayed that Theophano would come soon.

She was dreaming of Demetrios again: dreams which she had thought long banished. Over and over she lay as she had lain that bitter winter's night, saw the Varangians in her chamber, heard the sound of their axes hewing him down.

This time she did not wake screaming. Otto slept with the same restless energy he showed when he was awake. Gudrun snored gently. Ismail was close, across the passage. She took what comfort she could in their presence.

Five nights now. She lay trembling, fists clenched over the knot in her belly, and tried to breathe quietly. There was a dull throbbing behind her eyes: remembrance of the wine that she had drunk before she slept, in a futile effort to drown the dream.

She rose softly. Gudrun never stirred. Otto sprawled across the warm hollow where she had been. She drew on her robe, paused to light a taper from the lamp beside the bed, slipped out into the passage.

No one stirred. There were no guards at the doors, no monks stumbling sleepily to the night office.

Ismail had a cell to himself. No one in so ecclesiastical a city would share a bed with an infidel, and the servants had quarters of their own below.

He was asleep with his sometime companion, the large harlequin cat that belonged nominally to the archbishop, curled in the hollow of his belly. It opened a sleepy eye as she approached, and began to purr.

There was just room enough on the pallet for Aspasia. She fitted her front to his back, breathing in his scent. The cat, rousing, made its way up the ridge of his side to spread itself above their heads. Its purring rumbled in her skull.

Ismail neither moved nor tensed, but she knew that he was awake. She slid her hand down to the warmest part of him. It woke to her touch.

His voice was hardly louder than the cat's purr. "You shouldn't have come here."

"I know." She realized that her cheeks were cold. Wet. When had the tears fallen?

He turned in the circle of her arms. His frown did not fade, but his voice was gentler. "Dreams?" he asked her.

She nodded.

He dried her cheeks with the edge of the innermost coverlet and kissed her softly.

"I thought I was braver," she said, "or more sensible. We're in no danger. Cologne is strong, and provisioned for years of siege. That's why the empress chose it. She'll be here long before the year is up, with the army of the empire behind her, to drive this dog back to his kennel."

"The heart is seldom sensible," said Ismail. He smoothed her hair away from her face. "My lord archbishop would be rather less than delighted to find you here."

Even now Aspasia could smile at that. "Wouldn't he?" She shifted closer, body to body. He was hard and lean and furnace-warm. She ran her hands up and down his back where the skin was as smooth as a boy's, and sank her teeth gently into his shoulder.

They made love slowly at first, then more quickly. Half of Aspasia was caught up in it. The rest of her would settle on no one thought, but leaped from Otto to Demetrios to the archbishop to the camp outside the walls, then back into the city and the palace and this small chilly cell with the cat asleep at the bed's head.

Ismail's breath caught; his body stiffened. She held him inside her, legs wound about his middle, for as long as she could. As if he were a talisman; as if he could guard her against the dark and the fear and the sound of axes.

After that they shared the nights. Aspasia did not go to his bed until all was quiet; she left it always before the bell rang for matins. She did not dream again, except of harmless things.

On the tenth night of the siege, she was almost light of heart. She slept more deeply than she had in too long a while, a sleep without dreams.

The cat woke her, purring against her cheek. Wan grey light crept into the room. She sat up in shock.

"Good morning, my lady," said Henry of Bavaria.

He was in armor with his helmet under his arm. Years in captivity had thickened his body, thinned his hair; as if to make up for the latter, he had grown a rather impressive beard. It was red as his imperial cousin's had been, though his hair was still straw-fair. His smile was wide. No doubt he thought it wolfish.

Aspasia reached with dignity to draw the coverlet over her breasts. Ismail seemed deep asleep. She made no move to wake him. "Good morning," she said, "my lord. How did you take the city?"

"Bloodlessly," he said. He stepped into the room. Archbishop Warin peered over his shoulder. There were others behind him.

Aspasia smiled sweetly at them all. "Ah," she said. "I see. Treachery."

"Or loyalty." Henry held out his hand.

She ignored it, rising unaided, drawing with her the topmost blanket. No doubt she looked appalling with her hair tumbling wherever it would and her face still full of sleep: an aging, raddled wanton who lacked the sense to be afraid. She wrapped the blanket about herself and raised her chin. "I suppose you've come for his majesty."

"Wise lady," said Henry. His admiration seemed genuine even through the mockery.

This time she let him take her hand. She watched him consider pulling her to him.

"I would not," Ismail said gently, "if I were you."

She glanced back. He lay on his side, propped up on his elbow. There was no sleep in his eyes.

Aspasia closed her own. He was half the Saxon's size, naked and unarmed. *Dear God,* she prayed. *Don't let them fight.*

Henry laughed, but he let go Aspasia's hand. "Will it please your highness to conduct us to his majesty?"

She could refuse. Oh, easily. Let him find his own way across the passage, make his own peace with a startled and cross-grained young emperor.

But she had her pride, and she loved her princeling. He would be terrified if he woke to strange faces, loud voices, men in armor.

She swept past the rebel and the bishop into a corridor full of armed men. They goggled at her. The bishop muttered something that sounded like a curse.

At least they had not invaded Otto's chamber. Gudrun was still asleep. Otto was up with his tunic on backwards, playing on the floor with his army of wooden knights. He greeted Aspasia gravely. "There are men outside," he said. "Are they going to fight?"

"Not now," she said. She took time to dress and to put her hair in order, and to do the same for Otto. "Your cousin Henry is here. He wants to see you."

Otto frowned. He knew all about Cousin Henry. "Will he take me away?"

So clear, children's sight could be. Aspasia swallowed past the ache in her throat. "I don't know. I think so."

"I don't want to go," he said.

"We can't always have what we want." Aspasia took his hand. He did not try to escape her. He would howl, his face said, if he had to; but first he wanted to see what there was to see.

He liked all the men in armor. Cousin Henry frightened him a little, but he only stood the straighter for it, meeting the blue eyes with his brown ones and keeping his head up as a king should. Henry seemed somewhat disconcerted. He tried a hearty manner, a ruffle of the curls which Aspasia had combed so carefully. Otto did not duck or frown, but his stare was quellingly steady.

Henry's hand fell. "So," he said. "Well. This is the king's majesty. A fine little man."

Aspasia would have laughed if she had dared. Henry's men looked as uncomfortable as their lord. There was much shuffling of feet and rattling of weapons.

Henry sat on his haunches and offered the child his best smile. "Would you like to come riding with me?"

"On a horse?" Otto asked.

"On a warhorse."

Otto thought about it. "Can I hold the reins?"

Someone laughed. Henry grinned. "A rider, are you, then?"

"I rode here," said Otto, "on Master Ismail's horse. He let me hold the reins. His horse is better than yours. She's better than anybody's."

"No doubt she is," Henry said. He straightened in a creaking of leather and mail. He cocked his head toward one of the soldiers. "Marbod. Look after him."

Aspasia set herself between the child and the soldier. "I'll tend him. Go now, do whatever else you need to do. We'll be ready in an hour."

"Half an hour," said Henry.

"An hour." She herded Otto in front of her. Henry's men parted to let her by. One of them fell in behind. She took no notice.

She took the full hour, though she could easily have done it in a quarter of the time. She set the startled and stumbling Gudrun to packing all their belongings, and sent someone to fetch breakfast. Otto did not want to eat; she made him choke down a bite or two. Excitement had caught hold of him. "I'll ride a horse," he said. "All by myself."

"Not by yourself," she said, but he was not listening. Her lips kept going tight; her throat kept closing. Treachery did that to her. It would be a miracle if she could keep from spitting at his most loyal excellency the archbishop.

Ismail came in on the heels of the servant with breakfast,

robed and turbaned and much too calm. He sat but did not eat, listening with all apparent patience to Otto's chatter.

Aspasia watched him warily. God knew what the ruffians out there had said to him. They did not seem to have laid a hand on him. She wondered if any had tried.

Strange. The worst had happened, in every way she could imagine. Otto was betrayed, Henry was in the city, his whole army knew who was Aspasia's lover. And she felt light. Freed.

The sun was up and shining in the slit of window when Aspasia sent for her captor. He came, which amused her. A Byzantine would have known better than to give her any advantage.

"We are ready to ride," she said, "whenever you wish."

"So you are," said Henry. His amusement was more obvious than hers. He beckoned to Gudrun. "Here, bring the boy. These are all his things?"

"Not all, lord," said Gudrun. "Only these, and these. The rest are Lady Aspasia's."

"Take them," Henry said to the men who had come with him.

They took what Gudrun had pointed to. Aspasia suppressed a sigh. So: she was expected to carry her own baggage.

Gudrun led Otto out past Henry and the laden soldiers. Aspasia set hand to the more manageable of her boxes.

"No need for that, my lady," Henry said, and now surely he was laughing.

Aspasia turned on him. "Then send me a man who can help me."

"No need," Henry said again. "His excellency has agreed to be your host for yet a while." His glance flicked from her to Ismail; he shook his head. "It wasn't easy, I'll tell you. I had to promise him that you'd behave yourself. Poor man, you've shocked him abominably."

Aspasia tossed his words out of her head. "I don't need to behave myself. I'm going with his majesty."

"You are not," said Henry, and now there was steel in him.

"Of course I am. He needs me."

"He has his nurse. I have teachers waiting for him, kinswomen whom he'll be glad to know. Good women," said Henry. "Virtuous women. Who can teach by example as well as by precept."

Aspasia was cold. It was better, she thought distantly, than the fierce heat of a blush.

"You must admit," Henry said, "that I've been generous. I'm not throwing you in prison. Nor am I dealing with your paramour as the law says I ought, infidel that he is, who dares consort with a Christian and a princess. When we're well and safely gone, you'll be free to go. Even to your empress, if you're so minded. I've done nothing here that I care to hide."

He made a rather dreadful degree of sense. He had Otto, and with him the regency. Theophano would contest for it; he was certain that he would win. And he would have her kinswoman in his debt. Aspasia could be denounced, her lover castrated or killed; they could at the least have been flung in prison for as long and as hopelessly as Henry himself had been, for treason that was hardly a greater sin than Aspasia's sins of the flesh.

She could try to kill him, she supposed. It would help nothing, and it would certainly get Ismail killed for abetting her.

Looking into Henry's pale and prison-bloated face, she knew that he was afraid of her. Poison in his cup, a dagger in his back: he knew well what to expect from a royal Byzantine. But he dared not dispose of her altogether. She ranked too high.

Otto was gone, taken away. She had not even said good-bye. If she had been less whitely angry, she might have fought back tears.

She caught the gaze of the man who had taken him. She held it. She made it fall. She inclined her head in her most royal wise. "You may go," she said.

Twenty-Nine

Archbishop Warin was as glad to be rid of Aspasia as she was to be free of him. He might have been vindictive enough to cast her out in the snow, naked as he had found her, and her lover with her; but Henry's orders and his own native prudence gave her a proper escort. All that was hers, she was allowed to take. With Ismail's own belongings, and mules and horses for both of them, and servants to look after them, it made a respectable caravan.

The escort had their own orders. They were to see her on the road to Italy. She was not to veer from it either eastward, where Henry had gone with his stolen emperor, or westward, where lords of the Franks might be inclined to cast their lot with the empress. She had messages from Henry to Theophano, which she had every intention of delivering.

The archbishop did not give her the courtesy of a farewell. He had spoken to her once since Henry took Otto away: a summons to his workroom after the morning mass, which she had quite calmly attended. A young priest had given her Communion, not knowing, it seemed, who she was or what she had done. She hoped that he had not paid too high for his ignorance.

His excellency clearly had resolved to play the confessor. That she had a priest of her own, or had until he went with Otto, would matter little to so lofty a prelate. He greeted her with impressive aplomb and bade her sit in a chair that faced his worktable. He did not offer her wine, but that courtesy perhaps was beyond him.

He folded his hands on the table. They were beautifully gloved in fine white kid sewn with gold and amethysts; the amethyst of his ring glowed deep pure purple. "I trust," he said, "that you have confessed your sin with due contrition."

"I have my share of sins," she said.

"The body is a difficult servant. Often it undertakes to become the master. Every good Christian is enjoined to rule it; to keep it free of fleshly taint."

"The saints are to be admired," she said, "and virgin martyrs most of all."

He looked sharply at her, as if he sensed her irony. She had had ten years to prepare for this; to harden herself to the reality of her fault. She tried to keep her face quiet, her eyes downcast, like a proper penitent.

He shifted in his chair. It creaked. He was not an extraordinarily tall man, but he was amply broad: a big, florid, fair-haired German. Like most of his fellow princes of this barbarian Church, he was a temporal as well as a spiritual lord. He shared in the councils of the kingdom, ruled lands and people of his own, even rode to war.

He would not rule her, however he might try. She kept her eyes on her laced fingers. The knuckles were white. Carefully she eased them.

"You are sensible, surely," he said, "of the danger to your

soul. To sin in the flesh is deadly enough. To sin with a base Mohammedan—"

"Muslim," she said, soft but distinct.

He paused. "A worshipper of the false prophet Mahound—"

"They worship none but God," she said.

She heard the hiss of his breath. A quick glance showed his ruddy face grown ruddier. But he was still in control of himself. "It ill behooves a Christian woman to consort with the servant of a false god."

"Is that what Saint Helena's confessor told her when she was empress to a pagan emperor?"

"Saint Helena," he said, "dwelt with her husband in pure chastity, as brother and sister."

"And so she conceived her son."

Archbishop Warin half rose. "Is it your intention to attract a charge of heresy as well as that of adultery?"

Her eyes flashed up. She should be afraid, she knew. Later she would be. Now she was only angry. "I make no excuses for what I have done. From the first I have been as a wife to him, and he has been faithful to me as I to him. Our sin is only that no priest has blessed our union. In all other respects it has been as sacred to us as any bond of Christian marriage."

"That, with an infidel, it cannot be."

"And may I not hope that one day he will wake to the truth?" Which had been true enough when she began. This man did not need to know how long ago she had stopped hoping, or even wanting Ismail to be aught but what he was. "Was that not the hope of Helena and Radegund and many another woman united with an unbeliever?"

He could not answer that. He chose to tower over her and to thunder at her. "Then you repent? You will give him up?"

"No," she said.

That took him aback.

She rose. She was much smaller than he, but she knew

how to stand and how to hold her head. He would remember, she hoped, how she had faced his upstart duke just so, and made him come and go at her bidding. "Your objection, then," she said, "is only that he is a Muslim."

"You have sinned with him outside of sacred vows."

"So," she said, "I have." She paused. She tilted a brow. "I was grieved to hear of Frau Hedwig's death; and the child, so sadly lost. That is great sorrow for any man. And yet God can be merciful. He can if it pleases Him send another to be one's sweet friend. So I have found, who when I was a wife, loved my husband with all my heart."

The archbishop's face deepened from scarlet to crimson, and thence to royal purple.

She smiled gently and took her leave.

The smile that touched her lips as she rode out of Cologne had no gentleness in it. Archbishop Warin had learned what came of judging where he might himself be judged.

Ismail had been appalled when she told him. "He could have had you killed," he had said.

Not Archbishop Warin. He was too careful of his own skin. When he decided to turn it again and be his empress' loyal servant, he would not wish to be held to account for her kinswoman's death. However richly provoked.

It gained what she had hoped: it freed her much sooner than Henry had commanded. The morning after his departure, she was let go.

Winter's grip was iron-hard. The mountains would be hellish to cross. But cross them she would. Theophano would know how she had been betrayed, and yes, how Aspasia had failed her. If there was to be a punishment for that, Aspasia would bear it gladly.

She missed Otto. It surprised her more than a little how much she had come to rely on his presence, his stream of questions, even his noise and fret. Her arms were empty; her heart was sore. He had not even looked back. He had been too eager to ride a warhorse.

She would get him back. She made a vow of it, riding the wind out of Germany, steeling herself to face his mother.

The passes were open. Just. She was fortunate, the guides told her. She preferred to ascribe it to God's mercy. The snow that blanketed Germany had fallen more lightly here, and strong winds had blown much of it aside. They could, with care, negotiate the steep narrow tracks.

Urgency kept them on their feet. The archbishop's men had gone back to Cologne once their charges were in sight of the mountains. Those who rode with them now were hire-lings, but she thought they could be trusted. She could not be sure. At night she slept with Ismail for safety as much as for warmth. Both of them had knives, and he had a beauti-ful, wicked-edged sword, which he knew how to use. Whether that was enough, or whether her gold bound them, the guards attempted no betrayal.

God's hand again, she was certain. He seemed very close, up on the roof of the world. Warm in Ismail's arms while he slept and the wind strove to pluck their tent from its moor-ings, she felt as close to serene as she ever had. Was this what it was like to be holy? So quiet; so perfectly simple. So sure of what one was and what one must do.

She did not even hate Henry. He had done her prince no harm. Only broken prison, suborned an archbishop, taken a kingdom that was not his. Though maybe he believed that he was entitled to it. His father would have taught him as much from infancy: his father, who had found Byzantine law so convenient, and claimed the throne as *porphyro-genitus,* the first son born of a king after he had taken his throne, against great Otto who was born when their father was but Duke of Saxony. Now it was German law by which the son swore, and all his followers with him: whole flocks of bishops, lords in dozens, lesser folk following where the regalia were.

How single-minded a man could be when he cast his eyes on a throne. That was part of the reason why she had so loved Demetrios, why now she loved Ismail. They did not want to rule men. Only to know what there was to know; to make and to heal, and to be of use in the world. God had made them to be good, and her to love them.

What else she was for was as clear as the air at dawn before the last brutal descent, with Italy veiled in cloud below them and Pavia waiting for the message which she brought. She belonged to the empire; to her empress and to her young emperor. To have both love and destiny, even in such a reverse as this—that was a blessing.

Cold daylight calmed her fervor considerably, but the core of it was as solid as ever. They lost a mule going down, and almost lost the man who was leading it, but the man was only bruised and scared, and they salvaged most of the beast's burden. Soon enough the slope softened, the air warmed, the snow shrank. The plains of Lombardy were swept bare by a wind that, though strong, was gentler than any that blew in Germany.

Then at last they came in sight of Pavia. Their bone-tired beasts, sensing that they had come to haven, speeded their pace a fraction. Ismail's mare even tossed her head and snorted.

Aspasia straightened her aching back. This much could be said of riding too far too fast for any decent sense: one hardened to it somewhat. Her courses were on her, which made it worse. Not long now before she was done with that. She would be glad. It was one of the few prices of age which she was pleased to pay.

She nudged her mule from the middle of the company to its head. Ismail's mare moved aside for her. He acknowledged her with a glance.

Sadness touched her, brief but sharp. Here again they

would have to play their old secret game, conceal what they were, pretend to an indifference they had never felt. She almost reached for his hand, but stopped before she began. God knew, they would not need to hide much longer, with half the soldiers in Germany witness to her indiscretion.

But now she must be discreet and calm and perfectly the royal messenger. The news she brought was terrible enough. She must not complicate it with her own stupidity.

Pavia received them less quietly than she would have liked. She might have escaped recognition, wrapped in cloaks as she was, but there was no mistaking Ismail in his turban and his robes on his fine Arab horse. By the time they came to the palace they had gathered a sizable following. "What news?" they cried. "What news from Germany?"

The chief of the gate-guard, who had taken on himself the office of guide, shouted them down. "Let the empresses be the first to hear!"

The empresses were in the hall. It was the hour for public audience, and they both presided, seated side by side. Aspasia appreciated the meaning of that.

Empress Adelaide rose as Aspasia approached. Theophano did not. It looked like imperial dignity. Aspasia suspected that at least part of it was dread. She looked well. Tired, inevitably, but strong, even facing messengers who could have brought only one message.

She sat still as Aspasia and the others behind her accorded the empresses the full obeisance. Adelaide did not have to know how little of it was meant for her. She was slower than Theophano to understand what Aspasia's coming meant, or less willing to accept it. It was she who bade them rise, irritably, and made short work of the proper phrases. "What is it?" she demanded. "Why have you come here? Is the emperor with you?"

"No, majesty," Aspasia said.

The hall was still. Had it been so from the beginning? Surely they could hear how her heart beat, hammering against its walls.

"You left him? Or were you sent away?"

"We were sent," Aspasia said. "Majesty." Her eyes were on Theophano. The younger empress seemed barely to breathe. She could read what was in Aspasia's face. She would not say it. Aspasia almost hated her for that; for making her play out the rest of this bitter game.

"We were sent," she said, "as messengers. From the Archbishop of Cologne. And," she said, "from the one who calls himself Duke of Bavaria. And, now, Regent of Germany."

Her words fell one by one in the silence. "Henry of Bavaria," she said, "has escaped from his prison and taken the emperor and the regency. He bids you know that if you remain in Italy he will make no move against you. Germany is his by right, and has always been. Italy you may have until it pleases him to ask for it."

Adelaide sank down slowly to her throne. Her face was grey. It was not, Aspasia was careful to acknowledge, weakness. It was shock and cold fury.

"So," Theophano said, soft and calm. "After all you had the right of it. Are you going to rebuke me for my error?"

For a moment Aspasia did not understand her. "Rebuke you? My lady, it was I who lost him."

"No," Ismail said, startling her. "Two archbishops turned traitor: he of Utrecht, who set the rebel free, and he of Cologne, who let him into the city."

Adelaide's lips tightened. She could not have liked to hear such condemnation of churchmen, however richly deserved. Not from an infidel.

Theophano nodded slowly. "Of course. The Church would prefer milord Henry: man that he is and Saxon and, they might think, more easily manipulated than a woman from Byzantium. The more fool I, for trusting in an arch-bishop's loyalty."

Adelaide crossed herself. The gesture made Aspasia think of drawn swords. "God will judge His own," said Adelaide. "We will go to God's Vicar."

"The pope," said Theophano. "Yes." She rose at last, with unthinking grace. "He was Otto's man. He will hear the plea of Otto's mother and of Otto's queen."

"And," said Aspasia, "with God's help he will hear us first, before milord Henry thinks to secure him."

That gave Theophano pause. "Would he have thought of it?"

Aspasia shook her head, first slowly, then more firmly. "No. I think not. He was too full of his own triumph when we saw him. He'll reckon himself amply supported by all the bishops of Germany. It was always his failing," she said, musing, "and his father's before him: he never thinks of empire. Only of Germany."

For once Adelaide looked on her with something close to respect. "So he does. So his father did. His bishops may not be so eager to follow him if the Holy Father forbids them. Which you can be sure he will." She said it with grim satisfaction.

They took the rest of it into the private rooms, away from staring eyes and wagging tongues. Aspasia had time to shed her traveling clothes, to eat and drink, even to rest if she wished. But there was no sleep in her. She found the empresses in a small cluttered workroom, conferring with astonishing singleness of purpose. This war for the youngest Otto's crown had done what his father had never been able to do: persuaded them at last to bury their feud. There was amity between them, albeit with a barbed edge.

They allowed her into their council. There were others: Adelaide's chancellor, a bishop or three, a shifting company of noblemen and women.

Among them stood one whom Aspasia knew very well indeed. He had aged much too much since last she saw him. Two years had it been since the second Otto made him abbot of Bobbio? He was wearing an abbot's cope over Benedictine black.

Grey and haggard though he was, he brightened immeasurably on sight of her. With a glance that asked permission of the empresses, he rose and held out his arms. She embraced him, too well aware of the bones under the habit. "Gerbert," she said. "Gerbert, old friend, what brings you here?"

"Death," he answered starkly. He mustered a smile. "No, no, it's not as dreadful as that. His majesty made me abbot; his majesty is dead. I judged it best to leave my monks to contemplate their sins in peace, far from the one they've sinned against."

He was bitter. Aspasia grieved for him: clear-eyed, capable, blunt-tongued Gerbert, driven out of the abbacy he so richly deserved, bereft of the emperor whom he had loved.

"Is it so bad?" she asked him.

He shrugged. He did not want to talk about it. Not here, with so many ears to hear. She let him go, though her glance kept returning to him.

The others had been so courteous as to carry on without them. "Italy," Adelaide said, frowning with concentration. "That is ours. But we can hardly rely on it to provide us with troops, what with its own feuds and squabbles, and the Saracens in the south. Beyond the Alps . . . what have we?"

"Saxony," said Theophano, "beyond question. Duke Bernhard is truly loyal; I'd stake gold on it. As I shall, to aid him in arming his troops. Archbishop Willigis was always firmly ours. He'll know now what's fallen, and will be taking steps to secure the Church where he can. Outside of Germany . . . what of Burgundy?"

"Burgundy," said Adelaide, marking the tablet. "Swabia, incontestably: my lord duke is a loyal man. Lorraine . . . perhaps, perhaps not. The Franks—" She paused, turning her eyes on Gerbert. "My lord abbot"—Did no one but Aspasia see how he winced?—"will the Franks stand with us, do you think? Or will they turn to Henry?"

Gerbert shook his head. "I can hardly judge, majesty. But as I know them, I think that there may be hope. If the king stays out of it—if he remembers his truce with Otto, and not the war that went before it; if maybe your majesty should deign to intercede with her majesty the queen—his lords may come to us. If we send envoys to the strongest of them . . ."

"To as many as we can." Theophano had so far forgotten herself as to rise and pace. She still had a long colt's stride when she was not hobbling it with queenly dignity. She stopped suddenly, white-faced, clench-fisted. "God *damn* that man!"

There was a long, astonished pause. Theophano drew a shuddering breath. She returned to her seat and sat in it, calm again, queenly again, as if she had never burst out in temper.

Slowly they stirred, rousing. There were letters to be drawn up, plans to be made, forces to be gathered. It interested Aspasia to see how quickly it was all done, and how many women's voices there were, sharing counsel.

Almost, appallingly, she burst out in giggles. She had tried once on the road to Pavia to explain to Ismail why it struck her so to see so many widows and lady regents in the empire. "There's a very old play in Greek," she had said, "by a truly outrageous master. Aristophanes, his name was. It was all about how women set themselves to rule Athens."

His expression was thoroughly skeptical. "And what came of that?"

"Peace," she said, "and good sense. Though I don't think"—and now the giggles burst out, irrepressible—"that we could do as they did. Not in this world."

She thought that he would never ask. But in the end he did. "What did they do?"

"Refused the men their bodies," she answered. "It drove them mad."

"No doubt," he said, dust-dry.

Not that he would know. She kissed him long and deeply and raised herself over him, letting her hair curtain them both. The lamp's light caught the glints of silver in it. "You see why I thought of Aristophanes," she said. "So many women, ruling so strongly. Do you know what they'll call this? The War of the Empresses."

"It's very Muslim in its proportions," he said: "two empresses against one would-be emperor."

"So, then. At the least they're evenly matched. Although," said Aspasia, grinning down at him, "if I were to be consulted, I would opine that poor Cousin Henry is desperately outnumbered."

"The world turned upside down," he said. "Women ruling in the courts of kings. What will we see next? Fish sprouting wings? Stags swimming the sea?"

"Men succumbing to common sense."

"That," he had said, "is perfectly improbable."

Thirty

A spasia freed herself at last from the council. Gerbert had left somewhat before her. She found him in the first place she looked, the room that was Ismail's when he was in Pavia. It was one of the pleasanter chambers, up in one of the towers, with a good hearth and an ample bed and a fresco of leaves and flowers. He said that the woven traceries reminded him dimly of his own country.

Gerbert sat on the bed as if he had never been aught but a wide-eyed young monk. He did not, for all of that, look better than he had in the empresses' council. He had a cup in his hands, nearly empty, and wine that he had to have brought, since Ismail never drank it.

Aspasia accepted a cup for herself but did not drink from it. Once greetings were past, no one spoke. It was not an uncomfortable silence; their friendship was too close for that. But neither was it a peaceful one. Gerbert turned the cup in his fingers, turned and turned it.

When Aspasia was about to seize his hand to make him

stop, he set the cup on the floor and settled himself anew, cross-legged in the eastern fashion. He looked at them both. His eyes were deathly tired. "I suppose you want to know it all."

Aspasia shook her head. Ismail said, "Only what you want to tell."

Gerbert sighed. "You don't know," he said, "how good it is to sit here, and know you for friends, and know surely, down to the bone, that I can trust you. I had a dagger in the back once. Did you know that?"

"I knew that the abbey was resisting you," said Aspasia, "but not that it was so bad."

"Bad," he said. His voice faded to nothing. He shook his head. "I don't know that it was bad. Difficult, yes. I was an outsider. They had one of their own whom they wanted, and of course the Rule says that the monks may elect their abbot. When I was imposed on them by an emperor whom few of them had ever seen, and he a Saxon to boot, and I a Gaulishman . . . it was a sore strain on their vow of obedience."

"Still," said Aspasia, "they were under vow."

He laughed without mirth. "Exactly what I said to them! They hated me the more for it. Things had got lax, you see, and here I was, set over them against the Rule, telling them they had to obey the Rule or suffer the consequences. Rigor, that was my watchword. And every lord and bandit for miles about cast a greedy eye on the abbey and its lands and took what he pleased, as he pleased, while we were in disarray. They beset me within and without."

Ismail reached for him, held him with an arm about his shoulders. Aspasia said, "You did well to leave."

"Once we knew that Otto was dead, I had no choice." He scraped his hand across his face as if to scour away the grief. "Never mind. I'll go back if I can. If I can't, God wills it. Empress Adelaide has been kind; she took me in and asked no questions, and set me to work."

"Too hard, from the look of you," said Ismail.

"No harder than you," Gerbert shot back, somewhat too sharply.

Ismail was not at all dismayed. "Maybe not. Now that we're both well rebuked, will you have another cup of wine?"

"Strictly medicinally, of course," said Gerbert. He filled the cup, drank deep. "I don't intend to get drunk. Calm, only. Serene. Sanctified."

"Silly." Aspasia sipped from her own cup. It was good wine, lightly watered, strong and sweet: wine worthy of a lord abbot. "Laughter is a great curative."

"Even for death?" asked Gerbert.

"Death cures everything but bliss."

"Or hell," said Gerbert. "Don't forget hell."

"I'll not only forget it. I'll consign it to oblivion." She drank deeper. The fumes of the wine dizzied her, but her mind was clear. "The empresses have the right of it. Grief rules no kingdoms."

"Memory teaches," said Ismail. "Self-pity robs the mind of all good sense."

"Doesn't it?" said Gerbert. He essayed a smile. It was not too ghastly, for a first effort. "Did I tell you I have a new mule? Her name is Alba. She's almost as stubborn as I am."

"Impossible," said Ismail.

"Possible," said Gerbert, "only for a mule. She carried me nicely out of Bobbio, and a box of books with me. The library there . . . one could kill for it. Hundreds of books. Row on row of them."

"Hundreds?" Aspasia was skeptical. In the east she would believe it. Here, a few dozen would be a lasting marvel.

"Hundreds," said Gerbert. "And more in the making. Turbulent, contumelous, murderous sinners my monks may be, but in the scriptorium they turn to angels."

He was rapt, contemplating it. Then abruptly he returned

to himself. "The library is a joy and a marvel, but there's no school to speak of, and I'm only a middling penman. I'm good enough to write letters for royalty, but to do fair copies of Cicero and Boethius . . . not if there's anyone else to do it. Do you know what I've missed most?"

They shook their heads.

"Teaching," he said. "Taking minds as dull as lead and making them shine. I think, if Bobbio won't have me back, I'll go to Rheims. They've begged me more than once to come back and be master of the school again. Am I good enough for that, do you think?"

"Admirably," said Aspasia. She meant it. Everyone knew what a marvel he was in the schoolroom. He was amply brilliant outside of it, and for all his failure at Bobbio he was a ruler of no small skill, but when he was teaching he was most purely and joyously himself.

He sighed. "It's good for a man to know where his limits are. I found them in Bobbio. I can run a school. I can't rule an abbey that doesn't want me."

"It may," Aspasia said, "when it's had time to think."

"Maybe." He did not sound at all convinced. "One thing I know I can do: write letters for the empresses. I'm not anything in Francia, but my archbishop in Rheims, Adalberon—he's royal kin. I think he may be willing to help us."

Gerbert had had easily enough wine to make him drunk, but he sounded perfectly sober. He did not fill the cup again once he had drained it. He leaned forward, elbows on knees, once more his old irrepressible self. "I'm going to ask if I can be the ambassador to the Franks. I'm one myself, after all. And Adalberon is one of the most powerful churchmen in Gaul; it's his right to crown the king. He'll listen to me. He'll do what he can to keep the king in hand."

They were friends, Aspasia recalled: the lordly archbishop and the peasant's son from Aurillac. Gerbert never bragged about it; he would never think of it. But he had been happy when he met the archbishop of his newly adopted city and knew that they would like one another. His letter to Aspasia had been full of that joy.

A little of it touched him now, easing the taut lines of his face. As he grew older he became more distinguished to look at, with his strong blunt features and his clear eyes. She could understand why the monks of Bobbio disliked him so intensely. He was too honest. He said what he thought; he seldom stopped to consider prudence. Nor could he ever understand dishonesty. An abbey grown easy under slack rule would hate him.

It was not the letter of the Rule that bound him. It was a deeper fidelity: a clear-eyed common sense that accepted what Aspasia and Ismail were, because they were faithful to one another, and kept vows that were no less strong for that the Church would never acknowledge them.

He rested between them, content. "I'll do that," he said. "I'll go to Rheims, and wherever else the empresses ask. This is unconscionable, what the Quarreller has done with our emperor. I can't allow it." He laughed suddenly. "Listen to me! You'd think I was the lord pope."

"Someday," said Aspasia.

He shook his head, but he smiled. "You Byzantines. You lack the proper respect."

"We have it," she said, "but for our own Patriarch. A bishop in Rome, even if he holds the See of Peter . . . what is he?"

"God's Vicar on earth." Gerbert hiccuped lightly. "What an army you make! A pair of subtle Byzantines, a Lombard queen, and a dog of a Moor. And all your loyal confreres. Some of whom, I'm sure, are thinking hard about turning their fine new coats. It's enough to make the devil laugh."

"As long as he laughs," said Aspasia, "and thinks us less than we are, then I'm content. What can we do but pray, and ask God to help us?"

"And fight the good fight." Gerbert laid an arm about them both. "We can't help but win, can we?"

"With God's help," said Ismail.

"Well, yes. With that. And our own invincible obstinacy." He grinned. "A proud herd of mules in a righteous cause. We'll never lose."

"A drunken herd of mules," said Ismail. He eased Gerbert down, paying no attention to resistance. "There now. Sleep. Here of all places you can do that: here where you have friends."

"Friends." Gerbert's eyes were wet with wine-born tears, but he did not let them fall. He smiled through them. He was still smiling when, all at once, he dropped into sleep.

Thirty-One

"I'll not command you," Theophano said.

She was in her bedchamber in a robe of lapis-blue silk lined with sable, her hair freed but not yet braided for sleep. It streamed over her shoulders and down her back; when she had stood to greet the three of them, it had fallen to her knees.

She did not seem to know how beautiful she was. Alone with them, even her maids dismissed to the outer room, she let herself be herself, sitting on the wide bed and leaning toward them, intent. She spoke mostly to Aspasia and Ismail, but her eyes shifted more than once to Gerbert, who sat quiet in the corner. "I know how grim a journey you had; I won't compel you to make another so soon. But if you will—if you can—"

"Of course we will," Aspasia said, though she shrank from the thought of the Alpine passes. The embassy to the pope was settled already: a delegation of prelates would go, with an archbishop at its head, which was both wise and politic. It was the north that needed her, with the rank that she could claim and the knowledge she had of the empresses' counsels.

Theophano regarded her for a moment. She did not look away. The empress said, "You know that I trust no one as I trust you. You can say what needs to be said, do what needs to be done. People listen to you, I notice. Even when they would rather not."

Aspasia's brows went up. "They do?"

Theophano laughed, sudden and sweet. "You really don't know that? Believe me, Aspasia, there's no one better for what I'm asking. Still, there are others, if you don't want to face the passes again before spring."

Gerbert shifted slightly. "My lady—"

Theophano turned to him. "Yes, I was thinking of you. But I need you to go to Francia, if you will, if you can face the journey."

"Of course I can," he said. His tone was almost angry. "That's what I came to ask. That you send me. I should have known you'd be ahead of me."

"That is what an empress is," said Theophano. "Someone who is always ahead of the rest. An excellent position to be trampled; or to be abandoned."

"I won't abandon you," said Gerbert.

"Nor I," said Aspasia, bringing them both round to face her. She glanced at Ismail, who sat silent, listening. "Now that you have your physician back again—"

"He goes with you," Theophano said. "I want—need—his assurance that my son is well and safe. If the rebel allows him to stay, then he may; or he may elect to accompany you back to Pavia. I leave him free to choose."

Aspasia's cheeks warmed slightly. Not enough to be obvious, she hoped. Theophano did not know how Henry had found them. It was not something that could be said in front of a roomful of servants and the Empress Adelaide.

Ismail spoke for them both. "I think that his lordship will

prefer my absence to my presence. But I will go, if you will promise to remain here until matters are settled."

Theophano looked briefly disconcerted. One could, Aspasia thought, forget how fearless Ismail was where his craft was concerned.

"It is wise," Aspasia said, "to remain in a single guarded place where one's armies and embassies can know to come at need. Henry won't be crossing the Alps. He'll have his hands full securing Germany."

"Yes," Theophano said. "I had intended to play the spider in her web and lair in Pavia. Will my physician permit me to ride to Germany if the need demands it?"

"In great need," he said, "and in summer, yes. Until then you can trust to your loyal subjects. Of whom we are three."

She smiled, perhaps in spite of herself. "None more loyal, Master Ismail. Which should be a lesson to his most Christian and rebellious lordship and all his followers." She drew herself up, became again the empress as she was in the world's eye. "You may go when you wish. Messages will be given you; likewise all that you will need for the journey."

Aspasia bowed low. Theophano's eyes on her were deep and clear. Everything that she had not said was there to be read; everything that Aspasia needed to understand. Grief, anger, fierce refusal to bend or break. Henry had Otto. Theophano had the right to the empire.

Aspasia almost pitied the rebel. He did not know yet what an enemy he had made. An empress robbed of her empire; a mother robbed of her child.

Theophano held out her hands. Aspasia came into her embrace. They held for a long moment. Theophano was perfectly steady. It was Aspasia who had to bite back tears.

To Ismail too, and to Gerbert last but not least, the empress offered the honor of an embrace. They took it in their disparate fashions: Ismail with dignity, Gerbert with honest affection. There was a light on them both, like young warriors riding to their first battle. Aspasia might have smiled if she had not felt it in herself. It was foolish, maybe, but it bore her up.

"Go with God," said Theophano.

Empress Adelaide summoned Aspasia in the morning before mass. It was like her to expect that everyone be up for matins with herself and the nuns. Aspasia, whose body was remembering that it was no longer young, did what she could to put herself in order, with the page dangling and fidgeting without.

It surprised her very little once she had gone where she was bidden, to be kept waiting in an icy box of an antechamber. From the sound of it the empress was praying. Her piety was famous; she had shared it with her husband, passed it to her son. Aspasia, whose mind had a deplorable bent for the unorthodox, almost envied her. True piety would have passed the time in prayer. Aspasia could only sit and shiver and wish herself back in her warm bed. Preferably with Ismail beside her.

At last the page returned for her. She followed him into a room as stark as a nun's cell. Here was none of the comfort that Theophano favored. A hard narrow bed with a single rough coverlet and no bolster, a crucifix over it, a box for clothing, a niche with an image of the Virgin, a cushionless chair and a low stool. That was all.

The empress looked like a Benedictine in her stark and simple black, a black veil over her hair. No paint marked her face, no jewel relieved the starkness of her garb. Her belt was of plain leather, its clasp of iron without ornament. On her breast lay a simple silver cross.

Her temper had grown no sweeter, her spirit no gentler. She did not invite Aspasia to sit. Her women were there, and her priests wearing the bland, sated look of the well-sanctified. "You are going back to Germany," the empress said.

Aspasia inclined her head.

"You are not the worst of choices. Though why her highness would want to send you, with so many worthy clerics ready and eager to serve her . . ."

"Perhaps, your majesty," said Aspasia, "she thinks that I can convey her messages as she wishes them to be conveyed."

Adelaide's nostrils thinned. "No doubt."

"Does your majesty wish to question the choice?" Aspasia asked.

"Her highness," said Adelaide, "does as she pleases."

"Which, your majesty, is to share the regency which was given to her. She needs and welcomes your wisdom. Would you bid her send another in my place?"

"Would you obey?"

"I am obedient to my liege lady."

Adelaide smiled thinly. "Your oath was never given to me."

"Do you wish it?"

Adelaide was silent. Aspasia had hoped that she would be. There had been no oath given, no fealty sworn. Theophano had never asked. Aspasia served of her own free will, out of love and loyalty.

"I know," said Aspasia, "that I fulfilled ill the charge that was laid upon me to keep the emperor safe. This that I do now is meant for atonement." Truly: purgatory could be little more bitter than the Alps in winter.

"See that you remember that," said Adelaide. "Nor would it be amiss for you to pray now and then for God's guidance."

"So have I done; and all the more since my emperor was taken from me."

"That was an ill thing," said Adelaide. For a moment she looked weary, even sad. But she hardened again, eyes narrowing, chin setting within the veil. "That the bishops should resist us, that they should even betray us—God will judge them."

"That is my devoutest hope," said Aspasia.

The empress would never approve of her; but there was something like respect in her glance. "Your Greek arts may be of use after all. Henry will never budge; he was obstinate in his cradle. But the others about him, the Franks beyond his borders—them you can win. How you do it, I shall not wish to know."

So would she keep herself clean of sin if Aspasia must resort to it. Aspasia made no effort to hide the irony in her glance. "You set me free, then, your majesty?"

"I bid you do whatever you must to win back the child and the empire."

Aspasia paused. Here too was a woman who thought not simply of her own small kingdom but of the empire that was beyond it. "You know what Rome is," she said.

"I know that we have no empire unless that rebel gives up our emperor."

"You could," said Aspasia slowly, "let him do as he pleases. Italy is yours; you can hold it, rule it. You need not concern yourself with Germany's troubles."

"Without Germany there is no empire." Adelaide fixed her with a cold stare. "Do you think that I married an emperor for a whim? I was a queen in my own right. I was in prison when he found and freed me; my kingdom was contested, my crown in jeopardy. He would have been content to restore me to my place, to let me rule as his vassal. But I saw that I could have more: that God wished me to be not simply queen but empress."

"And empress you intend to remain." Aspasia nodded. "I am Roman myself; my father was an emperor. I understand."

"Do you? Do you know that Henry would marry you if you would have him?"

Aspasia's smile escaped before she could stop it. It was thin and faintly bitter. Yes, he would marry her, even now.

However black her sins, she was and always would be an emperor's daughter.

"He has asked," she said. "I will never accept."

"Why?"

Because she loved Ismail. Because she cherished her freedom. Because she did not wish to be an empress. "Because," she said, "I am loyal to my lady Theophano."

"What is loyalty beside a throne?"

"Everything," said Aspasia.

Adelaide did not believe her. No one did who reckoned a throne worth striving for. The empress snorted, not delicately, and dismissed her with a flick of the hand. "Go, begin your embassy. If you abandon it to be Henry's consort, we are hardly worse off than before."

"I shall not do that," Aspasia said quietly. She bowed just to the proper degree and no more. "God keep you, your majesty."

Thirty-Two

E aster came early in the year of Our Lord 984. In Italy, maybe, it was spring. In Germany the winter had only begun to break.

Aspasia tracked her quarry through the snows of the Saxon march. He was in Magdeburg on Palm Sunday. He would be in Quedlinburg at Easter, as had become the custom of the German kings.

It was a sore temptation to while the time in her beloved Frauenwald. But Aspasia was stronger than that. When this was over she would go home. Now she went where she must go.

She waited for Henry in Quedlinburg. The people there knew her; they received her politely if somewhat nervously. She had to unleash only a little royal temper to win lodging in the castle for herself and her escort. The escort had to bivouac in a barn near the outer wall, but she had a cell to herself above the hall; no one tried to remove the man who slept across its door. It was not, unfortunately, Ismail. He had a fine hand with his slender Toledo blade, but he was no soldier. After the first night he slept in the hall with the servants, winning for himself a place near the fire.

News from Magdeburg rode far ahead of the rebel and his train. Aspasia first knew of it from a man who came in toward evening of Holy Monday, a peddler of relics and quack medicines whom she knew from other years. While she picked over his stock of herbs and simples, he said, "It was a surprise to see you here, my lady. Don't tell me you've gone over to the new king."

"I was always Otto's servant," she said. She rubbed a ruddy tendril of saffron between thumb and forefinger, marked the stain it left, sniffed the sharp, astringent scent. "How long ago was this culled?"

"It's the first of the spring picking," he said. He leaned toward her and lowered his voice. "I'm not talking about Otto, lady. The two who died, or the one who lives."

She kept herself calm. "Henry?"

He nodded. "I heard it with my own ears, sitting in the hall at his lordship's feast. One of his bishops got up and blessed him and called him king. 'King by right and blood of all the Germans.'"

"Not the Italians, too?"

The peddler grinned, showing teeth that would have benefited from one of Ismail's powders. "He says he's going back to the old ways. Germany for the Germans; let the rest of the world go hang."

"And my emperor?"

"He wasn't there," said the peddler.

She realized that somehow she had managed to tear to shreds a quite costly scrap of the Magdalene's veil. She looked at it appalled, but not for its sake. Henry had wasted no time. And now, dear God, he did not need Otto. A child too young to be without his nurse, but like all children certain to grow, and grow into an enemy. The Greeks at Troy had known what to do with such an inconvenience. What the Germans at Magdeburg would have done . . .

The peddler mistook her expression. He winked at her. "No fear, lady. To good Christians it's the Magdalene's veil. Between the two of us, it's a cutting from my grandam's Sunday shift."

She hardly heard him. She chose packets at random, paid what he asked with no more than a token haggle, got rid of him.

Henry would arrive tomorrow or the day after. She could ride to meet him, for what good that would do. She would lose whatever advantage she had in being settled in his own stolen castle, eating his stores and commanding his servants.

Wait, she told herself. *Be patient.* If Otto was dead, nothing that she did would change it. If he was imprisoned, she would not free him by betraying her desperation.

She must be all royal and all Byzantine. Henry would see no weakness in her.

The maid whom she had appropriated for herself was young but capable, and delighted to learn how to wait on a princess of the Romans. Hilda loved the feel of crimson silk; she showed a genuine talent for weaving Aspasia's hair into the intricate plaits of Byzantine fashion.

It was all Aspasia could do not to fidget like a child. The castle was in uproar. Henry's outriders had come in; he was an hour or two behind them. She would, must, be in the hall when he came, the image of royal serenity.

"You look," said Hilda, "just like the lady on the walls in Ravenna."

Aspasia faced her in honest startlement. "How do you know Ravenna?"

"I went there," said Hilda proudly. "My gran used to be a waiting-woman for Empress Adelaide. She took me when I was small, to learn how to be a lady. We went too many places to remember, but I never forgot Ravenna, or the lady in the church. She was an empress, Gran said."

"Theodora," said Aspasia. "She was the greatest beauty of her day."

"You look like her. Those big eyes, and the nose."

Theodora had had, Aspasia admitted, a very long nose. "Beauty was different in those days," she said.

Hilda paused, struck. "Why, you must be descended from her!"

"Only indirectly," Aspasia said. "Our line comes from Basil the Macedonian. But kinship is at least as complicated in Constantinople as it is in Germany. If I traced all the branches and byways, no doubt I'd find myself kin to Theodora."

"Imagine," said Hilda, whose fingers had not ceased for a moment their flying progress through Aspasia's hair. "All those years and all those empresses. We've only just started here. Two hundred years ago we were pagans, and now look. We're going to make a new Rome, the way Charles the Frank wanted it, but he died and his sons squabbled over inheritances till there was nothing left."

Aspasia was beyond astonishment. "You are an educated woman."

"Hardly that," said Hilda. "I listen, that's all. My sister taught me to read a little. She's a nun in the abbey here; I was a year in the school. She wants me to be a nun, but I want to try the world first."

"Your father allows you so much choice?"

"My father died fighting Saracens. My brother is too busy being the empresses' man to pay attention to me. He'll remember me after this is over, I suppose, and find a husband for me."

"Do you want one?"

Hilda shrugged. "That depends on what he's like. If I don't take to him, I'll go to the convent."

So practical; so lighthearted about it. Aspasia considered the face above hers, intent on the last intricate weaving. A broad-cheeked, wide-mouthed, plain-pretty face under a crown of mouse-gold braids. She would do whatever she pleased, and do it well. "Would you like to travel with me," Aspasia asked, "until this is over?"

When Hilda smiled she was almost beautiful. "Everywhere? All over Germany? Even to Francia?"

"Francia has its own ambassador," Aspasia said. "But yes, wherever I go you may come with me. Even if we go no farther than the hall of this castle."

"We'll go far," Hilda said. "I'm sure of it."

Aspasia shook her head, but she smiled. "You don't think Henry will surrender to us?"

"Not he," said Hilda with confidence. "He's got the crown now. He's not about to let it go." She finished what she was doing, stood back to admire. "I'd love to go to Francia. I've never been there."

"Nor have I," said Aspasia, rising. "Maybe later, when this war is over, we can all go."

Hilda smoothed the folds of Aspasia's gown, tightened the jeweled girdle a fraction. Aspasia raised her chin. Hilda held up the precious bronze mirror which she had conjured from somewhere.

Aspasia did look rather like the Empress Theodora. She hoped that she would be as skilled in intrigue. She nodded, setting the pearls in her ears to swinging, and smoothed the last vestiges of the frown from her brow. "Now," she said.

Aspasia was in the hall when the would-be King of the Germans made his entrance. She had not presumed to occupy the throne. She sat on the dais next to the empress' place, with Ismail and the two most imposing of her escort at her back. Others were there in force, the whole of the court that was not openly opposed to Henry's claim, but none had dared to mount the dais, nor had any ventured to displace her. Her stillness was the perfect, hieratic stillness of the Empresses of the Romans.

Henry was too full of his own new-seized power to be

afraid, but he was disconcerted enough. When the rest of the court rose as one and hailed him as king, she did not move, not even to the eyes. She had learned long ago to stare straight ahead and still to see what passed on the fringes. Not everyone was wholeheartedly committed to the new order. Some only mouthed the words. Others looked uncomfortable. On those she might be able to work her wiles.

Henry advanced through the hall. It was not a steady progress. He paused often to give or receive a greeting, to slap a man on the back, to bow over a lady's hand. Aspasia had ample time to reckon the number and kind of his escort. Bishops in plenty, in a black cloud of priests. Lords of high rank in jeweled tunics. And, somewhat toward the rear, a gleam of white. Slavs, and at their head one with the torque of a chieftain, and on his head a glittering incongruity: a helmet that surely was of Persian make and fashion.

So. Henry had made a pact with the enemy. She might have been more disturbed if the sight behind them had been less devastating.

Franks. The embroidered tunics were unmistakable. One was wearing the purple of nobility over scarlet leggings cross-gartered with gold. Aspasia knew him; his glance acknowledged her. He was one of King Lothair's counsellors.

It took most of her strength of will to sit still, and not to sway in her seat. Too late after all. Too late for everything. Otto was nowhere in Henry's following, Francia was gone over to Henry, and Henry wore the crown as if he had a right to it. She hoped, vindictively, that he found it heavy.

He reached the dais at last and sprang up onto it. He landed lightly in a swirl of cloak, grinning as the shout went up.

"How it must please you," Aspasia said, "to wear the crown at last."

He swept a bow, still grinning. "And greetings to you also, my lady Theophano Porphyrogenita."

Her teeth set. She smiled. "My lady Theophano of the

Romans sends greetings but not, as surely you will understand, felicitations."

"No," he said. "She'd hardly send those, would she?" He took the seat that was the emperor's, leaning across the chair between and striking it lightly with his fist. "You know that if you said the word, you could sit beside me."

"And how is your lady wife?" she asked.

He flushed angrily, but he laughed. "As deadly as ever, I see. Are those Lombards behind you?"

"Empress Adelaide was so kind as to grant me a company of loyal horsemen."

"She couldn't have kept you about long. You've barely had time to travel there and back again."

"I was given a trust," said Aspasia. "I was pleased to accept it."

"Should I hire a taster, then? And a new troop of body-guards?"

"Your life is hardly at risk," she said. She turned her gaze back to the hall. In the way of courts, the gathering pursued their own concerns, leaving royalty private above them. It was a little dizzying to have such power.

Henry sat back on the throne. "What do the women want, then?"

He meant insult. She did not deign to acknowledge it. "They want what is theirs," she said. "The empire. The emperor."

Her voice was calm. It did not break on what she most craved to know.

"There is no emperor," he said. "Only a child crowned king unrightfully."

"How so?" she inquired. No tautness; no anger. Her gaze rested peacefully on the play of light above the eddies and currents of the court.

"The right is mine," he said, "as it was my father's before me. He was conquered by superior force. I have been more fortunate."

"Ah," she said. "The right is in the strength."

"And in the blood."

"Are you then the son of a ruling king?"

Henry paused. She could scent his anger, like hot iron. "Did you come to scold me like an unruly boy?"

"No," said Aspasia. "I came to inform you that your rebellion is hardly uncontested. Messengers have gone to the pope. Will the bishops follow you still under the threat of anathema?"

That shook him. "He may not yield to your pleas."

"Otto's creature, I believe you called him once. He will aid Otto's empress and his mother."

"My bishops are loyal to me. They will stand by me."

"So you can hope," said Aspasia. She was silent for a moment. Then, delicately, she asked, "And my emperor? How have you disposed of him, now that you no longer need him?"

"How is it done in Byzantium? Blinding, isn't it? Or a dagger in the dark?"

Her fingers tightened on the arms of her chair. She drew a long breath to steady herself, to master her voice. "This is not Byzantium."

"No," he said, abandoning mockery. "It's not. I'm no maimer of children. He's been docile enough, except when I tried to leave him in Magdeburg. He wanted to ride with us."

"He is here?"

"Here and healthy. Which is how and where he will stay. Who knows? He might be my heir someday, if I get no more of my own. Or he might want to take the cowl as my uncle Bruno did and be a saint, and maybe rise to pope. You see how I've set him free."

"I see how you have robbed him of what is his." She rose. She bowed as a daughter of the Porphyry Chamber to a nobleman of the royal kin. Not a degree more. Not a hair less.

He lacked the subtlety of her people. He did not think to command her; he said nothing to rebuke her. He let her go.

Thirty-Three

Otto was playing in the kitchen garden, where the snow had almost melted and the sun was almost warm. He had grown. The rest of him was blessedly unchanged.

Aspasia stood for a while unnoticed, watching him. His nurse's back was to her as the woman sat under the gnarled branches of the apple tree. Otto was engrossed in a game with a great brindled hound-puppy. From the look of his clothes, some of it had involved a roll in the mud.

The puppy, leaping and barking and licking Otto into giggles, caught sight of Aspasia. It lolloped toward her, ears flopping, barking with impressive ferocity.

She was glad of the mantle that protected her skirts. The puppy's guardianship was somewhat less than whole-hearted: it bounced to a halt in front of her, sniffed her foot, offered a tentative wag of the tail. She presented her hand for its inspection. Its tail quickened to a blur; it did its best to leap into her arms.

But Otto was there first. He nearly bowled Aspasia over. He did not say anything. His arms were tight around her neck; his body was shaking.

It was gladness, not weeping. The tears were her own. She carried the solid weight of him to the bench under the tree, and sat beside the startled and delighted Gudrun.

Otto pulled free abruptly. His cheeks were dry of tears, neither flushed nor pale; healthy. He grinned from ear to ear. Then the grin vanished; his brows drew together. "You didn't say good-bye," he said.

She could hardly point out that the fault was his. "But I came back," she said. "For a little while."

His frown deepened. "You're not going to stay?"

"I can't. I have to help your mother."

"Mother is in Italy," said Otto.

"Yes," Aspasia said.

Otto wriggled out of her lap and climbed onto the seat beside her. He kept his arms around her middle. "That is Wolf," he said, cocking his head toward the puppy. Cheated of its game, it had found a stick and flopped in the sun to gnaw on it. "He's mine. Cousin Henry gave him to me."

Aspasia swallowed to rid herself of the bile in her throat. "Cousin Henry has been kind to you?"

"He gave me Wolf," said Otto. "He lets me ride his horse."

That was more than kindness to a small boy. Aspasia did not like Henry the better for it. He had taken away Otto's birthright. Anything that he gave, however happy it made Otto, was poor payment for what he had stolen.

Otto was warm against her, but there was tension in him. "Cousin Henry says I'm going back to Cologne. I don't want to go. I don't like Archbishop Warin. He says you're bad."

Aspasia could imagine. "Maybe if you keep quiet and learn all your lessons and do as you're told, he'll let you be. Archbishops are busy men. They can't always be playing guardian." The more for that the child to be guarded was no longer a king.

"He says you're bad," said Otto with innocent persistence. "He called you Jer—Jen—Jezebel. What's a Jezebel?"

Gudrun was crimson. Aspasia's glance kept her from interfering. "A Jezebel is a bad woman," Aspasia said. That man—that mincing, sneering, hypocritical man—how dared he? She would teach him to poison her Otto's mind against her.

She let none of her anger show. She smiled and hugged Otto to her, smoothing his ruffled hair. "I suppose I am bad if an archbishop says so," she said. "But I still love you, and I'm very glad to see you."

"I love you," said Otto. "Why are you bad?"

"I don't like Archbishop Warin," said Aspasia, "or Cousin Henry. I do," she said, "like Master Ismail. Very much."

"So do I," Otto said. "Is he here? Did he come with you?"

"Would you like to see him?"

He nodded eagerly.

Ismail greeted the boy and his dog with becoming restraint. Aspasia knew how strongly he was affected: his voice was as soft as it was with the very sick, and he did not even mind that Otto, taking him by storm, knocked him off his feet. He did say mildly, "There are gentler ways to be glad to see someone."

Otto blushed and hung his head. "I was *glad,*" he said.

"So you were." Ismail let it be. His glance agreed with Aspasia's; his examination, disguised as a game, proved it. The child was whole, hale, and growing like a weed. Gudrun assured them that he was adequately fed. He was to go, she said, to the cathedral school in Cologne, where he would learn his manners and his letters.

Aspasia could hardly quarrel with that. It was what Theophano had wanted to begin with. But Archbishop Warin—"What does his excellency say to this?" she asked.

"His excellency," said Gudrun with a faint curl of the lip, "is pleased to entertain his majesty for as long as his so-called majesty commands."

Gudrun was not usually so clever with words. What she thought of it all was readily apparent. She made it even clearer as she said, "You haven't come to steal his majesty back, have you?"

For a moment Aspasia was almost inclined to say she had. But prudence was stronger than temper. She shook her head, not without regret. "I can't put him in danger. He'll be safe enough with you to look after him; in Cologne he should be well out of the fighting."

"There's going to be a war?" Gudrun looked half eager, half afraid.

"I hope not," said Aspasia. "The empresses have sent to the pope; they've asked him to intervene. They want to end this bloodlessly if they can."

Gudrun crossed herself. "Please God."

There was a pause. Otto was showing his pup to Ismail. Ismail regarded the beast with remarkable aplomb. He had never lost or even slightly mislaid his Muslim loathing of dogs.

Aspasia drew a slow breath. "I . . . see that Cousin Henry has acquired an ally or two."

"Slavs," said Gudrun. "Franks."

"So the Franks have gone to him?"

"King Lothair himself," said Gudrun, "with the promise of an army."

"At what price?"

"Lorraine," said Gudrun. "And for all I know, Charles the Great's old empire. Lothair somewhat fancies himself as a builder of empires."

It was not as if Aspasia had failed to expect it. The fine lord in his purple tunic, walking so close behind Henry, had been proof enough. But one could hope that the promises were not made; that the ambassador might still be open to persuasion.

"They sealed the accord on Palm Sunday," said Gudrun, "in front of the whole court. I was kept out, but I saw what I could, and I heard the rest."

Then there was no hope for Aspasia's embassy. Lothair's mother had been the first Otto's sister. His father had been the heir in direct line from Charlemagne himself. And his wife was daughter to Empress Adelaide by the King of the Lombards. He would reckon himself well rewarded with the title of protector of the German crown. Who knew what he would seek beyond it?

"Henry might do well to watch his throne," said Aspasia, "that Lothair doesn't snatch it out from under him."

"God knows," said Gudrun, "one has as much claim to it as the other." She smiled suddenly, a mirthless, warrior's smile. "There may be hope still. I listen, and sometimes I hear. Milord Henry isn't as secure as he'd like to be. The bishops follow him like fat sheep, but the little lords, the freemen with a bit of land cleared out of the wilderness, the good common Saxon folk—they don't cheer him when he rides by. They remember great Otto. They wish his son had lived longer. They'll follow his son's son."

Aspasia looked sharply at her. She was not given to flights of fancy. Gudrun believed what she said; she was grimly pleased with it. What had Henry and his toadies done besides steal Otto and his crown, to win her enmity?

What did men of that ilk ever do? Aspasia sighed inaudibly. Hope was large after the pinching of despair. It hurt.

"Archbishop Willigis will lead them," said Gudrun, "if they can screw up their courage to fight. They don't like to be reminded that they had a duly elected king, son and grandson of kings, and milord the Quarreller took him and his kingship without so much as a by-your-leave."

"If that is true," said Aspasia, "if it's not pure dream, my empress will be heart-glad."

"It's true," Gudrun said. She seemed offended that Aspasia should doubt her.

Aspasia had no apology to offer. "There are still the Franks," she said, "and the Slavs. The empresses have sent an ambassador to the Franks, as I was sent to the Germans. Now . . . I can hardly give up and go home. If King Lothair can be persuaded not to keep his promise . . . even if he delays, if he comes too late . . ."

"King Lothair is not all of Francia," said Ismail. Otto, bored with all the talk of kings and wars, played on the floor with his puppy. If he knew that he had lost his crown, he did not seem to mind it. Better for him, Aspasia supposed, than if he had known and raged and been helpless. There was strength in innocence.

"The Franks are hardly more united than the Germans," Ismail said. "How many of their lords, I wonder, would be willing to fight for the empresses in return for the proper concessions?"

Aspasia got up from her chair. The room was too small to pace in, with all that was in it: her bed and belongings, and chairs for the three grown folk, and Otto with the puppy. She went to the door, looked out. The guardroom was nearly empty. The captain, she remembered dimly, had said something about training exercises. One or two men stood desultory watch. They were alert enough; they kept their weapons close to hand.

She turned back to the smaller compass of the room. "I don't know how many Franks can be persuaded to turn against their king. But I know who can tell me."

They waited. Ismail knew what she was doing: there was a spark in his eye.

"Yes," she said as if he had spoken. "Gerbert."

Ismail nodded. "Gerbert will know anything worth knowing. Will you send him a letter?"

"I'll do better," said Aspasia. "I'll send myself."

* * *

It was just as difficult as Aspasia had expected to leave Otto behind in Cousin Henry's hands. Otto did not make it easier. He tried to bear the pain as a king should, but his lips quivered. Given even the whisper of a chance, he would break down and howl.

She fixed him with her sternest stare. "Remember," she said. "Whoever wears the crown, you are the king. I am going to get your kingdom back for you. Will you be strong, and learn all that you can, and wait for me?"

"You promise to come back?"

"I promise," she said.

His chin set. He dipped his head. The tears brimmed but did not fall. "Come back soon," he said.

Thirty-Four

⊕

Francia was not quite as wild a country as the marches of Germany. The Romans' presence had been stronger there when it was Gaul, and their memory lingered: roads as straight as spears, cleaving through hills, leaping rivers on arches of still-sturdy stone; great bridges built not to span rivers but to contain them, aqueducts bearing water to the old cities. Germania had such prodigies: Cologne had been a Roman town. But Francia had a more settled look. This was not outpost but province proper of the old empire.

Rheims, Saint Rémi's city, Durocortorum of the Romans, sat at the meeting of the ancient roads. A little river bounded it. On the far side stood the somewhat shabby monastery which housed in its chapel the tomb of the saint. On the near side behind walls of well-fitted stone lay the city, and on its hill the squat tower of the cathedral.

It was a small city, hardly more than a village beside the great City of the east, but it had its own dignity. And, Aspasia thought, its own considerable beauty. The light on it was wonderful, like pale golden wine, with a sparkle in it that could lift even a heart as heavy as hers.

She had sent no message ahead of her. She had seen for herself how the country armed to go to Henry's defense: levies mustering in the villages, and the ring of hammer on anvil, and swift ridings of messengers from city to city. What hope she had had was sunk low. She should have stayed with Otto; she should have tried to set him free.

Ismail never saw the use in brooding over what he could not help. It was the exile's wisdom. He could endure, or he could eat away at himself until he went mad.

Was she an exile, then? She never forgot the City; every night she prayed for it, and prayed to see it again someday before she died. But she had made the West her place. Home was where Theophano was.

No. Not any longer. It was where Otto was. And Otto was taken from her.

She did not know that she liked to know so much of herself. Theophano was as beloved as ever, the child to whom she had been as much sister as mother, whose friend she would never cease to be. But Otto was her king.

"You are like a cat," Ismail had said to her once. "No one owns you but yourself. Unless on occasion it pleases you to call someone master. Sometimes you even do his bidding."

She had not wanted to believe him then. She was a good servant, a loyal subject. Now she knew that he had seen her truly.

She served Theophano well enough in serving Theophano's son. With that to brace her, she entered the holy city of Rheims.

The archbishop's servants received her and her escort with commendable aplomb. They accepted the news of brigands away east, no threat to an armed company but dangerous enough else, and an ill sign. A kingdom that was well ruled did not suffer from brigands. They were showing themselves in Germany and throughout contested Lorraine.

"None this far west, thank God," said the majordomo who showed them to the guesthouse. They would share it with a party of pilgrims, but there was ample room for all of them. The archbishop would see them, the majordomo said, as soon as his duties permitted. Meanwhile, would they be pleased to accept food, baths, rest?

"All," said Aspasia, "and gladly. But we needn't trouble the archbishop quite yet. Is Master Gerbert in the city?"

The man's face brightened a little. "Master Gerbert? At this hour he would be in the school; he was kind enough when he came, to take the classes in mathematics and music for Master Heribert, who is ill. But he would wish to know of your coming, I am certain. I shall send to him."

Aspasia inclined her head. He bowed in return and withdrew.

Rheims had Roman baths, ancient, crumbling, but still devoted to the rites of cleanliness. Ismail went straight to them. A few of the escort, Lombards with more Italian blood than some, trailed after. Aspasia, seeking the women's side with Hilda behind her, heard Ismail within, instructing the bath-servants in the way of the eastern *hammam*.

That for all its pretensions was no more than the Roman way, and here they remembered it well. Aspasia had not been so clean since she left Aachen. There were no warm springs here, but the water in the caldarium was amply hot. It loosed her knotted muscles, scoured away the mud and the weariness of travel, lulled her almost into peace.

Hilda was in bliss. Aspasia had not asked leave to take her from Quedlinburg, had simply assumed that she would go. Had, if one wished to see it so, stolen her. There had been no pursuit. One lone woman whose brother was a partisan of the empresses would hardly seem worth fighting over.

Aspasia's black mood shadowed her not at all. She was wary of the bath, but if Aspasia went gladly to it, she was pleased to follow suit. "Charles the Great bathed every day," Aspasia told her. "Sometimes for hours together. He used to swim in the pools at Aachen, and even hold audience in them."

"In the water?" Hilda asked. She tried to be polite, but the incredulity shone through. "Naked?"

"So they say," said Aspasia, who bathed in her shift.

There was no one else in the women's bath. The servant, having seen her settled, had gone away, no doubt in pursuit of an interrupted nap. She decided suddenly and dropped her shift.

Hilda was not unduly shocked. She would have seen as much at any riverside in summer. She discarded her own camise, sinking gingerly into the steaming water.

Aspasia could not help but envy the smooth young body, unscarred by either years or childbearing, with its big firm breasts and its ample hips. And such skin—white as milk, veined like marble, with a fine golden down on legs and arms. Aspasia was fair-skinned for a Greek but never so fair as that; her pallor was a matter of will. A glimpse of sun turned her as brown as a peasant.

Maybe the monks had the right of it. Vanity was a woman's vice. With all the sins on Aspasia's soul, this one was hardly worth mentioning.

"I wish," Hilda said, "that I looked like you."

She would never understand why Aspasia laughed. It took a while to soothe her hurt feelings, and then the servant was back, to wrap them in thick soft cloths and lead them to the tepidarium.

Gerbert was waiting when they returned to the guesthouse. He rose from the chair in which he had been sitting, and held out his arms. Aspasia and Ismail came together into his embrace. They stayed there for a long moment, not speaking.

Aspasia was the first to disentangle herself. She smoothed her rumpled gown and said, "You know."

"I knew before you, I think," said Gerbert. "I did what I could, but it was too little and too late."

Her back wanted to sag. She would not let it. "So there's no hope."

He shook his head hard. "Hell is hopelessness. Earth only pretends to it." He pulled them both with him out of the warm dimness of the guesthouse into the open air. "You're tired, of course you are, but you can't rest like this. Look! There's the sun, growing bright now that winter's past, and promising a fair spring. There's the air, sweet as wine. There's my city on her hill, warm and huddled and human. What's despair in the face of that?"

He was wholly himself again. His eyes were bright; his face was eager. The shadows under his eyes were no more than one should expect of a man whose every day was full to bursting.

"Gaul is good for you," said Aspasia.

"It's home." He linked an arm through each of theirs and strode out down the stone-paved street. He stamped a foot on it, with pride. "Roman," he said. "They built to last."

"Italy was never your country," Aspasia said. "Nor Spain. This is where you belong."

He nodded. "I didn't know it myself until I came back. It's not just Gaul, you see. It's Rheims. The closer I came to it, the happier I was. When I rode through the gate I was singing."

Aspasia's smile felt odd, unpracticed, as if she had not smiled in too long. "I can tell that Rheims is glad to have you back. They've even put you to work in the school."

"Of course they have. With Heribert down—thank God you're here, Ismail, we've got no one who can call himself a doctor instead of a hog butcher—with Heribert sick, they've got no one to teach the advanced classes in music, and mathematics has always been a weakness here. You'd think they'd have the sense to bring in a younger master to teach the beginners, who can take on the older ones when there's need. They haven't done a thing worth doing since the last time I was here."

"Obviously they need you," said Ismail.

"They need plain common sense." Gerbert shook himself. "And here I promised myself that I wouldn't vent my spleen on you. Look at my city now, and tell me there's only darkness ahead of us."

He had led them to the door of the cathedral. The sun was westering, shining on the grey-gold stones of the tower and catching fire in the mosaic over the door. The pattern for it, Aspasia knew, had come from Ravenna. She turned from it to the city.

A huddle of thatched roofs, a pattern of streets that had been wrought in Rome; but the Franks had blurred the straight lines, filled them in with twists and turns. A patchwork of faded brightness was the market with its tradesmen's awnings. People bustled in it, never as many or as busy as in her own City, but many enough and lively enough to marvel at.

"Whatever we do," said Gerbert, "whoever calls himself their lord, they will go on. Poorly, maybe, under a bad lord, but people are like thistles. They thrive in hard places. None of them cares deeply whether Henry or Otto rules in Germania. No more does the sun or the sky or the ground under our feet.

"And yet," he said, "we do matter. A good lord is better for the people than a bad one; rightful rule is more to be wished for than rule by force or by falsehood. That's what I learned in Bobbio. That's why I came here."

"Amen," intoned Ismail, startling them both. He showed them a gleam of teeth. "If your devil may quote scripture, then a devil of a Moor can sing plainsong." Gerbert laughed; Aspasia smiled. Ismail went on, "All sermons aside, my friend, matters are at an ill pass. Can your archbishop do anything to better them?"

"You can ask him," said Gerbert, opening the postern and beckoning them inside.

The cathedral was dim in the light of vigil lamp and candle, with the flame of sunset softened and goldened by the glass of its windows. One along the north aisle was a rarity, an image made in colored glass like a mosaic hung in the air. Jewels of light swam in it: ruby and sapphire, emerald and diamond.

Later, maybe, Aspasia would take time to marvel at it. Gerbert led her past without a glance, pausing only to genuflect before the high altar.

Even when she had seen the cathedral properly, Aspasia would remember it as she saw it then, an edifice of shadow and of light. Columns marched away into the gloom, each bearing its high round arch, and above them the glitter of mosaics, a procession of saints standing guard over the roof. She had barely taken it in when she was hastened out of it into the bright enclosure of the sacristy.

It was not the light that dazzled her. One of the presses was open, a sacristan doing something with the vestments within: silk and damask and cloth of gold, a glitter of jewels on cope and chasuble, and in a corner by itself, the golden gleam of a crozier.

The sacristan turned. He was an oldish man, his sandcolored hair gone mostly grey, his beard silky white. He had a long, gentle face like a scholar's, and mild grey eyes. They lighted as they fell on Gerbert.

Gerbert went down on one knee, kissing the man's ring. Aspasia saw the amethyst and knew who he was. This was Archbishop Adalberon himself, smiling as Gerbert straightened, and standing patiently while Aspasia followed Gerbert's example. Ismail would not kiss a Christian priest's ring. He bowed with suitable respect; Adalberon looked on him, quite openly and contentedly fascinated. "So," he said. His voice fit his tall slender body: rather light but clear and melodious. "You are Master Gerbert's friend from Córdoba. He's spoken of you often."

Ismail inclined his head. "I am honored to meet the friend of my friend."

Adalberon smiled a wide sweet smile. And yet, Aspasia thought, he was neither a fool nor an innocent. Only Soissons ranked higher in the Church of Gaul; and Rheims crowned its kings. The Archbishop of Rheims would need to be as subtle as a Byzantine, if not perhaps as deadly. He said to Ismail, "If this place discomfits you, we can withdraw elsewhere."

Ismail's lips twitched. He was not so easily to be won over, but few princes of the church would have taken such thought for his comfort. When he spoke he spoke softly, without his wonted edge of impatience. "How can I be uncomfortable in a house of God?"

"Nothing frets Ismail," said Gerbert. "Except stupidity. Do we have any of that here?"

Adalberon laughed. "Only enough for me." He beckoned them to seats. There was a bench and a stool, and a tall chair which Adalberon took as one who had a perfect right to it. Aspasia claimed the stool, rather to Gerbert's disapproval. She flashed a grin at him. He rolled his eyes and sat beside Ismail on the bench.

She knew that she was hardly dignified, crouched on the low stool at the archbishop's feet, but she was comfortable. She folded her arms on her knees and smiled up at him. He smiled back. "And you," he said, "are the Princess Aspasia. Or would you prefer that I call you Theophano?"

"Aspasia, please, my lord," she said.

He nodded. There was no pretension in him. If there had been, she would have been as haughty as Gerbert could wish.

Gerbert shifted, restless. "My lord, you know what message these friends of mine bring."

"Yes," said Adalberon, "and in person as well. The Quarreller was so generous as to let you go?"

Ismail answered him. "We never asked. We simply went."

Adalberon blinked at that. Then he smiled. "How unpredictable! I see why you were sent as envoys on that most difficult of all the embassies."

"Anyone else would have had sense enough to ask permission." Aspasia sat straighter. She was beginning to regret the impulse that had led her away from the bench. "And, of course, never been granted it."

"Milord Henry is outmatched, I think," said the archbishop. The thought seemed to please him.

"Milord Henry has the King of the Franks at his back," Aspasia said.

Adalberon stroked his beard. "He does that; and the more shame for me, that Lothair is my kinsman. Greed drives him, I fear. He covets Lotharingia: Lorraine. A country named after another Lothair—how can he resist it?"

"You, then, disagree," said Ismail.

"I am Lotharingian," said Adalberon. "I see a greater right and clearer foresight in the regency of the empresses. This snatching of the crown from the head of the child who bears it . . . it smacks of the same avarice which besets our lord king. And it is sadly short-sighted. Henry thinks nothing of Italy. He promises too easily to give up lands that, rightly or wrongly, are part of his kingdom. Either he means to let them go and has no thought for the strength of his realm, or he intends to keep them, and therefore contemplates treachery."

"It's short-sightedness, I think," said Aspasia. "Though treachery is hardly beyond him. He knows how to look like a king, but not how to act like one."

"Not all kings are honorable," the archbishop said.

She laughed, sharp and short. "Where I come from,

'honor' and 'royal' are never spoken together. It's all power, and yes, greed. But emperors—and empresses—who manage to last more than a year or two, learn how to see beyond the moment. It's to their advantage to keep the empire strong; for only then can their thrones be secure. They do whatever they must to assure that stability."

"We shall have to hope," said Ismail, "that milord Henry fails to learn that essential truth."

"Until it's too late." Gerbert set his chin on his fist. "Well? What are we going to do? We're huddled like conspirators. What shall we conspire in?"

"Victory." Aspasia stood. She needed to move, to make her thoughts run faster. "My lord, if you agreed to meet with us as privately as this, you must have something to offer. If only your sympathies."

"Those are yours," said Adalberon, "and long have been. But there may be more." He paused. "I can hardly promise you a king. Will a nobleman do? My brother Godfrey is lord of Hainault, which is in Lorraine. He, like me, prefers to see Lorraine a German province. He can raise an army that may, if God wills, match that of the king."

Sternly Aspasia quelled her beating heart. She was too wise a courtier to trust to 'may' and 'might' and 'could.' "Will he speak with us, my lord?"

"I have sent," said Adalberon, "to ask. The messenger will return as soon as may be. Until he comes, you are welcome to the hospitality of my house."

Aspasia thanked him with the proper phrases. He lingered a little, speaking of small things, making it clear that their presence was not only necessary but welcome. His dismissal was as gentle as any Aspasia had heard. "Both of you, surely, would wish to see how we tend the sick in our city. Gerbert, will you show them?"

As they walked out of the cathedral, Ismail said, "That is a kind man."

Gerbert shook his head. "His excellency is a saint. That doesn't make him a weakling."

"I never called him that," said Ismail.

"You didn't need to. Kindness in him is as natural as breathing. So is implacable pursuit of what he believes is right. He's a stronger ally than you might guess; and his brother is very powerful in Lorraine. They're allies worth having."

"I don't doubt it," said Ismail.

Gerbert eyed him narrowly, but he was giving nothing away. Gerbert shrugged, half-smiled. "Saracens," he said.

"Moors," said Ismail with a gleam of teeth.

"Infidels." They glowered at one another, until suddenly Gerbert laughed. Ismail was a scant half-breath behind him.

Thirty-Five

Messire Godfrey of Hainault would speak with the German empresses' ambassadors. He regretted that he could not come to Rheims; would they consent to attend him in a manor of his holding, on the march of Lorraine?

Aspasia did not suspect a trap. Adalberon rode with them in the armor of his sanctity, and their escort, though small enough to avoid alarming their host, was ample to protect them. Between the bishop's standard and the envoy's banner they were safe from any but the most desperate predators. And those, as Gerbert observed, were off with King Lothair's army.

What she had not expected was to find indeed a manor and not a castle. It was both like Frauenwald and unlike. It had begun as a Roman villa. Franks had walled it and fortified it, but the heart of it was almost intact. Outside the walls, serfs who perhaps had been there, bound to the land, since the days of the old empire, tilled the wide peaceful fields. It was the spring planting: men drove the oxen with the plows or wielded plows themselves, and women sowed the seed, and children leaped and capered and made a joyous excess of noise to drive away the birds. Some of them paused to watch the high ones ride by, but most were too deep in their own concerns to care. They looked as if war had never touched them.

The house did not entirely give the lie to that. Time rather than men's hands had knocked down part of the wall, and they had repaired it somewhat unskillfully with native stone, rough and unsubtle beside plaster and Roman brick. The outbuildings were wood and thatch, but the stables had a Roman look, straight sturdy walls under the remains of a tiled roof.

The villa itself was closest of all to what it had been. The fountain in the atrium was gone; they had roofed the courtyard and built a hearth in the middle and made it a hall. But the inner rooms were little changed. The walls were still painted, although in some places the paint was nearly worn away, and in others stained beyond recognition by grease and soot. The chapel still had its beautiful mosaic floor, the image of a chalice wound with vines and flowers, which must have been close enough to Christian to pass muster.

Messire Godfrey received them at the gate and conducted them within. He was older than his brother, shorter, broader, still strong. Adalberon's long scholarly face in him was shortened and thickened, his eyes closer in color to flint than to water. A long scar seamed his cheek, which he kept shaven, as he kept his hair clipped short for the wearing of a helmet.

Aspasia found the sight of him peculiarly reassuring. They had scholars enough in their alliance. They needed a soldier.

He had an escort of his own: solid men, not excessively handsome in their dress, but every one well armed. They were clean, Aspasia noticed, and their armor and weapons were well looked after. They greeted their lord with evident respect but no servility.

She nodded to herself. So far, well enough. Godfrey's men stared at Ismail. One or two crossed themselves, but there was no muttering or glowering. They were curious, that was all. Not like Germans, for whom the memory of the second Otto's defeat at the hands of Saracens was still fresh enough to bleed.

Messire Godfrey accorded them all the courtesies before he troubled them with business. His wife, much younger than he and just beginning to swell with child, took Aspasia in hand. She had her share of snobbery, that one, but she had heard Aspasia greeted as a princess. Once she had made it clear that she was not to be cowed by royalty, she was sufficiently respectful.

Hilda thought her hilarious. "Did you see what she did when her husband called you 'your highness'? I thought she'd drop through the floor. I told you you shouldn't have worn that old thing. The poor woman must have thought I was the ambassador."

"That old thing is quite adequate to travel in," said Aspasia, undoing the laces of her plain black dress and standing to let Hilda slip it off. Hilda had the crimson silk out of Aspasia's baggage; Aspasia shook her head. "Not that, we're not at a royal court. The blue instead, and the pearls."

Hilda conceded that it would do. It was quiet magnificence, almost somber, but it was silk. It would remind their hosts that Aspasia was a Personage.

She took care to remind herself. As she grew older she found it harder to sustain what pretensions she had ever had. In front of Henry it was easier; here, where Romans had been, where she felt herself among allies, it was a sore temptation to slip into the simplicity with which she had faced Adalberon.

An archbishop could be different. A lord of the world needed to see that his guest was worthy of him. It mattered little that Messire Godfrey knew perfectly well what she was doing, and showed it in the irony of his glance. If she had not done it, he would have reckoned it an insult.

They dined together quite pleasantly, with Ismail seated at the table and pretending to eat. He would have broken his fast earlier with bread and meat prepared by his own cook. Messire Godfrey had given him a place of honor to the right of Adalberon. Aspasia, on the left beside Lady Constance, caught glimpses now and then: an inclination of the turban, a gesture of the long graceful hands. Ismail on his best behavior was beautiful to watch.

"A most unusual escort," said Lady Constance, marking the direction of her glance.

"My empress trusts him implicitly," said Aspasia.

"And yet he is a heathen?"

"A Muslim," said Aspasia as she so often had before. They always looked at him like that, half fearful, half fascinated. "He is a very good physician. He came with me to make certain that the little emperor was well."

"And yet he left the emperor to ride with you," the lady said.

She had large and rather prominent blue eyes. Aspasia met them with her blandest stare. "The emperor is well looked after. His empire is another matter. Master Ismail and Master Gerbert are friends, and have been so since they were both in the service of the lord pope. Master Ismail hoped that their friendship might help our cause."

Lady Constance took the bait. "The lord pope? He served the Holy Father?"

"And great Otto," said Aspasia, "and after him the Empress Theophano."

Lady Constance was duly impressed. "Such a . . . striking man. So fierce. One might be a little afraid of him."

"People often are," said Aspasia. She hoped that her smile was not too nasty. One did not have to like one's allies.

One did have to avoid offending them. Particularly when they were not yet secured.

Messire Godfrey at least was a man she could respect. Constance was his third wife; he hoped that she would give him the son he had never had. He was gentle with her, according her all the proper courtesies and taking scrupulous care that she did not exert herself excessively: more in fact like a father than a husband.

When the hall was cleared and Lady Constance sent to her rest, the lord and his guests withdrew to the solar. It might have been the master's room from oldest times: not large but spacious enough, with a vast and ancient table in it, and a fresco of dogs and deer and a hunt, and a fine hunting hound picked out in mosaic on the floor. Whoever had put in a hearth after the hypocaust failed had been careful not to spoil the beauty of the room. It was as lovely in its way as any Aspasia had seen, and warm enough even for Ismail, with a fire of applewood on the hearth, and warmed wine for the Christians and a tisane of herbs for the Muslim.

He sipped it with approval. Aspasia scented the freshness of mint, and something else more astringent: lemon balm, maybe.

The men spoke of the world and its wars. Aspasia listened in silence. After a glance or two they seemed to forget her. She was a woman, keeping still as a woman ought. They did not have to know what went on behind the demurely lowered eyes.

"Lothair will never be persuaded to come over to us," Godfrey said. "He's not likely to forget that he warred with the second Otto, and not so long ago either, over Duke Charles and Lorraine."

Aspasia nodded to herself. Now that Otto was dead, Lothair was delighted to assist Otto's oldest enemy. They had been fools to hope that he would enter into alliance with Otto's son.

"The empress would hardly be happy to ally with Lothair," Gerbert said, "seeing that she almost miscarried of Princess Mathilda on her flight out of Aachen."

"Empress Theophano is Byzantine," said Ismail. "She understands necessity."

"She may," Gerbert said. "Lothair never will."

"So we all understand," Adalberon said mildly. "Shall we consider what is possible? Lorraine should remain under the German crown; on that we all agree. Will Duke Charles assist us, do you think?"

Godfrey, having no beard to stroke, assisted his thinking by stroking his long chin. "Given time and sufficient encouragement, he might. I know what I have to offer. I can raise Hainault; that's no small thing."

"And in return?" asked Ismail.

Godfrey smiled at him, a brief baring of teeth. "Continuance of German rule will be more than enough. If your empress should deign to add a favor or two, I'd hardly take it amiss."

"Such as?"

Godfrey shrugged. "Who knows what need might rise? I'll give her an army at Lothair's back. If Lorraine stays in her hands, I'll leave the rest of my payment to her discretion."

Yes, Aspasia thought. That was wise of him. It showed that he trusted Theophano; that he expected her to keep faith. Other lords would hear it and remember.

The talk turned to numbers and provisions and lengths of march. Aspasia, who had never seen a battle closer than the retreat from Aachen, was more inclined to care for the disposition of the wounded. But they never spoke of that if they could help it.

She was glad that they had won an ally, and had not had to pay too high a price for him. She hoped that it would not come to open war. Maybe they would only march about and sack the odd town and threaten one another. That was the best way to fight a war, if there had to be a war at all.

Thirty-Six

Whether Aspasia willed it or no, the preparations for war went on apace. Messire Godfrey withdrew to another of his castles, this one closer to Aachen, where the muster would come when it was ready.

Aspasia and her escort rode with him. Archbishop Adalberon did not; he thought that he might better serve their purpose in Rheims. But Gerbert kept them company. "The empresses charged me," he said to Aspasia, "not simply to test the winds in Francia; to do what I could to turn the Church in Germany to the proper way of thinking." He held up his pen. The letter under his hand was half done.

Aspasia nodded. He had forgotten her already: he bent back to the page, writing quickly and firmly.

Ismail was plying his craft in the village. Aspasia should have been with him. That she was not had nothing to do with any abhorrence of dirt or rags or stink; and certainly not because she feared contagion. Her mood had been getting stranger. Woman's troubles, maybe, although her courses came and went still as regularly as the moon.

She wandered, she cared not where, until she found herself on the edge of the field where the army had begun to
gather. Tents were up: plain leather for plain soldiers,
painted tents for the lords. One looked as if it might be silk.
Reckless, that one, to throw away all his wealth on a simple
shelter against the rain.

Some of the young men had got together for a mock battle. The sun glinted on their shirts of close-woven mail,
glanced and gleamed off their peaked helmets. Each of them
had added something to it to mark himself out: scarlet leggings under the grey iron coat, a belt of tooled leather dyed
deep blue, a scrap of bright silk wound Saracen fashion
about a helmet.

A few fought on foot with their great heavy swords,
which did not look to have been blunted for the occasion.
More elected to skirmish on horseback. The clang of metal
on metal, the voices of men and horses, men crying chal-
lenges or calling for surrender, the big war-stallions trum-
peting to one another, all mingled together. Over the scent
of crushed grass and spring rode the tang of iron and blood,
the pungency of sweat, the ripeness of dung and standing
water and middens. Human scents, sharpened now, edged
with war.

None of them spared her more than a glance. She was
small, veiled, in black, a woman from town or castle, widow
or bereaved mother, watching them play their game of
death. If she had been young or pretty, she knew what they
would have done. Good fathers and brothers of the town
did not let their daughters or their sisters go out alone while
there were soldiers camped outside the walls. Only the day
before, one such had caught his daughter with a man-at-
arms and lost his temper. The man-at-arms had lost rather
more than that.

Ismail had been tight-lipped when he came back from the
summons. Late in the night, when he was almost asleep, he
had said, "This much I grant the good freeman. He has a

deft hand with a razor. The cut was clean and should not fester. The surgeons would admire him in the slave markets of Córdoba."

He did not often speak of Córdoba any longer. Once in a great while he had messages. He was always very quiet afterward, and dangerously, distractedly gentle. All he would ever say of the letters was that they bore no ill news.

There had been no letter yesterday. It was the wounded man, that was all. Here in Germany there were no eunuchs, except those who had earned it as the man-at-arms had; even Theophano kept none there, although the palace in Pavia had a few. Eunuchs were a foreign thing. Heathen, the Germans said.

She stood on the field's edge and watched the young warriors pretend to kill one another. When a voice spoke behind her, she jumped like a cat.

"Lady?" it said. She turned somewhat too quickly, to stare into the face of Messire Godfrey's oldest page. The boy was no beauty, alas, and succumbing already to a plague of spots, but he had honest eyes. She could not help but smile at him.

"Lady," the boy said, "there's a messenger in the hall. He says he'll talk to no one but you."

"How high-handed of him," murmured Aspasia. The page blinked at her. She straightened her smile and held out her hand, as regal as she knew how to be. "You may conduct me," she said.

Well, she thought as she made her stately way on his arm, she could still bewitch the pages.

She was lighthearted enough when she reached the hall and dismissed her gallant knight. Godfrey was there, and Gerbert; Ismail came in behind her. The messenger sat at a trestle near the hearth, disposing handily of a platter of bread and beef. He seemed insensible of the fact that he was keeping a count and an abbot waiting.

He caught sight of Aspasia and rose, gulping down a last

mouthful of bread. What she had taken for a bald head and a dark coat proved to be a monk's robe and tonsure. Still, he was wearing good boots under the habit, and he was built like the young noblemen in the field.

As he made her a reverence, she was sure of it. He was noble-born, probably noble-raised. They did not learn that kind of grace in the cloister.

"This is Brother Notker," said Gerbert, "in service to the Archbishop of Mainz."

"Archbishop Willigis? Is he well?" Aspasia was hard put not to seem too eager. She sat in the chair a servant brought, and smoothed her skirts. After a moment's consideration she lowered her veil. She should not be too much a foreigner here; and it blurred her sight rather more than she liked.

"My lord archbishop is in fine health, lady," the monk said, "and sends you greetings and all good wishes."

"To him in return," she said, "I send the same."

Brother Notker smiled. Good news, then. Very good, from the look of him. "He'll thank you, I'm certain, my lady, and he's desirous of doing it in his own person."

"We are almost ready to go to him," she said.

He nodded, but he said, "I think you may not want to wait."

"Why?" Gerbert demanded. "Has something happened?"

"Indeed," said Brother Notker. "Archbishop Willigis is pleased to inform her highness that the Saxons have chosen their regent, and the rest of Germany has seen fit to follow suit. They have risen up against the rebel; they have hounded him to his lair. His excellency asks if it would please your highness to join him in assembly at Bürstadt, where the lords and bishops of the Germans have gathered." As he spoke, people came to listen. The more he revealed, the louder they murmured. For the last of it, he had almost to shout. "Even as I stand here, I trust in God and

His Mother that the rebel is taken and his army scattered, and his trial begun."

Everyone was talking at once. Only Aspasia kept silent. She did not dare to be glad. Not quite yet. Henry was a sly fox. Much more likely than not, he had eluded the trap.

But if the pope's decree had come . . .

She managed to ask the question without quite raising her voice to a shriek. The others stopped their shouting; except for a stray rumble on the edges, the hall was quiet. It dizzied her, so much silence after so much noise.

Brother Notker nodded. "The Holy Father has spoken on the empresses' behalf. Most of the bishops have reconsidered their allegiances. The threat of anathema can change one's mind wonderfully."

"Indeed," said Aspasia. Maybe she would let herself be glad. A little. Just enough for the pope's message. The whole singing choir of it could wait until she saw Henry himself, stripped and in fetters, before the council of the kingdom. And Otto—dear God, if he had used Otto as a hostage—

She was like a woman in a dream. Whether it was marvel or nightmare she did not know. Her escort was ready within the hour. Hilda, blessed miracle, had all their mutual belongings packed and laden in the wagon. Even Gerbert, who had become somewhat of a prince, with a prince's train, managed to muster it before the sun had risen too high. He frowned only slightly when Ismail twitted him for it, and that was wonderful indeed. Gerbert was raw enough still about Bobbio to mind what people said of peasants and pretensions.

Today he did not care. He mustered his attendants like an army, even to the massive and imperious cook, whom the master himself undertook to coax out of the kitchen. He sang as he went about his business. *He* did not doubt that Willigis had captured Henry.

Messire Godfrey saw them off with a most peculiar expression. Aspasia could almost be sympathetic. If the war was won already, if Henry was taken and Germany gone wholly to the empresses, then there was no need for his fine strong army. And armies, as she well knew, were like enchanted swords. Once drawn, they needed blood; nor would they rest in scabbard until they had it.

He would come behind them to assure that there was no trap, and to ward her if there should be need at Bürstadt. But for that day at least they would ride as they had ridden into Hainault: a sizable company but no army, with their knights and their men-at-arms, and Gerbert's monks singing hymns.

The soldiers took up the tune, but the words they fit to it made Aspasia blush. They rode eastward singing, and the spring rode with them. War had touched Franconia but lightly. The worst of it was away north in Saxony, where the German empire had begun.

A new messenger found them just past the abbey of Prüm. Henry was taken. He would reach Bürstadt before them. Of the emperor, the messenger knew nothing. Aspasia remembered to thank him. He seemed not to notice how half-hearted those thanks were. What use to have Henry, if Otto was dead or hidden away?

It was not long after that that they met a band of marauders. It could not have been set there especially for them, or there would have been more men in it. As it was, they were evenly matched.

The escort made a game as they rode, of planning battles in the country round about them. It was good training, and it kept them alert. They agreed that this was a fine place for an ambush: a sharp bend in the road, a hill rising steep on one side, trees closing in on the other. Aspasia wondered why, if they were so deep in the game, they did not think to send out scouts. That they had never met an enemy did not mean they never would, and this was a country without a strong king.

Her mule shied. She snatched the reins, scrambling to stay in the saddle. She cursed the beast with feeling. What was there for it to shy at? There was not even a breeze blowing. No bird sang; no squirrel chittered. There was no sound at all but the manifold mumble of their passing.

Ismail, who was riding beside her, sat straight in the saddle. His mare slowed her stride, ears pricked. Very slowly, very quietly, he drew his sword.

She opened her mouth to ask him what he was doing.

It was raining. Black rain. Someone screamed in pain. Those were arrows falling so deceptively gently.

Something fell on her. She crashed to the ground. For a long while she could not breathe. Dying—dead—

She had only had the wind knocked out of her. Whoever had got her off the mule and out of the fight must have been one of theirs: he had not stayed to rape or rob her. She still had her knife in its sheath at her belt. Her fingers were clamped around the hilt as she lay on her face, working up the courage to raise her head.

There were trees all about her, black and thick-trunked, swaying dizzyingly. She blinked hard. Gerbert's monks in a circle, and trees beyond them. Hilda was there next to her, very white and still.

She got creakily to her feet. Her lip stung; she ran her tongue over it, tasted blood. Split. No matter. She pushed two burly monks aside.

It did not look like a battle in a book, or even like a game on a field. Knots of men hacked and flailed at one another. The arrows had stopped flying for fear of hitting the archers' own fellows. Most of the escort rallied round the wagons, where most of the attackers seemed minded to strike.

She peered with growing desperation. No turban. Nowhere a dark head wrapped in white.

A shrill, ululating cry brought her hard about, seeming to

sound from everywhere and nowhere, freezing even the enemy where they stood. *"Allah-il-allah! Allahu akbar!"*

A shrieking, spinning, slashing demon burst through the thickest knot of fighters. God alone knew where he had come from. His mare reared, slashed, kicked. He whirled his bright sword and howled like a damned soul.

Only Aspasia, and maybe Gerbert, knew what he was howling. It was a song, much admired in Córdoba for its subtlety of nuance, of a youth who expired of love.

He was splendid to watch, and supremely uncanny. The enemy slowed and wavered and broke. The smaller fights unraveled. The large one frayed at the edges.

Ismail brought his mare to a rearing, pawing halt. He was silent, all at once. He smiled with appalling sweetness.

The enemy turned tail and fled.

Someone in the escort laughed. Someone else took it up. In a moment they all were howling; but not, God help them, in courtly Arabic.

Ismail laughed as loudly as any of them. His sword gleamed bright and clean; no drop of blood sullied it. He slid it singing into its scabbard and let his mare dance for a bit, showing off his horsemanship. The escort cheered.

It did not take them long to put themselves in order. One man had an arrow in the arm; Aspasia looked after him. A mule was lamed by a stray sword-stroke. They had to cut its throat: it could not walk far, and however easily they had driven off their attackers, there was no certainty that they would not come back. Surely one of them at least, getting over the shock, would comprehend that it had been a man who beset them and no demon; and that he had done no harm to any of them.

Aspasia's mule, having lost its rider, had sensibly withdrawn to the edge of the melee and set to grazing. One of the men caught it for her. She mounted, trying not to groan as the bruises made themselves felt. Nothing was broken, she was sure. Once she was in the saddle, the pain shrank to a scattering of aches.

Ismail had a sheen on him still. He had enjoyed himself—not least, she suspected, because no one could ever have thought that he would do it. He was good at hiding it, but he loved to startle people.

"Is this something you've done before?" she asked him when they were on their way again, the cleft and the curve well behind them.

"Not lately," he said. His face was calm, but he was grinning underneath. "It only works in Germany, where the Saracen is a tale to frighten children. In Italy they simply turn and shoot."

Cold skittered down her spine. "What if these men had known what you were?"

"Obviously they did not." His mare tossed her head and danced sidewise. He was as full of himself as any boy, and looking it, too.

"You," she said, "are out of your wits."

He fixed her with a haughty stare. "Mad I may be, but dull I have never been. Would you rather I had left it to our escort? Capable as they are," he conceded, "and zealous in our defense. But they would never have ended it so quickly."

Or for so small a price. She shook her head. A smile twitched at her lips. "You were very dashing," she said. "And handsome, with your bright sword."

She watched the slow flush creep up from under his beard. She was a little sorry to see him remember that he was a man of years and dignity, and not a wild boy. The light of him dimmed but, she was glad to see, did not go out.

It stayed in him. He was like a lamp that had been left to itself for too long, and then suddenly someone had cleaned it. The old dark scourings of the years were rubbed away; not all of them came back. He was happy, she thought. Or as close to it as he could ever be, when he was not in Córdoba.

Thirty-Seven

❖

Long before they came to Bürstadt, they knew that it was near. The road began to fill with travelers, most of them going toward the town. On the verges here and there people had pitched camp: as elaborate as a noble's pavilion, as simple as a blanket on the ground. Even beggars flocked to the scent and sound of a synod, where the gleanings in food and alms and gossip were well worth the journey.

The town itself seemed as wide as a city. Only the highest of the princes could lodge inside the walls; the rest camped round about, the strongest companies claiming the best places, the weaker taking what they could get.

"Plague," muttered Ismail as they rode through the clamoring, thronging, reeking camp. "Pestilence for certain, if they stay much longer."

Aspasia's mule stepped fastidiously round a steaming pile of dung. The beggars were brazen: one eluded the armed escort and clung to her stirrup, hopping and grinning and thrusting a filthy hand under her nose. The nearest guard plucked him off his feet and tossed him into the mob of his fellows.

Aspasia found that she was shaking. She was used to beggars; God knew, she had seen enough of them. But she could never harden to them. It made her a bad physician. She could not separate herself from the world's sufferings, learn either to ignore them as most of the highborn did, or to transmute them all into prayer like a cloistered saint.

Later she would come with Ismail, and they would do what they could do. Bread, too; she would see that the people who came for tending had something to eat.

She would have been content to camp in the field, but the steward of the council would not hear of it. He was a round-bellied little man, bright-eyed and quick like a squirrel; if it taxed him to be set in charge of such a mob, he did not show it. He was shocked that she would think of lodging anywhere but with Archbishop Willigis himself. "But, your highness! How could you imagine—your highness, you speak for the empress herself. To take the leavings—to camp in the road or next to the forest, with gnats, beggars, wild animals—oh, no, no, no!"

He was so distraught that she swallowed her protests and let herself be led in considerable state to the archbishop's lodging. By the time she came there, the whole world knew that the empress' kinswoman—her aunt, imagine it, and royal Byzantine herself, born right in the Purple Chamber, people said, and true, God was a witness to it—had come to the council.

They were hot at it in the hall of the castle. Not all of the bishops, by any means, had come round to Archbishop Willigis' way of thinking, and some of the secular lords looked ready to leap at one another's throats.

Henry the Quarreller was full in the middle of it. He did not look like a prisoner. He was unarmed, but then every

armed man had had to leave his weapons at the door. No
rope or chain bound him. The men near him, big men in
Archbishop Willigis' livery, might have been the entourage
proper to any great lord.

He had lost his prison pallor, and some of the softness
that went with it. At the moment he was flushed with fury,
straining toward Archbishop Willigis as if he wanted to
clamp his hands about that worthy's throat. "I will not!" he
roared. "I will not yield!"

The archbishop was a weedy little man with a face like a
scared rabbit. The louder Henry roared, the more like a rabbit he looked.

At last Henry subsided. Willigis blinked. His eyes were
pale, red-rimmed, and perpetually watering. He dabbed at
them with a damp bit of linen, and sneezed. His voice when
he spoke was soft and rather thick with rheum, but surprisingly deep. There was nothing rabbity about it. "That then
is your final word?"

Henry's beard bristled. "I will not give up the crown."

The archbishop sighed, coughed, blew into his handker-
chief. "Your position is hardly conducive to intransigence.
Would you choose to die, then?"

"At least," said Henry, "I shall die a king."

Willigis flicked a finger. The guards closed about Henry.
Glowering, shaking just a little but keeping his head high, he
let himself be led away.

"He won't budge?" Aspasia asked.

Willigis sneezed. Poor man, he was worse every year, and
worst of all in the spring. It was the effect of the warm air on
his humours, Ismail said. Aspasia was inclined to think that
it had something to do with grass and flowers: he was all but
prostrate on the few occasions when he could not avoid
walking in a garden.

He wiped his streaming eyes and sniffed loudly. "That
man is intransigence made flesh."

They were in the solar behind the hall. Most of the council had dispersed once Henry was sent out and Aspasia welcomed with due ceremony. The few who remained were the most loyal of all, or the most useful.

"What are you offering him," Aspasia asked, "besides his life?"

"Isn't that enough?"

That was Duke Conrad of Swabia. He was Franconian, and he owed his duchy to the German crown; his loyalty was as dour as it was unshakable.

"Whether his life is payment enough for a throne," said Aspasia, "depends on what you want to do with him. Will you keep him a prisoner and trust that he won't escape as he did the last time? Will you turn him loose and hope that he won't simply go back to his war and his followers? Or will you pay him more, give him something worth the keeping, so that he's not tempted to turn rebel again?"

"What would you give him?" Willigis asked.

"Bavaria."

Someone growled. It was not the present Duke of Bavaria, who owed his duchy to Henry's rebellion; he was in his lodging like a sensible man, enjoying his dinner. But he had friends, and Henry had enemies in plenty. "Emperor Otto took Bavaria away from him for his quarreling and his treason. Now he's quarreled his way to a crown, you want to give him back all that he lost? What kind of punishment is that?"

"It's not," said Aspasia. "It's bribery and corruption." She widened her eyes, miming innocence. "But you of course, my lords, are far above that. You'll execute him cleanly, and let his infamy die with him."

"No!" Duke Conrad flushed under all their stares. He coughed, cleared his throat, glowered at no one in particular. "We can't put him to death. Whatever he's done, he's royal kin. People turn away from him now because they see where the right way lies. But if we kill him we'll make a martyr, with a blood feud on top of it."

Christian barbarians, Aspasia thought, were appalling beasts. "So it's not true what we've so long believed? His father didn't try to kill great Otto with his own hands?"

"That was brothers," said Conrad. "They'll fight; who can stop them? And he failed. Young Henry, now—he never tried to kill anyone. Even the little emperor."

"You see," said Willigis, "there's no royal blood on his hands. Ambition—that's deplorable, and one could call him a thief, but it would hardly be politic to kill him."

"It would not be politic to reward him for being a rebel," Conrad said. "Set him free, I say, but cut him down to a castle or two and a few men-at-arms, and swear him to obedience. Then if he breaks his word, kill him."

Most seemed to approve of that. Aspasia shook her head, wishing that she could seize each one of them and shake him until he saw sense. "All that will do will assure that he rises again; and probably before the year is out." She drew a deep, steadying breath. "My lords, think. He won't yield now. If I were he, I'd keep on resisting, and all the while I'd wait, and send what messages I could, and gather my forces together. But if we give him—not what he thinks he wants, which is the kingship, but what he is actually entitled to, the duchy that was his father's before him—if we give him that, and show him true Christian charity, who's to say that he won't decide to be content with it?"

"The more so," Gerbert said, "if there's steel in back of it and an oath on his head."

"He'll never take it," said Conrad. "Not while there's still any hope of the crown."

"There is not." Aspasia's voice was flat. "If I undertake to convince him of it, and offer him Bavaria in return for his honest fealty, will you stand with me?"

They glanced at one another. To their credit, only one

muttered about women getting above themselves. The others seemed to ponder carefully what she had said.

Willigis coughed. "I think that my lady's proposal has merit; and she speaks for the empress. I will stand with her."

One by one, with Gerbert leading, they muttered their assent. Even, last and most reluctant, the man who did not wish to see his ally robbed of Bavaria. "If you can do it," he said, "I'll stand by it. If you can't . . ."

"If I can't, then what have we lost?"

"Time," said Conrad. But he did not try again to dissuade her.

Otto was not in Bürstadt. Henry's men held him in one of Henry's castles. Aspasia could hardly admit to surprise. It explained much of Henry's intransigence. Each side had a hostage now; and Henry was far more able to take care of himself than a lone small child in an army of enemies.

They were keeping the rebel in the castle, in a room high up in the tower. It was furnished for comfort, as much as ever could be in a castle, and there were windows on all four sides, narrow but tall, to let in the light. Aspasia, thinking of the tiny cell which she shared with Hilda, reflected that the prisoner was rather better housed than his jailers.

Henry welcomed her with perfect courtesy. No glint of mockery; no twist of the lip to remind her of their last meeting.

Aspasia accepted the chair he offered. He stood by a window, his stillness of a kind that Aspasia knew too well: taut, coiled, as if left to himself he would break free and fly.

Five years within the same four walls could do that to a man. He was not quite sane, she thought. Sane men did not snatch at crowns or begin civil wars.

And she was gambling on his sanity. She sighed to herself. Hilda breathed at her back, light and shallow, like an animal in a trap.

The silence stretched. He broke it abruptly, his voice

sharper perhaps than he had intended. "You have a message for me, madam?"

"None from my empress," she said, "that you haven't heard before."

"Do you think I'll listen better now?"

She could not see his face clearly, with his back to the light. She knew that he meant it so. She allowed herself a very small smile. "I think you have no intention of listening at all."

"You're going to try to make me."

"You have my emperor still."

It took him a while to puzzle her meaning. He tried his own obliqueness. "And how fares Master Ismail?"

This time she smiled more widely. "Blackmail, sir?"

Her amusement disconcerted him. He came to stand over her. Mere size could not cow her; she looked up calmly into his face. He glared down. "What would the good bishops do, if they knew where I found you in Cologne?"

"What, Archbishop Warin didn't tell them?" She clicked her tongue. "Tch. He's neglecting his Christian duty."

"Archbishop Warin," said Henry, and his voice was tight, "was one of the first to change his allegiance."

"I expected that he would be." She let her head rest against the high back of the chair. "It wasn't what you thought it would be, after all. Was it?"

"It was—is—all that kingship should be."

"Was," she said. "You couldn't have won, you know. Not once you took the crown. If you could have been patient, kept the regency, let it go on for years, and all the while taken great care to prevent the emperor from proving himself fit to rule, at his majority you could well and easily have been given the kingship in his stead. Who knows? The world is a deadly place, and children are fragile. A sickness might have taken him long before you needed to displace him. Then you would have had what you wanted, and kept it."

She watched the anger swell. He could strike her. The guards were too far to stop him, and Hilda could not match his strength.

He kept his fists at his sides. "You have a tongue like a snake," he said.

"It's called truth," she said. "You should have studied patience."

"As you did with that Saracen?"

"Moor," she said, gently. "I know the nature and the number of my sins. I would never reach for a throne."

He looked at her in utter incomprehension. It had, she noticed, shocked him out of his rage. "You are an emperor's daughter."

"What is a daughter, even to a king?"

"Wealth beyond price. Right to an empire."

"That," she said, "is why they keep us all in convents."

"But not you."

She shook her head. "Not I. I proved myself harmless, in the men I chose, in the life I led."

He laughed, raw-throated. "Mother of God! You almost make me believe you."

"You know that I tell the truth. I want no more than I have. I stretch my hand to nothing that is not mine."

"So, then. You want to play confessor."

"Would you confess your sins to me, my lord of Bavaria?"

"Yes!" He had said it to shock her, but she watched him realize that he meant it. Then the rest struck him.

"I am not," he said, "lord of Bavaria."

He was quick-witted. She kept forgetting. Quickness where she came from was small and dark and sharp-nosed. Big and blunt and fair was barbarian and simple, and slow to understand subtlety.

"You can be," she said to him. "My lord duke."

"Should I be a mere duke, when I have been king?"

"Better that than dead."

"They won't kill me," he said with fine certainty. But he paused, because doubt was the most tenacious of demons.

"Most likely not," she said. "They'll take your oath and confine you to one of your castles."

The color drained from his face. "I won't," he said. "I won't go back to prison."

"Then when they've had enough they'll kill you. They can hardly let you loose, can they? Unless," she said, "they have certain cause to trust you. If you could have Bavaria back, with no condition but that of loyal service to the emperor and his regents, would you take it?"

"What makes you think that any of them will offer me so much?"

"Because I tell them to."

"You? Not the empresses?"

"The empresses trust me to do what is best."

He stared at her as if he had never seen her before. Maybe he had not. What he would have seen was never simply Aspasia. A scion of the Purple Chamber; a wanton found naked abed with an infidel; an envoy of the foreigner queen. Now maybe he saw her simply as she was.

"You," he said slowly, "are a prodigy of nature."

She laughed with honest mirth. "Most tactfully put! A monster, that is I. And yet I am nothing but what any woman is."

"No," he said. "No, you are different. Others, even queens—they do what is expected of them. You do what pleases you."

"So do we all. It's only that what pleases me is seldom what the world expects." She rose, slipping past him, and walked to the window. It looked southward over the huddled roofs of the town, across the bright confusion that was the camp, into the green darkness of the forest. She spoke without turning, clear enough for him to hear. "Bavaria is yours by right. If you take it, and if you serve the emperor with true devotion, all your sins will be forgiven. All of them, my lord. No blood feud from those whose kin your war has killed; no reprisal from the regents whose office you seized, or the emperor whose crown you usurped."

"Why?"

He truly did not understand. Which was why, she thought, he could not have remained king. She gave him that part of it which might satisfy him. "I was never fool enough to keep a falcon in a cage."

"Then you'd tame me to jesses and a hood, and fly me on the creance?"

"You can always choose the cage," she said.

He came to stand beside her. She wondered if he would touch her. He was as hot as a hearthfire, even at a judicious distance.

"I could abduct you," he said, "and force a marriage, and begin a new game."

"Which you would lose."

"You are very sure of that."

He wanted her. Her, not her rank or her imagined titles. Maybe he had realized it as recently as she. He did not seize her as another man might. He made no move to touch her at all.

That rocked her. Germans took what they wanted. Henry was living proof of it in all that he had done since great Otto died. But her, he did not take.

It would have been better if he had tried to rape her. Then she would have known what to do.

He was good to look at. She liked to talk to him; that too was a new understanding. For all that he had done, she did not hate him. He was like a child, fierce and heedless, taking what he fancied was his, not caring who went without. But, she thought, he was growing up. He was learning that not everything he wanted was his to have.

"If I do as you ask," he said, "will you do something in return?"

"I won't marry you," she said.

He shook his head. He was only a little annoyed. "Will you promise me that if Otto dies without issue, my son will be king?"

"That is hardly for me to promise," she said.

Now he was angry. "Don't lie to yourself. I've seen what you've made of Otto, even as young as he is. I want you to teach my son; I want you to make him the kind of man who can be an emperor. I'm not such a fool as to think you won't do everything in your power to get Otto wedded, bedded, and provided with heirs. But if that fails, my son will be king. Promise that and I'll bow to your will. I'll take Bavaria, swear the oath, be loyal until death to the emperor you chose."

Aspasia stared unseeing at the sky. She knew young Henry by report; he had never been in court when she had been there. Eleven years old, he would be now, a tall, fair, quiet child who had gone young to study with the monks. Everyone knew that he would be tonsured when he was older, and made an archbishop.

She turned to face Henry. "You would suffer a woman to teach your son?"

"You've been teaching Otto. I know you had a hand in instructing his father; and his mother is your pupil from the cradle. Teach my son, and I'll be your emperor's tame hawk. No tamer or more faithful will he ever see."

His voice was quiet, but there was truth in it. This oath he would not break. This faith he would keep.

The cynic in her observed that even he could see when he was defeated. No one would trust him with the regency again. He could not be certain that he would live to see Otto grown; or that Otto would not be too strong then to overthrow. He had gambled twice for the throne and lost. There would be no third game.

Except that this too was a gamble; the greatest of them all. To surrender, and serve the one who held the place he coveted, and trust that his son would rule. It was Byzantine, that choice. Of all that he had done, it was the most worthy of a king.

She bowed her head to it. "If your son will endure my instruction, then I will instruct him."

"He'll endure you," said Henry, as one who meant to make sure of it.

She raised a brow but held her peace. For all that she could do, excitement bloomed in her. Another child to teach. Older, this one; formed already, and likely rebellious. A challenge. She would have to talk to Gerbert, who knew so much more than she of taming wild things.

She almost forgot to bid Henry farewell. She atoned for it by bowing somewhat lower than was strictly necessary for one of her rank, and saying to him, "God keep you well, my lord duke."

The title served its purpose. It would never be anything but second best, but it was a very good second. He would learn to be content with it.

Thirty-Eight

🔘

H enry the Quarreller accepted the bargain that was offered him, and yielded before the council. Then they let him go. He had affairs to settle, a duchy to claim. On the feast of Saints Peter and Paul, he swore on sacred relics, he would appear before the Diet at Rara and make formal submission to the empresses and to the emperor whom he had so signally offended.

Henry departed, attended by men in the livery of Mainz and Swabia and Saxony as well as of Bavaria. The throngs about Bürstadt melted away. In a month they would all reappear like mayflies above a pond, in the lands about Rara.

Gerbert rode out with the rest to meet the empresses on their way up from Italy and to ride with them to Rara. Messire Godfrey, who had come to Bürstadt in time to witness Henry's surrender, kept him company. Aspasia went to Magdeburg. Otto was there as Henry had promised her, almost the last thing he had done before he left Bürstadt. He was healthy, he was going brown, and his puppy was now a great half-grown monster of a dog somewhat taller than he was.

The dog was the first she saw of Otto. It loomed out of the shadows of the nursery and set great paws on her shoulders, and kissed her with doggy enthusiasm.

"Wolf!" The voice was very young and most imperious. The dog lowered itself reluctantly to all fours.

"Dear heaven," said Aspasia. "A Molossian."

"He is a mastiff," said Otto proudly. He looked, next to the dog, like a warrior with his trusty steed. Then he was her Otto, leaping as exuberantly as the dog had, laughing and crying and trying to tell her everything at once.

He stopped suddenly, arms locked about her neck. "You're not going away this time. Are you?"

"No," she said. "Never again."

He nodded. In much the same way Archbishop Willigis and Duke Conrad had accepted Henry's promises: gracious, regal, and determined to see that they were kept.

Magdeburg with Otto in it was home. They were a week in Frauenwald, which was more than glad to see its mistress, but the city was more suitable for raising an emperor. Ismail had his house near the Jewry, where all day long people came to be healed, and where she was as often as Otto would let her go. She had Otto to teach and to look after, and Otto's sisters, and when she came back from Rara she would have Henry's son. A school for princes. Sometimes she laughed at the thought. Sometimes she was nearer to terror. But even that was bright and clean, the terror that went with all the great choices.

On a grey soft day near Midsummer, a little before they were to ride to Rara, Aspasia paused by the palace gate on her way to Ismail's house. She had her box of medicines, which needed replenishing, and her plainest black cloak and veil wrapped against the gentle rain. The streets would be quagmires; she stopped to put on the rough wooden clogs that all the countryfolk wore. The gate guards greeted her respectfully, knowing who she was. As she returned the greeting, she paused.

There were riders coming up from the town. Their banner—she peered. She did not know it. A foreign lord maybe, or an embassy. Two or three of the riders were turbaned Saracens.

That was unusual enough to stop her completely. Saracens were no great rarity around the court and the emperor, but they did not often come so far into Germany.

The rest looked German enough. The man under the banner announced himself in broad Bavarian as a vassal of Duke Henry. He seemed pleased to say so. "I come to give my daughter to the abbey," he said, patting the hand of the veiled and skirted figure who rode beside him. The girl looked less exalted than excited, craning round at all the sights.

"And," her father said, "I bring a gift from my duke to the Princess Aspasia. These gentry"—he did not spit, which Aspasia thought generous of him—"are looking for someone who speaks their jabber."

The gentry, all three of them, sat their fiery little horses and offered no word. Something about them made her step forward boldly and demand of the lord from Bavaria, "Was there no speaker of Arabic closer than Magdeburg?"

His lordship looked down from his tall horse. He would reckon her a servant: she was dressed like one. But he was kind enough to answer her. "The duke had a man who could piece together a word or two. He said the princess would understand better than anyone; so he sent them with me. Are you her woman? Can you take them to her?"

Aspasia studied the foreigners. Two were older men, and one was young. Very young. His beard was no more than a sheen on his cheeks. He sat straight in the saddle, eyes fixed haughtily ahead, refusing to be sullied by this alien place.

The others let their eyes rove with studied casualness, as if this were a city like any other, and they belonged as well here as anywhere. He was too young and, she thought, too wild. He made her think of a hawk just caught, a haggard still half in youngling plumage, yearning for the open sky.

She spoke to him in Arabic, politely but without submission. "I give you greeting, young sir, and welcome to the house of my emperor."

He started. His mare shied. He soothed her with skill which she knew well; was it inbred in every Arab? He glared down at Aspasia, more like a hawk than ever with his thin blade of nose. "You speak the tongue of the Faithful?" His voice was sharp, peremptory.

She inclined her head, which was a rebuke. He flushed, but he did not abate his arrogance. "I have some small knowledge," she said, "of the language of the Prophet, on whose name be blessing and peace. Will my lord and his companions please to enter my emperor's house?"

The eldest of them spoke before the boy could begin. "We shall be pleased to accept your emperor's hospitality." He was as smoothly courteous as the boy was rough. From the glint of his eye, he knew it very well indeed; but he loved the boy regardless, and honored him, and indulged his failings.

Aspasia had seen for herself that the child was terrified. She left the guards to look after the Bavarians, and attended the Saracens herself. She saw them dismounted, assured them that their horses would be well cared for—as they would; she had commanded that they be stabled with Ismail's beauties—and entrusted them to the steadiest of the menservants, who would offer them the rites of eastern hospitality.

She for her part debated. She did not need to give the visitors an audience until tomorrow at least; they would expect no less of a princess. She should go to Ismail, who would snarl at her for being late.

But she could not bring herself to go. It was not polite to

ask anything of a guest until he should have rested, bathed, and eaten. Yet this much they gave her to know: they were not from Italy or from Africa. They were from al-Andalus.

That in the end was why she stayed in the palace. Three Moors in Magdeburg who were part of no formal embassy—whatever had brought them here, she was certain, down to the heart of her, that it had to do with Ismail. And she did not want to see him or tell him, until she knew.

She bathed and put on a gown worthy of her rank, and called Hilda to put up her hair.

Hilda was sure that the riders were nothing to fret over. "There must be an embassy with the empresses," she said, "and these decided to travel on their own, with a letter for Master Ismail, maybe, for an excuse. One's a boy, you say? Then I'm right, you'll see. He's out gallivanting. I wonder if his father knows."

"He looks," said Aspasia, "very well brought up."

Hilda laughed. "Why, lady! You're in love with him!" She laughed the harder when Aspasia blushed, cursing herself the while, but knowing it was true. The child looked just exactly as she imagined Ismail had when he was young. She would laugh with him over it later, when he had his message.

Unless it was ill news: his wife or son dead, his sentence altered to death.

Then she would comfort him. He was safe here; he was happy. He would grieve no more than he must, and no less, and then he would go on. That was part of what she loved in him: that slender strength, that bent but never broke.

She received them in the evening, in the wide and shining room that was the empress' bower. The last of the light lay long upon the floor; already in corners the lamps were lit. She had Hilda with her, but no other attendant. Out of deference to their custom, and indeed to her own of Byzantium, she wore a veil over her face.

All three of them came, washed and rested and fed, in fresh robes and clean turbans. The boy's robe was the most handsome, silk embroidered with gold; he was beautiful in it, but he seemed not to know it. He bowed at her feet, proud in his humility.

He did not recognize her even when she bade him rise. How could he? She was veiled. But he might have known her voice.

He complimented her very prettily on her command of Arabic. She bit back a smile. His manners with his betters, even if they were infidels, were impeccable. "The one of us who spoke the barbarian tongues," he said, "was lost in the mountains, and we found no one who spoke proper Arabic. Rafiq," he said, indicating the eldest of them, "has a word or two of Frankish, and we made ourselves understood, after a fashion. But truly, O great lady, it is a wonder and a delight to hear in this benighted land the speech of my own people."

"So would I be glad," she said, "to hear good Greek, were there no one about me who spoke it."

He smiled. His smile was wonderful: it transformed his face. "I was told, great lady, that you were the soul of wisdom and of courtesy. Now I know that the tale is but a shadow of the truth."

"Ah," she said. "Such flattery. And may I know to whom I say it?"

He flushed scarlet. "Oh, my lady! I cry your pardon." He would have dropped down again and abased himself, if she had not forbidden him. It was all she could do not to burst out laughing.

He was cruelly embarrassed, but he kept his head up as he announced, "Nasir am I, Nasir al-Din Muhammad ibn Ismail ibn Suleiman ibn Abu Salim of Córdoba. He at my right hand is Rafiq ibn al-Adim, he at my left Karim ibn Jubair, faithful servants of my house."

Aspasia bowed her head to each. She did not know why

she was dizzy. Ismail was a common name in Córdoba. So too Suleiman. And who was to say that Abu Salim had not had many grandsons? This was not, of course this was not, Ismail's son.

But oh, dear God, now that she had eyes to see, this child was the very image of her lover.

"It is known to us," he said, "that one of my house dwells with you here. Do you know the name of Hafiz Ismail ibn Suleiman?"

She swayed, but caught herself before he could see. "He is known to us," she said.

His face lit like a lamp. "He is here? He is in this city?"

"You will pardon me," she said with great care, "if I choose not to answer you at once. We know that he is not in this country of his own will. If you have come to take him to his death, then do you know that he is under our protection."

The boy flushed, then paled. His eyes glittered. "Great lady, your caution is to be commended. I am no executioner, nor yet assassin. I am but a son who seeks his father."

"You . . . look like him." Aspasia's voice seemed to come from very far away. "Yes, he is in Magdeburg. We hold him in great honor. He is physician to the emperor, and to the empress mother."

Nasir was angry still, but not too angry to be glad. "I hardly remember him: I was but a child when he went away. But I was raised to honor him, and to pray for his return."

"Until you grew into a man and chose to seek him for yourself?"

"Oh, no, great lady," he said. "Or, yes, I chose to look for him, but I was sent." The anger was gone; there remained only gladness. "Such news I bring, great lady—such joy as it will be. His enemy is dead. His exile is lifted. I have come," said Nasir al-Din, "to bring my father home."

It was, Aspasia supposed, inevitable. She did not remember what she said to her guests after Nasir explained his errand. She thought of lies, sleights, deceptions. She could feign to send a messenger, inform him with regret that Master Ismail had left the city, send him far afield. Months, she could gain. Years, even.

She told Nasir where to find his father's house, and gave him a servant to guide him to it. She sat for a long while in the darkening room, staring at nothing, thinking nothing, being nothing but emptiness.

She vowed to let them be. Strangers who were father and son would want to be alone together. News such as Nasir brought needed solitude to be comprehended.

She finished the day well enough. No one looked at her oddly or asked if she was ill. She went to bed neither early nor late, and lay awake, while the slow hours crawled toward dawn.

In the morning she got up, washed, dressed as she always did. She went to mass. She ate with Otto and played with him, and gave him his lesson. It was as if another woman did all of it. She walked, spoke, even smiled, but she was not Aspasia. Aspasia was alone in the cold.

When the hour came for her to go to Ismail as she should have done the day before, she meant to do other things that needed doing. He would summon her when he wanted her, or come to fetch her. She found herself in her old cloak and her wooden clogs, picking her way through the streets.

His house looked no different. It was large as houses went in Magdeburg. The door was painted green; the walls were freshly limed so that they gleamed in the sun. She blinked. She had not even noticed how lovely a day it was.

Ismail was not in the room that was half physician's clinic, half apothecary's shop. It was empty of anything but dust and sun and the mingled scents of herbs and medicines. She walked through it to the inner room and the stair that led to the upper reaches.

The inner room was guarded. It was not Wilhelm the servant, who was often there attending his duties. He would have smiled and given her greeting and let her pass.

This one did not smile. She recognized the younger of Nasir's two companions, the one who had never spoken or smiled. He did neither now, simply refused to move aside from the stair.

She drew a careful breath. "I wish," she said as politely as she could, "to speak with Hafiz Ismail."

The man did not move. "The Hafiz is seeing no visitors," he said. "Come back tomorrow."

She must not let anger rule her. This man was only protecting his master from the importunate. "I am not a seeker after healing," she said, still politely. "I am a friend. He will wish to see me."

"Come back tomorrow," said the Moor.

Her hands were fists. She did not often mind that she was small and weak and a woman. There was so much else that one could do to get one's way, if one were royal Byzantine.

Did she want to, now? Maybe after all he did not want to see her. She would only remind him of his exile; he who was free at last, and summoned home.

Feet sounded on the stair. She was about to turn away; she paused.

Wilhelm greeted her with pleasure. "My lady! The master was just asking where you were."

The Moor did not understand German. He stood like a wall.

Wilhelm, looking at him, understood. "These barbarians," he muttered. He tapped the Moor lightly, with a smile to avoid giving offense, and stepped past him to bow low and with ostentatious reverence. "Your highness, if you will come with me."

Maybe Karim would have resisted, but he was not a fool. He stepped aside. She felt his scowl on her back as she went up the stair.

She decided to be amused. Wilhelm was righteously indignant, outraged that royalty should be kept dangling at the door like a beggar woman. She soothed him with a smile and let herself be ushered into the master's presence.

They were sitting on the floor, Ismail much as he always did, Nasir like a young image of him. Each had an arm about the other. There was food on a low table and drink in the good silver cups, but clearly it was long forgotten.

"No, no," Ismail was saying. "That was after I married your mother. Two wives being then beyond my means, and as for treating them equally . . ."

Nasir laughed, but with respect. "I'm going to marry," he said a little shyly, "when I go back. Her family wanted to settle it before, but Mother wanted your blessing on it."

"So?" asked Ismail. "And is it a good marriage?"

"Oh, yes," said Nasir eagerly. "I know it's hardly proper, but her brother and I are friends, we were in the *madrasa* together, and then we were pages to the same emir—a most respectable family, Father, and well thought of in court—and he assures me that she's very pretty. Spirited, too. I think," he said, "I should like a wife with spirit."

Aspasia was going to turn and go. There was nothing for her here. His own world had claimed him; his own proper kin.

Wilhelm's voice stopped her. He had been waiting judiciously for a pause. Now that there was one, he said, "Master; young sir. The Lady Aspasia."

They both turned. Nasir was curious, a little annoyed. Ismail was pure singing joy. Even when he was happiest, making long and lazy love to her or riding one of his half-wild horses or putting bandits to flight by sheer force of outrageousness, he had never looked like this. One forgot the grey in his beard, the lines in his face; one saw only how like he was to his son.

He leaped up and took her hands. Before she could free herself, he had drawn her into the room, and stood still holding her, smiling at Nasir. The boy was on his feet, transparently uncertain whether or how deeply to bow.

Him at least she could help. "Come," she said, "be at ease. I'm no princess here."

He knew her then; from the way the color came and went in his face, he knew not only that she was her royal highness, but that she had been the serving-woman in the gate.

"Princess indeed," said Ismail, half-laughing, "but friend as well, and kin."

That too Nasir would understand if he wished: Ismail would not let go her hand, and when he had led her to the chair she always sat in when she was there, he stayed by her.

She knew what she was supposed to do. She thought that she would not do it. What right had Ismail to presume that she would?

He presumed nothing. He did not even ask with a glance. He wanted his son to see, that was all; to know the truth. In their world it was nothing to be ashamed of.

She let fall her veil. Nasir was too well bred to stare. He did not seem disappointed. He greeted her very handsomely, first as princess, then as kin. "My father has been fortunate," he said.

"And well I know it," said Ismail.

"So you told us, Father," Nasir said. "Mother was pleased that you could be happy in your exile." He smiled at Aspasia, oh so innocently. "She bade me tell you that you will be welcome in Córdoba, as the beloved of her honored husband."

"Wife," said Ismail, and there was iron in that.

Nasir barely blushed. "Oh, of course. How not? I hope, lady, that you didn't mind yesterday when I made no reference to it."

"Not at all," said Aspasia. She was proud that she sounded so calm. "I understand. You were full of your search for your father; you had no room for anything else."

"Just so, my lady." He was delighted that she understood

so well. "He told us so much about you. How learned you are, and how gracious, and how beautiful."

Ismail, she was pleased to see, had gone slowly crimson.

"Oh," said his son, "but I'm babbling. I cry your pardon, lady. I'm so happy, you see. I can't keep it in."

"I see," said Aspasia before Ismail could erupt. He had let go of her hand at last. She held it out to Nasir. "I'm glad to see you so glad."

"He's charming," Aspasia said.

He was gone, exploring the city. Part of it was tact. Part was curiosity. He had Rafiq to guard him, and Wilhelm's eldest, who knew a bit of Arabic, to keep him out of trouble.

Ismail looked torn between a snarl and a smile. "He's an irresistible young idiot."

"And what were you, at seventeen?"

"He was still at the breast," said Ismail, "when I fled from Córdoba. Fifteen years. Impossible that it should be so long."

"Yes," Aspasia said.

Alone with her, without appearances to keep up, he sat at her feet and laid his head in her lap. She unwound the turban and combed his hair with her fingers. He had not shaved it this summer, because she liked it so well; he had cropped it short instead.

She realized with a shock that he was weeping. Not hard; not painfully. He could talk through it. "He came in while I was salving Hedda's eyes. They're better, but they would be better still if she would stop rubbing out the salve as soon as I put it on. He came in and watched, and I never knew, until I saw Rafiq. He taught me the sword, long ago. Did I ever tell you that? He stood watching me, and I said his name. He wept like a woman. But he wouldn't touch me or embrace me until I knew who Nasir was. It was," he said, and his voice was wry, "a very damp meeting."

She could not help but smile. "He wept on your neck?"

"And I on his. Neither of us slept last night. We were up almost till dawn, talking, and then we shared the dawn prayer." He breathed deep, as if to master himself. "Aspasia. Aspasia, I'm free. I can go home."

Her heart twisted exactly as she had known it would. Knowing did not make it easier.

"My enemy is dead," he said. "His wife, who was so unkind to me, has become a holy widow, devoted to good works. The first of which, once her husband was entrusted to Paradise, was to petition the Commander of the Faithful for my pardon. In his graciousness he granted it. All that I had when I fled is mine still, and it has grown fourfold: my wife has tended it more than wisely. I am a rich man, my lady, and if not a prince, then noble enough for the purpose. My son is to marry a prince's granddaughter."

"I am happy for you both," Aspasia said.

He raised his head. Either he had not heard the strangeness in her voice, or it did not matter to him. His cheeks were wet but his eyes were shining. "Nasir is enchanted with you. The first thing he said to me, once we were done weeping on one another's neck, was that you were the most regal lady he had ever seen."

"And how many has he seen?"

Ismail smiled his sudden smile. "How many does a boy ever need to see? He's fallen in love with you. He went so far as to inform me that if I omit to marry you and bring you back with me, he will never forgive me."

She could not find a smile for herself. "So it's settled, is it?"

"I had been concerned," he said, "that I would have difficulty in supporting a second wife as is fitting to her rank and station. Safiyah assures me through our son that I need have no such fears. If you would prefer to have your own house, with your own household—it would be irregular, but there would be no impediment, except perhaps Nasir's displeasure."

"Of course we must not displease Nasir."

He glanced sharply at her. It was dawning on him at long last that something was amiss. "You are jealous."

"No," she said. She was not. She was glad to see that he had so splendid a son. She was happy that his wife had protected his estates so well. Safiyah was all that a good wife should be. She might even, Aspasia thought, be someone whom Aspasia would be pleased to know.

It was not that she was jealous. It was that he was going home.

He rose to his knees, folding her hands in his. "When you see Córdoba," he said, "you will wonder that you ever doubted. Constantinople may be greater, Baghdad more magnificent. Córdoba is beautiful. And the people in it . . . the school of medicine may be the best in the world. The poets are as numerous as birds, and nigh as sweet to hear. The wise men, the learned scholars: all come to Córdoba to learn and to teach.

"There is a place for you there," he said. "For what you are, for what wisdom is in you, the city will fall at your feet."

"Even if I am a wife, and respectable?"

"I will never ask you to be aught but what you are."

Ah, she thought. But what was that?

She freed one of her hands, smoothed a wayward lock from his brow. He was smiling faintly, deep in his beard. He could not help himself. All that he had dreamed of, all that he had prayed for, was coming true.

He had not even for a moment thought that he could stay here.

It was that, that hurt. He loved her down to the heart of him. He had no thought of leaving her. She would come with him. She would be his wife; she would love him freely where there was no shame. She would live among civilized people in a civilized country that would look on her with respect and cherish all that she was.

"No more deception," he said. "No more loving in secret. No more dread of your dishonor."

Her head shook slowly. She did not know what she was denying. Confusion, maybe. Fear. By sheer grim will she had made this country her own. Must she go now, and begin it all again?

"You're in shock," he said, looking hard into her face. "Of course. What am I thinking? I'm as heedless as Nasir. This is too much to take in all at once; and well I should know it, who have had the night and the day, and have barely begun."

Shock, yes. She was cold. She had no will to move, though when he drew her to her feet, she came without resistance. He looked about for the cloak she had discarded, frowned at it, wrapped her instead in one of his own. Its scent of spices made her tremble. She could not stop. No tears—at least there were no tears.

He left her standing there, hunting in the chest for the wine she kept there, and a clean cup. He would want to put something in the wine, to steady her.

She shook her head. She almost fell. But she could walk. She walked straight to the door, and out of it, before he could have known that she was gone.

She kept walking. He did not come after her. She was piqued, a little. Maybe Nasir had come back; or something else had conspired to stop him.

She did not go to the palace but walked past it to the cathedral. At this hour the priests and the canons were at their labors elsewhere. There was one in a side chapel, seeing to the candles, but he took no notice of Aspasia.

Aspasia sat on the base of one of the pillars. She should kneel, she supposed, and try to pray. But there was no prayer in her.

Or maybe the whole of her was a prayer.

Córdoba. Beautiful, learned, world-wise Córdoba. She

even believed that it would be for her there as Ismail had said it would. Ismail was half wild with joy, but he was still Ismail; he did not indulge in fancies.

In the mosaic over the altar, Christ the King and the Mother of God sat enthroned in majesty, and beside them a haloed saint: Saint Mauritius in his armor, warrior saint for a warrior church, here on the marches of the east. Under his feet, but proud for all of that, knelt a crowned king. *Odo,* the legend said, *rex Germanorum;* and in letters that glinted somewhat newer, *magnus imperator.* Otto, king of the Germans, great emperor. Someday, maybe, someone would alter that in its turn, to make him emperor of the Romans.

He did not look much as she remembered. This was a Byzantine king, shaped by hands trained in Byzantium: dark, great-eyed, sternly serene. The sternness at least was like great Otto. Neither his son nor his grandson had it. They were gentler, more truly civilized.

Was that an ill thing? she wanted to ask him. Gentleness was no virtue in a king. And yet even God, who was Justice absolute, tempered that justice with mercy.

The youngest Otto, her Otto, could be the best of them. There was strength in him, even as young as he was, and a questing intelligence. He understood from birth not simply what it meant to be German, but what it was to be Roman. He could make the world anew.

Gerbert had spoken of it before he left, something that the wise were dreaming of, what Charlemagne had striven for and his successors lost again. *Renovatio imperii Romani.* Not only to create a barbarian empire in the west. To restore the empire that was Rome.

What was Byzantium but one long striving after its shattered sister in the west? Even Justinian had failed to win it back; he had won fragments only, and those lost and gained and lost again. The Romans themselves were all fallen from what they had been, a race of petty squabblers in a ruined city.

The strength was here. They were barbarians yet, these Franks and Germans and still-half-heathen Saxons, but they knew what more they could be. They were young, strong, ambitious. If they could be united, if they could learn to live in amity under a strong king, they could rule the world.

Or if not the world, then a goodly portion of it. Gallia, Germania, Italia; Hispania even, if God granted them strength and a degree of reckless daring. All that had been the Western Empire.

The pillar was cool and hard against her back. She had lost Ismail's cloak somewhere. She had her veil still: woman's instinct, to guard her modesty even in distraction.

She was not so lost in vanity as to imagine that the dream of empire was hers alone, or that it would die if she abandoned it. There were others who shared it; potent forces, some of them. Gerbert. Archbishop Adalberon in Rheims. Theophano herself, through whom Otto gained his fullest right to the Roman imperium. Aspasia was hardly irreplaceable. Even Henry, whose son she was to teach—there were other teachers, many better than she.

She was a coward, that was all. She clung to what she knew, in fear of what was new. Here she was purely a foreigner. In Córdoba they would understand her.

She laughed, a sharp, uneasy sound in the columned stillness. So: that was what she was made for. To be a stranger in a strange land. To go west and west, following the setting sun, until the land itself was gone, and nothing lay before her but the Stream of Ocean.

She would have to ask Ismail to take her to the sea. He might even understand why she wanted it. And if he did not, why then, she would plague him until he surrendered. She would be his wife, would she not? She knew how wives set about mastering their husbands.

Thirty-Nine

I n the town of Rara, on the Feast of Saints Peter and
Paul, Henry the Quarreller made formal submission to
the empresses whom he had wronged. He came barefoot
and in his shirt, as a penitent, and stood so before the assembly of the realm, with his head bowed in proper humility
and his voice as sweet a murmur as ever a man's voice could
be.

Aspasia thought that he knew very well how he looked.
The day was so warm and fair, the assembly so large, that
those in charge of it had chosen to gamble on the mercy of
heaven. There was a canopy for the highest, but for the rest
the open sky. For pavement there was the wide green field;
for walls, the town behind and the river beside and the hill
above and the wood all about.

Henry advanced through the many-colored splendor of
the lords and prelates. His head was bare, but the sun on his
hair was bright gold. He had shaved his beard. His face was
smooth and strong and young. His shirt was clean, and

white enough to dazzle. The wind tugged at it, molding it to his body. It was an excellent body, if somewhat thickened in the middle.

He walked slowly as a penitent should. At intervals he stopped to kneel and cross himself, sometimes for the blessing of bishop or abbot, sometimes, it seemed, simply to pray. A choir of novices from Fulda, bright-eyed and boisterous before their master called them to order, angelic now, raised up their sweet voices in the verse that began the great saints' mass:

> "*Nunc scio vere, quia misit Dominus Angelum suum: et eripuit me de manu Herodis. . . .*

"Now I know of a surety, that the Lord hath sent his angel, and hath delivered me out of the hand of Herod. . . ."

Aspasia, watching Henry, saw that his lips quirked. It would suit his fancy to be called the Herod of the Germans.

He judged his progress nicely. The choir, having shifted from verse to psalm, ended on a last, joyful *Alleluia!* In the same moment he halted before the dais of heaped turves on which sat the empresses, one on either side, and between them on a throne higher than either, Otto wrapped in silk and crowned with gold.

Otto was sitting very still. He understood why he was there, and what Henry had done. He had been angry when Aspasia explained. "How can he be king? *I* am the king."

"He wanted it," Aspasia had said, "and so he took it. But God would not let him keep it. Now he comes to give it back to you."

"When I am grown up," Otto said, "I will have a sword and a horse. I will kill him."

"You will not," said Aspasia, to his considerable displeasure. She went on undaunted. "If he says that he is sorry, and if he promises never to do it again, and if he keeps that promise, then you should be a good king. You should let him live, and let him serve you."

Otto frowned, but he did not argue. She knew better than to think that that was the end of it. Otto never said as much as he was thinking. And to be sure, that morning while she helped him dress he had said, "I am not going to kill Cousin Henry. I am going to make him my best servant."

Aspasia's throat closed. She forced it open. "That is what a king does," she said.

"I shall be a good king," said Otto.

Now, on the field of Rara, Otto watched as his cousin halted before him and went down on his knees, then on his face, prostrate in submission. The only sound was the wind snapping the canopy over Otto's head and tugging at the dragon banner, and far away a hawk's cry.

Henry's voice seemed to come out of the ground. "My lord king. Most august empresses. Most reverend bishops and lords of the realm. I have sinned through my most grievous fault. I seized what was never mine to seize; I stretched my hand to that to which I had no right. God and your sovereign power have cast me down. God and your gracious majesties have deigned to lift me up, to grant me life, to offer me the mercy of your pardon."

He was eloquent, that prince of quarrellers. His voice rolled on. He begged their pardon. He rose to his knees to give reverence to the empresses regent, and through them to the king. He prayed that he might serve them as heretofore he had betrayed them.

Empress Adelaide heard him tight-lipped, but she voiced no protest. Theophano sat in imperial stillness. She had accepted Aspasia's resolution of their difficulty, but she was not entirely sure of it. Nor was anyone except perhaps Henry. He was standing now while esquires in the livery of Bavaria clothed him as befit a duke.

His eye caught Aspasia's. He smiled very faintly. It was

promise enough. He knelt again, this time to accept the duchy of Bavaria and to swear fealty in its name.

He had a place of honor at the feast, in which he seemed comfortable. People were beginning to walk more easily around him. Their trust he would have to earn, but for this day they would accept him.

He spoke once, briefly, to Aspasia. "Are you content?" he asked her.

He could not know how she stiffened. She managed a cool smile, a suggestion of a nod.

"I will keep faith," he said, "while you keep your own."

She did not recall what more he said. As soon as she decently could, she fled.

Otto had left the feast somewhat before her, nodding on Gudrun's shoulder. Indulgent smiles had followed him. People were fond of their little king.

He was asleep now. Aspasia sat by him in the grey light of evening, a book forgotten in her lap. Within the fortnight she would leave him; she would never see him again.

She thought that she had hardened herself to it. He would miss her for a while. But he was a king. The whole world looked to him, flocked about him, paid him homage. In a very little time he would forget her. When he was grown, maybe, once in a rare while, in the night before he went to sleep, he would remember his first teacher: the little dark woman who went away and never came back.

A shadow fell across the light. Otto's pup raised its head and growled softly but did not bark.

Aspasia looked up. Theophano moved past her in a shimmer of silk, a sweetness of perfume. The empress mother bent over her son as if to kiss him, but hesitated. She straightened slowly.

When she turned, her face was composed. "I hardly know him," she said.

"He remembers you," said Aspasia.

"Truly," said Theophano. "As a stranger in silk who comes rarely and goes often, and brings him children's baubles when he would rather have a horse."

Aspasia's lips twitched at that. "When he's tall enough, he may have one. He knows that very well."

"Maybe we should break his dog to saddle." Theophano drew up a chair softly and sat in it. "I knew when I gave birth to him that he would never be my child as common women's sons are theirs. A king belongs to his kingdom. I thought that I had hardened my heart; that, God willing, I had no heart at all. Then," she said, "I saw him riding into Rara on Master Ismail's saddlebow, laughing when the beast danced, and I knew what a fool I was."

"A fool, maybe," said Aspasia, "but you were never made of stone. My fault. A teacher should keep herself to herself. She should not love her students, nor teach them to love her."

"Why not?"

Swift, that, and full of sudden passion. Aspasia looked at this woman, this empress, this ruler of the western world, and saw her small wild Phania who could never understand why the world would not bend to her will. It was to her that Aspasia said, "If I had been sterner, your son would grieve you less."

"No," said Theophano. "All things have their prices. I would rather this pain than be what my mother was. She was all cold, all given to the empire. Then because she would not open her heart, the Evil One opened it for her. She fell prey to one who was harder of heart than she."

Aspasia nodded. She remembered that elder Theophano, so beautiful and so cold, and Nikephoros whom she conspired to murder, and John who took what she offered and cast her away. They were all dead now. Phania's brothers, who had bided in varying degrees of patience until they were old enough to rule, shared the throne of Byzantium. Constantine was like his grandfather, Aspasia's father: quiet, diffident, reckoned a bit of a fool. Basil was a firebrand. He would take the throne to himself if he could, and the empire with it.

They seemed very far away. They were no part of her world.

Would this too sink into remoteness when she was a lady of Córdoba?

Theophano did not know that Aspasia was going. No one did, except Ismail and Nasir. Aspasia had kept her counsel for Henry's sake, that he should not break his half of the bargain before it was sworn and irrevocable. It was bad faith, yes. Byzantine faith, he would name it.

Now if ever she should speak. But she could not find the words, no more than she ever could when her sins had caught up with her. What could she say? "Be glad for me, I've found a husband, do you mind if I run away to Córdoba?"

Theophano sighed. "You'll go back to Magdeburg from here, I suppose. Henry the youngest will be waiting for you; and the princesses. Is Adelaide old enough to begin lessons in Latin, do you think?"

Aspasia opened her mouth, shut it again. Theophano was not looking at her. "I may send Sophia to Gandersheim ahead of her time, unless you can civilize her. She grows daily more intractable."

"Perhaps," said Aspasia, "Gandersheim would tame her. Isn't milord Henry's sister the abbess there? She has her brother's temper, I hear, and rather more talent for ruling a demesne."

Theophano smiled thinly. "Yes, Gerberga is abbess of Gandersheim. I wonder how far she can be trusted. In herself she has never offered rebellion, but if she has my daughter in her charge . . ."

"They should be a match for one another," said Aspasia.

"And yet," said Theophano, "a little time with you beforehand, a little more of your discipline, would be of good use to Sophia. Unless you would prefer—"

"Of course I'll do as you ask." Aspasia bit her tongue. Pride had tricked it out of her. Ismail was like that with horses. There was none that he could not tame, even the stallion that threw him and trampled him and well-nigh killed him, and kept him abed a whole winter. He went back in the spring, limping still, and broke the beast to saddle.

But she would not be there to tame Sophia. She was going to Córdoba.

Theophano rose. Her scent wafted over Aspasia, rich and complex, a perfume of Byzantium. Phania's smile shone bright and mischievous out of the empress' face. "Admit it, Aspasia. You welcome the challenge."

Aspasia stared at her, bereft of words. Maybe it looked like a haughty glare. Theophano laughed and went away.

Forty

L *et him kiss me with the kisses of his mouth. . . .*
    Aspasia wondered if every Christian woman re-
called the Song of Solomon when she went to her
lover's bed. It sang in her sometimes until she was hardly
aware of Ismail, or of anything but the words and the music
and the dance of body and body.

Tonight she was vividly, painfully aware of him. He was
hungry for her, as if they had not shared a bed every night
since they came to Rara. They were making no secret of it,
only being discreet as modest people should. Hilda minded
not at all that she had a bed to herself, and if Theophano
knew, she did not elect to mention it.

He covered her with kisses, murmuring love-words in Arabic. They were poetry, and such as would set a lord abbot
to thundering anathemas.

She caught his head suddenly and held it between her
breasts. "Have you been eating henbane?"

"And safflower and anise and rue, oysters and leeks and

apples of paradise." He laughed. "My lady, I hardly need encouragement."

"At your age," she said, "you should know better."

He raised his head. He was still laughing. "Grey I may be, but please God, I shall never grow wise."

"You look hardly older than Nasir." And truly, in the lamplight he did not. She took him suddenly, startling him, but he was more than willing. She caught his eagerness, if not his delight. She let it fill her.

He was quiet after. He held her in his arms. When she began to weep he said nothing, only tightened his embrace.

She did not cry long, only long enough to know why she did it. Then tears were too little a thing for the vast echoing emptiness that was in her.

For a long while she lay silent with her head on his breast, and he stroked her hair. At length he said, "When we are in Córdoba, your life will be too full for tears."

"I'm not going to Córdoba."

Vast, the empty spaces. Winds howled in them. She barely heard him, though his voice thrummed in her bones. "Of course you are going to Córdoba."

"No," she said. She shifted; he let her go. She sat up, scraping back her hair. "I can't, Ismail."

He refused to understand. His brows were knit, but in bafflement, not in anger. "There's no need to be afraid. You know how Nasir loves you. So will all our city, once it comes to know you."

"It's not fear." He did not believe her. She said it again. "I'm not afraid, Ismail. I can't go. Too much is binding me here. Theophano, Otto, Henry's son . . . now I'm to take Sophia and try to tame her before she goes to Gandersheim. Don't you see? I can't ride away and leave them."

"You left Byzantium."

"I left an emperor I hated, who was going to lock me in a

convent. I went to a new world with the child to whom I was both sister and mother."

He shook his head tightly. "And am I nothing to you?"

"You are everything to me." She wound her arms about herself, holding tight, as if she could keep her heart from flying to pieces. "But I cannot go to Córdoba."

"Then I shall stay here."

Her mouth was open. She shut it. "You can't."

"I love you," said Ismail.

For a moment—for a soaring, terrible moment—she believed that it could be. That he could stay. That he would be happy. That he would not eat himself away with yearning for his own country, from which he was exile no longer, which had sent the most potent messenger of all to beg him to return.

She shook her head. It was the hardest thing she had ever done. "It would kill you," she said. "But first you would come to hate me. No, my love, my heart. You must go. I must stay. So God has written it."

She made herself see the spark of sudden joyous relief, even through the grief that drowned it. "I will not leave you," he said. "I cannot."

"You can." She wanted to touch him. But if she did, all her resolve would crumble. "A dozen years, God gave us. And never for a moment did I regret it; not for the flicker of an instant did I cease to love you. Nor shall I, until we meet again in Paradise."

He curled his lip at her good Muslim philosophy. "Do you know what houris are? Perpetually, inviolably virgin. How much pleasure do you think they have?"

In spite of herself she laughed, sharp and short and painful. "With you I would happily be a houri for all eternity. Or maybe God will be kind and let us take turn and turn. Is virginity a great burden for a man?"

"Allah!" He looked as if he could not decide whether to laugh or to shake her. "I shall abduct you, and bear you away to Córdoba. When you are where God intends you to be, you will see sense."

"But I am," she said. "I do. This is where I must be. This is what I must do. I am *porphyrogenita*. My father was the Emperor of the Romans. I am the Eagle's daughter, Ismail. I cannot run away from it."

"You run away from nothing. You go to serve God as He meant you to serve Him."

"No," she said. "No, Ismail. If I deny this, then I deny myself."

Her eyes were burning dry. So too were his. Even in that they were matched: in anger and in grief, as in all else that they were. No more would he reach for her than she dared to reach for him. The handspan of bed that was between them was the width of a world.

She watched him draw in upon himself, into a world of which she was no part. It was no more than she willed herself to do. Did it hurt him as terribly as it hurt her? Or could a man steel himself and be strong, as a woman could not?

She knew what he would say to that. She, whose cruel strength had sundered them.

She rose. With hands that shook only a little, she drew on her clothes. He did not watch her. He lay on his back, eyes fixed on the carving of the beam above his head. His face had none of the warmth of carved wood. It was stone.

She could not touch it. She must not. She knotted her hands into fists. "God keep you," she said. She did not stay to hear if he answered.

He did not tell Nasir. It was not cowardice, Aspasia knew that. It was to spare them all.

They had decided not to return to Magdeburg. All that Ismail needed or wanted was here in Rara. It was Aspasia who would have had to go back, to find a tutor for young Henry. Now she would be his tutor as his father had wished.

She hoped that neither of them ever understood what that bargain had cost her.

She was going to stay close to Theophano and be endlessly dutiful and let them go. But when they gathered their caravan—there was plenty of it, for there were others departing by the same road, and they would travel together as long as they might—she was there, like a beast that, wounded to the death, licks and licks its wound.

She would not die of this. Demetrios' murder had come close to killing her. This was nothing beside it.

Someone came to stand with her. Gerbert laid a hand lightly, gently, on her shoulder. Neither of them had told him, but he was friend to them both. He could see that Ismail was ready to ride, and that Aspasia was not; and that they were scrupulous to avoid one another.

Nasir had just begun to understand. He was mounted, already eager to be off; he started to dismount. His father stopped him with a word. His eyes flicked from one to the other.

What wisdom held his tongue, Aspasia would never know. His father's, maybe. Ismail's glance was terrible. A stranger, caught in the path of it, flinched and ducked and ran for cover.

Aspasia found that her fists were knotted in Gerbert's cloak. She could not pry them free.

In the last instant before the line began to move, Ismail turned and looked at her. He said nothing. His face was utterly still.

Someday maybe he would forgive her.

His mare bucked, fretting. With a sudden movement he drew his sword. It flashed through the air, wheeling and spinning, and bit the earth at her feet.

He wheeled his mare about, touched heel to her side. She sprang into flight.

The sword lay where he had cast it. The sun struck fire on

the blade. There was carving on it. A flow of words in Arabic; a shape of wings and talons and fierce curved beak.

Gerbert took it up. Her hands were waiting to take it, no will of hers behind them. The steel was cold and smooth and mutely eloquent.

"An eagle," said Gerbert, "for the Eagle's daughter."

Author's Note

⊕

All of the major characters of *The Eagle's Daughter*, with the exception of Ismail, are historical figures. Aspasia's name, age, and history are of my own invention; I have taken the liberty of including her among the daughters of the Emperor Constantine VII Porphyrogenitos.

The parentage of Theophano is not definitely known, but scholars are inclined to believe that she was a daughter of the Emperor Romanos II and his empress Theophano, who was indeed the child of a tavernkeeper. The elder Theophano's plot to depose her second husband, the Emperor Nikephoros, in favor of John Tzimisces, is described in detail by Leo the Deacon. I am indebted to Harry Turtledove for the typescript of his English translation of Leo's history. Another side of Nikephoros appears in Liutprand's highly entertaining and frequently scurrilous account of his embassy to Constantinople, which can be found in English translation in *The Works of Liudprand of Cremona*, tr. F.A.

Wright (London, 1930). The tale of Queen Willa's girdle appears in this same volume, in the *Antapodosis* or (as Wright translates it) *Tit-for-Tat*.

I have taken considerable liberties with settings, particularly in Germany, and have made occasional changes in chronology for the sake of the story. I did not, however, invent the timing of the death of Otto II and the coronation of Otto III. Otto II died on 7 December 983; the news reached Aachen as Otto III was about to be crowned King of the East Franks.

This, it should be noted, is his proper title. I have called him and his predecessors Kings of the Germans, and their kingdom Germany, in order to avoid confusion with the kingdom of the West Franks—i.e., what is now known as France. The lands which the Ottos ruled corresponded more or less with the Roman province of Germania; it is under this name that they are now generally known.

The quarrel with Empress Adelaide and the war with King Lothair were much more closely related than my narrative may indicate. Lothair was the empress' son-in-law; his wife, Queen Emma, was Adelaide's daughter by her first marriage to the King of Lombardy. Adelaide's withdrawal to Burgundy, therefore, in addition to the reasons I have given, was motivated by her opposition to Otto's policy in Lorraine. To further complicate matters, Queen Emma was rumored to have been the mistress of Adalberon, called Ascelin, Bishop of Laon—who was, incidentally, the nephew and namesake of Adalberon of Rheims. The rumor was believed to have originated with Charles, and to have contributed to his flight from France. His presence in the Ottonian court, and his high standing there, would have been a sore reproach to the woman whose daughter he had slandered.

Empress Theophano was not in Germany when her husband died, but at his side in Italy. She left Rome after his funeral and went directly to Pavia, where Gerbert had taken sanctuary with Empress Adelaide. Gerbert was not however the empresses' ambassador to France; his task was to write letters encouraging the German bishops to support the empresses' cause. These letters, and others relevant to the events and characters of the novel, have been translated by H.P. Lattin in *The Letters of Gerbert* (New York, 1961).

I have conflated the events of Henry's usurpation and surrender into a single year. He was in fact captured in May 984 and forced to surrender Otto III to the empresses in Rara, but they did not restore to him the duchy of Bavaria. Early the next year he rebelled again in company with Otto's old rival, King Lothair of France. Lothair managed to win and hold the city of Verdun in Lorraine. Henry however, rather than provoke a full-scale war, surrendered again in June 985, a year after he had restored Otto III to his mother, and at last received Bavaria. He kept his oath of fealty until he died in 995. He is said to have repented sincerely of his several rebellions, and to have warned his son against turning rebel in his own turn.

Empress Theophano died suddenly in June, 991. Dowager Empress Adelaide took over the regency and held it until 994, when Otto III, who had been leading troops to battle since the age of seven, was judged by the Imperial Diet in Sohlingen to have reached his majority—that is, to be capable of bearing arms. In 996 Otto journeyed to Rome for the first time and was crowned Holy Roman Emperor by the newly installed Pope Gregory V, born Bruno of Carinthia, who was a great-grandson of Otto I by his first wife, Edith of England. Otto III clearly and explicitly intended a restoration of the Roman Empire; he was supported in this dream by his friend and teacher, Pope Sylvester II. Unfortunately, like his father before him, he died too young to accomplish his ambitions: in 1002, at the age of twenty-one, while awaiting the arrival of the Byzantine princess who would have been his bride. Italy killed him as it did his father, between the native fevers and the native resistance to

German domination. The throne passed to Henry II, son of Henry the Quarreller, who thereby fulfilled the imperial ambitions of both his father and his grandfather.

Empress Theophano bore at least four daughters before the birth of Otto III, one of whom seems to have died in infancy. The name and dates of the first Mathilda are my own invention. The historical Mathilda may also have died young. Both of her sisters were placed in convents in approved Byzantine fashion: Sophia in Gandersheim, Adelaide in Quedlinburg. They were, Theophano said, her tithe to God.

Of all Theophano's children, Princess Sophia seems to have been the most difficult. When at the age of nine she was received into the community of Gandersheim, she precipitated a battle between the Bishop of Hildesheim and the Archbishop of Mainz, over jurisdiction of the abbey. The question was not finally resolved until 1208, when Pope Innocent III declared Gandersheim a free imperial abbey. Sophia herself became Abbess of Gandersheim in 1002 after the death of her predecessor, Gerberga, sister of Henry the Quarreller. She died in 1039.

Gerbert of Aurillac was one of the great personalities of the tenth century, a renowned teacher whose pupils included Otto II, Otto III, King Robert the Pious of France, the historian Richer of Rheims, and several popes of the early eleventh century. Born a peasant's son in France, educated first in the abbey of Aurillac and then in Christian Spain, he arrived in Rome shortly before the Princess Theophano. The philosophical debate which made him famous actually occurred much later, before Otto II rather than Otto the Great, and was a prelude to his being appointed Abbot of Bobbio.

Gerbert's primary allegiance from the time of his meeting Otto the Great was to the Ottonian house; Bobbio was given him by Otto II. After his flight from the abbey in 983 he did not return, but went back to Rheims in the service of

Archbishop Adalberon. He was instrumental in raising Hugh Capet to the kingship of France; when Adalberon died in 989 he expected to receive the archbishopric of Rheims. Hugh, however, appointed another man, thus beginning a civil war and a long struggle for the see, which ended only when in 998 Gerbert was named Archbishop of Ravenna. A year later, when Pope Gregory V died, Otto III, who had become Gerbert's pupil and dear friend, raised him to the papacy. He took the name of Sylvester II; he died not long after his emperor, in 1003.

A good general account of all of these events and characters, in all their manifold complexity, is that of Eleanor Duckett in *Death and Life in the Tenth Century* (Ann Arbor, 1967).

The imperial crown of Otto I is still in existence, and is now in the collection of the Kunsthistorisches Museum in Vienna. A photograph of it appears in a nicely comprehensive small volume of primary and secondary sources, Boyd H. Hill, Jr.'s *The Rise of the First Reich: Germany in the Tenth Century* (New York, 1969).